Uncanny Vows

Also by Laura Anne Gilman

RETRIEVERS
Staying Dead
Curse the Dark
Bring It On
Burning Bridges
Free Fall
Blood from Stone

PARANORMAL SCENE INVESTIGATIONS
Hard Magic
Pack of Lies
Tricks of the Trade
Dragon Justice

STORY COLLECTIONS
Lightning Strikes
West Winds' Fool and Other Stories of the Devil's West
Darkly Human

GRAIL QUEST
The Camelot Spell
Morgain's Revenge
The Shadow Companion

THE VINEART WAR
Flesh and Fire
Weight of Stone
The Shattered Vine

Uncanny Vows

Laura Anne Gilman

SAGA PRESS

LONDON SYDNEY **NEW YORK** TORONTO NEW DELHI

SAGA PRESS

AN IMPRINT OF SIMON & SCHUSTER, INC.

1230 AVENUE OF THE AMERICAS, NEW YORK, NEW YORK 10020

First Saga Press trade paperback edition November 2023

SAGA PRESS and colophon are trademarks of Simon & Schuster, Inc.

For information about special discounts for bulk purchases, please contact Simon & Schuster Special Sales at 1-866-506-1949 or business@simonandschuster.com.

The Simon & Schuster Speakers Bureau can bring authors to your live event. For more information or to book an event, contact the Simon & Schuster Speakers Bureau at 1-866-248-3049 or visit our website at www.simonspeakers.com.

Interior design by Davina Mock Maniscalco

Manufactured in the United States of America

1   3   5   7   9   10   8   6   4   2

Library of Congress Cataloging-in-Publication Data is available.

ISBN 978-1-5344-1596-6
ISBN 978-1-5344-1597-3 (ebook)

For the team at MPT, who, much to my surprise and delight, really *are* a family. Thanks for letting me in.

One

WINTER WAS SLOWLY releasing its grip on New Haven. Across the campus, trees budded and bloomed, the midmorning sunlight just warm enough to convince the young men to open their coats and abandon hats, but chill enough that they did not linger, heads down, hands tucked into pockets, brightly colored scarves fluttering. Then the bells tolled eleventh hour, and the graveled paths cleared as though by magic, leaving the campus Green still once again.

At the western edge of the Green, a three-story house filled most of a corner lot. Surrounded by a low stone wall, a small plaque at the entrance announcing that the house was property of the university. It, too, was quiet. The white-trim porch boasted a comfortable-looking quartet of chairs and a low mahogany table, as though waiting for warmer afternoons for chess, or some other decorous pursuit.

Past the front door, however, that quiet gave way to chaos. Chairs had been overturned, rugs shoved aside, and the ornately papered walls had been ripped in places. In the middle of one room, Aaron Harker pivoted, arms windmilling as he tried to keep his balance without losing sight of his prey, a gray-green figure the size of a cat and the shape of a frog, if a frog were to rise up on two feet and scurry like a ferret.

"Stop them," a familiar, breathless voice called. "Stop them!" His sister Rosemary, across the room, was holding an iron poker in one hand and a broom in the other, looking like a demented version of Lady Liberty guarding not a harbor but the exit out of the room.

Aaron pivoted again and swore. "What the blazes do you think I'm trying to do?"

The imp he'd been struggling to catch slid between his legs, leaving a trail of slime across his boots, and Aaron, lifting one foot out of the mess, pivoted a third time, getting dizzy from his attempts to follow the creature. They'd managed to chivvy the creatures from the upstairs rooms, but evicting them from the building entire had been more of a challenge. There were at least eight that they'd caught sight of, but they hadn't exactly been able to line them up and count them.

"Slippery little bastards," he muttered, wiping the back of his hand across his forehead. He'd discarded his jacket and cap across a chair in the parlor, and sweat was making his shirt stick to the small of his back uncomfortably, as though it were deep summer rather than only mid-April.

"Above you!" Rosemary warned, and Aaron looked up to see an imp swinging from the chandelier, screeching insults when it realized it had been spotted. Aaron had just enough time to calculate the likely weight-bearing capabilities of the fixture before the chain gave way, the imp falling with an ear-piercing shriek, followed by the bulk of the chandelier.

Clear crystal beads rained down like hail, bouncing and rolling all over the floor.

Aaron threw himself backward just in time, almost tripping over another imp. "Goddamn it." It had been a long day, starting with an early-morning summons from the provost of the university, and Aaron was tired of playing nice. "Bother, I take it back. Eat them!"

The Molosser hound guarding the staircase gave a sharp bark, the sound resonating throughout the first floor and making the imps shriek again. Botheration let his lower jaw drop in what could almost be considered a grin, sharp white teeth and pink tongue visible, but since Aaron had not given an actual order countermanding the order to guard, he stayed put.

Most uncanny would wet themselves, coming into close quarters with a hound. Imps lacked that level of self-preservation.

"Pbbbttttthhhhtt!" They didn't have speech, as such, but the meaning was entirely clear, particularly with the gesture the fallen imp made, spoon-fingered hands cupping between its legs before scurrying out of reach. But that movement put it nearer Rosemary and her poker, and she took the opportunity to whack it face-first into the wall.

The remainder of the imps, rather than being dismayed, let out another round of rude cheers, sounding remarkably like the brothers of the university fraternity house they had infested.

"That's enough out of you." Two hours of this, and Aaron had reached his breaking point. Although he'd been doing his best to avoid touching them until now, Aaron reached down and grabbed the nearest one by the scruff of its slimy neck, punting it toward Rosemary. With the reflexes that made them an effective team, she swung her broom, hitting the imp square in the chest and sending it flying, falling in a crumpled heap by her previous target.

"Two down, six to go," she said with grim satisfaction, dropping the now-broken broom handle and hefting the poker with both hands. "Who's next?"

The remaining imps scrambled up the draperies and over furniture, but Rosemary was clearly just as tired of trying to do this peacefully. Within thirty minutes they had subdued the remaining creatures, leaving them groaning in a pile on the parquet floor.

"We asked you to leave quietly," Aaron reminded the pile. "It didn't have to be like this."

From the bottom of the pile, another rude noise sounded.

"They're imps. I told you asking nicely wasn't going to work."

Aaron glanced at his sister, her curls falling from the braid that had been coiled neatly that morning, her face flushed with exertion, then down to where her fingers still gripped the iron poker, and bit back the response he was going to make. Stepping closer, Aaron gently uncurled her fingers where they'd clenched hard enough around the metal bar to turn her knuckles white, taking the poker from her and putting it aside. "You all right?"

"Yes. Of course." She sounded offended that he'd even asked. "The day a pile of feral imps is anything more than an annoyance, it's time to retire. Let's just get them into the box and be done with this."

On a proper hunt, there would be a body to dispose of, either by burning, burial, or sinking in a deep body of water, ideally one without strong currents. But while imps were a nuisance to civilized folk—or university students—they weren't particularly dangerous, and their corpses would turn the soil noxious. While meeting with the provost, the Harkers had arranged for a wooden crate lined with flat iron plates to be left by the side of the house. Once they had secured the imps within, an employee of the university would haul them back out into the countryside. Odds were something out there would eat them before too long, which was likely why they'd come into town in the first place.

Their mistake, Huntsmen remedied.

After reclaiming his jacket, Aaron fixed his collar and slicked his hair back before replacing his cap. There was nothing to be done about the sweat, but from a distance, he looked respectable once again.

Taking the coal shovel from the fireplace, he used it to lift the first of the knocked-out imps, gingerly carrying it out the front door to where the box waited, half-hidden by the thick trunk of an elm tree. Unpainted wood, half as tall as Aaron and twice as wide, the stenciled lettering on the box's sides suggested an earlier incarnation, but it didn't need to be pretty to be effective.

It took several trips to clear the house, even with Rosemary disdaining the use of the shovel and merely dragging them out, one in each fist. Each body made a wet, hollow noise as it thumped against the others, and several of them twitched faintly but otherwise remained knocked out. The iron plates couldn't kill them, not merely by contact, but they did enough damage to keep them docile for a while. Hopefully, long enough for them to be dumped somewhere far away.

When the last of the pile had been deposited, Aaron let the lid drop shut a final time, the iron latch falling into place with a satisfying clank.

"And good riddance," Rosemary said. "We should do one more tour of the house, but I suspect they all came out to play once you threatened to set it on fire. Which, by the way, and I shouldn't need to remind you, is never the answer."

Aaron sniffed at his sleeve, then his hand, and made a face. "Fire might be the only thing that gets this smell out. And the ooze . . . ugh."

She clucked her tongue at him. "It's not that bad."

"No, it's worse."

Rosemary rolled her eyes. "And they say women are too dainty for this work. Fine. I'll clear; you wash your hands. Bother"—and she called the hound over from where he'd wandered to relieve himself—"guard!"

The hound settled himself a few feet from the box, nose on paws and gaze intent on his target. After using the garden pump to splash the worst off his skin, Aaron leaned against the stone wall and studied his four-legged companion. "A lot of help you were," he said. "Although I'll grant you I wouldn't want them in my teeth, either."

Bother's erect ear twitched, acknowledgment that he was being spoken to, but otherwise he did not respond.

Aaron shifted again, his skin twitching. Rosemary could tease him all she liked, but he could still feel the weight of imp ooze. It would take more than a splash of cold water to erase the memory.

"Mr. Harker?"

Knocked from his wistful thoughts of a long hot bath, Aaron's left hand reached for the bone-handled knife at his hip even as he turned, relaxing only when he saw the two men standing on the other side of the wall. The speaker was the provost, a stern-faced man with a slicked-back mustache that would have better suited a younger man, and a pinched look between his eyes. His suit was now covered by a long black coat, a fashionable derby set on top of his head, and a blue-and-white knit muffler similar to those worn by the students wrapped around his neck, but the sour expression on his face was the same they'd seen in his office a few hours earlier.

In comparison, the man next to him was an expressionless shadow in brown, a short coat and uniform with its polished black buttons up and down, and buffed black shoes underneath, immediately identifying him as a member of the Messenger Service. The service seemed to choose their employees based on unremarkableness; Aaron suspected that even if he stared for an hour, ten minutes later he wouldn't be able to recall the shape of the face under the cap or the color of his skin.

"Mr. Harker," the provost said again, clearly annoyed that Aaron had not responded already. Aaron was thankful Rosemary was still inside; beyond the fact that the man had summoned them like tradespeople, the provost clearly had little use for women, and Rosemary had no use for men who had little use for women.

Aaron nodded once, waiting; he saw no need to confirm that he was, yes, still Mr. Harker.

"It's done?" the provost asked, his tone somehow managing to be both hopeful and disdainful. In response, Aaron nodded toward the box, even as something within thumped once, weakly, and then fell silent. Then some mischief took over his tongue, and he said, "You should warn your boys about leaving food out. You never know what's going to come to dinner."

If possible, the provost's scowl deepened.

And then, because if he was going to be treated like a tradesman, he might as well act like one, Aaron said, "You have our fee?"

There was a moment where Aaron thought he might have pushed too far, but the provost reached inside his coat and withdrew a slender brown envelope, which he handed to Aaron over the wall.

There was a temptation to brush his hand against the man's sleeve, to see if he would jump back in polite horror, but the weight of the messenger waiting made Aaron simply take the envelope, slipping it into his own coat pocket.

Huntsmen worked for the greater good of humanity. But they had bills to pay, too.

The transaction completed, the provost wasted no time departing, acknowledging neither Aaron nor the messenger beyond a brusque nod.

Both men watched him leave, then the messenger turned back to Aaron.

"Aaron Harker?"

"That's me," he agreed. Unlike the provost, the messenger had reason to confirm his identity.

The man handed him an envelope of his own. This one was a simple cream-colored envelope, sealed with a delicate bronze drop of wax pressed with a plain signet. Despite its travel, the corners were undented, the paper itself unmarked, as though other letters had been afraid to touch it.

Orders from the Circle, in Boston.

There was a bitter irony somewhere, Aaron was certain, that now was the moment the Circle chose to resume contact. Not that there was a rule against Huntsmen working directly for anyone, thankfully. The stipend they received from the Circle covered the basics, but not much beyond that, and while the Harkers did not live extravagantly, there were books and wine and new shoes to be acquired on a regular basis, and Botheration was not inexpensive to feed.

And there had been no official hunts coming their way for several months now, which had meant a smaller stipend.

No hunts, no communication at all. Because of Brunson. Not that anyone would say so. But the Harkers had grown up knowing that they were slightly beyond the pale, knowing that they had to prove themselves more than others, and he knew, even if Rosemary wouldn't admit it, that they were being censured.

And yet, there was no way the Circle could know what had really happened in Brunson. Their report had been clear: an uncanny had murdered three people, and a fourth had died during the hunt, of causes unknown. All truth. Simply not . . . all the truth.

Sensing Aaron's mood, Bother chose that moment to stand up, drawing attention to himself. The messenger, to give him credit, didn't flinch at the approach of the massive beast but stood his ground, his gaze fixed on the human, not hound.

Aaron rubbed a thumb across the wax seal, though not

hard enough break it. "Are you supposed to wait for a response?"

"I was not requested to do so, Mr. Harker."

"Fine." Aaron tucked the letter into his pocket, equally careful not to crease it, and pulled a quarter coin from the other pocket, offering it to the man. "Thank you."

When Rosemary reappeared a few minutes later, her own attire and appearance repaired, both Aaron and Bother had their attention fixed on the imp box, only the envelopes heavy in his pocket proof anyone else had been there at all.

She stepped off the porch steps and stopped. "What happened?"

He couldn't resist. "Why do you think anything happened?"

She just stared, hands on her hips, until he relented, pulling the envelopes out to show her.

"Finally," she said, exhaling her relief, stepping forward to reach not for the envelope with their pay, but the one with their new assignment. He pulled it out of her reach just as her fingers touched it and, when she scowled at him, tilted his head to indicate the two burly workmen approaching from the Green, a heavy handcart pulled behind them.

"It can wait until we're home," he said.

Two

"AFTERNOON, MR. HARKER."

Aaron nodded and handed the check to the teller, waiting while the man went through the necessary motions to deposit it to his account. He envied Rosemary, outside with Bother; the air within the bank was stuffy, and he was all too aware of the fact that the walk from campus to town had only added to the sweat under his clothing. And the Harkers did not bring enough money to this bank for the teller to pretend he couldn't smell anything.

Then again, Aaron knew that he and his sister were known in town to be slightly odd, if still respectable. So long as Aaron didn't try to bring an uncanny into the bank itself, they would likely continue to pretend that he was simply a gentleman of eccentric means, who indulged his sister in her choice of canine companions.

If they knew what Bother actually was . . . That thought amused Aaron long enough for the teller to finish his work, sliding the deposit receipt back across the counter.

"Thank you." Despite blotting, the ink was still wet. Aaron

fluttered the receipt in his hand as he left the building, nodding politely to a woman he vaguely recognized before crossing the sidewalk to where his sister and Bother waited.

Rosemary had buttoned her coat while she was waiting, her gloved hands pushed into its pockets. The sun was starting to slide into the western sky, the air chilling as it went, and they still had the walk home ahead of them. If Bother had not been with them, they could have taken a trolley cross-town, but the last time they'd tried, a child had attempted to mount Bother like a pony, his mother had gone into hysterics, and the driver had asked them to leave, as though it had been their fault.

If they'd had an automotive, they wouldn't have been dependent on trollies or trains, or shank's mare. Rosemary, however, was less enthusiastic about the idea, even if they'd had the cash for it.

Deeming the ink dry enough, Aaron folded the receipt and handed it to Rosemary, taking Bother's lead in exchange as she tucked the slip of paper into the chatelaine purse at her waist, the slight bulk of it just enough to stash her Ladysmith pistol and a kerchief.

The conniptions the provost would have had if he'd known how heavily armed Rosemary was, even on a simple hunt like this, made Aaron chuckle.

"What?"

"Nothing, just . . . nothing." He'd learned the hard way that his sense of humor did not always amuse others, not even his sister.

He flicked the leather lead, and Bother rose to his feet, taking his usual position between and just ahead of them as they walked.

"Do we need anything from the store?"

Aaron shrugged. "Probably."

But neither of them paused as they went past the grocer's and the butcher's shops, both overly aware of the yet-unopened envelope in Aaron's pocket. There was no use in buying supplies if they'd be gone for a week or more. Their territory stretched as far north as the Canadian border and south to Maryland, and they never knew where they would be sent next.

"It will be good to be working again," Rosemary said. "But you think they'll want us to leave right away?"

"They might, but I won't. I need to bathe, and eat something, and ideally have a full night's sleep. And so do you."

She glanced at him, then turned her nose up in mock offense. "Are you telling me I stink?"

"Yes."

Her look of indignation lasted for a few seconds before it cracked. "Fair, fair."

The answer to all their questions would be found simply by opening the envelope, but Aaron knew his sister. Despite her eagerness back at the university, Rosemary enjoyed the moments of anticipation, the stretch of time when she knew an adventure was coming, but not what.

He disliked it almost as much as she enjoyed it, preferring to save that sort of anticipation for novels, but it was a minor discomfort. And they would know soon enough.

Their home was a three-story structure of Gothic revival design, similar to the other homes in the neighborhood, but at a point in the recent past it had been split into two apartments, although in the three years they had lived there, neither of them had met the occupants of the first-floor flat. Tonight, the windows were dark, the curtains drawn, the only sign of life a single light glowing from their own quarters.

When they reached the graveled path to the door, Bother stopped, turning to look up at his humans.

"The kennel for you, sir," Rosemary said in response, pointing toward the path that led to the back of the three-story house. Bother sighed heavily but padded in the direction ordered, Rosemary following to make sure the door was unlatched for him. The hound was reasonably intelligent, bred to think as well as react, but all the intelligence in the world did not make up for the lack of opposing thumbs.

Aaron continued onto the front porch, where it took him a few minutes searching the pockets of his jacket for the key before unlocking the door. Adjusting the lamp sconce, he stared up at the narrow stairwell to the second floor and sighed.

"You're getting old, son," he told his reflection in the pier glass. His reflection made a face back at him; there were Huntsmen three times his age out there. A morning chasing down imps should not leave him so worn. Inactivity was not good for them.

That thought was a reminder of the envelope still in his pocket. Knowing that Rosemary would be only a few minutes behind him, he hauled himself up the steps, checked the coal heater, and laid claim to the bathroom. Dropping his soiled clothing in the basket by the door, he took a sniff of his shoulder and grimaced. Once the water had filled the tub sufficiently, he stepped into the bath and reached blindly for the soap, applying it with generous precision before rinsing it off. Watching the grime and unidentifiable liquids circle the drain and disappear was satisfying, but if he lingered too long, Rosemary would kill him.

The tile flooring was cold under his feet, and he dried off quickly, then wrapped himself in the dressing gown hanging on a hook by the door. Wiping steam off the round mirror hung over the sink, he let his finger draw a sigil on the glass, a symbol for wealth, then erased it. Rosemary was slowly coming around to the idea that sigils were useful tools on a hunt, but if she knew he'd been drawing one in the house, even for their benefit, he'd have to listen to an hour's worth of reminders on why it wasn't smart, or safe.

"Because 'safe' is such an important part of our lives," he told his reflection. And he was tired of having to measure every penny. If their finances improved, they would be able to buy an automotive. Rosemary might not be convinced it would be that much of an improvement, with the inevitable noise and dust and rattled bones, but owning one would mean not having to wait on train schedules, or suffer the crowds and confusion of stations, and that was almost incentive enough for him to risk it.

A sharp knock on the door interrupted his thoughts. "Did you die in there?"

"Be right out," he said, hastily clearing the rest of the mirror and fastening the belt of his gown. His sister brushed past him when he opened the door, her hair already unbound, and her feet bare under her own robe.

"There had best be warm water left," she said.

"I make no promises." The kitchen boiler was modern, but occasionally cantankerous, and if anyone had been home in the flat below them, odds were good her bath would be tepid at best.

There was likely, in some book, a sigil for warming water. And if he found it, he wouldn't share. After all, she didn't trust such things. . . .

Grinning at the thought, he headed down the hall toward his bedroom.

"And make us something to eat!" she called before shutting the door.

By the time he'd changed into an old pair of trousers and a soft wool sweater, his feet encased in well-worn slippers, the water had stopped, and he could hear her humming quietly from behind the door, the hot water apparently having held out long enough for her to fill the tub again.

He headed into the kitchen and checked the cupboard and ice chest without much hope. A few eggs and a chunk of cheese would finish off the last of their perishables and were enough for a simple omelet.

Some men might sneer at the thought of mastering the domestic arts; Aaron had been raised with a more practical hand.

In the back of his attention, he heard the bathroom door open, and the door to Rosemary's bedroom open and then close again, unconsciously tracking his sister's movement. Once finished cooking, he plated the eggs and tucked forks on the edge of the tray, then retrieved the letter from his jacket pocket and placed it on the tray as well, and carried it all out into the main room, where Rosemary was now curled up in her favorite chair, hair wet-braided in a plait, hanging over her shoulder. Dressed in a plain blouse and skirt, a dark blue quilt drawn over her lap and house slippers on her feet, she could easily have been mistaken for a woman of gentle leisure save for the fact that instead of needlepoint, she was cleaning the hilt of a slender steel dagger, twin to the one she usually carried in her sleeve.

He waited until she'd put the blade aside and wiped her hands clean before handing her a plate, then placed the envelope on the tea table, positioned so they both could see the seal on the flap.

Rosemary took several bites of her supper, then lifted her chin toward the letter. "Hunt, or summons?"

And that was the crux of it, wasn't it? The reason they'd both been willing to wait to open it. The message was probably sending them on a hunt. But there was a possibility that it was an order for them to present themselves.

It was unlikely; since the Debacle of 1816 in Pittsburgh, the Circle had been wary of summoning Huntsmen in person. And if the Circle knew for certain that details had been omitted from their report, important details, they would have been summoned immediately, not nearly half a year later. But the silence of the past few months had left the Harkers wary.

It was easier to elide the truth in paper. Put to the test in person, Aaron wasn't sure he could lie, and he knew Rosemary didn't think he could, either. His sister would lie to shame the devil himself, if need be, but even she did not want to face the Huntsmen Circle and do so.

The utter unfairness of it pinched at him: they had filed their report, had answered all the questions with reasonable honesty, or at least no dishonesty, and if they had left out some particulars of what exactly they had faced and done . . .

He still had nightmares about Brunson. Nightmares of a human turned into a monster, the use of magics forbidden to humans—forbidden and, they'd thought, mercifully forgotten in the hundreds of years since the treaty had been signed.

The treaty was what held the fey out of this world, kept them from dipping malicious fingers into the doings of humanity. If it were to be known, even in a whisper, that one of the essential agreements had been broken . . .

Aaron had no desire to consider that, not even in the safety of his own thoughts. What they'd seen in Brunson was nothing good, and no good would come of it being known. They were doing the right thing, keeping quiet.

"Aaron." His sister was watching him. "The letter?"

After putting down his plate, he took up the envelope, swinging his legs up over the arm of the sofa and propping himself against the cushions before slitting open the flap and pulling out a thin sheet of paper.

The handwriting was familiar. "It's from Harry," he told her, and he saw the hand holding her fork pause, then resume its action, some of the tension leaving her shoulders and neck. Harrison McIntyre was the Archive Secretary and an old . . . perhaps "friend" wasn't the correct word, but someone they had known nearly all their lives. He had known their parents, and possibly even their grandparents, he was that old.

Her fork scraped against the plate, and she stabbed at the last piece of egg. "What does it say?"

"A moment."

He skimmed the letter, long experience letting him translate the half-legible marks into coherence. The Secretary may not have intentionally set out to create a cypher, but his short-hand was effectively that.

"Huh."

"What?"

He ignored her query and kept reading, then brought his gaze back to the top of the letter and started again, looking for anything he might have missed, overlooked. "There's something he wants us to look into. Officially, but not a hunt. Not yet, anyway."

It was a distinction without a true difference; if you sent Huntsmen, it was de facto a hunt. So why the cautious wording? That was not like Harry, not at all.

Unless this was some sort of test.

His sister narrowed her eyes and made a "get on with it" gesture with the hand holding the fork. "Details, Aaron, come on!"

"He says there's been a disturbance in a small town, name of Roughton, just southeast outside Boston. An otherwise unremarkable location, but apparently several of our more generous benefactors reside there."

They both heard the Secretary's dry tone in the words; Huntsmen did not like to consider themselves beholden to anyone, but there were expenses to be paid and offices to be maintained. Thankfully, there were also a number of well-to-do men who enjoyed the feeling of helping to save the world without actually having to do anything. So when one of these benefactors beckoned, Huntsmen jumped-to. Discreetly, and without servility, but definitely jumped.

The discretion portion might be why it was not officially an assigned hunt. Unofficially, there would be no record in the journals. Nothing to tie them to the Huntsmen at a later date, should it become inconvenient.

"Oh, they have my interest now." Rosemary had put aside plate and fork, her skirt tucked demurely around her legs, every inch the attentive audience. "Disturbances of what sort? A schoolteacher pummeled to death by a horse with the head of a man? Tiny men running amok in the grocers? A wolf speaking in tongues in the butcher's doorway?"

He grinned briefly at the sarcasm in her voice. "Nothing so simple. There have been a series of disruptions at our noble benefactor's abode. Broken windows, that sort of thing. Mischief only, annoying, but hardly pointing to the uncanny, unless the family has a resident gespenst."

"In which case it is a matter for a priest, not us," Rosemary said. Huntsmen dealt with things of flesh, not spirit.

"And Harry probably would have told them the same, until a few days ago, when a man was struck down by no visible weapon." Aaron reread the pertinent portion of the letter, then read out loud, "'He was, according to the doctors, physically unharmed; breathing, but unaware of his surroundings. He simply will not wake up.'"

". . . That's it?" Her tone was incredulous, and he didn't blame her. A man falling into a coma sounded like a medical mystery, not work for Huntsmen.

Aaron held up the letter as though something might fall out of the pages before continuing. "The victim is the brother-in-law of Walter Ballantine, aforementioned benefactor. We are to inquire gently"—and he emphasized the word—"and deal with anything that may or may not be occurring, while keeping the situation from escalating."

"And by escalating they mean making life uncomfortable for our well-to-do victims and their neighbors," Rosemary deduced, her sarcasm doubled. "Well, you had said it would be nice to be called in before someone died, for once."

Aaron wasn't so sanguine. "This isn't a hunt, Rosemary. It's not even a test to make sure we're still . . ." And he waved a hand about to indicate something, he wasn't quite sure what. "It's . . . busywork. It's politics. Even imps were better than this."

"Huntsmen answer the call," his sister intoned, a platitude drummed into them since childhood, then shrugged, clearly less distressed by this than he was. "If Harry thought it was important enough to send someone, then we go. Even if it turns out to be nothing, I don't care; it's still better than snatching imps."

"It'll be another stupendous waste of our time," Aaron muttered.

"Maybe so, but who would you suggest they send, instead? Sjunnson?"

That brightened Aaron's mood, just imagining it. Sjunnson was an excellent Huntsmen, with more experience than the two of them combined, but the rough exterior and rougher interior of a longshoreman. Not the soul one would choose to send into a nicer neighborhood, not unless you were looking to cause a ruckus rather than prevent one.

"But that's an excellent point; was there no one better suited to this they could call? It's not as though I'm known for my diplomatic conversation." Aaron was not whining, he told himself; he was being practical.

"You're an utter disaster at diplomacy," Rosemary agreed.

"Blunt as a stump. But I'm quite good at it, and Harry knows that. So you just need to stay quiet and look pretty, just like Bother."

When Aaron grumbled again, she pulled a small pillow out from under her arm and threw it at him. "I was joshing, but it may be true. It may be they want us to make a pretty face of it, scions of an established Huntsmen family, all the trimmings." Their parents and both sets of grandparents had been Huntsmen, after all, no matter how badly that had ended.

"That's worse, not better."

"It doesn't matter what we think about it." Rosemary's tone went from thoughtful to sharp. "We have tea with one of our much-appreciated moneybags, either kill an uncanny or confirm that it's a medical issue rather than an uncanny one, and job well done."

She picked up the dagger again, flipping it easily over her fingers, and slid it into the sheath on her forearm, just under the embroidery of her cuffs. "And then, a few days in Boston to do some shopping!"

Aaron was reasonably certain she hadn't meant that last bit as a threat. Probably. But the gleam in her eye suddenly had him more worried than anything that might be waiting for them in Massachusetts.

Rosemary knew she should be asleep, or at least tucked into her bed, a glass of warm milk on her nightstand. But they had no milk in the house—none that was still safe to drink, anyway—and her bed was suddenly too soft, her pillows too hard, and the mechanical clock tick-ticking its way through the night far too loud.

Which is how and why she found herself, wrapped in the quilt taken from her bed, sitting on the low front steps of their house in the small hours of the morning.

The first-floor flat was dark, as usual, and no one in the neighboring houses seemed to be astir, so she had the entire street to herself, just her and the low hoots of owls, and the occasional yip of something hunting near the creek that ran at the end of their street. The air was cold but clear, the stars thick overhead. Even without a lamp, it was bright enough for her to see the contents of the battered tin container in her hand.

Three glass vials, each half the length of her pinkie, each with a tiny needle attached, set in a bed of combed wool to keep them from rattling or breaking.

It had been almost three months since she'd opened the case, and even then it had merely been to check, to reassure herself that they were there, intact. She hadn't felt even a pinch of need. But now, suddenly, the drug called to her, reminding her of its presence, its promise.

Blast, they called it. The unholy combination of a drug created by a Polish scientist and a similar compound derived from the blood of centaurs. It cleared your thoughts, banished exhaustion. Just for a little while. Just enough to get you through a hunt. Just enough to keep you sharp.

Rosemary didn't need it. She'd proved that, going months without so much as looking at the case where it was tucked away in her unmentionables drawer.

But she wanted it. Wanted that rush of sudden alertness,

wanted the need for that sudden alertness, the exhilaration of life-or-death decisions, the feel of violence crashing through her bones.

Knowing that such wanting was dangerous did nothing to diminish it.

Rosemary needed to be careful.

There were only three vials left. She'd used one, just to test, when she first acquired the kit. One during the kelpie hunt, when Aaron had ended up in the hospital and she was too afraid to sleep for fear he might die while her eyes were closed. Another when they were helping track the uncanny down in New Jersey, the one they'd never been able to identify. And one in Brunson.

Three more, and God alone knew where or how she would be able to acquire more. If anyone knew . . . if Aaron knew . . .

Rosemary closed the lid, hiding the vials from sight as though that would make them disappear.

"Only when I need it," she told the owl overhead. "I promise."

Three

AFTER FINALLY CRAWLING back into bed just before dawn, Rosemary soundly resented the fact that her brother seemed to have gotten a full night's rest, even before she discovered what he had been doing in the hours before she woke up.

"Really?" She eyed the automotive, a clunky black monster waiting in front of the house dubiously. She hadn't even known you could hire an automotive until that morning. "How much did it cost?"

"Don't think about it," her brother said. Despite his studied casualness, he was practically bouncing on his heels. "Think about not having to deal with the train, or trusting our luggage to porters. Think about the time we will save, both getting there and getting back."

Aaron had few enthusiasms; she hated to dash cold water on anything he felt that strongly about, even if he had sprung it on her without warning, knowing how she felt about the things. But she had doubts that exceeded the mere cost.

"Do you know how to drive it?"

"I drove it here from the rental office," he said, which wasn't really an answer. Sensing she was about to voice more objections, or refuse entirely, he hurriedly went on. "I've put the milk and eggs order on hold until we get back. And Nancy will check for any mail or packages that might arrive."

Their neighbor had to be a hundred if she was a day, sour as lemon and bitter as pits, but she had an odd soft spot for Aaron, which he shamelessly exploited.

Without waiting on a response, Aaron took their bags from the porch where Rosemary had dropped them to the curb, then retrieved the stoutly built wooden trunk that held their extra weapons and ammunition. "Look! It all fits in the back, with room for Bother, too."

Aaron trying to placate her was more exhausting than Aaron in a fit of pique. Rosemary sighed, accepting the fact that they would not be taking the train. Her brother could be exceptionally single-minded when he decided on something, almost to the point of mania. And, in truth, the idea of not being tied to train schedules was appealing.

"What will we do for—"

"I had Nancy make us sandwiches, too," he said, lifting a paper sack in anticipation of her question.

Looking up, Rosemary saw Nancy watching them from the window of her house across the street and lifted a hand in thanks. "You're going to end up married to her, if she has anything to say about it," she warned him.

With that horrifying idea stuck in his mind, she felt somewhat revenged.

Leaving Aaron to finish loading their luggage, she went to release Bother from his kennel.

"No train today, Bother. Ready for something different?"

The hound looked as dubious as she felt, but when told "Bother, up!" he clambered into the back seat, squishing between strapped-down luggage and crate. With his shoulders and blunt head rising above them, one ear erect and nose lifted to take in the new smells, Rosemary thought he looked as though he might be posing for an advertisement for Mr. Ford.

"You too, huh?" she asked, scratching under his chin before settling herself into the passenger seat. It felt uncomfortably exposed, with only the windshield in front and nothing overhead. She reached up to make sure the pins of her hat were securely fastened, then reached down to where a soft wool rug was folded under her feet. She pulled it up, determining that it was meant to go over her lap.

Without anything else to do, she looked down the hood to where Aaron stood, frowning downward in an unreassuring manner. "Are you certain you know how to drive this?"

"It's very basic," Aaron said, although the look on his face was not one that inspired confidence. Consigning herself to her fate, Rosemary draped the wool rug over her legs, tucking the ends underneath her in the hope that it would protect her skirt from any dust or dirt kicked up from the road.

Aaron did something at the front of the hood that she couldn't see, and when the engine coughed and spluttered to life, he jumped into the driver's seat with a slightly mad grin on his face. "Hang on," he told her, then pulled a lever, and the vehicle lurched forward. Rosemary grabbed at the seat under her, fingers curling into the leather, as Aaron manhandled the wheel, turning the automotive into the street and on their way.

"Isn't this dilly?"

Rosemary had to admit, once they were underway, it was pleasant enough; for all the dust the wheels kicked up, it certainly produced less smoke than a train. And while Botheration no longer had room to lounge as he did on a train, the hound seemed content, occasionally leaning forward to rest his massive head on her shoulder but more often hanging half over the side of the automotive, tongue flapping ridiculously.

But there were disadvantages as well, and halfway there she insisted Aaron pull over to stretch their legs—and rest their backsides. The seats might be the finest Mr. Ford's company had to offer, she informed him, but they were sadly lacking in padding.

The plan had been to arrive at their destination before suppertime. By the watch pinned to Rosemary's sleeve, it was barely three p.m. when they drew up in front of the hotel's facade. Aaron caught her checking the time, and by the expression on his face clearly ready to launch into yet another extolling of the virtues of them buying an automotive of their own.

Rosemary pointedly ignored him, accepting the hand offered by a uniformed employee of the hotel to assist her out of the vehicle. Bother, thankfully, waited until the young man had stepped back before leaping out to join her.

"You'll be wanting to park this beauty?"

"Yes," Rosemary said before Aaron could respond, and she gave him a look that quieted any complaint he might have made. "We won't be needing it until we depart."

"You don't know that," Aaron whispered hotly, grabbing the bags from the back seat and handing Rosemary hers.

"Yes, I do," she said, and marched into the lobby, confident that he, Bother, and the porter carrying the weapons crate would follow.

The hotel was not particularly elegant, the paint slightly faded and the huge brass vases set by the door showing a hint of tarnish, but the air of a place just past its prime was what the Harkers preferred. In their line of work, coming back covered in mud or dirt—or blood, not always their own—was not an uncommon occurrence. It made sense to stay somewhere such things would be politely overlooked, so long as the bill was paid promptly.

"Try to remember to get rooms on the same floor this time," she said to Aaron as they passed a small sitting area, Bother padding along obediently between them at heel.

"It's not my fault they didn't believe you were my sister. The look on the maid's face, though, when you—"

His reminiscence was interrupted by a familiar, unwelcome voice echoing through the lobby.

"Well there. Hello, Harkers."

Rosemary stopped, forcing her face to remain in a mask of pleasant civility. "Jonathan?"

Behind her, she could hear a growl, but she wasn't certain if it came from Bother or Aaron. It could have been either, truly.

Rosemary noted the porter stopping a few feet away, placing the crate on the floor next to him and waiting close enough to be summoned, but not so close he might be accused of eavesdropping, before she had to return her full attention to the unexpected arrival.

It was, in fact, a fellow Huntsmen.

"I would say what a lovely surprise it is to see you here, but you wouldn't believe me." Jonathan Scheinberg stepped forward, taking Rosemary's hands in his own and pressing a gallant kiss on top of them before stepping back to nod at Aaron. "I'm here on an errand for Cubwell. You?"

Errand was a polite, public term for a hunt. Benedict Cubwell was a politician from the tip of his hat to the shine of his shoes; it made sense that he would have known about a disturbance irritating a benefactor, and Scheinberg was his chosen protégé. But Cubwell had no actual position in the Boston office, and Harry McIntyre did. If he'd sent Huntsmen in, when they'd already been assigned . . .

"McIntyre has us looking into a situation in town," Aaron said, and that was definitely a growl in his voice. Rosemary moved her heel back a half step, coming down hard on the tip of his shoe, a warning to behave.

Jonathan raised a well-manicured eyebrow, his smile unchanged, although his shoulders were stiffer. "Calm yourself, Harker. I'm simply staying for the night, my work takes me a few towns west. No need to fear I'll cast a shadow over you—or your hound."

There was a tone to the other man's voice, not quite sharp, but with a faintly unpleasant edge to it, undercutting his facade of civility. Rosemary bit back a sigh. Jonathan wasn't a bad sort, if prone to thinking in terms of chess when the game was hazards, but he clearly still wasn't over the fact that they'd been granted a Molosser. Bred and trained in Germany specifically for Huntsmen to use, the beasts were placed carefully. You couldn't buy one; the breeders chose you.

They had not chosen to choose Jonathan.

Since Rosemary still had no idea why they had been chosen, she merely smiled and shrugged, responding to the words rather than the tone. "Where we go, he goes." They had tried to leave him home, once, when he was still a pup. They'd learned then that a Molosser stayed in his kennel because he chose to, not because there was a lock on the gate.

The latch on his current kennel was more to keep others out.

"I'll check us in," Aaron said. "Scheinberg."

"Harker," the other man responded in exactly the same tone.

Jonathan watched him stalk toward the reception desk and sighed theatrically, without even the pretense of true regret. "He still doesn't like me much, does he?"

"You shouldn't take it personally," she said lightly, bringing Bother in to heel before any of the other hotel guests could take offense at his presence, or, heaven forbid, he took offense at theirs. "Aaron distrusts anyone more charming than himself."

Crooked white teeth flashed in a smile. "It's a wonder he can bear to be near you at all, then."

"Jonathan. Enough." She had no need to be flattered; they were all three here to work, not socialize, and she knew him too well to fall into that honeypot, or to think that he meant her to. It was merely habit, trained into them and honed during years of hunts; the easiest way to get information was to charm it out of someone.

But neither of them had anything the other needed, and she needed to save her energies for the diplomacy their contact would require.

He made a gesture of acceptance, then asked, "You're well, though?"

And that was the disarming thing about Jonathan, Rosemary thought: the question had been asked honestly, with actual concern.

"We're well," she assured him. Part of her wondered what he had heard, what gossip was being spread about them this time, and if she should bother to try to work it out of him. "Although imp spit is surprisingly difficult to remove from clothing, did you know that?"

"I did know that." And he made a comically pathetic face, willing to follow her lead into nonsensical small talk. "It also ruins the polish on ones shoes."

"Oh dear. My condolences to your valet."

Her sardonic reply earned her a half smirk, quickly erased as they saw Aaron returning, presumably with the keys to their rooms. He was moving more swiftly than usual, leaning forward and leading with his chin, which did not bode well for his mood. Rosemary sighed. He wasn't going to believe that Jonathan wasn't here to spy on them, even if they never ran into the man again.

Perhaps she would have a glass of sherry, rather than tea, before they went to visit their witness.

Jonathan, no fool, lifted a hand in farewell, well before her brother reached them. "I will leave you two—apologies, three—to be settled, then. Good hunting."

She smiled in response, keeping most of her attention on the oncoming storm that was her brother. "And to you."

By the time Aaron reached them, his pace had slowed,

Jonathan's departure removing the source of his vinegar. "I can't believe you encourage him."

"Honestly, Aaron," she said, half turning to summon the porter. "Really? I don't know why he upsets you so."

"He's a fancified upstart."

"He's first generation, and feels the need to prove himself," she corrected. "And he's more than competent, which I think is what you find truly unforgivable."

A huff was the only response she received, which effectively proved her point. If Jonathan had been less capable, less charming, Aaron would not have felt the need to measure himself against the other man and think himself lacking.

But she pointed out none of this, saying only, "He's not here to interfere with us."

Her brother sneered. "I wouldn't be so sure of that."

"Aaron."

"I don't like anyone that charming."

Despite herself, Rosemary laughed at the echo of her own words. "Move past it, Aaron."

He scowled and took the hound's lead back from her. "Bother, let's go."

Rosemary followed them toward the wide staircase at the center of the lobby, watching as people made way for the pair, like a railway train scattering a herd of sheep from the tracks.

Dear God, she hoped there was an uncanny to blame for whatever was going on here, some physical action to be taken. Aaron in a sulk was bad enough, Aaron in a sulk while she needed to be politic, rather than hunting, would be an unending headache.

She loved her brother, but there were days she wished she could lock him in the cupboard for a while.

"Men," she said, annoyance dripping from the word, and an older woman passing by chuckled in sympathetic response.

"Rosemary?" Aaron had paused at the foot of the steps, looking back at her impatiently, the porter and their luggage already out of sight.

"Yes, yes, I'm coming."

It couldn't be worse than imps, she supposed.

The stairs led to a half lobby and an ornate metal grille that opened to an electric elevator. Bother hesitated slightly when the doors opened but followed Aaron inside, staying close to his side as Rosemary and the porter joined them.

Rosemary admitted to a slight trepidation herself as the doors were cranked closed; she'd ridden in one a few times before and found them far preferable to climbing stairs, but something about being enclosed like this made her skin twitch.

"Third floor," Aaron told the ancient man standing by the controls. No doubt Jonathan had a room on one of the lower floors; rooms were invariably smaller and shabbier on the top floor, but traveling with Botheration, the Harkers had become accustomed to such accommodations. In truth, Rosemary wasn't sure she would have made a different decision, if she were on the other side of the desk.

But when the doors were cranked open again, they stepped into the clean if somewhat drably decorated hallway.

As requested, their rooms were next to each other, at the far end of the corridor.

Rosemary left Aaron to deal with the porter and took Bother in with her, noting as she turned the key that the lock was new and in good repair. The room, too, was in better shape than the hallway, the striped gray-and-white wallpaper clean and unfaded, the blue carpeting underfoot likewise, and if the bedspread was an unpleasant shade of gray blue, the bed itself was firm, and the pillow comfortable. Rosemary had stayed in better, but she had also seen much worse.

Tucked into one corner was a sink set into a wooden cabinet painted the same gray blue as the bedspread, the basin surprisingly large, and when she turned the handles, warm water flowed almost immediately.

Despite herself, Rosemary was impressed. She might still have to go down the hall to bathe, but considering how messy hunts could become, the ability to rinse herself—or her clothing—in the privacy of her own room was no small thing.

Bother pushed at her leg with his head, and she reached down to unsnap the lead from his collar. "All right, I hear you," she said, pulling a shallow steel bowl from her bag and filling it with water. While he slurped noisily, she unlaced her boots and put them by the door, then disrobed down to her chemise and petticoat before unpacking her kit, hanging her skirts and blouses in the narrow wardrobe. A quick glance in the mirror hung there showed that, despite her hat, there was still dust in her hair, and a smudge of dirt on her chin that both Aaron and Jonathan had failed to mention.

"Men," she said again, this time with resignation. Aaron

was likely simply oblivious; she supposed Jonathan thought it was more polite not to mention it.

Once Bother had finished drinking, he settled on the carpeting by the bed, watching as she washed her face and rinsed her mouth before brushing out her hair and putting it up into a stylish knot. She studied herself in the mirror, tucking stray hairs back into place with a distracted frown. When younger, Rosemary had spent time trying for the perfect wave, the idealized ringlets framing her face. But her thick curls would not be tamed, and the result had never matched the effort she put in. And it certainly wasn't practical to carry a Marcel iron with her on hunts

Practicality was a virtue for Huntsmen.

Her mother's hair, thick and curling like her children's, had fallen to her waist when loose. She had ignored the fashions of her day and worn it in a single plait coiled at the nape of her neck. Her father had joked that it was better than armor, that no uncanny's claw could cut through it.

Shaking off an old melancholy, Rosemary went back to the wardrobe, considering her clothing options. Although she favored the practicality of the unfashionable gored skirt for ease of movement, she suspected that something a touch more fashionable would be required here. Shaking out a simple brown-and-gold pleated hobble skirt, she eyed her boots and decided it would have to do.

She'd just finished fastening the buttons when Botheration stood and faced the door, his soft "woof" coming at the same time as the knock, a firm single rap.

"It's open," she called, knowing from Bother's reaction that it was Aaron, not a stranger.

Her brother hadn't bothered to change, his hair still ruffled from the drive, and she felt a familiar twinge of envy at the
lesser demands of male fashion. He carried his hat in his hand,
his coat over one arm, and a look of annoyance on his face.
"Your room is larger than mine."

Aaron had a tendency to become focused on details like
that; Rosemary was used to it. "Then it's a good thing Bother's
staying here, isn't it?"

"You'll get to walk him in the morning," he said, with the
air of someone making a fair trade. "Do you want to take him
with us to interview Mrs. Ballantine? If there's even a trace of
uncanny around her, he'll be able to tell."

Rosemary cast an eye at the hound, who was now curled
up on the carpet by the bed, seemingly content to let his
humans decide what he should do.

"Harry's letter said that she was the wife of the benefactor, but he didn't say how much she knows," she said slowly.
"Bringing Bother might . . . raise questions."

The hound's soft brindle coat and wide brown eyes often
reassured people, despite his muscled bulk, but there was no
way around the fact that he was considerably larger than most
dogs and had, on occasion, shown a wicked sense of humor.
Terrifying a witness might occasionally be useful, but she
doubted this would be one of those times.

"He stays here," she decided. "Bother, be good, stay quiet.
No howling at the chambermaids."

The look of utter innocence Botheration turned on her
made Aaron laugh, and she hoped it meant that he'd let go of
his earlier sour mood.

In truth, her experience with hotel maids was that they

were not taken aback by much, but Bother's bark was deep enough to unnerve even someone used to it, much less an innocent walking past or mistakenly opening a door. And while a sizable gratuity eased most problems, Rosemary knew the state of their finances down to the penny, and they didn't have the money to buy themselves out of trouble just then.

By unspoken agreement, they bypassed the elevator for the stairs, which clearly had not been maintained as well as the rest of the hotel, but for that reason were blessedly empty. If there was an exit from the building that did not lead through the main lobby, Rosemary decided that the hotel would be perfect.

Sadly, there was not.

Aaron paused just outside the building, looking wistful. "I don't suppose we could take—"

"No." Rosemary didn't even have to think about it. "I am not going to get in that contraption while you try to navigate city streets."

Aaron tipped his derby forward over his head and shoved his hands into his coat pockets. "Fine. Are we going to walk there, then?"

"Excuse me." Rosemary ignored him, instead calling to one of the uniformed employees. "Is there a trolley stop nearby?"

"Down around the corner, ma'am. Take you into Boston proper."

"We're looking for Allston Lane?"

The man rubbed his chin, then nodded. "Blue line'll get ya close. You'll need ta walk the rest of the way."

"Thank you." Rosemary shot a glance at her brother, who

made a gesture of surrender and started walking the direction the man had indicated.

———————

The trolley, its wheels clattering against the brick street, took them away from the clustered buildings of downtown, up a slight hill dotted with modest homes. As they reached the top of the hill, a brisk breeze hit them, filling their lungs with a briny, bracing scent. Rosemary knew that the harbor was miles away, and well out of sight, but for a moment she would have sworn she was standing on a rocky shore, hearing the waves build and crash in front of her.

"'I must go down to the seas again, to the lonely sea and sky,'" Aaron quoted from beside her, soft enough that she knew better than to respond.

They'd learned to sail from their father, in a tiny boat barely large enough for an adult and two children. The scent of seawater was the memory of him, still. Bittersweet, but comfort all the same.

It would have been easier if he had died with their mother, in that terrible hunt. Easier, cleaner, and kinder.

Thankfully for their mood, the driver called out their stop, and Aaron reached up to pull the cord that indicated they needed to get off. They were at the outskirts of town now, the shops and modest homes replaced by grander houses set on larger plots of land.

The address they'd been given was set back slightly from the road, behind a low wall of deep red brick. They paused by the gate, both of them self-consciously adjusting their clothing where it might have become disordered.

"It's just money," Aaron said, which Rosemary thought would have been more reassuring if he hadn't said it almost as a question.

The two-story home was built of the same deep red brick, the door and trim painted white, with a backdrop of thickly clustered trees just behind, creating a soothingly picturesque visual.

"A lot of money," Rosemary said. Not ostentatious, but clearly well-to-do. "But they're the ones who need us, not the other way around."

"Actually . . ."

"Oh shut up."

A smooth-raked white gravel path led from the gate to the front door. Crocuses were beginning to show their heads around the steps, along with what looked like bleeding heart. The sight of those homely flowers made some of the tension in Rosemary's neck and back ease, as Aaron stepped forward and rapped smartly with the door knocker.

They only had to wait a few minutes before the door opened, a woman in a drab brown shirtwaist and a starched apron eyeing them with caution.

"Rosemary and Aaron Harker, of the Boston Huntsmen, to see Mrs. Ballantine. I believe she will be expecting us." Rosemary made the introductions as smoothly as though they had been long-expected for tea, and in the face of that confidence, the woman ushered them inside without hesitation.

Aaron wanted to hate the Ballantine house, simply because it was something they would never be able to have. But he couldn't. Like the outside, the interior embraced the subtler side of wealth without the need to shout about itself. The brass fixtures on the door were polished to a muted gleam, and when they stepped inside, the carpet underfoot was clearly an antique, the chandelier overhead casting a gentle light over the space, but there was a comfortable, homey feel to it, too. Aaron could almost imagine children running down those stairs, an exasperated parent or maid calling after them to slow down, for God's sake.

And as they passed over the threshold, he looked down and noted the glitter of silver and iron shavings worked into the sill. More a warning than an actual deterrent, but Ballantine had clearly listened to at least some of the advice his donations had earned him. So the man was not a fool or, at least, not entirely one. That might make this easier.

"Mrs. Ballantine is expecting you?" Some doubt had slipped into the housekeeper's voice, and Rosemary was quick to reassure her.

"She is, although we did not set a particular time. It is a family matter."

Aaron once again admired his sister's ability to manipulate people. Her words were truth: they were here about a member of the Ballantine family. If the woman took that as implication that they were members of the family? Well, that was on the woman's head, not theirs.

Whatever the woman thought, she seemed reassured. Reaching off to the side, she tugged on a rope, and somewhere deep in the house, a bell chimed. Seemingly within seconds, a younger woman appeared behind the first, her deep-pocketed apron and thick-soled shoes identifying her as a housemaid.

She glanced at the woman, looking for instruction, then at the Harkers.

"I'll take your coats, sir, miss, if you don't mind?"

While Rosemary shrugged out of her long coat and unpinned her hat to give to the girl, Aaron gave his pockets a surreptitious pat-down to make sure he hadn't accidentally left a knife there before surrendering his coat. He had left his pistol in the hotel room, but his usual dagger was in its vest sheath, the silver-tipped jackknife tucked into his pants pocket.

It might be considered rude to pay a visit while armed, but since he knew that Rosemary would have at least one throwing knife tucked into her sleeve no matter where she went, he felt that breach of etiquette would not get him scolded, if discovered.

After all, if he needed it, then he'd have been right to have brought it, wouldn't he?

The girl disappeared with their piled coats over one arm, hats in the other, as the woman gave them another close look, as though judging their acceptability to be brought farther into the house. Aaron resisted the urge to run a hand through his hair and adjust his tie again.

Apparently they passed muster, because the woman nodded once, almost in approval, and said, "Follow me, please."

They were led down a paneled hallway, past several paintings of landscapes that were too ugly not to be expensive, and a number of mahogany doors, all closed. She stopped at one that looked no different from the others and knocked, then without waiting for an answer, opened it halfway. "Ma'am?"

A voice inside gave assent, and the housekeeper opened the door all the way, ushering them inside.

The room was not, as Aaron had been half expecting, a lady's parlor, but rather a library. More, it was a library clearly designed for someone to sit in and read, rather than storage or appearance, with leather chairs tucked into well-lit corners, and chestnut-wood bookcases filled with an eclectic assortment of spines and sizes. Aaron was, reluctantly, impressed. If one had money, this was an acceptable way to spend it.

Mrs. Ballantine was seated on a loveseat by one of the bookcases, the upholstery a muted brown that managed to somehow be a perfect backdrop for her pale green dress. She was younger than he'd anticipated, perhaps closer to forty than fifty, with only the faintest strands of silver in her fashionably coiffed hair and the slightest suggestion of wrinkles around mouth and eyes. Her husband, the one who had presumably made the appeal for their help, was nowhere in evidence.

But Mrs. Ballantine was not alone. A girl was seated comfortably in one of the armchairs, a book balanced on one knee, a cup of tea in her hands. Aaron took her in at a glance: slender build, certainly no more than thirteen and possibly younger. Dark hair, two plaits tight-woven against her scalp, simple skirt and blouse, the hands curled around the cup much darker than Mrs. Ballantine's, with an olive tone. Not a member of the family, then, unless someone had married outside their community, but not a servant, clearly comfortable in the household. A companion? She seemed young for such a position, but he supposed it was possible.

"Mr. and Miss Harker of the Boston Huntsmen, ma'am."

"Thank you, Mrs. Green. That will be all."

Clearly relieved to have made the right decision, the housekeeper bobbed her head once and closed the door behind her as she left.

There was silence for a moment, the three adults in the room watching each other; then Mrs. Ballantine smiled, polite if not welcoming. "Miss Harker, Mr. Harker. May I present Daniella Vaz de Peña? Daniella is the daughter of a family friend, and indeed a dear friend of mine, come to keep me company and distract me from my worries." The smile she gave Vaz de Peña was distinctly warmer, the smile a mother would give a child, and Aaron was surprised by the feeling it stirred in him. Sympathy, perhaps, mixed with something darker.

Jealousy, he realized with a physical shock, even as Rosemary turned to acknowledge the girl with a polite smile and an offered handshake, giving her equal status with the other adult in the room. The girl straightened up and smiled back, clearly delighted to be given such attention.

"Please, sit down, join us." Mrs. Ballantine gestured to one of the empty chairs near her settee. "Dr. Collins has not been able to explain what happened to my brother, or how to cure him, but Walter seems convinced you might know more?"

There was a question in the woman's voice, and Aaron threw a glance toward his sister, waiting to see how they were going to play this. There were some instances where Aaron was forced to lead, where a woman could not, but they'd agreed on the way over that this was not likely to be one of those times.

Rosemary did not acknowledge his glance, sitting gracefully on the loveseat next to Mrs. Ballantine and taking the woman's hands in her own in a practiced, soothing manner that claimed the woman's attention. "Your husband has asked us to look into the recent unfortunate events involving your brother, yes. I assure you, we will be both thorough and discreet."

Aaron took a chair that was close enough for conversation, but still a polite distance away, and sat down. His role now was to be attentive, to let his sister guide the conversation and watch what was revealed.

But the presence of the girl in the room was a complication they had not planned on. Huntsmen were not a secret society, particularly or by design, but anonymity was preferred, and a child could not be expected to have any particular discretion. He worried slightly at a cuticle, wondering if Rosemary would be able to address that before more was said.

Thankfully, at that same moment, Mrs. Ballantine seemed to realize that this might be a matter the girl should not overhear.

"Daniella, make sure you see Macy in the kitchen before you leave. I suspect she has a plate of cookies she has no idea what to do with that you may as well bring home."

From the smile on the girl's face, extra cookies were a frequent occurrence, and if she was aware that she was being sent away, she showed none of it in her expression, murmuring a polite farewell to the Harkers before leaving the room.

The woman waited until the door had closed again before visibly settling herself. "Forgive me. This is difficult, speaking of . . . of what happened that day."

"How much has your husband told you of what we do, Mrs. Ballantine?"

The woman shook her head. "Only that you had experience with this sort of thing, and that I should tell you what I saw. But I fear . . . I know that it sounds mad, that I sound mad."

"There is very little you can say to us that will sound mad." Both Mrs. Ballantine and Rosemary turned to look at Aaron at that, his sister's eyebrow rising slightly as though to ask what he was doing, deviating from the script, and he half lifted one shoulder in a shrug.

The woman gave him a look of what might have been gratitude, so he thought he hadn't put his foot in it too badly. When she looked back to his sister, Rosemary had smoothed her expression into nothing but focused concern. "My brother is correct: there's no need to feel self-conscious. In our line of work we have heard and seen things that the rest of the world would deem impossible, and yet were true. Tell us as much as you can remember, without worrying about how it might sound."

Mrs. Ballantine placed her hands in her lap, clasped as though to keep them from moving. She wore a sapphire on her left hand, Aaron noted, slightly larger than the diamond on her right. "It was Tuesday, a little after noon. I had come into the office to discuss some matters with Franklin. He works for the firm."

Franklin was the brother who had been struck down, Aaron presumed. Harry hadn't given them a name.

Rosemary nodded, all sympathetic attention. "He's a lawyer?"

"Yes, although quite junior. He's young yet, but Mr. George, the head of the firm, took him on as a secretary when he was still in school, and expects he will have a great future ahead of him."

She was speaking of him in the present tense, Aaron noted, although it sounded as though he had not woken since the attack.

"And the matters you came in to discuss?"

"Aren't relevant." The words were polite but firm; Rosemary had been put in her place. She took it with grace, moving on to the next question without a flinch.

"It was an ordinary day, then?" Rosemary asked. "There had been no indication of anything in your brother's life, no upsets or confrontations? No one who might have wished harm on him?"

Oh, Aaron hoped it wasn't a pukwudgie. Every hunt he'd ever read about them was chaos from start to end.

"No." Mrs. Ballantine shook her head. "I mean, we were all concerned about the damage that had been done to the windows—Walter had even discussed buying a guard dog to patrol the grounds—but that was here. Franklin didn't mention anything happening to him, and he would have told me."

She sounded certain about that, and Rosemary let it drop.

"So that day, when you arrived . . ."

"I was at the front desk saying good morning to Mr. Parker, another one of the partners, when we heard a noise from Franklin's office." Mrs. Ballantine gave a delicate shudder, almost too tiny to see. "It sounded like something hitting against the wall, so I went inside, Mr. Parker with me."

"And you saw . . . ?"

The woman swallowed.

"Franklin. He was lying on the floor, papers scattered all

around him, as though a gust of wind had knocked everything awry. I thought at first he had fallen, hit his head, but then I saw . . ."

The Huntsmen waited.

Mrs. Ballantine shook her head slightly, barely a sideways twitch, and pressed the back of her hand against her mouth before continuing. "I couldn't have seen anything; it must have been shadows, the day was very bright outside, and—"

"It's all right," Rosemary said, her voice calm and soft, a cushion to fall into. "Tell us what you saw."

"A shape," Mrs. Ballantine said, her eyes looking somewhere distant. It was a look they'd encountered before, the look of someone who'd seen things rational thought told them were impossible. "Slender, I think. Greenish, or bluish, shifting, the way water changes color? And it was leaning over Franklin, like . . . as though it had pushed him down. As though it was going to do something worse. But when I came in the door, it . . . it disappeared."

She looked away from Rosemary, as though seeking something else in the room, no, as though *afraid* something else was in the room, before turning back to them. "It was there— I saw it. No matter what Mr. George claims, I saw something. How could it just disappear?"

Her blue eyes were wide and uncertain, the lines of her face deepening in her distress. She wasn't lying or exaggerating; she'd seen what she described. He'd eat Rosemary's best hat if he was wrong, and he wasn't. She simply didn't have the context to describe it properly, that was all. Uncanny were too far outside modern sensibilities, common sense leading witnesses either to deny what they'd seen entirely, or forcing the memories into vagueness, that much easier to dismiss.

Aaron had no idea what sort of uncanny could disappear in the middle of an office, but there were any number of uncanny that could and did hide in shadows, using them to trick human eyes. They simply needed to determine which one this was, then find and dispatch it.

Rosemary kept going, her hands now curled around Mrs. Ballantine's, her voice velvet-soft and sympathetic. "And Mr. Parker, did he see anything?"

"No. Or, if he did, he said nothing." Mrs. Ballantine lifted her chin, but her eyes were still uneasy. "He called for someone to call a doctor, then tried to get me to leave the room, as though I'd leave Franklin just lying there!"

"And you haven't spoken to anyone else about this?"

The more people who were aware, the more cautious the Harkers would need to be. Particularly if the local authorities were involved.

"No." Mrs. Ballantine was firm on that. "When Franklin wouldn't wake up, I told Walter what I saw, but . . . what were we to do, call the police?" She laughed, but there was very little humor in the sound.

A wealthy woman would be considered eccentric rather than mad, at least officially, but she was right: the police would at best ignore her report, chalk it up to hysteria. Fear of ridicule had done the Harkers a good turn; less official involvement was better.

"And your brother has not woken since?"

"No. No matter what the doctors tried, they just . . . they

said we should just make him comfortable, and pray." Her expression said what she thought of that advice. "Dr. Collins thought it was apoplexy, at first. And then he asked me if my brother was using opium. Franklin! He barely drank wine, much less . . . But he won't wake up. He just lays there, barely breathing, and he won't wake up."

Aaron caught Rosemary's eye, raising one eyebrow, and she gave a faint nod. Medical science might not recognize the symptoms, but Huntsmen did. Giambattista Basile had first documented instances of uncanny-influenced sleep back in the seventeenth century, but the phenomena was far older than that. The Sleeping Beauty myth had its roots in actual hunts, from all over the globe.

Aaron felt anticipation starting to work its way up his spine, his blood starting to move a little faster. From the tiny smile curling his sister's mouth, entirely inappropriate, she felt the same.

And if the disruptions that had preceded the attack did not match any of those stories, and nothing in what Mrs. Ballantine had said explained why her brother had been attacked, if he was still a target—and if others in the house were at risk as well? That just made it more of a challenge.

Huntsmen, like hounds, were bred to hunt.

––––––––

They took their leave of Mrs. Ballantine after acquiring the address of the law firm where her brother worked, and a promise that, should there be any change in her brother's condition, she would alert them directly at their hotel.

The sun had dipped below the horizon while they had

been inside, and the air was noticeably colder, making the walk back to the trolley stop more bracing than Rosemary generally enjoyed, and she was beginning to feel the lack of sleep the night before.

"So. What do you think?"

Rosemary took a moment to consider everything they had learned—and what they had not—before responding. "I think whatever she did see, she's likely forgotten half, and embroidered half. But we have no way of knowing which half."

"Do you know of any uncanny that can actually disappear?"

"There are none." Rosemary was certain of that: invisibility was impossible.

Her brother made a noise deep in his throat that sounded like doubt, but he didn't contradict her.

A quick supper at a little café near the hotel served to fill their stomachs and supply them with a barely cooked steak for Bother, who greeted them with relief on their return, pushing his bulk against Rosemary's legs as though he'd been left alone for days, rather than only a few hours.

After the hound had licked the last of the meat off his jowls, she attached the lead to his collar, then, once in the hallway, knocked on Aaron's door. He answered, already in his nightclothes, his glasses perched on the edge of his nose and a slender journal open in his hands.

"*Spindacker's Boston Tribes*," he said at her look. "I'm hoping there's some mention of a local uncanny that plays tricks on eyesight."

Uncanny, as a rule, were territorial. There were some that moved about, and many that migrated, but you started from the assumption that your prey was known to den in the area.

"I'm taking Bother out for his constitutional, and then I'm turning in. I'll have the front desk knock us at eight?"

Her brother nodded, then closed the door without so much as a "good night," his nose already back in the journal. Rosemary, used to such behavior, merely tapped the leash and directed Bother toward the stairs.

A good night's sleep, and hopefully the morning would bring them better hunting.

Four

THE NEXT MORNING started cloudy but warm, and after a quick breakfast at a café in town, another trolley ride took the Harkers, minus Bother, to a less residential part of town, where squat storefronts and taller brownstone buildings with more discreet signage sat side by side, the rattle of bicycles and wagons going past interspersed with the chime and clang of the trolley as it rolled back along its track. Well-dressed pedestrians pushed past them as Rosemary stopped in front of their destination, her mouth set in a flat line.

"What are you thinking?"

"That I dislike lawyers a great deal. They thrive on the misery of others."

Aaron had no response to that, so he stayed silent, waiting. Finally, she sighed, visibly shaking off whatever mood had struck her, and he asked, "Your calling cards or mine?"

"Yours. They won't take me seriously."

She wasn't wrong. And yet. "That's why you always win."

His quip only got a faint smile from her as they stepped up to the front door and pushed inside.

Where the Ballantine home had not made a fuss about their wealth, the law offices of Parker, George, and Heddle practically oozed New Money and Ambition, from the thick pile of the carpets underfoot to the carved moldings overhead, and the immaculately groomed young man sitting behind the reception desk.

"We should have brought Bother," Aaron murmured as the door closed behind them, cutting off the noise of the street outside. It was difficult to imagine anything being so crude as to interrupt the hushed quiet of this space.

The young man looked up, politely, professionally alert. "May I help you?"

"Yes," Aaron said, handing over his card, a simple square of thick cardstock with his name and *New Haven, Connecticut* in a masculine copperplate. "We had an appointment with Franklin Congdon." It wasn't enough to project confidence, their mother used to say; people in authority meet confidence with confidence. Arrogance, however, got you in most doors without question.

"Oh." The young man took a moment to be flustered. "Yes. Ah. I'm afraid that Mr. Congdon is, um, not in today."

Rosemary lifted her head just enough that she could look down her nose at the young man, who likely was closer to Aaron's twenty than her twenty-six. "I beg your pardon? But we have an appointment."

He blinked at her, now completely flummoxed by the pair of them. "Yes, I . . . Let me see if there is someone else who can explain the situation. Please, have a seat?"

They might not take her seriously, but Aaron would always put his money on Rosemary, for good reason.

The chairs they were ushered to were a match to the rest of the front office, mahogany and brocade, and deeply uncomfortable. Rosemary arranged her skirt and attempted to make the best of it, but Aaron bounced back up, choosing instead to lean against the paneled wall, hands shoved into his pockets and a bored expression fixed on his features. He hated this part, the waiting. They had discussed their approach on the trip over, had agreed on what they would say and what they were looking for, and yet his thoughts kept going around and around, imagining variations on how it might go, all the ways it could go wrong, and rehearsing how he would deal with it. Should they not have given their actual names? Would it have been better to use false ones? How much could they tell, and what should they elide about why they were here? His brain was like a maddened squirrel, racing inside his skull.

"Stop it," Rosemary said quietly.

"That never helps, you know. You telling me to stop it."

They'd had this conversation a thousand and ten times before and would likely have it another thousand and ten times to come; he suspected that she started it simply to give him something else to think about. He hated the fact that it always worked. Although thinking of all the ways he couldn't behave properly—too intense, too direct in his behavior, even for Huntsmen—wasn't all that much of an improvement.

"Throwback," they'd whispered when he was younger, when his parents or Rosemary couldn't hear, but not caring that he did. He supposed they'd meant for him to hear, to know that they knew he wasn't quite right, that he didn't belong . . .

"Excuse me."

Aaron looked up to see the young man had returned, this time accompanied by an older gentleman, his waistcoat buttoned smartly across a wide stomach, his chin covered by a strip of hair in a style fashionable a decade ago.

"I am Archibald George, senior partner. Hawthorn here says you had an appointment with our Mr. Congdon? I'm afraid you weren't on his books."

"Oh. Oh dear." Rosemary fluttered in a way that would have made Aaron laugh like a cat if he hadn't been prepared for it. "Aaron, dear, did your secretary not confirm our appointment?"

"Of course he did. Jonathan is most efficient." He turned his attention back to the older man, doing his best to exude expensive disappointment. "Where is Mr. Congdon?"

"Please . . ." And Mr. George gestured for them to follow. "This is best discussed in my office."

Aaron thought it was all going well, but the door to the office had scarcely closed behind them, trapping them in a luxuriously furnished space, when the senior partner perched on the edge of his desk and crossed his arms over his chest. "You're not here to meet with Congdon."

Aaron's thoughts slammed to a halt as though they'd been introduced to a stone wall, and Rosemary, who had clearly been ready to lay on the charm, took a figurative step backward, although she did not move. "I—no. We aren't."

Her admission stopped the other man cold; clearly he had been expecting them to prevaricate. But once you'd been found out, there wasn't much point.

Since he'd brought them to his office to confront them in

private, Aaron thought it safe to assume he didn't plan to call the police on them, at least not right away. With a nonchalance he didn't feel, he dropped into one of the chairs set in front of the desk. They were much more comfortable than the ones out front. Rosemary, following his lead, took off her hat and sank into the chair next to him, placing the hat on her lap and smoothing the simple goose feather with one finger in a move that, if you didn't know better, might look like a nervous twitch.

"I thought not," George said with grim satisfaction. "Congdon was many things, but slapdash was never one of them. If you'd had an appointment, we would have found it in his daybook."

"Was? Is he dead, then?" Aaron leaned forward, dropping his disinterested facade for the sharper-nosed curiosity of a newshound, complete with the small notebook he fished from the inside pocket of his coat, a pencil tied to it with a scrap of ribbon. The plan had been to claim to be potential clients and hope that they'd be handed off to a junior partner, who might be coaxed into gossip—or, if they were lucky, actual facts. But good Huntsmen, or at least smart Huntsmen, could shift to a new plan on a moment's notice.

"Ghoul," the lawyer labeled him in mild disgust, and Aaron bit his tongue to keep from retorting that he did not eat decaying human flesh, thank you very much. Although in truth, there were some newspapermen he wouldn't be so certain didn't.

"No, he's not dead," the lawyer went on. "But he might as well be. Apoplexy, the doctors say." He shook his head, that momentary lapse into cold pragmatism now replaced by a well-composed portrait of sadness. "There had been no warning. I'd seen him just that morning and he seemed perfectly fine, and then . . . well. Terrible tragedy, he was a promising young man."

Rosemary let just enough horrified fascination color her words. "You saw it happen?"

He frowned at her, as though the question was offensive. "No one did. He was alone in his office, and then we heard a thump and ran in to find him, face down on the floor. Gave us all quite the turn."

Interesting, Aaron noted, that he didn't mention the man's sister had been there as well. Chivalry, to shield her from a pair of muckrakers? A request from her husband? Or something else entirely?

George's gaze seemed to soften around the edges, some real emotion moving behind the facade; then his face sharpened again. "So, newsmen? And lady?" he corrected himself. "What paper, so I'll know who should receive my complaint."

Rosemary shook her head. "We're not with any newspaper."

The negation, as hoped, threw the senior partner off-balance for a moment, then: "You're from Health Assurance, then." He sounded resigned now, not angry, as though he'd been expecting something of the sort. "You could have just come to me in the first place. We're not keeping any secrets."

Aaron privately doubted that; it had been his observation that everyone kept secrets. Most of those secrets simply didn't matter to anyone other than those holding them.

All that was a distraction. If Mr. George thought they were from an assurance company, that gave them another chance.

Conversations were just another hunt: circle around and catch them from the side, see what falls out once they've been shaken. They couldn't prove he was lying, but he had omitted information, and knowing that gave them the advantage.

"Mr. George, you said he was alone. Had there been anyone with him, just prior to that?"

There was a slight shift in his expression, barely noticeable behind the facial hair, then he shook his head. "No."

Aaron let himself glance at Rosemary, whose attention was entirely on the man, as though his every word dripped pearls. But she didn't believe him, either. Mr. George was definitely keeping secrets.

But lies sometimes could tell you more than truth.

"No meetings that morning?" Rosemary took up the thread, lifting her eyebrows in polite surprise. "It's been my experience that an office of your reputation rarely leaves their junior people sitting idle."

Oh, he did not like being challenged by a woman, puffing up like a banty rooster, his cheeks pinking slightly. "Congdon had been working on some research for one of our clients. If he saw anyone that morning, it was not an official meeting."

Nothing that they could confirm in writing, in other words. But that told Aaron that there had been a meeting that morning. Or at least that Congdon had seen someone who had not been written down in his datebook. But why would Mr. George not want to acknowledge it?

The man had been unmarried, so it was unlikely he was having an affair, and even more unlikely that he would have arranged an assignation at his place of employment, although Aaron, admittedly, had no experience in such things. Had it been something of dubious legality, a client who could not officially be listed or recognized? Aaron knew little about such things, either: Huntsmen did not end up in courts of law.

If Congdon had seen someone just before he was attacked, there was the strong possibility that it had been an uncanny. But if so, how had it managed to make its way into the offices? There were uncanny who could mask themselves as human, briefly and in poor lighting. But to come into an office, surrounded by humans? That was not normal uncanny behavior. They lurked in woods, abandoned spaces, or dark alleys, not well-lit, occupied buildings. And even the few uncanny that were human-shaped, who could pass as human at a distance or at night, would be obvious under light and direct observation, their eyes or scapes or sucker-mouths giving them away.

Congdon's sister was married to Ballantine, who knew about Huntsmen . . . had Congdon known about Huntsmen as well, and by extension the uncanny? Aaron almost choked on the idea that the man had taken an uncanny on as a client, knowingly or otherwise. Or, God help them all, if he had tried to make a deal. That sort of thing never ended well, for the human.

Aaron had a dozen or more questions he wanted to ask, but the expression on George's face was that of a man who had given enough time to foolishness. Even Aaron could tell that they would get no further with that line of questioning and were likely to be removed from the premises if they lingered.

Time to be blunt, and Rosemary could yell at him later.

"We had been led to understand that a . . ." Aaron made as though to consult something written on the notepad he had pulled from his jacket pocket. "A Mrs. Ballantine was the one who found him?"

A flicker of the man's eyes was the only indication that Aaron had hit on something George had hoped to keep hidden. "Yes, if you know that already, there's no point denying it. Congdon's sister was here. She'd brought him lunch. But there's no need for her name to be brought into this; it was a sad moment for her, one she has no need to relive."

"Indeed," Aaron murmured, wondering if this man had ever actually spoken with a woman, or if every female in his life was indeed that delicate. "She was the one who called for help, on finding him?"

"Yes."

Another lie, or Mrs. Ballantine was lying about another partner being with her. Aaron found himself inclined to trust her word more. Although, not entirely. People lied for all sorts of reasons, and sometimes for no reason at all. If Mrs. Ballantine enjoyed being the focus of attention, she might embroider her role.

But then she would say *she* had been the one to call, not give that role to someone else.

People made Aaron's head hurt.

As though aware he'd just spoken himself into a corner, George backtracked slightly. "We telephoned the operator for help, but I'm afraid whatever had happened, it was already too late." George shook his head again. "We will miss him here. He was a good man, a hard worker." It didn't take the other man standing up, clearly ready to show them out, to know that they had run out of time. With this avenue, at least. Aaron was desperately trying to come up with some excuse to see Congdon's daybook when Rosemary leaned forward in her chair.

"We've taken up too much of your time already, our apologies. If you could have someone show us Mr. Congdon's office, and have someone provide us with a list of all his clients?" Her words were polite, but it was clear from her tone that she wasn't asking a question.

"Of course." Aaron felt an urge to applaud the man's stiff-jawed professionalism, when he clearly wanted nothing more than to wash his hands of them entirely. But for whatever reason, the idea that they were from an assurance company made him more obliging than he might have been otherwise, and while Huntsmen were not encouraged to lie as such, nowhere had they been taught they needed to correct misapprehensions. Particularly when they worked in their favor.

Mr. George escorted them out of his office, handing them over to a fresh-faced boy with the air of someone done with the entire business. "David, please take them to Congdon's office. Let them look things over, but under no circumstances remove anything."

"And the list of clients?" Rosemary reminded him.

"If you can establish that you have need of those names, we will provide them. Until then, we protect the privacy of our clients. Good day, Miss Harker, Mr. Harker."

———

Unlike the senior partner's office, Congdon's barely earned the name, four bare walls and a plain desk covered with dog-eared folders and a stack of dry-looking books. There was a tea-colored stain in the shape of a wide ring next to the books, and Rosemary traced her fingers over it, as though it would tell her something. "Someone forgot to use a coaster."

"You two would have gotten along, then," Aaron said, picking up one of the books and riffling through the pages, then putting it back down. There wasn't much else to look at: no bookcases or cabinets to snoop through, no photos to examine, just the desk and the walls. Rosemary thought it must have been a dreary place to spend so much time in. Had they removed items? She was better versed in reading blood trails and branch-marks than this.

Their escort had paused just inside the door, clearly planning on watching them the entire time they were there. His face was smooth-cheeked, almost innocent, but Rosemary thought that his eyes were as suspicious as a cop's.

"You can search us when we're done, make sure we haven't taken any of the clearly valuable belongings when we leave," she said tartly, and he flushed bright pink.

"I was told—"

"You were told to bring us here, not to guard us. But if you must . . ." Rosemary turned toward the boy, drawing his attention and using her body to block a direct view of whatever Aaron was doing. Without Bother, they couldn't tell if there had been uncanny in the room prior to this, but Aaron was both clever and quick-fingered, and she trusted that if there was anything that looked suspicious—or useful—he would find and pocket it while the boy was distracted.

She let her shoulders soften a little, leaning in just slightly. Too young to be even a junior partner, likely an office errands boy of some sort. But old enough to be distracted by an attractive young woman paying attention to him. "Did you work with Mr. Congdon?"

"No, miss, ah, ma'am. Mostly I run errands for the partners. I'm to go to Litchfield in the spring, though."

Rosemary nodded as though that meant something to her.

"Mr. Congdon was—is—a good fellow, though. Always a 'good morning' to us all, and he'd remember your name first time he met you. Listened real good, clients liked that. Is he going to be all right?"

Rosemary found herself wanting to give the boy good news. "They don't know yet."

"And they don't know what happened?" Beyond the senior partner's hearing, once the boy started speaking, the words seemed to tumble out of him. "Because I saw him just before, and he was fine. Was laughing, even."

She didn't dare look over at Aaron. "When you say 'just before,' you mean earlier that day?"

"No, miss. It was . . ." He tilted his head back as though to think better. "I hadn't gone to fetch lunch yet, so it was maybe eleven? They were walking in the hallway. I guess he was walking them out? And they said something and he laughed. I was going the other way so I didn't hear what it was, but it must have been funny the way he burst out." The boy looked thoughtful for a moment. "People don't laugh much, in here. So I noticed."

"Paying attention to details is important, the mark of a good lawyer," Rosemary said approvingly, and watched his chest broaden under the praise. "Did you notice anything about his companions? Their appearances, how they walked?"

A number of uncanny were human-shaped, but there was always something about them that would seem odd, something the human brain would notice and be wary of.

He frowned, then shook his head. "No. He looked perfectly ordinary. A little younger than me, though, that's why I noticed. I would have thought he was Mr. Congdon's brother, only I know he doesn't have one."

Rosemary's blood chilled for an instant. Uncanny were, for the most part, beasts. Cunning, even clever, but beasts. The only uncanny that could manage extended human interaction, who would look youthful even when full-grown, were the fey.

Please, she let the heartfelt prayer rise up to a deity she didn't entirely believe in. *Please, not that.*

Behind her, she heard Aaron slam the desk drawer shut, and the boy's attention flicked to him, giving her a moment to compose herself.

"I think we've learned all we can," her brother said, coming to stand next to her, the press of his arm against hers a welcome comfort. "Please inform Mr. George that we will be in touch, should we need more from him."

———————

Emerging from the building back into the noise of the street was almost a relief, despite the chill air slipping underneath the cloth of her coat and nipping at her nose, a reminder that spring in New England was considered winter elsewhere. But it wasn't enough to calm Rosemary's nerves.

"Did you hear? Did you hear what he said?"

Her brother took her arm, on the surface a sweet, fraternal gesture, but his fingers pressed hard enough to leave a bruise through the layers of cloth. "Breathe, Rosemary."

"I am breathing. Aaron. Did you hear? If the fey are here, if the fey are involved . . ."

"We don't know that. We have no cause to think that, save pure conjecture off a piece of unverified information. Breathe."

Irritated, she nonetheless took an exaggeratedly deep breath, exhaling slowly, then a series of smaller, actually calming breaths. He steered her away from the office, walking them back toward the trolley stop. The sun had emerged from the morning clouds, warming the air enough that it was slightly more pleasant, and there was a corresponding increase in the number of people on the sidewalks, forcing Rosemary to don at least a veneer of calm.

"You're right," she said finally. "I know you're right. But—"

But even the thought of a fey here, anywhere near mortals, was deeply troubling. And by "deeply troubling" Rosemary wasn't afraid to admit she meant "horrifying."

There were reasons, many reasons, why the fey were forbidden to walk the world of mortals. The treaty that kept fey and mortals apart was generations old, with strict penalties for breaking on both sides, even if most mortals knew nothing of it. Huntsmen were the guardians of that treaty—and the enforcers of it, should it come to that, by the weight of their blood.

The last known—and dealt with—breach had been over a hundred years ago.

The events in Brunson had risked a crack in that protection, if the fey were to notice, and who could tell what they noticed, or did not? That uncertainty had been enough to give both Harkers nightmares for weeks after their return home. Rosemary had scoured the newspapers, dug into every source of gossip she could without being obvious, listened for any rumor or whisper that might be fey intrusion, had waited with a sick pit in her stomach for word to come from the Circle that Huntsmen were being called to war. Only when the second month had passed with no indication of further magic loosed in the world had they begun to relax.

Had she stopped worrying too soon? If a fey was here, was it in response to that crack? Or had one of the fey chosen to break the treaty of their own accord?

Rosemary wasn't sure which possibility terrified her more.

"Don't borrow disaster," Aaron said, knowing exactly where her thoughts had gone. "It may be that it was a nephew, or the son of another partner, or the boy was wrong and it was simply a youthful-looking but otherwise ordinary man on perfectly ordinary business."

"An ordinary man who was the last to be with the victim before he fell into a strange, unexplained sleep?"

"It's possible. And since that option would make our job more difficult, I'm going to say the odds of it being true increase."

Aaron's customary cynicism was oddly reassuring.

"So, we are back to a random uncanny who could walk through a busy office at midday, attack a man, and leave, and nobody noticed?"

"Except Mrs. Ballantine."

"Who claimed that the figure she saw *disappeared*." She

paused speaking while they passed an older couple, white heads bent together, then went on. "I liked her, Aaron, but I'm not sure that we can consider her a reliable witness. Not unless your research last night turned up an uncanny who could turn into thin air?"

"Regrettably, no. Sprout wings, yes, but not disappear."

"So what, then? A hungry rover? Doors don't stop them, and the doctors wouldn't know to look for the bruising they leave, or they would have thought it was from the fall itself. They're simple enough to deal with, once you've identified them." Wrap a rowan branch around the neck and burn the body to ashes, and the victims recover, weak but alive, in a few weeks.

Aaron considered that for a moment. "If it were a rover, they'd be feeding on more than one man. We need to discover if anyone else has fallen victim to a mysterious sleeping sickness. Is that the sort of thing that's likely to be in the papers?"

"Not until it's too late to be of use to us." Not for the first time, Rosemary wished for a swifter source of news, a telegraph system dedicated to such reports. "We need to find a font of gossip. Perhaps Mrs. Ballantine can be of use again."

Rosemary liked cities, enjoyed the noise and bustle, but her experience had been that for the finding of useful gossip, small towns were better. Still, uncanny, like humans, were often lazy. If the first victim had been from one social group, the odds were good that others would be as well, simply because the uncanny had discovered a way in.

"We need to get Bother into that office, soon." The hound would be able to tell immediately if an uncanny had been in the office, even if he couldn't tell them what kind, if they managed it before the scent faded.

"Or," her brother said, drawing his words out, "we need to have Bother scent something from the office." And, with a careful, completely pointless look around, he pulled a wire-framed pair of glasses from his pocket. "Mr. Congdon's spectacles. Either they fell off when he collapsed, or someone removed them. But considering the amount of paperwork he appeared to be handling, it's likely he was wearing them, or at the very least had them on his person, when he was attacked."

"You really think Bother could pick anything off a pair of glasses?" She respected the hound's abilities, had seen him track an uncanny from even the faintest trace on the ground, but spectacles? That seemed a bit of a reach.

Her brother shrugged. "We won't know until we try, and it's certainly more practical than trying to sneak him into the office. Especially if it were a fey." Molosser hounds were trained to scent and follow uncanny, but even the hint of a fey would, they'd been told, send them into full hellhound mode, and a hound on the hunt left nothing but chaos behind.

The thought made Rosemary wince. A Molosser's claws were designed to rend flesh; what they could do to floors and furniture was almost as painful. They had been sent to do this *quietly*.

They arrived at the trolley stop and found a place slightly away from the other folk waiting, to continue their conversation. "If it was fey . . . would that explain what Mrs. Ballantine saw?" The journals said that fey magic could do seemingly impossible things, works of wonder and horror, but they never clarified what those works *were*.

"If it was a fey, we've got worse problems than one sleeping prince. But it's far more likely that whatever she saw clouded her mind and slipped away in the confusion."

"And nobody else saw it?"

"An office full of bullheaded, fact-minded lawyers? They'd make themselves forget it, even if a kobold came up and bit them on the nose."

She wasn't sure she agreed with his dismissal of Mrs. Ballantine, but it was a strong argument, particularly about the lawyers. She could not imagine Mr. George ever acknowledging anything he could not explain.

"Rosemary, why did you ask for the client list? You must have known he would refuse to give it to us. Nobody would be willing to hire a legal firm who might spill any of their dirty details."

Rosemary welcomed the change of subject. "I know. But it gave him something to deny us, which makes him feel as though he won that exchange. That way, if we have to go back and ask for something else, he might be more willing to give it."

"That . . . I would never have thought of that. It's—hey!"

Although the trolley stop was not particularly crowded, a woman walking quickly, her head down, from the opposite direction, had bumped into him, sending Aaron staggering sideways and crashing against Rosemary.

Instinctively, even though he knew better, his hand went to where his wallet was tucked inside his coat. His hand paused; then he spun on his heel to stare after the woman. "She took my knife!"

Rosemary turned as well, searching the crowd, even

though the woman had already disappeared around the corner, and to race after her would raise more interest than they could afford. She reached out to grab Aaron's shoulder; while their instinct was to chase, their orders were to settle things quietly, with discretion. And chasing after a woman in public, in broad daylight, would definitely cause a scene.

Using her grip on him as a handle, she pulled him toward her, moving them both forward again. "Plain steel?"

"Silver-edged!" He calmed slightly. "But I liked that one. I've had it for years. It saved me from a—"

"You can replace steel," she interrupted him. "So long as it wasn't . . ." And she hesitated, reminded that they were in public, too closely surrounded by ordinary folk who were already giving them curious glances. She tugged him closer, tilting her head so that her voice reached only his ear. "*That* knife."

That knife carried poison within it and was nothing to be left in the hands of the ignorant—or the malicious.

"You think I'd be carrying that today? Pfffft." Aaron made a rude noise, offended that she thought he'd thought he might need it to deal with lawyers. "I just . . . I was used to it, that's all. But why take the blade and not my wallet?"

"When it turns up stuck between someone's shoulder blades, we'll know. Next time, pay more attention when someone bumps you. Honestly," she said with asperity, "it's as though you've never been pickpocketed before."

"That's not the—" He paused, turning slightly to let another woman pass by him, his gaze suspicious until she had moved on without incident. "That's not the point. Why did she take the knife, and not my wallet?"

Rosemary shrugged, not particularly worried as she dug in her purse, handing him one of the coins as they heard a trolley rattling down the street. "Probably because she could tell at a touch you were stone-poor. An opportunistic thief is hardly uncanny, and if it's not uncanny, Aaron, it's not our business."

Grumbling under his breath, he dropped his coin in the ticket box and followed her onto the trolley.

Five

WHILE THE TOWN of Roughton was not large compared to New Haven, much less Boston, it sprawled over a surprisingly wide area, much of it hilly. Rosemary found herself thankful for the trolleys that crisscrossed the city, allowing them to get from point to point with a minimum of walking—or Aaron arguing to take the automotive.

Despite her brother's continued grumbling about the loss of his blade, Rosemary took advantage of the time to study the town in daylight. The buildings they passed were a pleasant mix of old and new, well maintained with fresh paint and clean bricks, the streets clearly laid out, with trees planted at regular intervals, and the people going about their day were dressed neatly but not overly fashionable. On the surface, it seemed like the town was doing well for itself.

But surfaces were often misleading. Somewhere there was an uncanny, or possibly an entire den of them. One man had already been attacked, for reasons or causes unknown; what else might be happening that simply hadn't been discovered yet?

The lack of information was infuriating, and Rosemary felt a strong urge to return to the Ballantine house and demand the woman give them more information.

Because there was no way that would go badly.

"Geography is as important as mythology," she said softly, almost to herself. "I wonder if there's a history to this town."

"It's New England," her brother said, pausing his grumbles to answer her. "Of course there's a history. Either someone was a witch or they were a royalist who ended badly, or they were a patriot who also ended badly but heroically, or they were a royalist witch who cursed half the founding families down to the final generation."

Aaron was being sarcastic, but he wasn't entirely wrong. At least two plaques they'd passed indicated the town dated back to the Revolution, if not earlier.

"Harry didn't mention anything about curses."

"Harry hasn't been in the field since Hector was a pup. Probably more worried about the curse of money stopping to think about anything else. There are so many uncanny native to this area, Rosemary, it could take us a year to run them all down. But none of them match the nature of the assault."

"Well, if you can think of a way to ask the Ballantines if any of their ancestors were witches, or ran afoul of witches, let me know."

The trolley stopped, and they swung down onto the street, making their way up the block to the hotel, trading increasingly lunatic ideas on how to ask Mrs. Ballantine about possible witches in her family.

They both fell silent when they entered the hotel, as much habit as actual fear that anyone would eavesdrop, but—

"Am I paranoid, or are we getting odd looks?" her brother asked out of the side of his mouth.

"I'm not going to say you aren't, but we definitely are. Do we look terribly disheveled?" She had a sudden thought. "Oh, if Bother caught a scent here while we were away . . ."

Her brother cracked a grin, despite his worry. "Wouldn't be the first time. Remember Broad Street Station?"

Rosemary turned a pained expression on him. "Please never mention that again."

They'd been much younger then, Botheration new to them, and it had been the first time they'd heard his hunting howl, a blood-chilling sound inherited from his hellhound ancestors. That would have been bad enough, but then he led them—and half a dozen idiot policemen in hot pursuit—on a merry chase through the rail station before finally bringing them to a den hidden in the train sheds below the building itself.

It had been almost a year before other Huntsmen stopped making train sounds at them.

Rosemary stopped at the front desk to retrieve their keys from the clerk. Thankfully, there was no complaint about noises coming from their rooms, and when she opened the door to her room, the hound merely lifted his head from the floor where he had been dozing, the midday sunlight coming through the window and dappling his short tawny fur. A quick glance showed that there had been no disturbances, the tell-tales she had placed around the room still intact. Not that she had expected otherwise, but caution was preferable to unfortunate surprises.

She suspected Aaron was using sigils to protect his room,

rather than thread and chalk, but she wasn't going to ask. Better not to know for certain.

"Tired of being cooped up?" she asked the hound. "Come on, let's get you some air."

The hound got to his feet, stretching and yawning, then presented himself for the leash. They followed the same path they had the night before but had to move more cautiously, with so many people around. There was a small park across the street she hadn't noticed earlier, barely large enough to earn the name, but someone had taken great care in laying out graveled paths around thimble-sized gardens. A mother sat with her infant on the bench, both of them wide-eyed as they watched Botheration approach.

"Is that a dog?"

"Either that or a pony, we're never quite sure," Rosemary responded, and the woman laughed, bouncing the infant on her knee. Bother sniffed at the baby, then, losing interest, tugged on the leash to indicate that he wanted to move on.

"You find ordinary people terribly boring, don't you," she said, as they came to the end of the path and went back out into the street. "I'll tell you a secret: so do I."

Rosemary and Aaron had been raised entirely within the Huntsmen community. The adults they knew, the children they grew up with, all became Huntsmen. Even the few relatives they had who didn't still knew what the Harkers did, what they were. Unfortunately, with so many Huntsmen sent over to help in Europe, there were few opportunities to gather with people she would find interesting. The few times Rosemary had tried socializing outside the community, she had been bored to tears before the end of the evening.

"Good thing I have Aaron," she told Bother. "And you, of course."

Someday she might marry, although at her age she was beginning to doubt it. Aaron . . . she loved her brother but had no illusions about his suitability to be someone's husband. It would be an utter disaster.

It was only when her boots began to pinch at the toes that Rosemary realized they'd walked well past the center of town, and by the time they turned around and returned to the hotel, her stomach was informing her that it had been far too long since breakfast.

She'd barely had time to hang up her coat and unpin her hat, placing it on the shelf of the wardrobe, before there was a knock on her door a half second before it opened, and Aaron poked his head in, hat off and his collar loosened.

"The café next door had lunch available," he said, holding up packages wrapped in brown paper. "I doubt they're as good as the ones Pepe makes, over on Wooster, but it should hold us over until dinner. We were too tired last night, but the clerk at the front desk said that the hotel dining room makes an excellent Delmonico."

Rosemary took one of the packages from him, unwrapping it to reveal slices of cold ham and several slices of buttered bread. Not her first choice, but Aaron's preferences were narrower than hers. "I wonder if Jonathan is back yet, and if he would like to join us for dinner."

Aaron came all the way into the room, closing the door behind him, and sat on the floor next to Bother with a solid thump, scowling at her over his own lunch. "Why would you want to—"

"He's a fellow Huntsmen," she interrupted Aaron. "And whatever your feelings about him, a competent one as well. I would welcome his opinions."

"I wouldn't."

"You're being a child."

She ignored his under-his-breath retort to that, pulling the chair out from the writing desk, then settling herself in it. For a few moments, the only sound in the room was that of rustling paper and chewing, plus the occasional snap of canine jaws as Aaron offered the hound scraps of ham and bread.

Rosemary finished first, crumpling the wrapper into the waste basket and washing her hands at the sink before returning to the desk. Uncapping and posting her pen, she pulled a piece of notepaper toward her and began making a list.

"This all started with basic nuisance behavior, according to Harry. Their mail being soaked through, one of the windows broken. As Mrs. Ballantine said, nothing serious."

Her brother leaned back against the side of the bed, looking up at the ceiling while Bother licked the grease off the papers. "Mischief like that would suggest someone had broken a deal with brownies."

But brownies were not known for directly attacking humans. And, as far as the Harkers knew, had no ability to send a victim into such a deep sleep.

"Even allowing for panic in the moment," Rosemary said out loud, "I don't think a brownie would match what Mrs. Ballantine saw."

"Not unless someone stretched it in a taffy pull," her brother agreed, his tone suggesting that he wouldn't mind seeing that happen. "Oh! Which reminds me." He pulled the spectacles from a pocket, shaking them open with two fingers and presenting them to Bother, who, food gone, had draped his head over Aaron's knee.

"Scent, Bother. Wittern."

The hound lifted his head at the command, black nostrils flaring as he identified what Aaron was asking him to smell, then ducked closer to practically inhale the metal and glass.

The Harkers waited one second, then another, and a few more, until Bother exhaled and lowered his head back to Aaron's knee.

"It was a good idea," Rosemary said, when Aaron just stared at the rejected spectacles. "It might just have been too long for any scent to hold on metal."

"Or maybe there wasn't an uncanny in the office at all."

"We're back to thinking it's merely a medical condition?"

Aaron considered the notion a moment, his hand absently stroking Bother's ear, then shook his head. "No. There's something uncanny going on here. But all we have is some petty vandalism, and the claims of a woman who might well have been having hysterics."

Rosemary curbed an odd impulse to leap to the other woman's defense. "Neither of us thought she was hysterical."

"She might well have been."

"Aaron. Are you arguing with me just to argue?"

"No. No! I just . . . It keeps coming back that she's the only one who admits to seeing anything, but what she saw? It's not in the book, not in any of the books I've read."

They were both well-schooled in the uncanny of their area, as all Huntsmen were, but over the years Aaron had developed a fascination with traits and tendencies of uncanny not just locally, but as far west as Ohio. If he said it wasn't in his books, she believed him.

Rosemary added that to her list, the scratch of her pen on paper the only sound, other than Bother's occasional quiet grunts of pleasure as Aaron found a particularly itchy spot.

"Lacking a medical explanation, and the fact that a sleeping death does fit other uncanny attacks elsewhere, I think we need to continue with the presumption of an uncanny behind this. But how does the mischief fit into that?"

Aaron shrugged. "Escalation? Mischief, and then when that didn't get their attention, violence?"

"Maybe. But why did it *want* their attention? To what purpose?"

"And we're back to the family history. Family history, Rosemary. You need to find out if they're hiding anything."

Rosemary pressed too hard with the pen, and ink blotted the paper, making her hiss with exasperation. "Harry sent us here to smooth things over, not rile them up."

Frustration clouded her ability to think, and the lure of the box with the three vials, hidden on the shelf of the wardrobe, was an almost physical pull. *Not yet,* she thought, and she forced her attention back to the painfully short list of what they knew for certain.

"Franklin Congdon. Unmarried, with no known offspring, one sister. Gainfully employed, no obvious connection to anything uncanny, save through his brother-in-law's affiliation with us. No medical issues, no known enemies."

"He's a lawyer, however junior. Of course he has enemies. Do you want speculation?"

She rested the nib of the pen above the paper. "Go on."

Aaron held up a thumb, ticking off his points. "We have a witness who says that the victim met with an individual of unknown origin, young and apparently charming, before falling ill. If it wasn't a client, who was it? And before you begin to panic again over the idea of it being fey—"

He paused, but Rosemary couldn't deny that she had panicked, and merely waved for him to go on.

"The last thing a fey would want to do if they were sneaking past treaty lines would be draw Huntsmen attention."

"Unless drawing Huntsmen attention is exactly what it wants to do." She frowned. "Why?"

"I have no idea. You asked for speculation."

"Useful speculation, please."

"I don't think the individual with him was fey—or any kind of uncanny. Too public, too visible, too many chances they might be seen. But they were the last ones to be in contact with the victim, so we need to find out who they were. It's possible that they were the intended victim, and our man was simply in the way."

Rosemary winced. "But it doesn't explain the damage to the Ballantines' home. Miserable coincidence?"

"We have no reason to presume it's uncanny-related except for the fact that a member of the family was attacked, but he does not live in the house, so . . . yes? Coincidence."

"An idea," Rosemary said, holding up a hand to stop him. "While we both agree that it was unlikely to be a random attack, we need to consider that it might not be random, but also not directed at the victim himself."

Aaron sat up abruptly, dislodging Bother. "The brother-in-law?"

"He is the connection to us. More, he's an active supporter of our work. If an uncanny were to learn that?"

"You think the damage to the house, and the attack on a family member, was meant as a warning, to stop him from supporting us?" Aaron considered the idea for a moment. "That's . . . far-fetched."

"It's extremely far-fetched," she agreed. "It's also possible."

Huntsmen training said that the uncanny were creatures of emotion and instinct, not logical thought, barely above beasts in their thinking. But the Harkers had recently learned that this was not always the truth—and that some uncanny were not only thinking creatures, but thoughtful.

Rosemary quickly added all of that to the "speculation" side of the paper. "We're definitely going to have to speak with Mrs. Ballantine again." Poking a beehive, to see what flew out. "And her husband."

Aaron looked decidedly unenthusiastic about that idea. "Do we want to meet with them together or separately?"

"Separately, I think. Divide and conquer. Woman-to-woman for sympathy, and man-to-man practicality. Quietly." *And politely,* she didn't add, but the look she gave her brother spoke volumes. Aaron had the training, and a sharp mind, but his edges were sharp as well, and his ability to empathize with other people was sometimes sadly lacking.

"Are you sure you don't want to coquette with Ballantine, and let me be mothered by the missus?"

She considered it for a moment; he wasn't wrong—it had possibilities. But: "No. If we had a better handle—any handle—on Ballantine, maybe. But if he takes a woman being sent as an insult, we're worse off than if you are too blunt with him."

Huntsmen, in theory, did not discriminate between the sexes; too many women over the centuries had battled the uncanny for that to be possible. But the rest of the world had not quite caught up yet. There were days she doubted it ever would, suffrage protests notwithstanding.

"The front desk had a telephone. I'll see if they will let me use it. If not, I'll send a message requesting another meeting."

"Do we want to give them time to prepare?"

Rosemary tilted her head. "You think that would be a problem?"

"If there is a connection, we're more likely to discover it if we keep them off-guard. Asking to meet with them both—"

"Urgh." Rosemary capped the pen and dropped it onto the desk, pinching the bridge of her nose between thumb and forefinger. "You're right, of course you're right, hush. But we need to be politic about it, or the Circle will have our heads."

Family pride aside, the Huntsmen stipend was what kept them housed and fed. Rosemary was aware that she was not suited for life in domestic service, although she thought she might do well as a nurse, should it come to that. Aaron, on the other hand, would be miserable in any kind of office job, leaving either labor or military service, and neither would welcome his sort of blunt speaking.

While she was muttering to herself, considering and discarding the best ways to approach the Ballantines, Aaron left the room, returning a few minutes later. She looked up, pen at the ready, whatever she was about to say halted by the sight of another knife in his hand, slightly larger than the one that had been stolen.

He flipped it back and forth in his hand before slipping it into the now-empty sheath under his vest, then moved his arm back and forth, testing the feel of the replacement. "I don't like it," he said. "But it's better than not having anything there at all."

"Is that the one Joshua sent you, before he went overseas?"

"Mmm. Plain steel, though."

Rosemary suspected that her expression indicated a significant lack of sympathy. Her knives were weighted specifically for throwing; his were more replaceable.

But the knife was an unwelcome reminder that they hadn't heard from Joshua in months, had no idea if their cousin was still in Latvia, or if he had been reassigned elsewhere. Some of the Huntsmen who had been sent to help deal with the rise in uncanny activity in Europe had come home; he had not.

Yet. He had not come home yet. She refused to assume the worst. But it was difficult, with the bits of news that reached American newspapers, the rumbles of unrest seemingly everywhere. Change was in the air, change and violence, and Rosemary did not like it.

"Enough." Aaron swung around, his mood shifting from pensive to manic. "I'm tired of thinking. Come on, Bother. Let's go for a walk."

The hound heaved himself to his feet, brown eyes clearly telling Rosemary that he didn't *have* to go outside, that he was only doing it because *Aaron* needed to go outside.

"You boys have fun," she said, turning back to her list.

The lobby was oddly empty when Aaron and Bother exited the elevator. The hound sniffed once at the carpeting, checked out the single man sitting in one of the chairs off to the side of the lobby, but otherwise showed no particular interest until they went outside, at which point he stopped dead in the walkway and lifted his nose to scent the air.

"You're just smelling dinner," Aaron told him.

Dusk had crept into town while they were upstairs, the sidewalks, like the lobby, emptier than they had been earlier. Aaron took a moment to look around, enjoying the feeling of not having to rush off to catch a trolley. The hotel was set on the corner of a three-way intersection, with a cluster of stores, most of them closed for the night, to the right, while down the street to the left the glow of lamps advertised a restaurant open for dinner. A lone delivery truck moved along the street, the clop of hooves and wooden-spoked wheels squeaking under the weight of whatever it carried, two men on bicycles passing it heading the other direction. Boston, with its tall buildings and bustle, might have been a hundred miles away, not ten. Aaron reached into his coat and pulled out a silver case, tapping at it before replacing it in his pocket. He knew the restlessness in him, even if he didn't like it, and it was nothing a cigarette could fix.

Bother pushed at his knee, as though reminding him that

they had come outside for a purpose, and Aaron flicked the leash, telling the hound to move.

Life with Botheration was simpler back home, where they could open the door and allow the hound to take care of his business, knowing he would let them know when he was done. But their neighbors knew the hound, knew that he wouldn't cause trouble. When they traveled, unless they were in the countryside, a leash and a human were required. A 120-pound animal wandering the street alone, even without Bother's obvious musculature, would have someone calling the police or, worse, trying to capture him themselves.

Bother did not take well to anyone other than the Harkers putting a leash on him.

Rosemary had mentioned a small park nearby, tucked between a tiny stone-walled church and an electricians' supply store, and he directed Bother toward that. In Aaron's opinion, calling it a park was giving it far too much credit; it was a pocket-sized patch of greenery, probably lovely in the summer, with broad-trunked chestnut trees lining a graveled path, but Bother's attention was on the patch of winter-brown grass, currently unoccupied.

"Go, do." There wasn't anyone else there at the moment, so Aaron let the lead drop, leather strap dragging behind the hound as he sniffed at the dry grass, looking for the perfect spot.

Still restless, Aaron walked after Bother, keeping a few paces back. Roughton, as befitted its affluent population, had installed incandescent streetlamps that illuminated the street surprisingly well, but did not quite reach into the parklet. He had shrugged into his coat before going outside, but the air was nippier than he'd expected, a reminder that it wasn't spring quite yet, and he turned the collar of his coat up against his neck.

"Hurry up, will you?"

The hound ignored him.

With a sigh, Aaron started pacing along the path, trusting Bother to catch up with him when he was done. Lacking distraction, he found himself rethinking the events of the day, and the conversation with Rosemary, his mind chasing down options and discarding them almost as swiftly.

"I wonder if Ballantine golfs. I could lose to him—that might make him open up."

And a golf club was a singularly useful weapon, should they be attacked. Although he supposed it was too early in the year for such an outing, and he hadn't brought an appropriate outfit.

Bother seemed to have found a worthy spot, getting down to business. Aaron turned away, giving the beast a modicum of privacy, when something tugged at the base of his brain, warning him that something was nearby, watching him.

"Bother." But there was no need to alert the hound; he had already paused, head lifted, even his flopped-over ear trying to stand erect. His tail was perfectly still, chest barely rising or falling, but the muscles under his plush coat were bunched, ready to spring into action in an instant. And his eyes, normally soft brown, now sparked with a deep red glow.

That was confirmation, had he needed it: there was an uncanny nearby. One Bother considered dangerous.

"Where is it, Bother?" He moved closer to the hound, slipping open his jacket for access to the knife he'd just holstered there. He had left his pistol in his room, which was just idiot carelessness. They were on a hunt, as peaceful as this town seemed.

The hound rumbled, deep in his chest, but didn't move. Either the hound couldn't tell where it was, or it was right in front of them.

This was a bad place and time for a confrontation. Leaving the park would be the smart idea, if the uncanny let them. But Aaron was curious. Was this their quarry? Or something else?

"Are you here to cause trouble," he asked the unseen presence. "Or are you just watching, waiting to see what we'll do?"

He wasn't expecting a response, although recent experiences had taught him not to presume. But Huntsmen training said that if an uncanny was causing no problems, they were to be left-be. Not out of any policy of tolerance, but because there were only so many Huntsmen, and far too many uncanny in the world. The odds were not in the Huntsmen's favor, ever.

Bother moved to Aaron's side, pressing lightly against his knee and letting out a low rumbling noise, not quite a growl, not quite a whine. "Easy, boy," Aaron said quietly, bending at the knee slowly to pick up Bother's lead. Despite the cold, his palm was sweaty against the leather loop. "Easy. This isn't the time or place to pick a fight."

The uncanny seemed to agree, because a few seconds after Bother gave the warning, the feeling of being watched was gone.

Back in the room, Rosemary put down her notes and listened to Aaron's report, her eyes following Bother take a turn around the room, clearly still on alert.

"Whatever it was, it didn't follow us across the street." Bother's hackles had gone down the moment they left the park, and by the time they'd entered the hotel, Aaron would have sworn the hound had forgotten about the incident entirely. Aaron was not so fortunate.

"But you didn't see anything."

"No." He hadn't heard anything, either. Or smelled anything. But that didn't mean it hadn't been there. He might misdoubt his own senses, on this, but never Botheration's.

"And it didn't—"

"It didn't do anything," he said, frustrated by her questions. "It just *was*."

He hadn't expected her to question him like this, as though she hadn't known him his entire life, hadn't trained with him, for days and weeks, from the time they were old enough to understand that their family was different. That even for Huntsmen, he was different.

They never talked about it, he and Rosemary. He rarely let himself think about it. But he heard the whispers, and the sometimes not-whispers. Huntsmen all had fey blood, far back in their family lines. That was *why* they were Huntsmen. But Aaron, the whispers said, had too much. Was a throwback.

Other Huntsmen didn't trust him. But he'd expected more from Rosemary.

"I felt it, Rosie. We both did. There was an uncanny, maybe more, in that park with us. Something dangerous."

Something in his voice must have convinced her, because she stopped watching Bother and turned to look at him. "All right. Do you think it's whatever we're looking for?"

Did he think whatever they were hunting was aware of them, looking for them, was what she was really asking. Were the Huntsmen also being hunted.

"No." His response was instinctive, immediate. "I'm not certain. But I don't think it was. I'm not sensitive to things like you are, but I didn't feel threatened."

Bother had, though.

Bother's odd rumble, deep in his chest, and the way he'd stiffened, canine companion gone and in its place a purpose-bred hellhound. He should tell Rosemary that. He knew he should.

"All I know is that Bother did not like it, at all."

And had he? Aaron wasn't sure what he had felt. Concern, yes, a touch of fear, but also curiosity. And something else, something he was trying hard not to think about.

Rosemary tapped her fingers on the leather surface of the writing desk, a nervous twitch. "There are a great many things Bother doesn't like. Squirrels, for one." She took a deep breath and let it out again, obviously resetting her own nerves. "I don't like this. Whatever it was, it's a probable risk, and if it's not what we're looking for, Bother's reaction says someone is going to have to deal with it. Do you think it lives here?"

"Here, the city, or here, that park?" She gave him a glare he probably deserved. "I don't know." He changed his mind after a moment of reflection. "No. The park was too small. The way Bother reacted, it had to be large, or there had to be a lot of them, and they'd be too noticeable either way. I think we surprised it on its way somewhere else."

Gut deep, he knew what it had been, what it had to have been. But if Rosemary wasn't coming to the same conclusion, maybe he was wrong. Maybe Bother was wrong.

It had been months since Brunson, and they'd heard no whispers, no rumors. There had been no alarms. There was no reason to believe that the fey had come back.

But he would be adding more protective sigils to their rooms, and Rosemary could just live with it.

———

Outside the hotel, the town was closing up for the day, offices shut, lights dimmed or gone dark, the evening stillness broken only when a trolley rattled by on metal tracks, its bell chiming out the stops, the harsh scrape of its brakes like a wound in the air.

A young couple disembarked from the trolley when it paused, walking arm in arm halfway down the street before disappearing through a doorway filled with light and noise. The door swung shut behind them, and quiet returned. The night was still too chill for anyone to linger when there were warmer places, filled with comfort or cheer, waiting.

An owl called out in the distance, barely audible, hunting for its dinner.

The lamp near the park flickered, then went out.

Under the trees a darker shadow appeared, then disappeared, then appeared again, farther down the street, as though drawn by a string. Overhead, the soft flap of wings and a flash of white showed the owl, following after until they came to a squat stone building set by the edge of the road, sloping lawns bordered by tall elms. The shadow settled there, fading to invisibility, waiting. Watching.

A man in a cassock stood by a lighted window on the second floor, an open book in his hands. He turned a page, then another before flipping it shut, turning away from the window. A moment later, the lamp winked out, the window going dark.

In the shadows between two elms, something shifted, then stilled again, the faintest glimmer of a pale green light visible in the growing dusk. The owl called again, followed by the shriek of something caught up in talons, and somewhere nearby a church bell tolled the seven o'clock hour.

The front door of the house opened, and the man came out, wrapped in a dark coat, a slanted fedora casting smaller shadows over his features. He paused, shifting the book to his left hand in order to lock the door, then adjusted the muffler around his neck before striding off down the street, a destination clearly in mind.

The pale green flicker emerged from the woods and followed.

Six

BREAKFAST IN THE hotel the next morning was a quiet affair, Aaron glaring down at his marmalade and toast, to the point where he did not even notice that his sister had poured him coffee, not tea, until he took a sip.

"Really?" He squinted at her, clearly unamused.

"My apologies," she said, not even trying to sound apologetic. She took the cup away from him, keeping it for herself while she poured a proper cup of tea from the waiting teapot and offered it to him. Not mollified, he took a cautious sip before returning his attention to the bread, the glower returning.

She sighed, stretching her leg out under the table to kick at him, gently. "Either eat it or set it aside. It hasn't done you any harm, to glare at it like that."

As she'd hoped, the interruption got him talking about whatever'd had his tail in a twist since she'd come back from taking Bother for his morning walk. "I don't like it, Rosemary."

She looked up from her own breakfast, making her eyes go wide in contrived confusion. "What, the toast?"

His glare, redirected, did not impress her. She was pushing him, deliberately. There was something going on in his head, something he was trying to keep from her, and that was not acceptable while they were on a hunt.

"Is it about last night? If it's not what we're hunting"—she wasn't convinced of that but was trusting Aaron's instincts for now—"then it's not our problem. And if it was, there's nothing we can do about it now save pray it didn't realize we're here for it."

And *that* was bothering her a great deal, but it wouldn't be the first time they'd hunted something that knew they were coming. "But that's not what's bothering you, is it?"

She was watching his face as she spoke, catching every minute flicker of muscle around his eyes and mouth, the telltale way he shifted his jaw. Rosemary knew her brother. Knew when he was plotting his next move, turning over facts in his head to formulate a response—or when he was chewing on something that had no answer, and no end. This morning, it was the latter.

"Aaron."

"I'm just worried." He put down his toast, still untouched, and looked her in the eye. "Not about last night."

A lie, but she let it pass, for now.

"About Mrs. Ballantine's story. Her description is so vague, it could be anything. Including a hysterical hallucination. And don't give me that look," he said, even though she knew she wasn't giving him any look at all. "We both know what she saw was upsetting, even without anything uncanny involved, and there's no way you're going to convince me that she's ever faced anything more upsetting than a servant breaking the good china before."

Rosemary thought he was being particularly unfair, but she put down her coffee cup, letting him know she was listening.

"Months without so much as a wink from the Circle, and suddenly we're being sent to deal with a maybe-nothing hunt that involves a benefactor? I think this is a test, one we've been set up to fail."

She opened her mouth to say something, she wasn't sure what, and he rode roughshod over her. "No, hear me out. I've been thinking about it all night. Jonathan being here? I don't like him, but he's far better suited to this sort of thing than we are. They could have sent us on his hunt, and let him handle this."

Aaron wasn't wrong, so Rosemary stayed quiet.

"But they didn't. They sent us . . . and there he is lurking in the background."

Also unfair, as they hadn't seen Jonathan since that first encounter, but Aaron was still talking.

"If there's nothing here, if we can't spread oil on the waters and keep our particular benefactor happy? They have an excuse to sideline us, permanently this time. They'll use that as justification, say that we're not up for the work anymore. Oh, they'll be gracious about it, no doubt. Offer us a pension, maybe ask us to work in Documents, where nobody has to see us."

"You're overthinking this again." And by overthinking, she meant indulging in paranoia.

He shook his head. "Tell me I'm where I'm wrong. Tell me it doesn't all fit together."

Rosemary tapped a pattern on the table with her forefinger and index finger, rat-tat-rat-tat.

"If they knew what really happened in Brunson, if they even suspected anything, really, the Circle would already have pensioned us off into obscurity."

They'd had this argument multiple times since leaving Brunson, and it always came back to the fact that Rosemary had agreed: nobody, not even the Circle, could know that a human had used magic. The fact that the Harkers had stopped it, had kept more magic from reentering the world, would not erase the fact that the most basic terms of the treaty had been broken. Keeping silent had been their only hope of preventing that fact from being learned by anyone—human or fey—who would have taken it as an excuse to cause more chaos.

But beyond that, and the reason Rosemary had agreed to keep silent, was that an uncanny had helped the Harkers kill a human. Never mind that they'd all been working for the good of this world; there was an accepted order to things, and even the faintest suspicion of Aaron being complicit in upending that order? That was Rosemary's greatest fear, from the time she was old enough to understand the risk.

Even just the suspicion that they hadn't been entirely forthright in their report had earned them nearly six months of being sidelined. If anyone knew . . .

They'd done the wrong thing for the right reason, and there was no comfort in that.

"They don't need to know," Aaron said. "They only need to *think*. If they decide we can't be trusted at all, what happens to us? Rosie, what happens if they take Bother away from us?"

"They won't. They can't." She stared at him, her appetite gone. "Could they?"

Hounds were bred by Huntsmen order. They belonged to the Huntsmen. If the Harkers were no longer Huntsmen . . . Such a thing had never been done. That didn't mean it couldn't happen.

"No." Rosemary said it so firmly, she believed it herself. "The Circle wouldn't—*Harry* wouldn't. It may be a test, but I believe Mrs. Ballantine." She had to believe her, because Aaron's theory was horrible. "We will find the uncanny, we will take care of it, and nobody will have reason to question us. About anything."

Her eyes dared Aaron to contradict her, and he looked away first.

———————

After breakfast, the Harkers split up, Aaron to confront Mr. Ballantine, Rosemary to see what she could learn from Mrs. Ballantine.

"Take Bother," Aaron had said. "Just . . . don't argue with me, Rosie. Take him."

Thankfully, the trolley car had been mostly empty at that hour, and the hound had only garnered a few sideways looks. Now, standing outside the Ballantines' house, the hound leaned slightly against Rosemary's leg, her gloved hand resting atop Botheration's head and his bulk a warm, comforting presence.

"Behave yourself, Bother," she told the hound. "This is a nice place we're going into, filled with nice people. Nice. They're not used to hounds like you. So just . . . be a good dog?"

The hound shook his head once, his one erect ear twitching backward as though the better to catch her words.

"I know you know how to do it," she said, and started up the steps, Bother in perfect synchronization with her.

The Circle couldn't take Bother from them. She couldn't imagine it. She wouldn't let it happen.

Unlike their previous visit, today Rosemary had one of the silver-edged knives from the chest sheathed under her skirt, as well as her Browning pistol tucked into a pocket of her coat and one of her throwing knives hidden under the pleated sleeve of her blouse. It was a trifle much, for having tea with a society matron, but while Aaron might not think that the uncanny he'd encountered was hunting them, neither of them were the sort to take the chance that he was wrong.

A firm hand on the knocker gave three raps that echoed inside the house, and after a short wait, the housekeeper opened the door.

"Rosemary Harker, here to see Mrs. Ballantine, if she's available."

She had decided against calling ahead. Arranging a meeting would have guaranteed her availability, but it could also have given the woman the opportunity to avoid it. The element of surprise should always favor Huntsmen.

The housekeeper's face could have been made out of wood, but Rosemary thought she could see just a hint of distaste there, quickly hidden. If the distaste was for her or Bother, Rosemary wasn't certain, but resisted the urge to check for a blemish on her face or stain on her blouse.

"Come in. I will see if Mrs. Ballantine is available."

Well, they hadn't been turned away at the door; that was a good sign.

Bother's claws clicked on the parquet floor, and Rosemary

hoped that they wouldn't leave scratches. "Sit, boy," she asked. He dropped into position at her heels, still as a statue save for his single erect ear, which twitched every now and again from some noise only he could hear. But he remained calm, his eyes soft and jaw hanging slightly open.

Whatever had caused the earlier mischief had either been human or had not lingered long enough for the scent to remain. Rosemary wasn't sure which option she'd prefer.

Minutes passed, and she entertained herself by trying to estimate how much the gently worn Persian carpet under her feet had cost. More than an automotive but less than a year's rent on their apartment she'd decided, when the maid from the other day returned. "Mrs. Ballantine has company, but she will see you." Rosemary refused to react to the implied insult of the housekeeper handing her off to a lesser servant, merely slipping off her coat, making sure the pistol was secured in its pocket, and handing it and her hat to the girl, who promptly deposited them behind a door in the hallway before gesturing for Rosemary to follow her.

"That's an awfully big dog, miss," the girl said. "What's her name?"

"His name is Botheration." It wasn't, really. His actual name, translated from the German, was Ironblood Dawn Treader. But he'd been Bother since he came to them, a gawky, oversized, half-trained puppy. Ironblood Dawn Treader belonged to the Huntsmen. Bother belonged to *them*.

"Is he? A bother, I mean."

Rosemary's hand dropped to Bother's head again, a gentle touch as she smiled down at him. "Often."

The girl led her to the same door as before, and rapped

gently. Unlike the housekeeper, she did not wait for a voice to call out but pushed the door open and ushered Rosemary and Bother inside.

"Thank you, Macy," Mrs. Ballantine said, dismissing the maid.

The company turned out to be a woman, slightly younger than Mrs. Ballantine, dark blond hair drawn up in a soft knot covered by a simple little hat, her attire a somber skirt and jacket in dark purple over a fitted shirtwaist unadorned by any jewelry. Overall, she gave the impression of a woman who faded into the paneling, save for the fact that she was, in fact, the very first thing Rosemary noticed when she walked in. Charisma, subdued to the setting, but filling the room none-theless. Rosemary did not share her brother's suspicion of anyone more charming than herself, but rather appreciated the evidence of it.

"Miss Harker." Mrs. Ballantine drew Rosemary's attention back to her hostess, who eyed Botheration cautiously before returning her gaze to Rosemary's face. "I was not expecting to see you again so soon. And where is your brother?"

There was no point in prevarication; if the Ballantines spoke to each other at all, they would inevitably discover what the Harkers had been doing, and honesty might give her an advantage later. "Aaron is bearding your husband at his office. We felt it would be more fruitful to approach you separately."

To give Mrs. Ballantine credit, her polite-interest facade didn't crack, although Rosemary thought she saw a glint of humor in the woman's eye. "A lion in his den, indeed. Con-sidering how difficult it is to catch him at home these days, I suspect that was a wise choice. Please, do sit down. Oh. And your dog, will he—"

"Bother," Rosemary said as she took the offered chair. "Lie down."

He settled at her feet, but she noted that his gaze was on the yet-unnamed woman, who seemed equally fascinated by him. Bother's use was not limited to sniffing out uncanny.

"You may pet him, if you like," Rosemary said invitingly. "He looks fierce, but the slightest encouragement and he will roll on his back for belly rubs."

"Oh." The woman seemed taken aback. "It seems too presumptuous to do any such thing. He is . . ." Words seemed to fail her, before she finished, "A very special dog, is he not?"

Rosemary was torn between the woman's obvious approval and a faint shock at her words. "Yes, he is."

The woman smiled, a satisfied, not quite smug expression. "I thought so."

"My apologies," Mrs. Ballantine said hastily. "Miss Rosemary Harker, this is Madame Betanne Sweet. She is a *medium*."

Rosemary managed to keep a pleasant expression on her face, despite feeling the urge to roll her eyes at that revelation. Spiritualism as a movement was bunk, but despite many of its so-called practitioners having been exposed as frauds, the movement remained popular among the grieving, who needed something more solid than the assurances offered by the Church. And it contained just enough truth to potentially pry open doors Huntsmen were vowed to keep shut.

"You have doubts about my work." Madame Betanne waved off disclaimers Rosemary did not intend to make. "I am not offended. My work does not depend on the belief of others; I do not work to make believers, but to comfort those in need."

Rosemary smiled politely. The fact that she could see Bother was more than an ordinary hound suggested the woman might have some fey in her bloodline, enough to manipulate those already ready to believe, but nothing more.

And she might not in fact be able to see anything special about Bother at all, but was instead playing the confidence game. If so, it would gain her nothing: Rosemary had no money to be grifted out of. But if she could keep Mrs. Ballantine from being taken in as well, perhaps Mr. Ballantine would be grateful enough to put in an extra word for them with the Circle.

Not that she shared Aaron's paranoia. Not exactly. But a little extra help would never go amiss.

"If you're here, dare I hope that you have news to impart?"

Rosemary did not look at the medium; if Mrs. Ballantine felt it was acceptable to speak in front of her, unlike the young girl yesterday, then that was what they would do. But . . . cautiously. "Discovered, yes. Confirmed . . . not yet. But it looks as though your husband was right to call us in." Rosemary didn't know how much Mrs. Ballantine knew about the Huntsmen, or her husband's support of them, but she apparently believed—or wanted to believe—that there was more to the world than what was taught in schools or from the pulpit. If playing into that belief was what it took to get the woman to confide in Rosemary, then that was what she would do.

"I was right," Mrs. Ballantine said to Madame Betanne, "it was nothing—how did you say it—mundane that caused my brother's illness." Then she turned back to Rosemary. "So what I saw . . . Do you know yet what it was?"

Rosemary hesitated. It was too early to promise anything, or be trapped by assertions they couldn't prove, particularly with Aaron's doubts about Mrs. Ballantine's veracity lingering, like an unpleasant guest. "We aren't certain yet. But it does seem that something . . . unusual caused the . . . incident."

"Supernatural, you mean," Madame Betanne said, nodding her head sagely. "My dear, I feel certain that Franklin has much to tell you."

If Rosemary had had ears like Bother's, they would have pricked up at that. "Has he woken up?"

"Oh. No," Mrs. Ballantine said sadly. "But Madame says that she will be able to speak with him, via the spirits."

Madame nodded, her eyes bright. "He sleeps only beyond our reach. The spirits will be able to hear him, and I can hear them."

Rosemary bit the inside of her lip hard enough to leave the taste of blood in her mouth. Ghosts did not speak. They were silent, senseless specters, subsisting on the grief of those left behind. A noisy spirit was simply one with enough strength to create havoc—

She stopped, struck by a thought. Had there been a death here, or in the family, that might have resulted in a haunting? Had that been the cause of the destruction, separate from the actual attack?

"Oh, we're so busy chatting, I did not ask if you would like tea," Mrs. Ballantine said, touching the handle of the teapot with one well-manicured finger. She did not wait for an answer but poured the steaming liquid into one of the thin-edged cups waiting on a lacquered tray. It had been set for four, Rosemary noted, and wondered if Mrs. Ballantine had been expecting other guests, or if she had assumed Rosemary and Aaron would be returning at some point.

The tea was jasmine-scented, just cool enough to drink without burning her tongue, and Rosemary shook her head when offered the sugar bowl and creamer.

"You are also a student of the immaterial world, Miss Harker?"

Mrs. Ballantine might feel comfortable speaking freely in front of Madame Betanne, but Rosemary did not. She took another sip of tea and lifted her gaze to the medium, pulling all the charm, both natural and learned, she possessed into that look. "My feet are firmly planted in the material world, but my brother and I have had some experience in things modern science cannot yet explain."

"Indeed." The woman was matching look for look, aware that a challenge had been issued. "But surely you cannot think science can explain everything."

At another time, in another place, Rosemary would have risen to the argument and enjoyed it immensely. But she was too aware of Mrs. Ballantine watching them, and the reminder of their charge to finish this hunt without bringing attention to themselves.

"I think I do not know enough to make such a determination. All I may do is collect the facts, and work from that. And that is why I am here this afternoon," she said, turning her face to look at Mrs. Ballantine. Let the medium think she had won that little battle; Rosemary had work to do.

"Mrs. Ballantine, I apologize if my questions seem intrusive, but can you think of anything, anything, that might have brought your brother to the attention of . . ." She hesitated, glancing at the spiritualist, then back at Mrs. Ballantine. "Of anyone who might have cause for a grudge? Or a desire to harm him?"

Rather than answering right away, Mrs. Ballantine put her cup down and reached for one of the tiny sandwiches set on a plate next to the teapot, then pulled her hand away and placed it firmly in her lap, twisting the ring on her right hand in a nervous gesture.

"A man in his position, even at a junior level, they are bound to make enemies. People who've had rulings go against them, or—but that's not what you meant, was it."

Rosemary waited, pushing as much sympathy and support into her gaze as she could, pretending that it was only the two of them in the room, a safe connection.

"I don't know," Mrs. Ballantine said. "I don't even know how one *might* give offense, in such a case."

There were as many ways to run afoul of an uncanny as there were uncanny. But few that would cause one to go after a human in such a manner. "Trespassing, often. Intruding into the space they consider their own. Was your brother one to go into the woods, or across fields?"

That made Mrs. Ballantine laugh, a delicate peal of amusement.

"I take it that would be a no."

"Franklin is very much a creature of the city," Mrs. Ballantine said with fondness. "His idea of the wilderness is a town without streetlamps."

That didn't quite eliminate any uncanny from Rosemary's

list, but it made several of them much less probable. Dryads were vindictive as hell and were the right shape to have been the figure Mrs. Ballantine had seen, but the only thing that drove them to that was damage to their grove—and they would be far more likely to kill everything in the room, rather than disappear. A hungry rover could drop its victims into a deep sleep until their soul-energy was renewed, but it was an opportunistic creature, more prone to waylaying a drunk on the street than a sober man in his office.

If there were marks on the body, teeth or suckers or something else entirely, that would tell them a great deal. But there was no way Rosemary could ask such a thing of the man's sister. When there was a corpse, the Harkers could find a way to examine it, even if that meant digging up the grave. But a living, insensible victim?

This meeting was not going well. Rosemary could feel the restlessness building in her, the bone-deep twitch to be on her feet and hunting.

"Mrs. Ballantine. I hesitate to ask, but—"

"You want to see Franklin."

That hadn't been what she was about to ask, but: "Yes."

The woman nodded, as though it were a perfectly natural request, to visit a sleeping man.

"My brother rests upstairs, Miss Harker. I was just about to introduce Madame Betanne to him, but please, join us."

———

Aaron had waited until Rosemary had departed with Bother to set out on his own errand. He had originally intended to retrieve the rental automotive and drive into Boston proper, but when he'd mentioned this to the front clerk, planning to ask for directions, the man had laughed at him.

"You don't want to be driving there," the old man said. "One wrong turn'll run into one of those contraptions coming the other way, and you're both stuck. Those streets were built to let horses past, and not much more."

Aaron had thought the trip from New Haven had taught him how to handle the automotive with reasonable skill, but the thought of Rosemary's expression if anything went wrong, particularly if it cost them more money, was enough to make him rethink his plans.

Instead, he caught a midmorning trolley into Boston, crammed up between a gaggle of well-dressed ladies clearly heading in for the shopping Rosemary had gotten starry-eyed about and a tight cluster of men in suits and bowlers, their mouths pinched and minds already on the day's work ahead.

Aaron supposed the jolting of the mechanized car as it ran along the tracks was better than being tossed into the back of a horse-drawn wagon, but not by a significant amount. If they could only afford an automotive of their own, he could learn how to drive in a city . . . but he knew the state of their finances as well as Rosemary. Unless their small investments suddenly took off, that was a distant dream.

On the advice of the trolley driver, he got off the stop before they entered the city proper and walked the mile or so to his destination, pacing himself to avoid arriving sweaty or windblown. It had been a few years since Aaron had been in Boston, but it hadn't changed much, as far as he could tell. The old man had been right: many of the streets were little more than wide alleys, particularly as he made his way closer to the waterfront.

The offices of Ballantine & Brothers Shipping was a narrow but deep brick-fronted building, clearly having started its life as a warehouse, and still used for such, on the first level. The only sign of their occupancy was a small bronze plaque by the door with their name in simple script, and a bell. Aaron looked up, then to the side, noting the heads of iron nails driven into the wood at regular points and the faded wreath of herbs tucked over the lintel, where it could be mistaken for the remains of a bird's nest. Looking farther up, Aaron noted more bundles and what looked like silver wire strung across the windows.

Like the house, Ballantine had followed through on what he'd been told; the building was warded against the most basic of uncanny.

But only the most basic. That gave Aaron an idea

He rang the bell.

A workman whose rough clothing matched a face that had not seen the sharp end of a razor in several days let him in and, when Aaron said he was there to see Mr. Ballantine, jerked his thumb up a narrow wooden staircase, clearly disinterested in what his business might be. Aaron took the stairs, stepping carefully on treads that creaked as though they were considering giving way at any moment.

Pausing on the landing, Aaron removed his hat and used two fingers to ensure that his hair lay flat, then took the last two stairs and passed through the doorway.

While the first floor had not moved far from its first life as a warehouse, the second floor was clearly office space. Unlike the legal firm yesterday, there was no display of wealth or style; the offices were Spartan, the furnishings obviously chosen for durability rather than comfort, and there was no young man seated behind a desk to greet visitors. There was no desk at all. Instead, a small, wizened old man with tufts of hair slicked against his scalp tottered through the space, then stopped and peered at Aaron.

"Who're you?"

"Aaron Harker." *And what are you?* almost escaped Aaron's mouth before he bit it back. The man only looked like an uncanny; he was as human as Aaron himself, and likely more so. "I'm here to see Mr. Ballantine. He will know what it's about."

"Well then, why're you standing there like a lummox? Go!" And the little man flapped his hands at Aaron, driving him toward the left-hand hallway.

Despite himself, Aaron began to grin. If Ballantine was anything like his employees, this interview might not be so terrible after all.

In keeping with the rest of the building, Walter Ballantine did not have a plush office. In fact, Aaron would not call the space he found his quarry in an office at all, merely a wide wooden desk in the middle of a large space, surrounded by men scurrying back and forth on unknown but obviously very important errands.

"Mr. Ballantine?"

The man looked up as Aaron approached, and his sharp

gaze made Aaron slow his steps, unsure if he wanted to be noticed. "That's me."

The man, like the building, was not what Aaron had expected. Rather than an elegant, elongated figure, Ballantine was a thick block of a man, broad-shouldered, with a rough-hewn face, square-jawed as a boxer, shirtsleeves rolled up under a startlingly bright pair of yellow suspenders.

But those sharp eyes gleamed with intelligence, and Aaron knew better than to judge by appearances.

"So you're who the Huntsmen sent, hmm?" Ballantine didn't seem particularly impressed, and he did not invite Aaron to be seated. Aaron tried not to take it personally. His suit might not be the newest style, but the wool was quality, and there was nothing to be done about his youth except survive it. He had tried growing a mustache, to make himself look older, and his sister had laughed herself into tears before sending him to the washroom to shave it off.

"I am." He had learned too early in life that attempting to defend against implied failures rarely succeeded and often made things worse.

"So why are you here, bothering me, instead of hunting that thing down?"

Aaron bit back his instinctive response, smoothing the pleat in his pants to buy himself a second to formulate his thoughts. Rosemary would placate the man, soothe his temper. But Aaron knew, in his gut, that it would be seen as weakness if Aaron were to try that, man to man. He took a moment, trying to look at the man the way Rosemary would, to see beyond what he was saying to what he *meant*.

Go strong, Aaron decided. This was a man who didn't

need to prove himself, who expected results when he asked for them, not polite words, no matter what Harry said.

"You deal with maritime issues," Aaron said, gesturing at the warehouse around them. A guess, based on the invoices and manifests on Ballantine's desk. "So you know a ship doesn't sail blindly into the deep. The captain charts a course, based on all available knowledge of the tides and stars, yes? Huntsmen do the same: we learn all we can, so we know what it is we hunt—so we can hunt it successfully, with a minimum of disturbance to those around us."

That last was a complete and utter lie, particularly when Bother was involved. But while Aaron might be terrible at lying, he also wasn't an idiot. Ballantine wanted this dealt with quickly, but he wasn't going to be happy if a hellhound tore through his pretty grounds.

Ballantine narrowed his eyes and turned down the corners of his mouth. "Hrmph." But it wasn't an unhappy noise, or a scornful one. The man was thinking, Aaron decided, and stayed silent, letting the man come to his own conclusions.

"I don't see why you needed to bother me, since you've already spoken with my wife. I wasn't there; I didn't see anything." Ballantine leaned back in his chair, hooking a thumb in one suspender and peering at Aaron from under thick, graying eyebrows. But the blue eyes had gone from alert to suspicious. Aaron needed to step carefully.

"This isn't about what was seen. It's about what we haven't seen. Yet."

Those eyebrows went up an inch. "Excuse me?"

Aaron wondered for an instant if he had overstepped. But it was too late to back down. "Mr. Ballantine, the uncanny have long preyed on humans. You know this—you support our work. But they are . . . reactive. Opportunistic. Attacks like this, within a building filled with people, seemingly out of nowhere? They are rare, and rarely random."

It took a second for that to sink in; then Ballantine leaned forward slightly. "You're saying that Franklin was attacked for a reason? What, that he invited this attack on himself?"

Aaron lifted his hands, spreading them in a "Who can say?" motion before placing them by his sides, carefully non-confrontational. "I am saying that we are taking this seriously and looking into all possible avenues. Including the possibility that, yes, your brother-in-law was targeted for some reason.

"And that's why I'm here. You know that we've spoken with your wife, but there are things that your brother-in-law might not have shared with her, perhaps something he didn't want her to worry about?"

Ballantine scoffed. "And you think he might have told me?"

With a silent wish that Rosemary never learned that these words came out of his mouth, Aaron said, "There are some things men understand better."

Ballantine let out a laugh that turned into a harsh cough. "If you think Congdon ever told me anything, you've been barking up the wrong tree. He was a good man, don't get me wrong, and I was damned fond of him, but the only thing we had in common was Dorothy.

"Wait. If you think he was a target—is Dorothy in danger?" Ballantine's body shifted again, but Aaron couldn't tell if it was in disquiet or surprise or some other emotion. Give him a text in German or French or Latin, and Aaron could translate on the fly. Show him a patch of broken branches or bent grasses, and he could tell you which way an uncanny had gone. But the language of expression and movement eluded him, no matter how much he tried.

But the man was waiting for an answer.

"It's entirely possible that he was targeted, yes. Lawyers, because of the nature of their work, seem to draw uncanny attention more often than not. The matters of oaths and obligations—" He stopped, the man's expression reminding him that even his sister did not share his fascination on that topic. "As to your wife's safety . . ." There was his opening. Aaron paused as though considering the situation. "As there was only minor damage done to your home, I assume that you have taken all the usual precautions around your house. Silver and iron, herbal banes, sigils of protection?"

Ballantine had begun nodding agreement, then stopped so abruptly Aaron was surprised he hadn't sprained his chin.

"Wait. That last."

"Sigils?" Aaron feigned surprise. "Yes. They are not common, and most folk would never need them, but they arc quite effective."

He was walking a thin and potentially dangerous line here. Sigils were nothing this man would have been told about, no matter how much money he gave.

Huntsmen used a variety of tools. Some were physical, practical: handguns, edged weapons like knives, Rosemary's bow, and, occasionally, hand-to-hand combat. Hounds, for those granted one. Some were mental: logic, intuition, deduction. Instinct.

And some were . . . neither of those things. Fairy lights,

illumination of fey manufacture, were inert; they required nothing to use beyond knowing the spell-words that turned them on and off, and so Huntsmen used them, if carefully, as they could not be replaced if lost or broken. Spell-craft, the summoning and invoking of loose magic, was expressly forbidden humans by the treaty.

Sigils fell somewhere in between. They could be excused as folk magic, that repository of fey spells that had been lost to time and Huntsmen-promoted obscuration. They were tools, and like any tool, they could be misused, or mishandled, even by Huntsmen.

An uncontrolled sigil had been what killed their mother and left their father half-mad.

Aaron slammed the door shut on that memory, wrenching his attention back to the man in front of him. Summoning what few acting skills he had, he cocked his head as though considering an option, then tapped a finger to his mouth and said, "I suppose I could add a few to your protections, both here and at your home . . ."

Ballantine was no fool. "And what would you expect in return?"

The urge to ask for money slid in like a snake, and Aaron smothered it; they could and did ask for compensation in some circumstances, but not formal assignments. And particularly not from a benefactor. The Circle would not be amused.

"We need your brother-in-law's datebook, to determine who he saw on the day he was attacked. Unfortunately, his employer declined to share it with us."

The datebook might not give them any useful information, but Aaron had decided that he did not like Mr. George, and Mr. George had not wanted to give it to them. Therefore, Aaron wanted it.

"And you think I can get that for you?"

Gently, he heard Rosemary's voice whisper in his ear. *Gently.*

"I believe that you are a man of some influence," Aaron said, meeting his gaze evenly. "So, yes."

Ballantine waited just long enough for Aaron to began to sweat, thinking he'd misplayed his hand, before saying, "You'll put these . . . sigils on the house and here?"

"House and here," Aaron agreed.

Seven

AT MRS. BALLANTINE'S request, they left Botheration in the library, once Rosemary assured her that the hound would wait quietly.

Rosemary waited for the other two women to precede her out of the library, holding back to give Bother a "wait-not-guard" hand signal. The maid might come in to clear away the remains of tea, and there was no need to terrify the poor girl. The hound had simply sighed and curled up by the chair Rosemary had been sitting in, nose tucked under one paw.

When she caught up with the two women, they were shoulder to shoulder, the incline of their bodies suggesting a surprising level of comfortable confidences. Rosemary recognized the stance because it was one she often used herself, when coaxing witnesses to speak with her. Everything about the spiritualist, from her half-mourning attire to her diffident modesty, felt like a confidence act, but there was something about the woman that made Rosemary hesitate to dismiss her. There was a slim chance that Madame Betanne might in fact be a true sensitive, able to feel the presence of uncanny things around her and labeling them spirits. If so, Rosemary thought, she could be useful.

"Of course I insisted that he be brought here," Mrs. Ballantine was saying as she led them down a hallway of closed doors to the farthest one, clearly chosen to be as far from the rest of the house as possible. Rosemary approved of the caution. If he had been carrying a sickness, that was wise. If he was still the target of an uncanny . . . it was also wise, although it would have been wiser still to have him housed elsewhere.

"His quarters are perfectly fine for a bachelor, but I wouldn't have been able to rest, not knowing if he was being cared for properly."

"Of course," Madame Betanne murmured.

Rosemary could also understand wanting to keep a sibling close.

Their hostess did not bother to knock on the door, pulling it open without fanfare.

The room was spacious, easily the size of both Harkers' hotel rooms, but the figure on the bed seemed to fill all the available space. Franklin Congdon lay on his back, the sheets turned down across his chest, smooth as though the bed had just been made. His hair, brown to his sister's silvering blond, fell into his face without the use of oils or pomade, and his expression was placid, almost slack, whatever worries he had carried in life eased away as though by sleep.

But he was not asleep. Rosemary could forgive his loved ones for thinking he was; his chest moved slowly up and down, with no sign of injury or illness on his body. She might have been fooled as well, if she had not seen firsthand this sort of thing before.

She had been eleven, her hand tucked into her mother's as they walked down the hallway of a sanatorium. Her mother's heels had made a tap-tap-tap noise on the floor, and young Rosemary had thought it the sound of authority, of competence. She had tried to make her own flat-soled shoes create the same sound but failed utterly.

So caught up in her effort, Rosemary had failed to notice where they were going, until her mother paused in front of a door.

"Poor girl," her mother had said. "Look, Rosie. Look carefully."

Wanting to please her mother, Rosemary had. She had looked long and hard at the girl in the bed, noting the stillness of her body, the way her hands rested lax at her side, the way her chest barely moved, and her porcelain features were untroubled by thought.

"What happened to her?" Because even at eleven, Rosemary had known enough to know this was no natural sleep.

"She angered a night hag. Simply for being beautiful. It's an uncanny sleep, and there's nothing we can do to break it, no matter how often her parents ask."

"Nothing? Not even true love's kiss?" Because while she had been attending to her studies, Rosemary had also been reading the stories, and a sleeping princess, as this girl surely must be, could always be awoken by true love's kiss.

"Not even true love's kiss," her mother had said. "The only thing that breaks this sleep is the death of the one who forced it."

Her parents had found the uncanny, found and killed it, and the girl awoke. Rosemary had wondered, for months after, if she'd dreamed while asleep, and if they'd been beautiful dreams.

"Oh," a voice said, startling Rosemary from her memories. "Oh, he's right there, Dorothy. He's right there waiting for you."

The spiritualist brushed past Rosemary to catch up Mrs. Ballantine's hand in her own, pressing it to her bosom. "He's waiting for you."

Rosemary managed not to roll her eyes. The woman might be sensitive; she was also a terrible actress. But Mrs. Ballantine lapped it up, begging the woman to tell her brother that she was there, that she was doing everything she could to bring him back.

There was a nurse by Congdon's bedside, her back ruler-straight, hair pulled back in a severe bun, and by the expression on her face, less than impressed with either woman in front of her.

"Has he moved at all?" Rosemary asked her.

"A few times, miss." She managed the interesting feat of looking at Rosemary without taking her eyes off her patient. "His fingers have twitched a few times when I poked the flesh of his palm, and his leg jerked once, as though he had stumbled."

"Nothing else?"

"No, ma'am."

The girl her mother had shown her had been motionless, even when poked or pinched.

Not willing to break into the nonsense happening by the bed, Rosemary studied the room. Following Mrs. Ballantine up the stairs and down the hallway, she had seen more gleaming hardwood and brass, vases of fresh flowers set on narrow tables. But there was none of that here, only the simple wood-frame bed and the chair the nurse sat in, and a small wooden table with a covered pitcher and a cut-glass tumbler. The walls were simple plaster, bare of art or ornamentation, the single window tightly shut, a sheer curtain drawn over it. There were arguments that said fresh air was better for patients who were bedridden, but an open window was also a potential entrance for an uncanny. Better to keep it closed, for now.

"Franklin. Sweetheart, can you hear me?" Mrs. Ballantine had moved to the other side of the bed, taking her brother's hand in her own. Rosemary imagined seeing her own brother there, herself in the position of trying to call him back by sheer force of their bond, and winced, her sympathy returning. It wouldn't work, any more than true love's kiss would. Fairy tales held a kernel of truth, but they had been reshaped to give hope, rather than serving their original purpose of warning.

"He hears you," Sweet said, dolefully encouraging. "He's trying to answer, but something holds him back."

Huntsmen had no business interfering with spirits; they left that to the Church.

She thought of Bother waiting downstairs and turned back to the nurse. "Has he been bathed?"

The nurse looked at her then, clearly deeply offended. "Of course."

"Damn." She hadn't meant to say it out loud, but really, damn. She was all for advances in modern medicine, but it would have been easier back when people were afraid of someone with the sleeping sickness and refused to touch them. If he'd been bathed, not even Bother's nose would be able to find any trace of uncanny contamination.

She stared at the motionless body, bedclothes pulled up to his chest, red-striped pajamas making his pallor more obvious.

Wait.

Stepping forward to where Mrs. Ballantine was now kneeling by the bedside, she asked, "Do you still have the clothing he was wearing when he collapsed?"

The woman didn't look away from her brother's face. "Yes. It was one of his favorite suits; I wouldn't let them get rid of it. It's hanging in the closet there." Rosemary turned, saw a narrow door with a simple latch-handle.

Madame Betanne turned to look as well, then glanced at Rosemary. "You think it might tell us something?"

"It's possible." It had been several days, but if there was still a scent left on it, Bother would be able to follow it. *Please,* she thought as she reached to open the door, *please don't be lined with cedar or stuffed with lavender sachets. . . .*

She gave an exhale of relief when the door opened to only the faintest smell of dust and lemon.

"I will need to take this with me." She offered no room for argument, favorite suit or not. Mrs. Ballantine merely nodded, her attention returned to the figure on the bed. "Madame Betanne, can he tell you what happened?"

Rosemary paused in the act of folding the suit over her arm, waiting to hear the woman's response.

". . . He says it was dark, a darkness fell on him. But he knows no more—I am sorry."

The woman was no more sensitive than herself. Shaking

her head, Rosemary let herself out of the room and descended back down the stairs to reclaim her hound.

If they were very lucky, this would be the break they needed.

As she'd half expected, the maid was in the process of clearing the tea table, one wary eye on Bother, who was still on the stay position Rosemary had left him in, jaw hanging open and tongue lolling to one side in what, Rosemary acknowledged, could be terrifying to someone who didn't know him.

The maid glanced at her, taking in the suit hanging over Rosemary's arm, then looked back at Botheration. "He's grinning at me, isn't he, miss?"

Rosemary bit back a smile of her own. "Yes, yes he is. Macy, isn't it?"

"Yes, ma'am."

"Rosemary, please. You've worked for the Ballantines long?"

"Four years ma—Miss Rosemary. Started as day help, then they asked me to come on full last year."

"It seems like a good household to work for."

"Oh it is. The Mister, he's not much on conversation, but they treat us well."

"Have they lived here long?"

"Raised three girls here," the maid said, bobbing her head. "They've all gone on, started their own families."

"It seems like a happy house. I mean, until recent events. No tragedies dogging them."

"No, indeed. Mrs. Ballantine often said they were blessed." The maid paused to touch the saint's medal around her neck. "You're looking into what happened to Mr. Congdon?"

Rosemary saw no reason to deny it. "We are. Is there anything you know, anything at all that might help us?"

The maid shook her head. "He's a pleasant-spoken gentleman, always here to see his sister, but other than coming and going, and at dinners, we don't see much of him. I'm afraid I couldn't tell you anything."

And even if she could, odds were she wouldn't; Rosemary might be an interesting stranger, but she was a stranger, and a poorly chosen confidence could cost her what appeared to be an excellent placement.

"Will you be wanting your coat now, Miss Rosemary?"

Rosemary gave Bother the "release" sign, snapping the lead back onto his collar. "Yes, thank you."

It took longer than Aaron expected to finish up and return to the hotel, having to share the trolley car with a bunch of youngsters returning from a vaudeville matinee. Aaron had hoped to get back to his room and cleaned up before Rosemary spotted him. But she was sitting in the lobby drinking tea and reading a newspaper when he came in, and her head lifted as though she'd Bother's ability to scent him.

He took a quick whiff of himself and admitted that it was entirely possible.

"Aaron."

"Rosemary," he said, mimicking her tone.

"You're . . . What is that on your clothing?"

He looked down at the splash of green paint across the front of his shirt, having thoughtlessly unbuttoned his coat when he walked in.

"Paint. I'm not used to using brushes to mark sigils, and green's not the best color for it, but that's what they had available."

He walked past her, heading for the elevator. He hated the things, certain every time he got on that this would be the time a cable snapped, and he would either die alone, or squished by every person in there with him. But he hoped it would buy him a little time before he had to deal with Rosemary.

He misjudged how quickly she could walk; she caught up to him while he waited for the elevator to descend to the lobby. The operator looked the sort to eavesdrop shamelessly, thankfully, so she was reduced to shooting him the occasional sideways glare. That would not last long, once they were on their own floor.

He moved past her, walking quickly, but did not bother to shut the door to his room behind him; she would just pick the lock, anyway.

He dropped his coat on the bed and went into the washroom, turning the water on and letting it run to warm up.

"Aaron."

He hated how she could pack so many words into his name like that.

"What?"

Rosemary was standing in the doorway, staring at him as though his skin had just turned green, rather than simply scrubbing green paint from under his fingernails. "You did what?"

He sighed, his shoulders slumping. "I painted protective sigils around Ballantine's office. And tomorrow I will do the same for his house. And in return, he will get us Congdon's datebook." Aaron stared at his fingers, wiggling them under the stream of water. Maybe he shouldn't even bother scrubbing it off, if he was only going to have to paint again in the morning.

"Are you mad?" Rosemary's voice, normally a carefully cultivated smoothness, cracked dramatically. "If anyone finds out . . ."

Once his nails were clean, he turned off the spigot and wiped his hands on the towel hanging by the sink before turning to his sister, still blocking the doorway. "Who is Ballantine going to tell? His wife? He doesn't want her to worry; he's not going to tell her there's any risk. His employees? They'd think him mad. Harry?" That was a possibility. Still. "Even if he does . . . Harry will have our backs."

Rosemary shook her head, obviously not convinced.

He understood her concern, but at the same time it irritated him beyond measure. "What would you have had me do, Rosemary? We needed information—he could get it for us. But he isn't the sort to deliver favors for free. And it wasn't as though I could slip the man a coin and be done with it."

Feeding a man's wallet was a time-honored Huntsmen's tool, but useless here, where the man in question likely spent more than they earned in a year just on his shoes. Aaron rarely felt envy; there was no point to it. But the past six months had sharpened his awareness of how close to the edge he and his sister lived, and if not envy there was a tinge of bitterness to his thoughts now, when he considered the Ballantines and their ilk.

Putting those thoughts away, he pushed past his sister, shrugging out of his paint-splashed shirt and reaching for the one he had worn the day before, pausing to sniff it first. It would do well enough for dinner, he supposed.

"And there's no way any of this will end badly," Rosemary muttered, clearly not letting it go.

"I made a decision, and it's done," he said, exasperated. "I may be younger, but I'm as much a Huntsmen as you."

"That's not—"

"It really is. You don't trust my judgment."

"I don't trust *sigils*."

"I'm not teaching him how to use them. He didn't even watch me draw them, any more than he'd bother watching his gardener trim the rosebushes."

They stared at each other, Bother letting out a low, unhappy whine as he picked up the tension in the air.

"If it provides a clue that leads anywhere," Rosemary started.

"If the datebook provides a lead, I will expect an apology. A real one."

Rosemary flapped her hand at him, as much of an apology as he was likely to get, and summoned Bother to her side with two fingers against the side of her skirt. "Put on a clean shirt," she told him, "then come next door."

It only took him a few minutes to replace the shirt, leaving the stained one in the sink to soak in the faint hope that the paint would come out. He knocked once on Rosemary's door, then, making sure there was no one else in the hallway, turned the knob and went in.

She was sitting at the desk, writing something on a sheet of paper, Bother sprawled at her feet, to all appearances sound asleep. Aaron knew better.

There was no other chair in the room, so he moved to sit on the bed. "Huh. You looking for a change of wardrobe?" And he indicated the man's suit jacket and pants draped across the bedspread. "Not that I don't think you'd look stunning in it, but I thought we were supposed to avoid gathering attention?"

She didn't smile, proof she was still upset with him. "Congdon was wearing it when he was struck down. I'd hoped that Bother would be able to pick something up from it."

Cloth would hold scent better than the metal of his spectacles; it was a smart move. He looked to the floor, where Bother emitted a heavy sigh, as though aware nobody believed he was sleeping. "No luck?"

She exhaled, a resigned noise that he would never tell her sounded a great deal like Bother's. "He was definitely interested in the smell—I will need to apologize to their laundress for the drool now decorating the pants leg—but beyond that, nothing, no."

He was almost afraid to ask, but . . . "Was Mrs. Ballantine able to give you any more detail on possible family history, or . . ."

"It was not a good time to ask," she told him. "Mrs. Ballantine called in a spiritualist."

Aaron winced, as much at her tone as the words.

"She trotted the two of us up to see him. She's stashed him in a guest room, with a nurse watching him breathe. And before you ask, no, Madame Betanne, as she styles herself, was useless. Same as most of them. And I asked; the nurse had already washed his body."

He nodded, his half-formed hope of another chance to

pick up a scent dashed. That was how their luck was going, it seemed.

He slapped his hands against his thighs, the noise making one of Bother's ears prick up. "There's no point in bemoaning what could have been." And he was telling himself as much as her. "We were called in before there was a chance for the usual bodies to accumulate, and Bother's good, but even he's going to have trouble picking up a days-old scent in the middle of so many people. So we're back to tracking down who the mysterious visitor was, to see if they know anything more. And thanks to my sigil painting, we should have that information by tomorrow."

He waited for her to say something, but she only turned back to her notepad, making another notation, then crossing it out.

"Rosemary."

She put down the pen at that. "I keep thinking that we're missing something." She made a gesture at the paper. "The maid claims it's a happy household, at least for the years she's worked there. And the clerk at the desk—poor man, he's so terribly bored—couldn't come up with a single tragedy in town for the past *fifty* years. This town is so boring, I'm amazed any uncanny stopped here, much less stayed. But we know there's at least one—two, if you're right that the one who stalked you—"

"It wasn't stalking," Aaron muttered.

"And yet there's absolutely no indication . . . We're missing something. Maybe a lot of something."

He had no response to that: she was entirely correct. But he'd seen her in this mode before: while he could put his frustration aside, hers would eat at her, which would keep her from resting, which would drive her to the drug in the vials she thought he didn't know about.

A bottle of wine might help her sleep, though.

He gave an elaborate stretch, making no attempt to make it seem realistic. "There's nothing more we can do right now, so what say we go have dinner, and call it an early night?"

Her expression shifted from discontent to a familiar amusement. "Let me guess: You have a new novel you want to read?"

He willingly sacrificed himself to her mockery. "A woman writer, name of Cather. I've heard it's excellent."

She shook her head, but a smile was threatening to escape, which he took as a win. Rosemary did not understand his fascination with modern fiction, did not understand the pleasure he took in slipping into a world without uncanny, without Huntsmen, but she indulged him, and that was occasionally useful.

"Come on," he said. "I will deny my evening read long enough to take you somewhere swell. Put your hair back up and let's go."

She stared down at the sheet of paper, then sighed, not even giving him the expected lecture on the state of their finances. "Give me ten to get Bother settled?"

But he had no sooner returned to his own room, intending to restyle his hair and change his tie for something better suiting a nice restaurant, than there was a knock on the door.

He opened it with an irritated flourish. "You're ready alr—"

But it wasn't Rosemary.

The uniformed employee, who couldn't have been more

than fifteen, didn't blink at his behavior. "Mr. Harker? Message for you, sir."

"Thank you," he said, even as the envelope was placed in his palm. Only after the door was closed again did he remember that he should have given the boy a tip.

With a shrug, he stripped off his tie with one hand, turning the envelope around in his other, to see if there was an address on it.

There wasn't, only his name in a strongly masculine hand. He frowned and touched the ink with the edge of his thumb. Blue joined the lingering trace of green paint: the ink was still damp. Whoever had addressed it had done so recently, meaning it had been rushed to them. Struck by that urgency, Aaron slid the envelope open. A few words in, and he was at Rosemary's door again, heedless of his half-undressed state, or the thought that his sister might likewise still be dressing.

"There's been an attack at the Ballantine house."

Eight

VEN WITH THE time it took to retrieve the rental automotive from where it had been parked, it took less time
to get across town than it would have in a trolley, particularly
as night was falling. Thankfully, the streets were empty, and
Aaron was able to park directly in front of the Ballantines'
home.

He had half expected to see the house ablaze with light
and activity, perhaps with a few policemen standing about
being useless. But to his surprise and relief, the house was still
and quiet, no sign of anything awry from the front.

Once the front door opened, that illusion was shattered.

From their first, admittedly brief meeting, Aaron would
have said that Mrs. Ballantine had a stone core, or maybe one
of maple, bending to the wind but rarely breaking. But tonight
she was a ragged mess, standing in the hallway, her dress a sil-
houette of green silk that shimmered slightly, but that finery
could not hide the fact that her eyes were red, and the handkerchief she clutched in one hand suggested the redness was
from tears. Or sneezing, but he suspected tears.

Rosemary stepped past him, past the housekeeper, whose mouth was a firm line of definite disapproval, to place a gentle hand on Mrs. Ballantine's arm. "Is your brother all right?"

"Yes. Yes, he's fine. Not fine," she corrected herself. "He hasn't moved, or been disturbed."

"He's the only thing that hasn't been disturbed," her husband said, coming down the hallway to join them. He was dressed far more formally than he had been that afternoon, but his tie had been loosened, and his hair ruffled. Aaron couldn't tell if the edge in his voice was anger or something else. Fear, maybe, but the sort that would make a man like this angry to feel. "We came home after seeing a play with friends to discover . . . Well, come see for yourself."

He turned as though to lead them down the hallway, but Botheration moved out front, taking point. The man glanced at the hound, doing a familiar-to-the-Harkers double take.

"That's Bother," his wife said. "I told you he was large."

Ballantine stared at the hound, then back at the Harkers, then back to the hound, before making an overly grand gesture to indicate that the hound should lead the way.

Rosemary moved with Mrs. Ballantine, Aaron behind, the housekeeper bringing up the rear of their strange little parade. Bother did not pause at the stairs, or any of the other doors along the hallway, but went directly to the door to the library. It was open, light spilling out into the hallway. Bother hesitated, then went through the doorway, the Harkers right behind.

"Dear God." Rosemary sounded as though someone had punched her in the stomach as they stared at the wreckage of what had been the library. Books had been pulled down, pages scattered across the floor, the upholstery slashed open to reveal its innards, ink splatters staining the previously exquisite rug.

It was too much for Aaron to take in, the weight of too much strong emotion around him. He breathed in through his nose, drawing himself inward until he could focus only on the room in front of him, rather than the people around him.

To the untrained eye, the destruction might look like the work of human hands, and human temper, but every instinct and every bit of training told Aaron otherwise, even if Bother remained still and silent by his side.

"This is more than mischief," he said, as much to himself as to his sister, who merely nodded, wordless, before moving past him into the room.

"What happened?" she asked.

"That's what I was expecting you could tell me." Ballantine, standing behind them, had regained control of his voice, but Aaron did not doubt that the man was furious. Even from a quick glance, he had cause to be. And Aaron didn't need Rosemary to tell him that they would be the next targets of that fury, if they weren't careful.

And maybe even if they were.

Rosemary was already prowling the edges of the room, one hand tapping restlessly against the fabric of her skirt. Only someone who knew her as well as he did would know that she was reassuring herself that her knives, one sheathed against her arm, the other tucked into a weighted pocket in her skirt, were there and ready. He'd sheathed his own knives and loaded his pistol, now tucked under the back of his jacket, but without knowing what it was they were hunting, it was uncertain if the bullets would do any good. Too many uncanny would not stop for anything less than cold iron, silver-tips, or bitebane-infused bullets.

But there was nothing to fight here. Not anymore.

"When was this discovered?" Aaron asked Ballantine, but it was his wife who answered.

"A little over an hour ago. The maid came in to freshen the flowers, and . . ."

"You weren't home yet?"

"No. Walter sent a message for you as soon as we saw . . ." The hanky came into play again as Mrs. Ballantine wiped at her eyes. "Saw that."

Aaron took a step into the room just as Rosemary went to the pair of French doors, her hand lifting to pull back the drapes, and Bother growled, a low, ominous sound. Rosemary and Aaron both refocused their attention on him. Unfortunately, so did the Ballantines.

"Shhh," Aaron said, holding up a hand before anyone could say anything. "Bother?" The way he was acting, they might not be alone in the room after all.

The hound lifted his head, soft brown eyes glinting with a hint of red. His jaw dropped open, and he took a gulping mouthful of air, then blew it out, his massive square head dropping again.

There was something in the room, some scent that made the hound react, but it was not strong enough to find the source. Too many people in the room, diluting the scent? Or had the uncanny masked itself, somehow?

"A simple hunt, that's all I ask for," Aaron muttered, frustrated. "No more surprises."

"We just had a simple one," his sister reminded him,

keeping her voice low as she joined him, aware that they had an audience. "You wanted more."

"It's not as though the universe has ever listened to me before."

Rosemary glanced at the Ballantines, noting movement in the hallway behind them: staff members, most likely, wanting to see what was happening. "We need to control the situation," Rosemary said. "Before they start demanding things we can't provide." When he nodded, she raised her voice deliberately, so it would carry across the room. "Botheration. Find."

The hound's head lifted again, and Aaron thought if he could speak, he would say, *I tried,* in the tone of an aggrieved child. Instead, he put his nose to the carpet again and huffed, then turned to the left, blunt head swinging back and forth in minute measure.

Ballantine moved forward then, arms crossed over his chest as he watched the hound work. "What is it doing?"

"What he was bred to do," Rosemary said. "Finding the trail of an uncanny."

"A dog can do that?"

"He's a little more than a dog," Rosemary said, but the man ignored her, focused on Bother's movements. Aaron might not be able to read people the way his sister did, but he could almost see Ballantine thinking he could breed and train his own dogs to do the same. *Good luck with that,* Aaron thought, amused. Bother's foundation line had been particularly bred and trained for this purpose; trying to train an ordinary dog to do the same would be an exercise in frustration for all concerned.

"What will he do once he finds the scent?" Mrs. Ballantine was also staring at Bother with a fascination only slightly different from her husband's, her kerchief still clasped in one hand.

"Track it, wherever it went."

Aaron was half hoping that the trail would lead to the bedroom they were keeping Congdon in; that would increase the probability that the man had been the target, and hopefully only victim. But Mrs. Ballantine said that he hadn't been disturbed.

It took a while for the hound to finish his investigation of the room, paying particular attention to the curtains and upholstered furniture. He circled back to one of the carpets, then stopped at a bookcase, staring at the upper shelves before moving on again. Aaron looked at Rosemary, and she nodded: at some point, one of them would need to check that bookcase and likely quietly remove some volumes. There were some works that should not be in private homes, for everyone's safety.

Bother made another pass at the overturned sofas, sniffing at cushions that had fallen to the floor before returning to Rosemary's side, indicating that he was finished.

"And?" Ballantine sounded confused. "Did he not find anything?"

Rosemary was busy rewarding Bother with a treat from her pocket, reassuring him that he'd done a good job, even if he hadn't flushed anything out.

"An uncanny was here," Aaron said. "His initial reaction confirms that." And it had been here long enough to saturate the room with its presence. "But whatever it was, it didn't leave a trail he could follow."

Which shouldn't have been possible. If an uncanny had been here, Bother could track it. Out the door, through the windows, up the chimney, Bother could find the exit point. Unless . . .

Rosemary must have had the same thought, as she turned back to Mrs. Ballantine, placing a hand on her arm and gently ushering her out of the room. "Come, let's check in on your brother, shall we?"

Aaron caught Ballantine's eye and jerked his head in the direction of the hallway, willing the man not to be stubborn, or oblivious. On any other day, Ballantine might have protested being ordered about in his own house, but the events had shaken him enough that he merely followed his wife and Rosemary back out into the hallway, lifting his voice to speak to whoever had been hovering and leaving Aaron and Bother alone in the room.

Or perhaps not alone.

"It's just us here now," Aaron said into the room, his voice echoing oddly against the overturned furniture. "The others are gone, evened the odds a little. So why don't you show yourself?"

In general, it was unwise to challenge an uncanny. Like taunting a bull, it could end badly—and quickly—for the challenger. But there were . . . not rules, as such, but *traditions* for some. A challenge was a game of sorts to them, and they couldn't help but respond.

Aaron waited, but there was only a heavy silence, the sole noise Bother's damp breathing. He should have sent the hound out with the others if he truly wanted the uncanny to reveal itself, but there was a fine line between taking a risk and being an idiot, and he tried not to step over that line if he could avoid it. It saved on lectures from Rosemary later.

He glanced down at Bother sitting at his side, motionless as though he'd been carved out of fawn-colored stone. Even his ears, normally a clear indicator of his mood, were still, the erect ear facing forward, the folded one resting softly against his head.

He reached down to rub gently at the back of the hound's neck, a familiar, soothing—for both of them—caress. Bother had the sensitivity Aaron lacked, had been bred specifically for it. In the face of the hound's calm, doubt crept in.

But the hound had confirmed that an uncanny had been in the room—and had not left.

"Come on, then," he tried again. "If you're wanting to send a message, I'm right here to listen."

He wasn't expecting an actual response to his invitation. Although about half the documented uncanny had the ability to at least mimic human speech, it was rare to encounter one able to communicate more than basic emotions. And the ones that could generally weren't dangerous—or at least weren't *generally* dangerous. Brownies and gnomes were more annoyances, and occasionally useful, if you flattered or bribed them. But even they could and would turn on humans, given half a reason. Fairy tales were right in that regard. The Harkers might have worked with an uncanny in Brunson, but neither of them had *trusted* it.

Aaron waited another moment, feeling Bother stir slightly under his hand. "I trust you, boy," he said quietly, and the hound stilled.

A challenge hadn't worked, so he tried another approach,

on the off chance that this uncanny shared at least one trait with humans: the need to complain.

"I don't suppose you could tell us what this is all about? Clearly you're angry." And he gestured at the debris of the room. "Is it anything we can fix?"

Silence.

Doubt grew into second-guessing.

He gave the room another look, noting the placement of furniture and lamps, the shadows cast by bookcases and curtains. To be hiding in the room, and not be visible, the uncanny would have to be small. But nothing small had done this damage, not even if there were a dozen of them.

If they were to believe Mrs. Ballantine, what she had seen looming over her brother had not been small.

Aaron settled his shoulders and looked over the evidence the way they'd been taught.

Bother had alerted them to an uncanny in the room, and Molosser hounds were never wrong about that.

The uncanny had been here within the past six hours, based on when the Ballantines had left for their play and when the destruction had been discovered. Bother could track uncanny scents older than that, if rain or running water had not erased them. In a closed room? It should have taken him minutes, at most.

And yet, Bother had not been able to find a trail out of the room.

Conclusion: the uncanny was still somewhere in the room.

Aaron's logic was sound. But was it right?

Aaron forced himself to inhale deeply, then exhale, letting his fingers relax, rather than tensing for the grip of knife or pistol. "Think it through again," he whispered to himself, no longer worrying if the uncanny was listening.

Fact: there was nowhere in this room for an uncanny to hide where Bother wouldn't be able to find it. But Bother hadn't been able to find anything.

"It left without leaving a trail," he said. "But that's—"

Aaron spun on his heel, fast enough that Bother yelped, a high-pitched, undignified noise, scrambling to follow him out the door.

Ballantine was waiting in the hallway. "What—"

"It may have ridden someone out, stolen their face to escape. Who was in the room with you before we came? Other than your wife." If either of the Ballantines had been ridden, Bother would have alerted them the moment he came into contact. Staff. They had servants in the house, a maid, a cook? Or children? There had been a girl here, their first visit. Children were easy prey to uncanny.

"What?" The man stared at him. "They can do that?"

"Some can." Ballantine would sleep better without knowing how many uncanny could cloud the mind until you saw what they wanted you to see. "Answer me, man."

"No one. Um, the maid, Macy. She was the one who found the room like this. There wasn't anyone else . . . our house-keeper, Mrs. Green, lives here, and Macy; the rest are day servants only and had already gone home for the night. With the children grown, we've no need of a full staff."

"That's plain living, certainly." The moment the words were out of his mouth, Aaron could practically hear his sister's sigh. Thankfully, Ballantine was still too distracted to take offense.

"So, nobody in the house besides you four." The housekeeper had opened the door; if there'd been a scent on her, Bother would have clocked it at once. "Where are they now?"

"I . . . I don't know. The kitchen?"

"Take me there."

Aaron hoped to hell that the man knew where his own kitchen was.

———

Mrs. Ballantine led the way up the stairs, and Rosemary noted with interest that the destruction had been clearly limited, not only to the downstairs, but to that one room. She filed that thought away as they arrived at the room at the end of the hall to discover that Franklin Congdon was in fact resting peacefully in his bed. The nurse was gone, the maid Rosemary had spoken with before sitting by the bed in her place.

"He's resting peacefully, ma'am," she said, in response to Mrs. Ballantine's anxious flutter. "Nothing's changed."

"Thank you, Macy. You may go now."

The look on the girl's face suggested that, with the memory of the damaged room fresh in her mind, she wasn't thrilled to be sent back downstairs. Rosemary was honestly surprised the girl hadn't slammed out of the house and never come back. The Ballantines must be good employers, or at least pay well enough to put up with such disruptions.

The girl was barely out of her chair before Mrs. Ballantine had moved to her brother's side, smoothing a lock of hair needlessly, then straightening the already perfectly placed fold of the blanket across his chest.

"Madame Betanne said she could see him here. She could sense him, see him, but something binds him from speaking."

Rosemary was surprised the spiritualist hadn't claimed some sort of message had been passed along. Being able to see the spirits was no guarantee of moral fiber, and wealthy people would often pay handsomely for even a sliver of hope. But maybe the woman had come with good intent after all.

And maybe pigs would fly.

"I was supposed to look after him," Mrs. Ballantine said, her hand still resting atop his chest. "He was the baby of the family, and Mama said I should look after him. Even when he grew up. I still looked out for him."

Rosemary felt a reluctant sympathy. She and Aaron looked out for each other, but she knew that feeling of responsibility. Still, taking blame for the act of an uncanny was ridiculous. "You still are looking out for him. You're keeping him safe. You called us in, to find out what did this to him."

"You haven't had much luck in that, have you?"

Rosemary was accustomed to bitterness, and she let it wash past her without comment. But her hostess winced. "I apologize. You've only just arrived, and . . . my nerves are not what they should be tonight."

Even if she hadn't been under orders to be on best behavior, Rosemary couldn't have refused that apology, or the almost-timid glance the woman threw her. "I've often found that some tea and honey, and just a dash of bourbon, settles the nerves well."

Mrs. Ballantine gave her a faint, conspiratorial smile. "I've heard tell of that, as well."

She looked back at her brother, touching his cheek. "We're here, darling," she said. "There's a very large dog downstairs, and brave people here to keep you safe and bring you home."

Then she stood and turned to Rosemary, her eyes still red, that faint smile quivering uncertainly on her lips. "Will you join me in that tea, Miss Harker?"

———————

By the time they reached the kitchen, Rosemary had been invited to call Mrs. Ballantine by her first name, Dorothy—"You've seen me at my very worst; it seems foolish to stand on ceremony"—and learned that she and her husband had been married for twenty-seven years, that her baby brother had been ten when they married, growing up more as a brother to her own daughters than an uncle. A kind ear, a sympathetic shoulder, and most people would tell you everything they knew.

"Oh, the girls. I don't know how to tell them. . . . I suppose I keep hoping I won't have to. That he will just wake up, and . . . and it will all be over."

Mrs. Ballantine stopped and shuddered. "When we had the first trouble, the . . . disturbances, I thought it was hobos, or hooligans from town, or . . . something ordinary. Unpleasant, but ordinary. But this . . . oh God. Whatever tore up my library, you think it was the same thing that did that to him? It was in my house. If we hadn't gone out . . . I would have been there, reading."

"But you weren't," Rosemary said reassuringly, even as her thoughts were working furiously. Mrs. Ballantine hadn't been there. And the uncanny had been furious enough to tear up an entire room, and only that room. It hadn't even tried, as far as they could tell, to go upstairs—Bother had shown no interest whatsoever in the stairs.

"The earlier disturbances, they had all been outside the house, only?"

"Yes. A few windows had been coated in something, soap, I think? And a few more broken, and some of my rose-bushes had been damaged; someone poured salt water all over them."

"Which windows?"

"Oh. The French doors in the library, and in the conservatory."

Rooms, Rosemary would put money on, Mrs. Ballantine used more than her husband.

Those things might not be connected. Might not. But Rosemary would put a month's stipend check against it being mere coincidence.

She needed to speak with Aaron. Alone.

"Do you think . . . What does it all mean?"

"We'll find out," Rosemary said, touching her arm again in reassurance. "For now, some tea and a night's sleep, and this will all look better in the morning."

They went through a door off to the side of the main hall, into a hallway of plain plaster walls and white-tiled floors that went down three shallow steps into the kitchen. "We'll just—oh."

To Rosemary's surprise, Aaron and Mr. Ballantine were already there, as were both the housekeeper and the maid, Macy, who looked as though she would rather be anywhere else, even back in the library.

"Walter?" Mrs. Ballantine sounded as surprised as Rosemary felt.

Rosemary frowned at her brother, then checked for

Bother, who had settled in under a heavy wood table, as though trying to stay out of the way. "Aaron?"

Her brother lifted his hand slightly, fingers moving in silent signs for "wait," and "all clear." Reassured, she waited.

"They're both human," her brother said to Mr. Ballantine, who did not seem relieved by this. Rosemary could feel her eyebrows lift; Aaron had thought one of the staff might be an uncanny? Well, that would be one explanation. It had happened before, God knew.

"So it's still in the house?"

Aaron frowned, more thoughtful than upset. "I don't think so. I don't know how it got out, but it did."

"I don't want possibles; I want surety." Ballantine didn't sound like he'd believe Aaron, no matter what he said.

"It's not in the house," Aaron repeated, and Rosemary could see that the two of them were perilously close to butting heads.

"I understand that this has been terribly upsetting to the household," she said, stepping forward to draw Ballantine's attention away from her brother. "If there is anything we can do to ease your mind—"

"You can find the thing that's doing this," Ballantine snapped. "I was told that you were competent, but so far I haven't—"

"Stop it," Mrs. Ballantine said, interrupting him. "Walter, I don't know what is going on, entirely, but I do know that they're not your workers, to be shouted into obedience."

Rosemary wasn't entirely certain, but she thought Ballantine's cheeks pinked a little at that, and the housekeeper's lips, if possible, compressed into an even thinner line.

Ballantine took a deep breath. "Fine. Yes. I apologize, Mr. Harker, Miss Harker." But the look in his eye was not apologetic.

"We will spend the night in the library," Aaron volunteered. "To make sure it doesn't come back."

Giving them unrestricted access to the rest of the house while the Ballantines slept. Much better than Rosemary's plan, which had been to come back in the morning. Ballantine looked inclined to accept, but—"No, oh no"—Mrs. Ballantine was shaking her head, looking scandalized. "I will not have you sleeping in there. The furniture is a disaster; there's not even a place to sit, much less lie down."

Rosemary was about to explain that they would be working, not sleeping, when she went on. "Mrs. Green, if you could make up the rose and the ivy bedrooms?"

If Mrs. Green's lips tightened any further, Rosemary thought with morbid fascination, her entire face might sink in after them.

Aaron glanced at Rosemary, clearly uncertain, but there was no way to gracefully refuse.

"Thank you," she said for both of them. "That's very gracious of you."

"The beds aren't terribly comfortable, but I suspect you won't be sleeping much." Ballantine might have accepted his wife's decision, but his meaning was clear: they were not guests; this was not hospitality without strings.

Since that matched their intentions perfectly, Rosemary merely smiled and nodded agreement.

"Our automotive," Aaron started to say, and Ballantine waved a hand. "Unless you're worried about your uncanny taking a shine to it, it will be perfectly safe where it is. Just have it moved in the morning, before the milk truck comes by."

Something nudged at Rosemary's hand, and she automatically petted it, feeling Bother's thick plush fur under her fingertips. His head was solid as a brick, but somehow softer than velvet, and exuded silent comfort.

Mrs. Green departed, presumably to set up bedrooms somewhere in the house.

"With your permission, we will take a tour of the grounds before turning in," Aaron said.

"In the dark? But what if that . . . thing comes back?" Mrs. Ballantine asked.

Rosemary almost chuckled at the woman's clear dismay.

"Then we will dispatch it," Aaron said calmly, reaching under his coat to pull out his pistol just enough to be identified, and then sliding it back into its holster.

"Oh. But if you kill it . . ."

"Once we know what it is, we will know how to wake your brother," Rosemary assured her, hoping that she wasn't lying.

"Let them work, my dear," Ballantine said, offering his wife his arm, clearly intending to escort her back to the main house. She made a face at him, exasperated but affectionate, but took his arm. "Macy, if you could bring a pot of tea to my room? With the special honey."

"Of course, ma'am." The look between mistress and maid caused Rosemary to duck a smile into her hand. Dorothy would be getting her toddy after all, despite the interruption.

With that, the Ballantines left the kitchen, leaving the three—and hound—staring at each other awkwardly. They were being treated as guests, but at the same time it had been made clear that they were not.

"If you could—" Rosemary started, just as Macy said, "Would you be liking some tea as well, Miss Rosemary, Mr. Harker? It's no more bother making it for three as one."

"Thank you, yes." Rosemary was exhausted and, she was only now remembering, starving. "And if there's perhaps some bread and butter . . . ?"

The girl recoiled, her expression going from shy to shocked. "Oh, bless the Lord, they called you away from dinner, didn't they. And not even a thought in their heads about that, of course they didn't." And with that, awkwardness disappeared. "You two, sit down there. And you too, Mr. Bother, you sit down and I'll fetch you something, too."

While she bustled off to the other end of the kitchen, where a massive iron stove hulked, Rosemary leaned forward, intending to ask Aaron what he'd discovered. But before she could even shape the words, he burst out, "The uncanny left no trail Bother could pick up. It's as though it just . . . disappeared. Melted."

"Exactly what Mrs. Ballantine described seeing in the office."

"I know, I know, no need to rub my nose in it," he said. "But that doesn't make it any less impossible."

"What was that you were saying to Mr. Ballantine when we came in?"

"Oh." Her brother rubbed the back of his neck, looking slightly sheepish. "I'd a thought it might have ridden someone out."

Rosemary stared at him. "What, like a spiritus monstrum?

It would fit the type of assault, certainly, and the description of what Mrs. Ballantine saw, but . . ."

"But it wouldn't have been able to create the destruction in that room. I know. And I don't think it's a shape-stealer, not really."

"They do tend to leave debris behind," she agreed. "Bits and pieces and the occasional hand or foot."

"But there was something in that room, and then there wasn't, and the trail went utterly cold. And Ballantine was staring at me like Jacob at his most disappointed."

The old Huntsmen had a stare that had cowed two generations of his students. "And you panicked."

"Like a virgin in a brothel," he admitted. "But the maid and the housekeeper both passed Bother's sniff test: the only thing he reacted to was a bit of dried fish caught in the maid's apron pocket. And they were the only ones in the house; no one else came or left between the last time the maid saw the room intact, and when we arrived. So we know it's not a shaper, and it's not a spirit."

"Process of elimination will take us time we don't have. This escalation of physical destruction—"

"You think it will make another attempt on its victim, try to finish him off?"

"Or someone else. We can't rule out another member of the household being a target." But the maid came back before Rosemary could say more. The girl might know some, or all, of what was happening, and certainly knew that the Harkers were in the thick of it, but Huntsmen habits ran deep. The fewer people involved in a hunt, the better. Bystanders too often meant bodies.

Oblivious to their silence, Macy was busily moving about the kitchen, putting down the loaf of bread she had brought and slicing it, then cutting several chunks off a wheel of cheese and adding that to a platter. She didn't seem inclined to speak, content to let them sit at the table while she hummed a little tune under her breath. Rosemary finally broke the silence.

"Macy. You said you've worked for the Ballantines for a few years?"

"Yes, ma'am, since just after I left school. The youngest daughter had just gotten married and went down to Virginia, where her husband's people are from."

Rosemary nodded, as though she'd already known that fact. "And Mrs. Ballantine and her brother, they're close?"

"Oh yes, close as kittens. Mr. Ballantine likes to say he got a wife and a brother when he married Mrs. Ballantine." Macy shook her head and dashed back to the other side of the kitchen when the kettle began to whistle, deftly plucking it from the hob and pouring the heated water into a teapot sitting ready. The warm smell of good tea reached Rosemary's nose, and she could almost feel her shoulders ease. She preferred coffee, yes, but there was something about the smell of tea that said things couldn't be all that bad.

"That's why all this feels so funny," Macy went on, before putting the kettle back and bringing the stove down. "Never seen a family less likely to be cursed."

"Cursed?" Aaron's ears couldn't perk up the way Bother's did, but if they could have, they would have.

"Well, that's what this has to be, isn't it? First Mr. Congdon, then this?" Macy shook her head, acting for all the world like an old granny, not a girl barely out of pigtails. "It's not natural. We're not so far from that place, you know."

"That place?" Aaron mouthed silently to his sister. She gave a tiny shrug. Like he'd said, this state was full of history; there were any of a dozen locations that could be "that place." Salem, likely, if Macy was the sort to consider curses. Or Fall River. Tragedy bred superstition.

Only the fey could curse, though, and make it stick.

Oblivious to their exchange, the maid took cups down from the cupboard, then disappeared for a moment into a narrow closet, emerging with a piece of dried beef that she placed on the tray next to two china cups and saucers.

Rosemary had the impulse to offer to help the girl carry everything to the table but was afraid that the interruption would make her realize she was being indiscreet and stop her talking. Across the table from her, Aaron had steepled his fingers together, holding them to his lips as though to keep himself from blurting something. If they could keep her talking, gently direct the conversation to anything unusual the girl might have seen or heard . . .

The tray settled on the table, Rosemary delivered the jerky to Bother, who took it delicately with his teeth, then made himself comfortable under the table again, his head resting on her boots as he chewed. Aaron, meanwhile, took over the tea, dropping a soft lump of sugar into each cup before pouring the steaming liquid, his hands deft enough that it barely made a splash.

"You enjoy working for them." It wasn't a question, but the maid responded as though it had been.

"I do. They're good people, they are," she said, turning

back to the counter to prepare her mistress's tray, now that the guests were settled. "Toplofty, sure, but not like some. They treat people well, even them as they shouldn't."

"Oh?" Aaron paused with the teacup halfway to his mouth, looking to her for clarification.

"Not you," the maid rushed to assure them, picking up something in his tone. "It's just . . . like the way they treat Miss Daniella. Like I said, they have daughters, long grown and married now. But Mrs. Ballantine treats that girl like she was family."

"And she's not?" Rosemary was asking for verification; she had been introduced as a friend's daughter, but there had been stranger surprises in past hunts, and surprises were never good.

The maid huffed a faint, surprised laugh. "Not with that skin, she's not. Dusky as a foreigner, isn't she? Mrs. Green says her father the Captain's a friend of Mr. Congdon's, and it's good of the Missus to take an interest in the girl, but she's not—"

"Macy." The housekeeper had returned. "Please take the tea up to the master parlor; Mrs. Ballantine is waiting." *And you are gossiping* was unspoken but clearly heard.

"Yes, ma'am." The girl bobbed her head at both Harkers and fled. Rosemary closed her eyes, reining in the frustration she felt at the interruption. When she opened her eyes again and turned to look at the housekeeper, she was met with a steely look that warned Rosemary from asking questions— or offering opinions.

"Your rooms are ready." It was a flat statement, inviting neither thanks nor questions, and the Harkers offered neither but finished what was left of the bread and cheese, washed it down with the last of the tea, and followed her meekly to their appointed chambers.

The bedroom Aaron had been assigned was small but well-appointed, and the housekeeper, whatever her personal feelings about the Harkers, had laid out a towel and soap on the dresser, and a flannel nightshirt on the bed. It was close enough to his size that he guessed it belonged to Congdon, not Ballantine.

Ignoring the toiletries, he opened the bag of weapons he'd taken from the automotive, then unloaded the contents of his pockets onto the bed and considered his options. He'd loaded six rounds into the Colt before leaving the hotel but now took another from a cardboard box pulled from the case and added it to the magazine. "Full house," he announced, before placing the pistol back on the bed and looking over his knives.

The loss of his favorite blade had left him feeling off-kilter, the new one not quite the same feel or heft. Given time, he would adjust, but they didn't have time. He shed his vest, the new steel blade going under his left arm, a smaller iron one under his right, adjusting them both for access. He then slid his jacket back on, flexing his shoulders and swinging his arms to make sure he could move easily. His silver-edged jackknife went back into his front pocket, the box with additional ammo tucked into one pocket of his jacket, the pistol placed carefully into the other. The remaining knife, a larger Bowie, he considered, then instead tucked under the pillow, then locked the case and pushed it under the bed, out of sight.

That left two slender boxes still on the bed. Opening one

of the boxes, he withdrew a slender piece of white chalk and moved about the room, lightly marking sigils on each wall, high up enough that they would not be seen at a casual glance, ending with one over the door. If anyone—or anything—other than himself entered the room, a resulting glow would alert him when he returned.

Before turning to rejoin Rosemary, he put the chalk away and tucked both boxes into the inside pocket of his jacket, patting them once to make sure they were lying flat, then closed the door quietly behind him and descended the stairs to where his sister was already waiting.

She had left her hat and drawstring purse behind and loosened the gathers of her skirt to give her a longer stride. Once again, he appreciated how much simpler his life was, clothing-wise. To look at her standing in the entrance hall, there was no way to guess that she had a knife tucked at her waist and another sheathed on her throwing arm, or that her skirt's pocket was modified to allow easy access not to a handkerchief but a pistol. In a fight, she was as likely to get off the first shot as Aaron—and he wasn't ashamed to admit that she'd be more likely to make it count.

"The odds of the uncanny lurking about the house are slim," she said, fully aware that he had been cataloging her armory.

"But not nil." Neither Harker was prone to impulsive behavior, but Aaron was determined that they not be caught by surprise. And if he was thinking not so much of the uncanny they were hunting as the uncanny that had been lurking outside their hotel, he didn't need to say it. Not so long as Rosemary was armed.

She was the champion worrier in the family, but he'd learned from the best, after all.

———————

Warmer weather might be coming, but night still came quickly, cold shadows pooling in every corner, turning the landscape into a potential battlefield. Neither of them thought the uncanny might be lingering, but that did not mean it couldn't surprise them, or that other things might not be out there as well.

The lighter tone they'd held earlier dropped away as they stepped over the threshold and into the night. As they moved away from the house, Rosemary clicked on the tungsten flash, playing the light over the path in front of them.

"Hold a moment." Aaron crouched in front of the gate, pushing aside a tendril of vine before extracting a slender piece from the box of chalks, this one green, to carefully begin drawing sigils of protection on the red brick.

"That won't last a hard rain," Rosemary said, looking over his shoulder, as though he wasn't perfectly aware of that fact.

"It just has to last the night. Maybe the morning. Anyway, I promised I would, and I'm not giving him any chance to wiggle out of our agreement. Are you going to help, or . . . ?"

"Or," she said on cue, flicking Bother's lead to get the hound's attention and setting the flash down so that it illuminated Aaron's work. "Find us when you're done."

Sigils only looked simple; they were passive, but complicated, particularly when you tried to layer them. But the more you were able to layer, the more power they had. Assuming you did them correctly, anyway.

He studied his marks, then bent to erase a line and redraw it to his satisfaction.

Rosemary didn't trust sigils. Didn't want him using them. It was the single point they argued over, again and again. And, Aaron knew, she had a point. Sigils had a cost. Their mother still would have died in that last hunt. Their father still would have been a broken man, his last memory of holding her bloodied body in his arms. But he might have died with her then, rather than lingering on, lost to reason, if not life.

Aaron was more careful. He understood them, used them with respect. Did not expect them to do more than they were created to do.

Throwback, something ugly whispered into his thoughts. But he had nearly fifteen years learning how to ignore those whispers, and his hand barely shook.

"Protection, well-being, safety." He spoke the sigils' names as he laid each one down, swift strokes on the red brick of the gate-piece, then at the four corners of the house. His mother had claimed that human will made them work, that belief powered them, and as such they were more faith than magic. Aaron wasn't sure he still believed that, wasn't certain the gray area was quite as gray as she'd taught him, but they were too useful a tool to lay aside.

Finished with the last one, he double-checked their placement, clearing up some chalk dust from the edges, and stood, feeling his knees crack disturbingly. Despite several broken limbs over the years, and an impressive number of wounds and bruises, he didn't think they should be making that noise before he'd even reached a quarter of a century.

"You're not allowed to fall apart before Rosemary's do," he

told his bones, pocketing the chalk and clicking off the flash to allow his sight to adjust to the dark. "I'd never hear the end of it."

Fortunately for his search, the Ballantines' house, while impressive, did not have much in the way of grounds up front, their gate set against the road and their neighbors a hard stone's throw on either side. Behind the house, a lawn sloped down a gentle hill leading to a higher brick wall running along the edge of the property, topped with iron knobs to discourage anyone who might think to climb over. Aaron found handholds, hoisting himself up just enough to see over the edge, and discovered a steeper slope down to what sounded like a swiftly moving stream, a darker shadow of trees on the other side. Iron knobs, running water, and no bridge that he could see in the dark. Good. Running water was decent protection, particularly if it was deep. A pity that moats had never come into fashion in America.

Letting himself back down to the ground, he turned around to survey the house itself. Only a few windows were still lit, all on the upper floors. The master and the mistress of the house, no doubt, warm and cozy. The ground floor's windows were dark, curtains drawn against the chill. He approved of the way the now-dormant rosebush hedge had been planted, making a thorny deterrent while keeping several feet around the house clear of anywhere something might lurk.

There was nothing, no amount of silver, iron, or water, that could keep out a determined uncanny, but there was no need to make it inviting for them.

A shadow shifted to his left, and Aaron tensed, then recognized the shape of a human and hound, and relaxed as his sister and Botheration rejoined him.

"Nothing of note?"

He couldn't make out her expression, but Rosemary sounded resigned. "We sniffed outside every wall, and Bother didn't so much as twitch an ear. I have no idea how anything got in or out. If he hadn't reacted the way he did inside, I'd have sworn the damage was human-caused. Could he be wrong?"

They both looked down at the hound, currently scratching behind one ear with a massive paw.

"I suppose it could happen," Aaron said dubiously. "But."

"Yes," his sister agreed. "But." But it never had, not with him, and not that they had ever heard, in the history of his line. Molosser hounds were bred for one purpose, and they did not make mistakes.

Something uncanny had been in that house, had torn up the library and left again, without Bother being able to find a trail to follow.

Aaron scratched at his chin, reminded that he hadn't shaved that day. "Do you think . . . it flew?"

"What, up the chimney? Turn into mist, like Count Dracula?"

They'd both had nightmares after reading that book, until their uncle had reassured them that no uncanny had such abilities, that the author had taken many different uncanny and combined them into one creature.

"Windows?"

"Shut and locked, so were the French doors, and no re-action from Bother when we approached from the outside."

Aaron sighed. "So our best hope is that it comes back for another round. There's no point both of us going without sleep. Do you want to take first watch, or should I?"

Nine

THE FIRST THING Rosemary did, after winning the coin toss, was check the library's fireplace for any sign of disturbance, some suggestion that an uncanny might have used it as an exit. But Macy, or whoever had done the cleaning, had been too efficient; the hearth was clean, the ashes neatly swept away, the flue securely closed.

"If there are uncanny who can turn themselves into mist," she muttered, "I quit."

This was the part of hunting that Rosemary hated. Give her someone to charm, something to chase, some way to make her heart beat faster, and all was right with her world. But this? Waiting, particularly waiting for something she didn't even know would happen, made her want to scream.

"An uncanny that can send someone into a motionless sleep, *and* disappear from a crowded room, or at least seem to, *and* is strong enough to do all this, without being caught." She had memorized entire lists of uncanny and their attributes before she'd had her first menses, but none of that was helping her now. They had an entire library at home, nearly a dozen works of uncanny lore and Huntsmen's journals, but most were too delicate or dangerous to bring with them.

Aaron would take that as another reason why they should buy an automotive, so that they could bring more weapons, more books.

Needing something to do with her hands, Rosemary began picking up the bits and pieces of destroyed books and placing them into a pile for disposal. She righted a few of the overturned chairs, but the larger pieces of furniture were too much for her, even if she hadn't been worried about making noise. Botheration had taken up guard duty by the door, his upright ear flicking every now and again as her voice caught his attention, but otherwise not moving.

"Books and furniture," she noted, putting aside a volume that had been ripped in two. "Not the rugs, not the curtains, even though cloth would certainly be a simple matter to stain or rip. And the walls . . . no claw marks." It was a puzzle, but she felt as though she were being asked to do it blindfolded. Every time she passed by the French doors, she had to resist the urge to twitch the curtains aside and open the doors, inviting whatever might be lurking to come back already.

By the time Aaron came to relieve her at one in the morning, Rosemary was both exhausted and bored.

"Not so much as a mouse," she reported. "Maybe that's it. The uncanny is the size of a mouse, and there were hundreds of them, standing on each other's shoulders; then they scattered into the walls?"

Aaron gave that idea the consideration it deserved for all of a second, before shoving her out the door. "Because I love you, I won't remind you in the morning that you said that."

The stairs seemed longer and steeper than they had earlier that evening, but she finally made it to the room she'd been given and barely managed to remove her shoes and clothing, draping them haphazardly over a chair and placing her knives under her pillow before putting on the nightgown that had been left for her and falling into bed. She recognized that the pillow was soft, and the sheets smelled of lavender, and then it was all darkness until a soft, scratching noise made her sit upright, one hand reaching under the pillow for her knife, her exhausted brain imagining of hundreds of uncanny mice.

For a moment she was disoriented, the room unfamiliar and far grander in furnishings than she and Aaron could ever afford. And a girl she'd never seen before, standing a few feet from the bed, her eyes wide, Rosemary's clothing in her hands.

"I'm sorry, miss," the girl squeaked. "I was just placing your things back." And she made good her promise, placing the clothing back over the chair next to her stockings and corset.

Rosemary squinted, still not quite awake, her eyes gritty from lack of sleep and her body complaining about the too-soft mattress and too-warm room.

"Breakfast will be ready soon," the girl squeaked again, and fled the room, closing the door behind her.

A maid. The Ballantines. Aaron.

Rosemary pushed back the coverlet, swinging her legs over the bed only to find a pair of house slippers waiting for her feet. She shuffled over to the chair and discovered that her shirt-waist and skirt had been freshly pressed, smelling of the same lavender as the sheets.

She must have been beyond exhausted, to not wake despite the maid coming in to take the clothing for pressing. She was only thankful she hadn't thrown a knife at the poor girl in her sleep.

Thankful for the relative simplicity of her attire, she dressed quickly, keeping the slippers rather than lacing up her boots. A glance out the window said it was barely morning, and a mirror on the wall confirmed that her hair was a useless riot of curls. She finger-combed it as best she could before coiling it into a knot and securing it in place.

"No alarms in the night," she told her reflection. "That's good news, right?"

Leaving the room, she paused in the hallway, listening, before descending the stairs. The house was still, save for faint noise coming from the kitchen. The day staff, no doubt, preparing breakfast. Her stomach rumbled, the previous night's bread and tea nowhere near enough to make up for the dinner they'd missed. But she did not follow the noise, instead retracing last night's steps to the library.

The door was closed, and when she paused just outside, there was a faint huffing sound indicating that Botheration had scented and recognized her, but he didn't let out a bark to tell Aaron she was there.

She crouched to check the door handle, noting a faint layer of chalk dust there, unsmudged by touch, and a thread stuck in the jamb, rather than fallen to the floor or blown elsewhere by the motion of the door opening. It was a simple trick, but effective.

Satisfied that Aaron had left the library, she gave a low whistle, a single note, to tell Bother she was coming in, and pushed open the door.

Bother met her on the other side, sitting just beyond the door's swing. If it had been anyone else, the sight of the beast, his jaw dropped open to show a row of sharp white teeth, would have had them slamming the door shut in a panic.

Rosemary lifted her left hand, palm up, then curled her fingers inward, and Bother eased out of his guarding stance, coming to rest his heavy square head against her leg in greeting.

"Good boy. All quiet?"

If it hadn't been, she would have known the moment any-thing had happened. Or, more likely, the entire house would have known. Bother rarely barked, but his howl could wake the dead into cold sweats.

"Where did Aaron go off to, hmm?" The answer to that was likely in search of tea. Preferably with toast and eggs to go with it. Her stomach rumbled again at the thought, and she patted Bother's head absently, wondering if they would be expected to eat with the servants or not. She rather thought she'd prefer it if they were.

A startled masculine yelp made Rosemary swing toward the door, her arm twisting out so that her throwing knife could drop into her hand. Fortunately for the young man standing in the hallway, she hadn't strapped it to her arm when she dressed.

"What happened here?"

"Who are you?"

They both spoke at the same time, words overlaying each other. It could have turned into a stalemate, but he blinked first.

"Billy. I'm Mrs. Ballantine's driver." He flushed a little,

looking absurdly young, then asked again, "What happened here?"

Rosemary turned to look back at the room. Aaron had clearly followed her lead, trying to put the room back to rights: the scattered papers had all been placed in piles on the desk, a sofa set upright, and the stuffing torn from cushions disposed of somewhere, but there had been nothing to be done with the damaged furniture, particularly in the case of the once-delicate writing desk, splintered into pieces. She could see the boy taking it in, then turning to give her a direct, vaguely suspicious stare.

"There was a break-in last night, while only Macy and Mrs. Green were home," she said. Which was, technically, the truth. "Mrs. Ballantine asked my brother and me to look into it."

He went from suspicious to intrigued in the space of a heartbeat. "You're not a copper." His eyes widened. "You're a detective?"

Rosemary supposed she was, of a sort. If of mysteries most folk would rather not hear about.

"Never heard of a girl detective before."

Maybe it was his obvious youth, or her exhaustion, or the strain of having to mind every word out of her mouth until now, but the response escaped before she could stop herself. "Because men don't like us to talk about it."

That got a surprised snort out of him, and he blushed an even deeper red. "Begging pardon, ma'am. I didn't mean to take it funny."

Rosemary rather thought she preferred being called miss. "It's fine, I'm not offended. It was funny."

Bother shifted, and Billy's gaze went to the hound, as though suddenly realizing he was there. The blush disappeared, leaving his skin chalk white. It was a not uncommon reaction to the hound, particularly when he stretched and yawned like that, slow and deliberate.

"It's all right. That's Botheration. Bother, sit back down, please."

"What the hell is that?"

Billy was closer than he knew. But Rosemary didn't think telling him that would help matters.

"It's all right. He's mine. Bother, please. Sit down."

The hound sat, more because he'd determined that there was no need to eat the newcomer than any trained obedience. That was both the problem and the best thing with Huntsmen-bred hounds: they were smarter than many people and saw no reason to pretend otherwise.

"I, um, I'll just go back to the kitchen, and let them know they'll need to feed him, too?"

She was reasonably certain Macy, who had clearly developed a soft spot for the hound, would have taken care of it, but she let him use that excuse to make a graceful escape.

"Aaron left you here to do morning duty, hmm?" she asked, scratching behind one of Bother's ears while taking in the room in the first rays of sunlight. She had been right; the curtains over the French doors hadn't been damaged at all, neither the smooth velvet nor the lace overlay. Twitching them aside now, she confirmed that the brass key was still in the lock, turned from the inside, and there wasn't so much as a scratch marring the smooth wood and plaster to indicate they'd been used as entry—or exit.

"Furniture and books," she repeated. "What made it damage some things and not others?" It might be random chance . . . or it might be terribly important. The feeling of something just outside her grasp, something they weren't seeing yet, returned to taunt her.

A brother-in-law, attacked in his place of work. A wife's refuge, destroyed, but nothing else. More pieces of the puzzle.

Had anything else been damaged? She didn't think Ballantine would withhold information, but what if he didn't realize it?

Rosemary let the curtains drop, even as Ballantine's voice greeted her.

"Miss Harker."

She had heard him coming, the tap-tapping of his soles on the floor heavier than anyone else's. "Good morning, Mr. Ballantine." She turned to face him, composing her face into a facade of competent assurance. "I hope you slept well."

"After all this?" The controlled anger of the night before was gone, and she could practically see the sarcasm dripping from his words before he collected himself. "Save me the delicacy—I think we've gone beyond make nice and placating the panicky benefactors, yes?"

Rosemary could feel her eyelids flicker, her thoughts running faster: Was he sincere? Or was this a trap, another test? If she was blunt with him, would he then turn around and complain about her to Huntsmen leadership?

"You're correct, we have. Make my job easier, and answer one question. What have you done, that your family would be targeted by an uncanny?"

"I beg your pardon?"

Ballantine was offended, possibly taken aback, but not angry. Not yet, anyway. If he had done anything, Rosemary judged, it was possible that he didn't know it. She pushed on, not giving him time to think of excuses or escapes.

"Most uncanny are reactive creatures. They're vicious, occasionally malicious, and dangerous to humanity, but they rarely randomly pick someone out for attack."

Unless they were hungry, but that wasn't the case here, and she thought it best not to even mention those instances.

"You think I—" He was spluttering.

"I think that it's highly probable that you, or someone in your family, encountered and somehow angered an uncanny, yes. Unknowingly or otherwise." Uncanny could be touchy as a biddy aunt, and just as quick to take offense. "The earlier mischief was a warning. The attack on your brother-in-law might have been chance, or something he encountered in the course of his work, but the uncanny came here last night looking for your wife, and when it couldn't find her, it tore up this room in a rage."

It had been a vague suspicion, sifting through her brain as she slept, but the moment she spoke it, it felt right. The pieces weren't clicking together properly yet, but she was beginning to see where some fit. Family. This was about family.

Ballantine wasn't impressed. "So go find the thing, and kill it. Don't stand here and accuse my family of, of God alone knows what sort of nonsense. As though we'd have any dealing with, with . . . that sort of thing!"

Rosemary waited while Ballantine blustered to a halt, one hand resting on top of Botheration's broad head, as much for her own calm as to keep him still. What she was about to say was the opposite of politic, but Ballantine was less the pompous bone-top she'd expected.

"Uncanny rarely attack without cause. For them to come back and target your family again, what would you have me think?"

His eyes narrowed, and his mouth thinned. "You don't know what it is, do you."

"We have an idea." They had several ideas and not enough facts. You couldn't hunt if you didn't know what you were hunting; there were too many variables, which gave the uncanny the advantage. They always knew how to kill Huntsmen.

"The more information we have, the more detailed the information, the more successful the hunt. So please. For your family's sake. Do you know of any way someone in your family might have encountered an uncanny? Anyone who seemed a little odd, a little out of place?"

She would give him credit; he thought about it, then slowly shook his head.

"Dorothy would have told me if anything odd had occurred to her. Franklin . . . he couldn't resist a good story. There's no way I would not have heard about it, even if he didn't know what it was he'd encountered. My children . . ."

"We can likely leave out anyone living in a different state," she said, before he could start to worry about them. With few exceptions, American uncanny tended to be territorial, not leaving their region unless forced out, and highly resistant to sharing with newcomers.

At that, he exhaled, seeming to deflate slightly.

"And there's nothing you can recall, yourself?"

"To be brutally honest, Miss Harker, until Franklin fell ill, and Dorothy told me what she had seen, I thought talk of these uncanny was a bit of bunkum."

Rosemary's eyebrows lifted. "But you supported our work?"

For the first time, she saw a curve of humor in his face. "I tithe to the Church as well. I do not necessarily believe that God's angels are perched on my shoulder."

"Hedging your bets." No, not a bone-top at all.

"As a good businessman, I try to ensure that my assets are protected. But no, in answer to your question, prior to this I had no encounter with anything not obviously human or of human manufacture."

That wasn't a guarantee, as many a would-be lover had learned to their dismay. But a lack of noticeably odd encounters did rule out a few more possibilities. Not a stone-wife, for example, which had been her odds-on favorite.

"You said last night that you only have a small household. Did you lay off or hire any of them recently?" There had been a hunt the previous century, an indentured servant who'd been turned off without cause and without pay. The master had discovered too late, after his entire family had died in the woods, that she had been a dryad's daughter.

He frowned. "Dorothy handles the hiring, but no. We had another maid when the girls were younger, because the house would have been overrun otherwise, but she left us on excellent terms several years ago. Billy, our driver, has only been with me for a year, but his father worked in our stable, when we kept one; he practically grew up underfoot. The others, they've been with us for years. More than a decade, in Mrs. Green's case."

His gaze flicked to her, sharp with understanding. "You think they'd be considered part of the family, being with us for so long. That maybe it was one of them who offended it?"

"It's unlikely, but it's possible," she allowed. Especially with staff who had been with them long enough to form attachments. Like the protective stance of the housekeeper, the silent, amused understanding between the mistress of the house and her maid. "We will need to speak with them—all of them. As soon as possible, please."

And she needed to find Aaron, to catch him up on what had happened.

Ten

IT WOULD TAKE a while for the entire staff to be gathered, as one of the maids had the day off and needed to be summoned and brought to the house. Leaving Botheration in the custody of Macy, who was shamelessly feeding him scraps from her hand, Rosemary and Aaron drove back to their hotel.

The clerk eyed them curiously when they reclaimed their keys at the front desk, clearly drawing the worst conclusion from them returning at such an early hour, but handed over the keys without comment.

They rode the elevator in silence, the operator openly smirking at them, before getting off at their floor.

"We can get changed, pick up a few more tools from the weapons case, and get back before—"

"The bathroom has a shower," Rosemary said, in the same tone a priest might announce that his church had a holy relic. "I intend to stand under it for as long as the hot water holds out, and to hell with anyone else."

"I will pack up what we need," Aaron continued, as though that was what he'd meant to say all along. "Should I summon you breakfast as well?" He'd already eaten with the staff, before Rosemary had woken up.

His sister waved a vague hand in his direction as she unlocked her door; he took that to mean yes. He went into his own room, shedding his coat and jacket and toeing off his shoes, listening for the sound of her door opening and closing again. When it came, he waited another moment, then went back into the hallway in time to see the door to the bathroom down the hall close and to hear the sound of the lock turning from within. Counting off the time in his head, Aaron went to her door, making quick work of picking the lock, and slipped inside.

Ignoring the clothing scattered on the bed, he went to her bag, opening it cautiously. "Not there." He closed it again, careful to replace it exactly as it was, and looked around the room. "Where did you put it? Where . . ."

He went to the wardrobe, opening the doors and scanning the contents, careful not to touch anything. "Where, where, where would you . . . there."

After lifting the small case off the shelf where it had been hidden, Aaron, holding his breath, opened it.

Three vials were nestled within, tiny, filled with a liquid that, while clear, almost shimmered when he held one up to the light. "Still three."

The urge to hide them, or better yet, dash them against the wall, rattled Aaron hard enough that he almost gave in to temptation. Instead, he closed the case again and replaced it on the shelf, and let himself out of his sister's room, returning to his own. He loved his sister, and he trusted her with his life, and more. But those vials worried him.

Hot water did not quite replace a full night's sleep, Rosemary thought, but it made the day seem far more manageable, as did the opportunity to change into fresh underclothes. Although so far there had been little to complain about; normally by now they would have been covered in dirt, if not other, less savory materials.

"And that is an excellent way to jinx yourself, isn't it?" she muttered, opening the wardrobe and staring at her options. After almost being arrested for indecent exposure two years ago, when she'd had to hike her skirt up to her knees in order to keep up with a stone-wife, Rosemary had given up on fashion for practicality. However, all of the outfits she'd brought this time had been chosen to create a certain socially appropriate facade. And socially appropriate ladies did not run, much less tackle anything.

At this point, she decided, that cat was well and truly out of the bag, and Ballantine didn't seem inclined to rat them out. Retrieving her penknife and sewing kit, Rosemary set to work, ripping seams and restitching them to allow for easier movement.

Finished, Rosemary considered her appearance in the room's single mirror, then decided it would have to do. Instead of the fashionable upsweep of the day before, she simply pinned her hair into a serviceable knot at the back of her neck. Damp tendrils escaped immediately, curling around her ears and forehead, and she made an exasperated face at them before shrugging. It would have to do. Lacing her boots, then replaced her knives in their sheaths, secured her pistol in her bag, and went into the hallway to knock on Aaron's door.

———————

Aaron's skill at navigating the streets was improving, although Rosemary still found herself gripping the side of the automotive as he took corners, or when another automotive seemed headed directly toward them.

Halfway there, Aaron asked, "How much should we tell them? The staff, I mean."

"As little as possible."

"Obviously. But they will ask questions—"

"No they won't. They'll want to know as little as possible."

Aaron opened his mouth, clearly intending to argue, then shut it again as he took the automotive around a corner at far too fast a speed, and Rosemary grabbed the edge of her door again. "But—"

"They won't want to know, because they have to keep working in that house, after. Gossip? Gossip makes a dreary day more interesting. Knowing something for a fact? That's uncomfortable."

They traveled the rest of the way in silence.

Mrs. Green let them in, her expression seemingly now permanently affixed in a sniff of disapproval. "This way," she said, leading them not to the library, nor the kitchen, but a sunroom at the back of the house. Through the windows, Rosemary could see the lawn they'd been walking through the night before, all the way down to the stone wall, and the thicket of trees beyond, although not the creek Aaron had said lay on the other side. No neighbors were visible, giving it the feeling of being isolated out in the country, rather than the outskirts of town, at the outskirts of Boston proper.

Just before they entered the room, Rosemary reached into the pocket of her brother's jacket and pulled out a small black notebook. The cloth cover was battered and worn, nearly all the pages filled with notes or sketches, and the pencil attached by a frayed black ribbon was worn to a nub. She made a mental note to buy a replacement before it literally fell apart on them, then slipped it into her own pocket.

"As you requested," Mrs. Ballantine said when they entered. "You've already met Macy and Mrs. Green. This is Billy, our driver"—and the boy ducked his head, hands gripping his cap as though he wasn't sure what to do with it—"Chef Paul"—and a tall, lean man with sallow skin stared back at them, dark eyes withholding judgment—"and Therese and Beth, our day-maids."

Therese was the one who had to be called in on her day off, and her service-polite expression barely hid a sullen undercurrent. Rosemary couldn't blame her, but she was also determined not to become the whipping boy for the girl's annoyance.

"My name is Aaron Harker, and this is my sister Rosemary," Aaron said, taking over introductions, while Rosemary, Bother now at her side, tried to fade into the background. "As some of you already know, we are here looking into the recent events in the household. And we'd like to ask you a few questions."

"I don't see why you need to gather us all here like criminals," Mrs. Green said, her status and seniority allowing her to say what Rosemary suspected they were all thinking.

"Nobody here would do such a thing as what happened last night, even if they'd been in the house, and I assure you, they were not."

"None of you are suspected of being involved," Rosemary said gently. "We only need to ask a few questions." There was no point in taking offense at the woman's tone, any more than at the maid's irritation. They were disrupting her household; it would be a rare housekeeper who did not take offense, and Rosemary and Aaron were the only targets she could attack.

Rosemary caught her brother's gaze and lifted her fingers in a reminder for caution. The household was already on edge; they would get nothing out of them if he antagonized them further.

Unfortunately, she had to let him lead. One-to-one, Rosemary could coax information, but a man asking questions carried more gravitas, could get more answers, with less effort. It wasn't fair, but it was true.

Aaron nodded slightly, and she let her fingers drop— a sudden memory of the curly-headed boy who had clung to her hand overlaying the tall, seemingly confident man in front of her—and wished, with a pain she hadn't felt in years, that their mother could see him now.

"You all know about the incident yesterday evening." Aaron didn't make it a question. Macy looked somewhat abashed as the others nodded. It was exactly the way she'd told Aaron: gossip was lifeblood. Speculation was entertainment. Rosemary didn't judge, particularly when it made their job easier.

Rosemary moved her gaze from her brother to the gathered staff. Billy was watching Aaron with fascination, but the chef obviously did not care to be there at all, his arms crossed over his chest and his gaze hooded. The three young women clustered together, leaning shoulder to shoulder as though for comfort, while Mrs. Green stood off to the side, looking not at Aaron, but the wall behind him.

They were listening, but they didn't want to be. She couldn't pick up any signs of guilt, or regret, only a disquiet, the reluctance to accept that such a thing could happen here. Rosemary had seen it before, and it never ceased to annoy her.

Behind her, she could hear the rustle of Mrs. Ballantine's skirts and wished there'd been some way to ban her and her husband from the room while they questioned the staff, but even the hint of it had raised Ballantine's hackles, and the Harkers had backed down.

"What you may or may not know is that there have been similar disruptions earlier, outside the house. This is the first time they've gotten inside, however. We have cause to believe that it was the act of someone with a grudge against the household."

That got their attention, the chef looking up abruptly and muttering in French, while one of the day-maids, Beth, pressed both hands to her mouth as though to stifle a gasp.

"We believe that this is someone who might feel that a member of the family, or someone in the family's employ, had done them ill. It may not have been anything intended, but they would have taken it as an insult nonetheless."

"And what do you want from us?" The housekeeper put undue emphasis on "us," and Rosemary might be feeling too sensitive, but the implication felt plain, that the Harkers should be able to deal with this alone.

On consideration, Rosemary decided that yes, she was being too sensitive, but also, yes, that was exactly what the housekeeper was saying.

Aaron, bless him, took her words literally. "We need to know if you've encountered anyone in the past few weeks whom you might have offended, or even annoyed. Think back to anyone who might have taken offense at a thing you did or said. Likely, they'd be someone you considered somewhat odd, or off, although there's nothing in particular you could name, why you feel that way."

Rosemary was amused by the realization that her brother had been questioned by the police often enough over the years to have borrowed their approach.

"How are we supposed to remember such a thing?" Chef Paul continued to be unimpressed by the whole matter.

"Your employers are at risk from this person," Aaron said, and then slipped into fluent French, speaking directly to the man. "We may be all that stands between you and unemployment. Without work, the Naturalization Committee might decide to take a long look at you."

Rosemary could only follow some of what her brother said, but it seemed to have been effective, from the way the man blanched, then nodded.

"His face is offense enough," Billy said, sotto voce, and the girls giggled, Chef Paul muttering, "You little shit," before Mrs. Green cut them off with a look. Despite herself, Rosemary was impressed.

"We need you to cooperate," Ballantine said, and as simply as that, as though a key had been turned in a lock, the tone of the room shifted. Rosemary bit back a sigh: He couldn't have told them that before they started?

The day-maids turned to Macy, who in turn looked at Mrs. Green, then asked, "Are you talking about local folk, or visitors? Because there hasn't been anyone to the house since Mr. Franklin fell ill."

"Or the week before," Therese said, and Mrs. Green nodded.

"The Missus hosted a dinner party the week before, but other than that, there've only been tradesmen and family through the door."

Which would rule out any of the shorter-tempered or short-memories uncanny. But there were some that carried grudges for months or even lifetimes. This was getting them nowhere.

"And no one you've encountered outside the house?"

There was a pause while they all seemed to be thinking over their past interactions.

"They might be local," Aaron added. "The sort you only see every now and again, or even someone you see often, but rarely has anything to say to anyone."

"Like Mr. Isaac."

"Who?" Aaron turned to Ballantine, but it was his wife who answered.

"Isaac Reever. He must be eighty if he's a day. Owns a bookshop, although it's a wonder he can make ends meet. When he finds something particularly old or interesting, he will bring it to us—" She paused, then explained, "My mother collected older volumes, and Franklin and I kept up her collection. But he's"—and she was about to say something, switching it at the last moment to—"harmless."

Human. Rosemary would wager her last dollar Mrs. Ballantine was going to say "human."

Aaron turned back to the staff. "Have any of you had an encounter with this Isaac recently? Think back, as many months as you can."

There were a few murmurs, but slowly, each of them shook their heads.

"We should still check on it," Rosemary said, pulling out the notebook to make a note of the name. Particularly if he had been the source of the books Botheration had alerted on in the library. Beyond that, any hope that the staff might be useful was fading. Not only did they not want to know anything, they didn't seem interested in seeing anything, either. Not even in their own lives.

"Excuse me, sir." Therese, her face no longer quite so sullen, got Aaron's attention. "Is this—" She stopped, glancing at the Ballantines as though asking permission. When neither of them said anything, she bulled forward. "Is this related to Mr. Franklin falling ill? I mean . . ." She flushed, looking deeply uncomfortable, as though she wished she'd never opened her mouth.

"What?" Aaron didn't mean to sound harsh; Rosemary would have encouraged her more gently, but the word seemed enough to push her forward.

"Misfortune. My nan used to say that misfortune came in threes. If she was right—and she was always right—that's two." She looked around nervously. "Which means there's a third to come."

"Enough." Mrs. Green tapped her hard on the shoulder in reprimand. "There will be no such superstitious foolery spoken here."

Aaron licked his lips, a clear sign that he was uncertain how to respond. It was superstitions foolery, as the housekeeper said. But it also wasn't wrong that the two were connected. Rosemary simply hadn't expected any of them to make the connection, and certainly not to say it out loud in front of their employers, and she admitted she'd been caught as flat-footed as her brother.

"If it would make you feel better," Mrs. Ballantine said, deftly avoiding the actual question, "I will ask Father Phillip to come in and bless the house."

She glanced sideways at Rosemary after she spoke, as though seeking her approval. While not officially acknowledging their existence, the Church's stance was that the entire Huntsmen line was damned for the sin of their bloodline. In turn, Huntsmen had little use for the Church—or any religion—and most of the uncanny didn't care about it one way or the other. But a few pious words would do no harm.

"Thank you, ma'am." The girl didn't seem entirely appeased, but that was the Ballantines' problem, not theirs. Aaron caught Rosemary's eye, and she nodded.

"Thank you for your time," he said. "If you remember anything later, anything at all that seemed strange, or seems strange to you now, please let us know."

He offered their cards to the staff, having written the name of the hotel they were staying at on the back. Only the housekeeper and Billy took one, the boy turning it over in his hands as though something new might be written there if he looked enough times. Rosemary didn't understand his intensity: they were simple cards, plain white stock embossed only with their names. The Huntsmen had no crest, no motto, and no recruitment. If you heard the call, you answered it.

Still, she supposed the three of them were novelty enough to make even ordinary cards interesting.

"You may go," Ballantine said, finally, and the room cleared with commendable speed, Billy giving one last look over his shoulder and almost running into the doorframe.

"That boy," Mrs. Ballantine sighed, but she sounded fond. "Fortunately, he drives more competently than he walks."

"I hope that you were able to find something of use out of that." Ballantine didn't sound as though he thought they had.

"It was useful," Rosemary said, before Aaron could respond. She glanced down at Bother, who had remained settled at her feet the entire time, heavy muzzle resting on his front paws. "Although it would have been convenient for one of them to tell us that they had, in fact, mortally offended an uncanny three weeks prior, the fact that none of them could recollect anything unusual in that time frame eliminated some possibilities. Now we can focus on the remaining ones."

It was possible to encounter an uncanny and not realize it at the moment, but when asked to recall any oddities, most people would remember something that had struck them, even if it hadn't seemed important at the time. That was where the name "uncanny" came from, that instinctive reaction humanity had to that which was almost-but-not-quite human, the unease felt around things they could not understand.

Her gut feeling from the previous night was firming into a

conviction that whatever had targeted this household, it was focused on the Ballantines themselves.

"You'd best be on to it, then," Ballantine said.

Rosemary forced her face into a pleasant, obedient smile that she hoped hid none of her disdain for his tone.

Mrs. Ballantine rose from the chair she had been sitting in, obviously intending to escort them out, since the housekeeper had left with the rest of the staff. Aaron, who had already started for the door, seemed to lose his balance, knocking into her hard enough to make them both stumble. "Oh!" He jumped back, already spluttering apologies. "My clumsiness, inexcusable."

"It's fine." Mrs. Ballantine patted him on the shoulder, a motherly gesture accompanied by a kind smile. "I've tripped on this rug myself before." It was clearly a lie, meant to make him feel better, but Aaron smiled in return, indicating she should lead the way.

Rosemary followed, her eyes narrowed, but she held her tongue until they had left the house, safely seated in the automotive, Botheration a warm bulk on the seat behind them.

"What was that?"

Aaron didn't even pretend to not know what she was talking about. "I stumbled?"

"Aaron."

He sighed, and she knew she wasn't going to like whatever came out of his mouth next. But instead, he took one hand off the wheel, which made her brace herself more firmly in the seat, as though they would crash immediately, reached into his pocket, and pulled out several silver-blond hairs now bound up in a silver and iron clip.

Rosemary forgot to be nervous about the way he was driving, mild suspicion flaring into gut-churning anger. "Tell me you did not," she said, despite the proof that he had, in fact, done exactly that.

He was looking at the road, but she could tell he rolled his eyes at her. "Don't act as though I ripped skin from her body. There were a few hairs on her sleeve; I took them, that's all."

"And what exactly are you planning on doing with them?" She glared at the long silvery-blond hairs, afraid that she knew exactly what he was planning, or what he hoped to plan, but she needed to hear him say it. Out loud.

"We're stuck, Rosemary. We've been here four days, and we have absolutely no idea how to find this uncanny, much less how to convince or force it to release Congdon and leave the Ballantines alone. And the Circle is watching—you know they are."

"All the more reason to *not* do anything foolish." But Rosemary could hear the weakness in her own voice. Aaron had a point. The Ballantines had been surprisingly polite, but it had been made clear that Ballantine at least didn't give a damn why they had been targeted; he only wanted it to be over. He expected the Huntsmen to kill whatever it was that was stalking them. And he expected it to happen soon. If they didn't, even the friendship his wife had offered Rosemary would not save the Harkers from the results of that failure.

Rosemary asked again, "What are you planning, Aaron?"

He glanced at her, briefly, before returning his gaze to the road, then pulled the automotive over to the side of the road, letting a horse-drawn wagon move past them, the driver giving them a curious glance. "Tracking the uncanny down, with what little we know, will take too long. We need to draw it out."

She waited.

"Last night, it was angry that it couldn't reach Mrs. Ballantine."

Rosemary nodded. "That was my feeling, too, yes."

"It's a good theory; everything we do know supports it. Strike down the brother, go after the sister. But she wasn't home. So we need to give it what it wants, offer it another chance at her."

Her anger went up another notch. "No. I'm not going to put another innocent—"

"I know." He interrupted her. "Rosemary, I know." She knew he didn't understand why she'd been so upset about that hunt in Corpus Christi, but the fact that she hadn't approved had apparently finally made an impact. "That's why I took the hairs. I can use them."

She figured out what he was after, and crossed her arms. "No."

"Rosemary, yes. You know as well as I do that even if this wasn't a test, it's still a test. Our entire lives, it's been a test. Ever since Mother—"

"Don't." She stared him down until he dropped his gaze, but he kept talking, his voice softer but no less certain.

"Ever since Mother died, there've been questions. About us, about our bloodline. Why do you think they didn't send me to Europe with nearly every other unmarried Huntsmen my age?"

"Because they couldn't send me, and they knew you wouldn't go without me."

"If they'd sent me, I would've gone. But they didn't; they won't. Not just because of what Papa did. I know how some of them look at me. I know what they think."

"They're idiots."

"But they're not wrong."

"Aaron—"

"No. I'm not . . . I don't behave right; I don't think right. You protected me from all of it; you and Mother and Papa all protected me. But I know what they said. What they still say. That I'm a throwback, a sport. More fey than human."

Every Huntsmen had fey ancestry in their blood—that was what made them Huntsmen. What tied them to the treaty and subjected them to the call. Why the Church called them damned. But it was a few drops here, a few drops there, family trees occasionally crossing and producing Huntsmen with more sensitivity, better hunting skills. Sometimes, it faded from a family entirely.

And sometimes, in some families, a throwback appeared.

Rosemary had first heard the whispers when Aaron was still a child, too young to understand. Their parents had shielded them both, but Rosemary still heard them. The whispers that the fey blood had surged in the Harker line. That the boy-child was a throwback. That the fey would come and claim him, soon enough.

Rosemary licked her lips. "To hell with them. But that's why you can't do this."

True magic was forbidden to humans. Sigils, fairy lights, those were all in a gray area, frowned upon but still used. What their father had done, whatever had gone wrong, it had gotten their mother killed and broken his mind. Bad enough, terrible enough that she should never have let Aaron use even the most basic of sigils. And yet she had, had looked away and told herself it was no better or worse than others did, that they got the work done and that was what mattered.

But what Aaron was suggesting now, there was no prettying it up. It was a violation of a treaty thousands of years old.

They'd risked everything to bury even the whisper of violation, their last hunt, and now Aaron wanted to use it himself? If anyone found out, they'd call him a traitor, or worse.

They'd burn him.

"Magic, Aaron. You're talking about magic."

"Passive magic." As though that would make any difference. "We need results, Rosemary. And we need them now."

He was right. But being right didn't make him right. It was the same thing they'd faced in Brunson, except they did not have the defense of ignorance.

"If anyone finds out . . ." She didn't specify who she meant by anyone; she wasn't certain she knew herself. Neither option was good.

"They haven't come for me yet; they're not going to now."

She narrowed her eyes at him. Something about his words, the way he said them, set off a warning chime. He was keeping something from her.

He narrowed his eyes right back at her, matching stubborn to stubborn. "If you have a better idea, something that will work now, I'll take it. Happily, with both hands."

He waited, hands folded in his lap, and she sighed. "Tell me the plan."

Eleven

FRANKLIN CONGDON HAD lived a town over, in a neighborhood very different from his sister and brother-in-law's. Children were playing stickball in the street, scattering when Aaron and Rosemary drove up and regrouping at a safe distance to gawk, either at the automotive or at Bother—or, likely, both.

"Bother, guard."

Not that he thought anyone would try to steal the vehicle, but it gave the hound something to do.

"Which building?" Rosemary came up beside him, looking down the street at the nearly identical row houses.

"Third from the end, with the blue shutters." Billy had driven Congdon home from dinner at the Ballantines' more than a few times and had volunteered the information with enthusiasm. "He lives on the second floor."

Offering her his arm, they strolled down the street without garnering any more attention, the boys losing interest when Bother showed no inclination to come out and join them, and resuming their game. There was no gate, only three brick steps up to the main door, which swung open with a touch of the handle.

"We locked the house, didn't we?" she asked, half joking, before stepping inside, Aaron close behind. There was a door directly to their right, presumably leading to the first-floor flat, and a wooden staircase in front of them that led up to the second floor and their destination.

That door, unlike the front, was locked. Aaron pulled a pinholder and pick from his pocket and bent to work, while Rosemary stood back and kept watch. It was not encouraged for Huntsmen to break the law, but there were any number of things that polite society might frown on that were essential for their work.

The lock did not provide much of a challenge, giving way almost immediately. Aaron straightened, turning the knob and pushing open the door as though he had every right to be there, before stepping back to allow Rosemary room to go first. She moved past him, throwing arm held at chest level, ready to defend herself if anything was waiting inside, while Aaron brought up the rear, left hand resting on the stock of his pistol.

"Well, it's clear that a bachelor lives here," Rosemary said, stepping carefully across the main room, her arm lowering when it became clear there was no one else there.

A few steps behind her, Aaron looked for whatever had caused her to say that, then shrugged. There was a leather sofa at one end, a blanket strewn across it, a short stack of books on the floor next to it, and a wineglass balanced precariously on top of that. A thick-legged oak desk took up much of the remaining wall, next to an old-fashioned stove. The walls were covered with framed prints, mostly landscapes, with a few photographs interspersed between. He might not agree with Congdon's style, but there wasn't anything particularly objectionable about it.

"We need something personal," he reminded his sister, who had already disappeared into what he assumed was the kitchen. "Ideally something family-related."

There was the rattle of the icebox opening, and a sound of disgust, Rosemary coming back out with a hand over her nose. "Mrs. Ballantine may be a doting sister, but she did not think to have anyone clean out his perishables. There's a cheese in there that might be earning uncanny status as we speak."

"Something personal," he reminded her, opening the lid of the desk and then sorting through the papers there. He picked up one of the pens and weighed it in his hand before putting it down again.

"This would have been easier if you'd thought to take something from the Ballantines' house last night."

"And if I'd thought of it last night, I would have." His temper flickered, and he pushed it down. Rosemary wasn't trying to pick a fight; she was just voicing her unhappiness with the plan. "But since we don't have the option of going back and asking them for items of a personal nature . . ."

He had suggested that, and Rosemary had said no. Actually, she had said more words than that, but it came down to no. Her willingness to go along with his plan rested on no one ever knowing they had done it, and if they'd asked the Ballantines, there would have been questions. Questions, she pointed out, that it was almost inevitable the Circle would hear.

Aaron was perfectly willing to admit, to himself, when his sister was right.

"Aaron."

His sister was standing in the middle of the room, hands on her hips, and he got the feeling she'd called his name at least once before.

"What?"

"I'll look here. You take his bedroom."

A petty part of him wanted to refuse, just to see how she would respond, but he suspected that the momentary satisfaction would be followed by days, if not weeks, of regret at her hand. "All right."

The bedroom looked as though a strong wind had blown through, despite there being no windows. The bedspread was thrown back, the pillow tossed to the side of the mattress, dresser drawers halfway pulled out. "Was that you in a hurry, or did someone come in here looking for something?" He hadn't noticed any scratches on the lock to indicate that someone had picked it before they arrived, but they were dealing with an uncanny who could disappear without trace or trail; there was no reason to think it couldn't enter the same way.

Aaron suddenly wished they hadn't left Bother down on the street, but while a well-dressed couple entering an apartment might not be memorable, that same couple with a massive hound would be. He thought about calling a warning to Rosemary, but common sense asserted itself: the flat was only three rooms. As with the Ballantines' library, if an uncanny had been here, it was long gone now.

He opened the wardrobe and rummaged through the pockets of the suits hanging there, coming up with a few coins and some lint, but nothing useful. The bedside table sported a leather tray of the sort that might normally hold a watch or ring, but when he gingerly shifted a used handkerchief that had been dropped there, he found only a handful more coins and a ticket stub.

There was nothing underneath the pillow or bedspread, either.

"How can you live somewhere and have so little to show for it?" In Aaron's bedroom, there was an entire basket of wooden toys his father had made for him when he was a boy. He hadn't even looked at them in years, but he could name each one and tell you how old he had been when it was given to him. But Congdon seemed to have nothing like that here, only clothing and toiletries.

Bending down again, Aaron peered underneath the bed.

"Aha." Pulling out a long wooden box, he opened the lid.

"Did you find something?"

Aaron closed the lid again, not looking at his sister. "Nothing useful." While he had no doubt that the materials in the books were intensely personal, even he drew the line at using a man's stash of pornographic images.

"Fortunately, I did."

He twisted slightly, looking up at his sister, who held a piece of paper between her fingers. She turned it so he could see it was a collodion print, slightly faded from handling, showing a young family, mother and father standing stiffly, and two fair-haired children at their feet.

"The Congdons, I presume?"

"It was in his desk, tucked in the family Bible, so one would assume, yes." She turned it again so she could look at the image. "I think it's safe to say he valued this."

"Bring the Bible, too," Aaron said. "Just in case."

Twelve

THANKFULLY, THERE WERE no new messages waiting for them back at the hotel. After depositing their finds, and Bother, in Rosemary's room, the Harkers went down to the hotel's dining room just as it opened. It was far earlier than they usually preferred to eat, well before sundown, but the past few days had been scattershot with regard to meals, and both their stomachs were beginning to complain on the matter.

The food was nothing to write home about, and Aaron would be just as thankful to never eat there again, but his chicken cutlet had been competently made, and filling, and someone else had prepared it. On those three points, Aaron could not complain.

"Would it be possible to wrap up the remains?" Aaron was prepared for the waiter to give them an odd look at Rosemary's request, when she pointed to what was left of her lamb, but the man barely blinked. "You're the folk with the dog the size of a pony, yeah? I imagine he eats a considerable amount."

"He does," Rosemary agreed.

"Tell ya what—after you finish, come back around to the kitchen. There're always scraps that go to waste, tell Betty Robert said you was to have 'em for your boy. Keep him from eating one of the porters." And the man let an exaggerated wink drop before collecting their plates and moving on.

"I'll fetch it," Aaron said, wiping his mouth with his napkin before dropping it back down onto his lap. "You take him for his walk."

They normally split responsibility for walking the hound when they were traveling, but Aaron wondered if Rosemary would sense an uncanny watching her, if she were the one to take Bother out. If she did, it was possible it was simply curious—worried—about a hound nearby, or it was keeping an eye on them both. If it was no longer lurking, it might have moved on. Or it might have been interested specifically in Aaron.

Not that they could do anything about it, not while they were still on another hunt. But he was curious.

No. Aaron stood as Rosemary got up to leave the table, then followed her out of the dining hall, going their separate ways in the lobby. Not curious.

Afraid.

Being afraid is smart, not a sin. Jacob's voice, the old man sitting on the porch of his house, Rosemary and Aaron sitting at his feet, still children, but already learning what it meant to be Huntsmen. *You were born with instincts, telling you what's what. Something scares you, look at it. The answer's there.*

Aaron knew what he was afraid of. He just didn't know what to do about it.

———————

The kitchen was larger than Aaron had expected and filled with the bustle he had expected. But when he flagged down a harried-looking man swathed in a stained apron and told him what he was there for, the man nodded and directed him to an older woman who was busy chopping what looked like an endless number of carrots.

"You're Betty?"

"You're the man with the dog." Bother's presence was a matter of gossip wherever they went; the Harkers were used to it. Sometimes, like now, it was useful. Betty reached with the hand not holding the knife and retrieved a battered tin pail from a shelf below her table. "Got some beef scraps, bit a chicken, and some cooked vegetables scraped off plates, if he's not too picky."

"This is perfect, thank you." The hound had a gut that could handle everything from filet mignon to days-old carrion, but he was more pleasant to live with when he had a steady diet of chicken and cooked vegetables. Making sure the cover on the pail was secure, Aaron slipped a small bill into her hand, where it disappeared with a speed that was almost magical.

Aaron, pail in hand, retraced his steps along the narrow corridor that connected the kitchen to the dining area, hotel employees moving around him with practiced ease. But rather than head directly upstairs, Aaron took his time, thankful that the pail was neither heavy nor particularly pungent. It had only taken a few minutes to fetch the scraps; Rosemary and Bother would not be back from the hound's nightly constitutional yet. And while he loved his sister, couldn't imagine working with anyone else, there were times a man just needed space and time to think.

What he was planning to do was more difficult than he'd let on to Rosemary, and he was under no illusions that there would not be consequences if they were discovered.

By anyone.

If he was right, if his worst fear was right, and the uncanny in the park that night had been a fey . . . if it sensed what he was going to do, if it felt the magic being shaped, that would be confirmation that the treaty was being bent, if not outrightly broken.

"I might be wrong." It wasn't as though anyone *knew* what a fey felt like, or even what one looked like. The last Huntsmen to have encountered one had died of old age before Rosemary had been born. It was entirely possible that what he and Bother had sensed that night was nothing more or less than a local uncanny, maybe even the one they were hunting, who had been as startled by them as they were by it. Perfectly ordinary, if unnerving, like encountering a bear during an early morning walk.

Which would still leave them with the worry that the *Circle* would discover what they—what *he*—were doing.

The Harkers were, bluntly, between a sharply pointed rock and a very hard place, and the only way out was to do what they had to, quickly, and hope no one noticed.

And that what they learned made it all worthwhile.

Aaron came to the end of the hallway and pushed open the door that he knew exited into an alcove behind the main stairs, just catty-corner to the marble reception desk.

"Jesus, man."

Aaron only just managed not to slap the dinner pail into the face of the man he'd startled midway through lighting a cigarette, and it took several seconds before he recognized the voice.

"Jonathan. You're still here?"

"Aaron." There was a tinge of mockery in his voice but, Aaron admitted, probably not as much as he deserved for flinching like a rabbit. "And yes," Jonathan went on. "Regrettably. Complications. I hope to have it finished in the next day or so."

Aaron's first instinct was to say something cutting about competence, but Rosemary's admonitions to be politic and polite stopped his tongue in time.

"And you? Any progress?" Jonathan asked, when Aaron didn't say anything further. "In your business here."

"Some." Aaron would be damned if he'd say more.

The other man laughed, but there was little humor in it, and he took a long drag off his cigarette, pulling the smoke down into his lungs and holding it there before exhaling a perfect smoke ring. "I'm looking forward to being able to spend some time at home, honestly. It's been a busy winter."

A busy winter the Harkers had mostly been left out of. Aaron didn't know if Jonathan's comment had been intended as a barb or not, but he kept his face still and didn't let anything show.

Jonathan shook his head. "In all honestly, my hunt was the sort of thing that could have been handled by a first-year trainee with a butterfly net. But we go where we are sent and do as we are told."

It should have made Aaron feel better, to learn that Golden Jonathan was sent on the same sort of cleanup hunts, too. Instead, it rewoke his suspicions. A nothing hunt, overlapping theirs, that had him staying in the same hotel the Harkers had been booked into?

He opened his mouth to say something, he wasn't quite sure what, when a small voice in his head reminded him that this, too, might be a trap. Huntsmen answered to the Circle, and both obedience and adherence were expected. Jonathan might have been blowing off steam, in safe company. Or he might have been testing to see what Aaron might say in response to even implicit criticism of the Circle.

"We answer the call," he said, giving the other man a crooked smile, infusing all the humility and obedience he could fake into his expression.

"We answer the call," Jonathan agreed, dropping the remains of his cigarette onto the tiled floor and grinding it out with the toe of his shoe. "Good hunting, Harker. See you around."

While Aaron gave Bother dinner in his room, Rosemary made use of the sink in her room to sponge off all trace of scent or cosmetics. If they'd been home, he would have told her to take a full bath, but this would have to do.

"I'm not sure this would work even if we did everything to the letter and the spirit," he told the hound, who didn't lift his head from the pail to acknowledge Aaron's words. "But don't tell Rosemary that."

Every text Aaron had read, and he likely had read more

than any other Huntsmen alive, said that magic, passive or active, borrowed or true, needed one element to work: belief. If you scorned it, if you scoffed, that lack of belief would become reality, and it would not work for you.

Rosemary didn't like magic. She didn't trust magic. But she knew better than to disbelieve in it. It was just that they both had to believe *he* could do it.

He got up before his brain began to cycle into self-doubt and knocked once on Rosemary's door before opening it.

She was seated on the edge of the bed, her hair down and loose, dressed in a long white robe, barefoot, with a stressed expression on her face.

"Nothing I packed matched the clothing someone like Dorothy Ballantine would wear, even for staying home, much less going out in public."

He stared at her, his own worries forgotten for a moment. "Do you really think an uncanny will know, much less care, about fashion? Really?"

She flushed, then grabbed a pile of clothing and disappeared behind the wardrobe door, only her stockinged feet and the top of her head visible as she finished dressing.

Aaron turned his back to her, knowing he shouldn't be so amused. He'd been the one to explain that they needed objects of personal and emotional value, to create the illusion. Her logic—that the more detail they provided, the better the illusion would be—was sound. Despite his determination to do this, Aaron knew he was playing with fire. So to mitigate the risk, he wouldn't be attempting to create a true illusion, merely the illusion of one.

He'd been honest with Rosemary: if she'd come up with

a better idea, he would happily have abandoned his. But he'd known, even as he said it, that she didn't have one.

All that remained was to put the ingredients together. On the desk, the hairs he'd taken off Mrs. Ballantine's dress were braided into a thin rope with several of Rosemary's own hairs, the black woven through the silver blond. Now he took out his jackknife and carefully sliced the photograph into narrow sections, folding them together with the hair rope until they formed an odd-looking bracelet just long enough to fit around Rosemary's wrist.

The magic would work better with some skin, or better yet blood, but he'd acted on impulse when he saw the hairs glinting on Mrs. Ballantine's sleeve, and there hadn't been a chance to take more. Which was just as well; Rosemary might have balked if blood had been involved.

When she coughed, he turned around. She was attired now in a simple dark brown dress that made her look older than her twenty-six years, hair piled into a complicated-looking tumble of curls at the crown of her head. He crooked a finger at her, drawing her closer, and fastened the braid-and-photograph rope around her left wrist, securing it under her cuff with thread from her sewing kit. She tested the feel of it, adjusting the fabric for better positioning.

"It'll hold," she said in response to his raised eyebrows. "So long as I don't fling my arms about."

"Please don't," he agreed. "I don't know how long the illusion will last, so we'll wait until we're in position to trigger it."

She nodded her understanding, then turned back to the wardrobe to claim her coat. Slipping a long cloth bag over her shoulder, she checking her pistol before sliding it into the pocket of her coat, then stepped in front of the mirror to adjust her hat.

"You need extra ammunition?"

She patted the bag reassuringly, letting him know he wasn't the only one who had restocked, before frowning at her reflection and adjusting her hat to a more fetching angle.

Aaron shook a cigarette from his case and lit the end to a glowing ember, taking a long drag and holding the smoke in his lungs, then letting it out again, enjoying the sharply bitter burn of his throat and mouth. He took another, shorter, inhale, then offered the cigarette to Rosemary, who took it with a grimace. She didn't particularly enjoy it, he knew, but it was a ritual between the two of them, before every hunt, and while Huntsmen were not superstitious as such, there was no earthly reason to break what worked simply to prove that fact.

Another deep inhale of smoke, and he crushed the glowing end between two fingers, watching as a thin tendril of smoke rose into the air and faded, then tucked the extinguished cigarette back into the case. Jonathan might throw away his half-finished bones, but Aaron had no such luxury.

Leaving Rosemary to finish her primping, he went back to his room. Coat, hat, scarf went on in order, then he holstered his own Colt, adjusting it until it rested comfortably against his spine, and slipped a box of mixed ammunition into the largest of his coat pockets. A finely worked metal chain went into another pocket, along with his lockpick kit and the notebook they used for sketching. A familiar anticipation rose in his throat, the mixture of excitement, uncertainty, and fear as comforting as Botheration's snores.

Picking up the hound's lead, he snapped it once. "Up, Bother."

The command wasn't necessary; the moment his hand had touched the leather, the hound had gotten to his feet, stretching once before padding over to Aaron's side and waiting patiently while the lead was attached to his collar.

Bother carried only his muscle and his teeth. Aaron had considered crafting him a harness to carry more ammunition, but when he'd tried to measure the hound for the leather straps, the hound had made his objections clear, and Rosemary had put an end to it.

They left the hotel without fanfare, leaving the automotive behind and instead taking the trolley back toward the Ballantines' home. The farther they were from things that were theirs, even temporarily, the better the illusion would work. Aaron hoped.

They got off the trolley a few blocks from their destination, Bother, having made friends with a man with a sandwich he was willing to share, following with slightly more regret.

The streets here were nearly empty, too far from the center of town to encourage traffic, and the few people they passed on the narrow concrete sidewalks gave Bother careful looks but otherwise accepted the Harkers as part of the scenery. To an observer, they looked like a young couple and their dog having an early evening stroll, only the oddly shaped bag over Rosemary's shoulder out of place in the picture.

The anticipation he'd felt earlier was fading, settling into equally familiar calm determination. Aaron reached into his pocket, touching the case of extra ammunition and visualizing the contents. "Two silver, six lead, six iron . . ." He counted off the bullets as though he was praying a rosary.

"Mountain ash?"

He stopped short, causing Bother to stop as well and turn his head as though to ask what was wrong. "Damn." He hadn't even thought of that. Not many uncanny were stopped by wooden bullets, but there were some.

Rosemary reached over her shoulder and lifted her bag up just enough for him to see the four arrow shafts inside. "Extra ammunition," she said with a grin. "I might not have been able to bring my bow, but I had these waiting to be fletched."

"What, you're going to beat something to death with those?" She loved her bow, and no matter how many times she had to leave it behind, would never accept that it was a wildly impractical weapon.

"Steel tips," she said with a fierce grin. "Shoved with enough force, even a Rovin' Mary would choke on it."

"That's what we love about you, your practical bloodthirstiness." He was teasing, but it was also true. Others might think he was dangerously odd, but Rosemary was everything Huntsmen valued. He tried not to let that bother him.

Rosemary glanced at her brother as they continued down the sidewalk, Bother pacing between and slightly ahead of them. Aaron's hat was pulled down over his forehead, hiding his eyes, but she knew that cast of his chin. He was chewing on something unpleasant.

It could be anything; her brother wasn't a wide thinker, but he went deep. Still, if it had to do with the hunt, she trusted he would have told her, and for anything else, she knew better than to ask. Prying at Aaron had the same result as poking: he turned into a clam and refused to open.

Instead, she tried to enjoy their stroll, able this time to look around rather than focusing on finding a destination, or trying not to think about Aaron's driving. This part of town was attractive, if somehow boring, every house fronted by a gate, some more unwelcoming than others. Daylight was lingering longer than even a week before, but the gardens behind those gates were holding on to their winter barrenness, only the occasional hint of pale green beginning to push through in leaf and blade.

Rosemary preferred winter hunts: it was colder, yes, but there were fewer places for something to lurk, fewer places an ambush might come from. Plus, there were uncanny that went dormant in the winter. Of course they then came out in spring hungrier than they'd gone in.

And that was a thought she'd rather not contemplate right now.

"We're almost to the house." When he only grunted, she leaned briefly against his shoulder. "Come on, time to ante up. What's your bet?"

"I'm hoping for vampire." He saw her look and shrugged defensively. "A victim sent into a strange sleep, a mysterious figure looming over him, getting access to a home with no sign of entry or exit? Vampire."

"There's never been a verified vampire sighting in North America. They're trapped in Europe." Nightflyers were the closest they'd had to face, but those left physical marks on their victims and tended not to leave them alive.

"Fine. Your bet?"

She pursed her lips, thinking. "A mara."

He scoffed. "We're going to need a lot more ash, if you're right."

She'd brought four shafts. He was right, that wouldn't be enough.

Maybe they needed a different topic. "Do you think Ballantine is going to follow through on his end of the deal?" When they'd left the hotel, the datebook had not yet been delivered.

Her brother shrugged. "I don't see why not, although I'm even less convinced now it will be useful. The damage in the library says that whoever the uncanny went to the house for, it wasn't aimed at Congdon—he was upstairs, but easy enough to find. A brownie could have done him in, much less anything with the ability to tear the room like that. It wasn't looking for him, which suggests the cause doesn't originate from the law office, or anyone he saw there."

She'd been thinking the same. Still. "I'd hate to let Ballantine think he could squirm out of his side of the deal."

Her brother laughed, and it wasn't a pretty sound. "If he does, I'm sure he will make it up with an additional show of support for our work."

That thought was appealing. Rosemary didn't like to think of herself as a mercenary, but the Ballantines could clearly afford to increase their donations. The salary of just one of the Ballantines' staff would cover the living and travel expenses of several Huntsmen. And if it were known that the Harkers had brought that extra money in . . .

That could buy Aaron a great deal of leeway.

"Here we go," he said, interrupting her thoughts as they turned a corner onto the Ballantines' street. "Feel ready?"

"No. Do it anyway."

They were passing by the Ballantines' home, the low gate closed, the chalk marks still visible, if you knew where to look.

"Touch the gate, as though you were opening it, about to go home," he told her. "In that moment, *be* her, as much as you can."

Rosemary placed a hand on the metal latch and took a deep breath, bracing herself. *Think like Dorothy Ballantine. Worry for her brother, bone-deep. Worry for her husband, her family.* Rosemary thought of their mentor Jacob, retired now, battle-scarred and sarcastic, of their friends still somewhere in Europe, facing unknown risks. Fear of the unknown, lurking outside their gate, outside their knowledge.

Next to her, but distantly, she heard Aaron speaking. Fey words, nonsense words. She did not understand how they invoked magic, she did not want to know, and he would never tell her. If anyone asked, she could say under oath that she knew nothing of magic save what she had heard through story and gossip.

Splitting hairs, she thought, disgusted at herself. This was too deep in the gray area for her to make excuses. But the moment they'd withheld information from the Circle, she'd known there would be a price to pay, one way or another.

Please, God, she thought. *Please, God, let no one ever know.*

They were past the gate now, although she did not remember letting go of the latch. Rosemary looked down at her hands. Still her hands. Still her toes, the tips of her boots peeping out from under the movement of her skirt as she walked. Still the weight of her weapons, reassuring against her body, and the scratch of the bracelet tight against her wrist.

"Did it work?"

"It worked."

To the external observer, the moment they passed the Ballantines' gate, she was Dorothy Ballantine, down to the way she smelled.

At least for a little while.

Now it was time for the second part of their plan. Aaron let go of her arm, slowing his pace so that he and Bother fell behind several feet. If there was an uncanny lurking nearby, scheming a way to get at the Ballantines, Rosemary should look like an easy treat.

Rosemary touched a hand just behind her ear, as though she was adjusting the tilt of her hat, letting Aaron know that she was all right, then folded her fingers over the cord of her bag. She hated having to wear gloves, hated the way they made her fingers slide on the hilt of her knives; even the slightest shift could throw her aim off, to disastrous results. But Dorothy Ballantine would never be caught in public without them, smooth kidskin gloves that buttoned up the side.

Be Dorothy Ballantine, she reminded herself. Out for a walk. Nothing in her thoughts except how lovely the weather was . . .

And that something was following her.

They weren't alone. Aaron knew it, suddenly, the way he knew the sound of Bother's claws on the sidewalk, or the particular sway of Rosemary's body when she walked. Not the Sense, but lifelong training, learning to pay attention to every sight, every sound, every feeling. Learning to trust your instincts. And all those things told him that an uncanny had taken the bait.

Bother, who had paused to sniff at a patch of dried grass, stiffened in that same moment, his head staying low but the rest of his body tensing, muscles flexing as he picked up the scent.

"Wait," Aaron said quietly. The hound whined, a faint noise deep in his chest, but held still, the instinct to give chase muted by training. Aaron tried to look unconcerned, while still keeping Rosemary in full sight. She was several paces ahead of them and pulling away as they lingered, but he estimated that Bother could reach her in a matter of seconds, if need be.

He watched Bother's ears, the set of his neck and body. Definitely an uncanny. But was it the right uncanny? There were things that lurked even in fine neighborhoods like this, picking off stragglers or the lost, the unwary.

The sensation of being watched faded, but neither man nor beast eased their awareness; all that meant was that it wasn't interested in them. Which was the point of the trap.

Aaron reached into his pocket, feeling the thin iron chain coiled there.

"Let's go," he told the hound, and started walking again, intentionally keeping them both to a slow stroll. Bother's head stayed low, but his ears twitched back and forth, alert to every sound. Aaron's heart thudded loudly in his breast, his knees bent for sudden movement, a slight headache forming from trying to keep his gaze focused rather than flicking about, gauging the directions of the threat.

Even braced for it, the attack took them both by surprise, coming not from a nearby tree or the lower coverage of a shrub, but the road itself, a figure suddenly there where a second before it had not been, a swing of greenish-blue cloak seeming to rise out of nowhere.

Rosemary startled back, even as the uncanny reached for her, and Aaron would have bet every coin in his wallet that the cloaked form was female, although he couldn't have said with certainty why.

Botheration growled, seeing his mistress in danger, and Aaron dropped a hand to the top of his head, pressing down gently in signal to wait.

Despite his sister's agility, the fabric of her skirt caught under her heel, and she fell, landing hard on the cobblestones. With a sound that might have been a gasp or a cry, the uncanny bent toward, her, exactly the pose Mrs. Ballantine had described standing over her brother.

"Hunt!" Aaron commanded, and dropped the leash just as the hound leapt forward, jaws open in anticipation of closing on the uncanny and dragging it to the ground. Aaron followed, retrieving his pistol as he ran, the movements second nature since childhood.

The uncanny must have heard them, because it turned, the hood falling away from its head, and Aaron almost missed his step, staring at the most beautiful face he had ever seen, square jawed and luminous.

It was beautiful, and furious, mouth filled with too many teeth snapping at the air. Then Botheration was upon it, his mouth closing on the outstretched arm with equally sharp teeth and dragging it down. Aaron felt a shout of protest rise in his chest, even as the uncanny folded forward, screeching a high thin note that should have shattered glass, if there was any nearby.

Rosemary clapped her hands over her ears, and Aaron winced but tucked his chin into his chest and barreled forward, halfway uncertain if he was going to capture the uncanny or demand to see its face again.

"Hold!" he called needlessly; a hound, once it bit down, did not let go short of death or order. But when he reached the hound, Bother was alone, jaws soaking wet and red-rimmed eyes, his canine expression deeply confused.

Aaron pulled up, gun suddenly useless. "The hell?" But it was gone, as swiftly and silently as it had appeared.

"What," Rosemary said from the ground, sitting halfway up and bracing herself on an elbow, "and where the hell did it go?"

Aaron shook his head. "I have no idea."

Thirteen

THANKFULLY, THERE HAD been no one walking nearby to observe what had happened, and the houses were set too far from the road for inquisitive eyes, even if the residents were so gauche as to pay attention to anything happening on the street.

Aaron, once he'd determined that Rosemary was all right, had scouted both sides of the street, Bother at his heels, desperate to find some trace of the creature, some hint as to how it had appeared and then disappeared. But there was nothing, no trace of cloth or skin, and the sun had sunk low enough that they would have needed flashes or fairy lights to search further.

"Just like in the house," Aaron muttered. "But how?"

Rosemary, her ears still ringing from the screech the uncanny had let out, could only shake her head.

"It walked upright," she remembered, looking to Aaron to see if he concurred. "Humanlike form."

"It was slightly shorter than you, but wider in the shoulder," he agreed. "Female?"

"I have no idea. The skin was . . . It felt strange, when it grabbed at me. Rough, but . . . slippery. Like the skin wasn't quite attached to the body? And its face . . ."

"What did it look like to you?"

"To me?" She glanced at him, puzzled, then her mouth shaped an *Oh!* in understanding. "Yes. It was lovely. Terrible, but lovely. As though someone had painted the perfect face, but only as a mask? A siren, maybe? Except . . . nothing else fits for that. And the skin being loose . . . that would suggest a shifter, but . . ."

"But nothing else fits for that," Aaron agreed, taking his hat off and slapping it against his leg in a rare expression of frustration. "It's like trying to put together a puzzle made of mismatched pieces."

"Or we're missing the piece that makes it all fit." Rosemary finished brushing herself off, then stopped and looked at her wrist, now bare of anything except the glove. "The bracelet's gone. It must have gotten knocked off when it attacked. Would the illusion break then?"

"Probably." Aaron let out a bark of laughter. "That must have startled it."

"And it ran. It didn't want to hurt someone who wasn't Mrs. Ballantine?" She turned, peering down at the cobblestones where she'd landed. "Aaron, I don't see the bracelet anywhere."

"Leave it," Aaron said. "Odds are it went into the drains, will be washed out to the bay soon enough. Safer than even if we'd disposed of it ourselves; running water will wash the last traces away."

She was just as glad to see it go; the skin where it had

rested still tingled unpleasantly, as though it had left behind a rash.

They walked back to the trolley stop, Aaron's hand on her arm perhaps a bit tighter than usual. The attack itself had been nothing worth noting; Rosemary had taken worse during workouts with Aaron in their backyard back home, particularly when Bother decided to join in. But the suddenness of it, the uncanny appearing and disappearing like that, out of plain sight, on a clear evening, had left them both slightly shaken.

Bother, on the other hand, kept shaking his head and licking his chops, as though reliving the moment when he'd bitten down, and wondering why he'd nothing to show for it.

Rosemary was beginning to realize that her skirts had done little to cushion the impact of cobblestones on delicate flesh, each step sending a jolt of pain. Bother hung close to her side, occasionally leaning against her in a manner that may have been meant as supportive but kept pushing her off-balance.

"Enough, Bother," she snapped, then sighed, placing her hand on the top of his skull, her thumb stroking the plush-thick fur there. "Sorry. I'm annoyed, but not at you. You did the best you could."

Nothing escaped a hound's jaws, not if it didn't want to let go. That was a fact. And yet.

Rosemary mused sourly that many previously unquestioned facts were falling by the wayside recently. Humans could use the higher magics, and hellhounds could lose their prey. She didn't want to know what would be third to fall; the first two were bad enough.

"At least," Aaron said, in a determinedly optimistic tone, "we know for a fact now that it is lurking after the Ballantines."

"I'm not so sure about that, either," Rosemary said. "I've been thinking." Aaron made a face but nodded to show he was listening. "We've been saying the *house* is under attack, the family. But the external damage? The French door in the library. The rosebushes torn up . . . outside the library. It was Mrs. Ballantine who made use of that room, first with the girl, and then the spiritualist. No sign of her husband. Even the morning after the attack, he didn't really come in, but waited outside. The library is her room, not his."

She looked at Aaron, to see if he was following her thoughts, but his expression was blank, waiting for her to continue.

"I think everyone has made assumptions, Aaron, including us, and they're all wrong. It's not about the Ballantines. It's the Congdons. Mrs. Ballantine and her brother. There was no attempt to attack Mr. Ballantine, not at his office, not at home . . . his spaces were left alone."

"Huh." Aaron was chewing over that, rearranging the pieces they thought they knew. "What do we know about that family?"

Rosemary ticked the items off on her fingers. "He's much younger than she is, from late in their parents' marriage. They're close; there doesn't seem to be a lady friend in the picture. No, nor a gentleman friend, either. As far as anyone's admitted, he's a model of good behavior. Hard worker, clean living. Likes children."

"And she's the model mother and wife?"

"I don't know about mother, but . . . yes. Typical upper-class marriage, but having watched them together, I think the Ballantines truly love each other."

"So probably not a siren. Could be a succubus."

"Succubi don't hold grudges."

"We don't know it's a grudge. They might have drawn its attention another way. Maybe their father stole something, and it wants it back from his heirs."

"You think that's not a grudge?"

Aaron frowned. "Grudges are emotional. Reclaiming something stolen can be simply a matter of balancing ledgers. There's an entire catalog of uncanny who will not rest until ledgers are balanced."

Rosemary looked sideways at him, but arguing lore with Aaron was pointlessly frustrating, because eight times out of ten his memory was better than hers.

"So we need to find out if they, or their parents, took anything that didn't belong to them. I'm sure asking that of a wealthy family, with significant social rank, will end well for all concerned. We'll be lucky if the Circle lets us file paperwork, when we're done."

"There's no need to be rude," Aaron said. "Just because you bruised your pride, doesn't mean things can't go our way. Maybe the datebook from Congdon's office will tell us something, after all."

They reached the trolley stop just as one of the cars rattled up, most of the seats empty. Aaron helped Rosemary up, then jumped on after her, Botheration at his heels.

"Do you think we should warn her? Mrs. Ballantine, I mean."

Aaron shrugged, checking over his shoulder to make sure

that the driver wasn't listening. "What good would that do? She's already aware of the threat, and the house is protected; I doubt she'll leave it any time soon, and if she does, she's a fool who deserves what happens."

"Very diplomatic," she said dryly. "So we go back to the hotel and do some research." A late dinner and a date with *The Blackburn Compendium*: Rosemary had lost track of how many nights they had spent that way.

But when they arrived back at the hotel, Walter Ballantine was waiting for them.

Fourteen

BALLANTINE STOOD JUST off to the side, a long black coat perfectly tailored over his form, a dark brown fedora on his head, and a package wrapped in brown paper in his hands, and he had clearly been waiting some time for them. "Mr. Harker. Miss Harker."

Something was terribly wrong. Aaron barely knew the man, and even he could tell that.

"Is there somewhere we can speak, privately?"

He clearly did not wish to be seen in public with them. Looking at his sister, the hotel's electric lights clearly showing her disarray, then down at his own pant legs and shoes, now covered in street dust, Aaron couldn't quite blame the man. They were already beginning to attract more than the usual number of sidelong looks from others in the lobby and behind the front desk.

Their hotel rooms were private, but impossible: they raised enough eyebrows when he went into his sister's room; a man unrelated to her absolutely could not, particularly not an unrelated, married man. Not that Rosemary would care, Aaron suspected, but she would care that others would care.

"There is a private parlor," Rosemary said, indicating a pair of doors half-hidden behind two monstrous potted palms.

The parlor required a key to open, and the hotel employee closed the door behind him with the air of a man who was too well-paid to eavesdrop. Yet another thing money could buy: privacy, with no questions asked.

The room was no better than the rest of the hotel, but there were well-upholstered chairs, and a comfortable-looking loveseat. None of them sat down, Ballantine because he was too agitated, and Rosemary, Aaron suspected, because if she sat down, she might not have the strength to get up again. And Aaron stood because sitting would have made him feel awkward, with the other two standing there, each waiting for someone else to say something.

So he did.

"You have the datebook?"

"What?" Ballantine looked down at the brown envelope he held. "Oh. Yes. I had to do some quick talking to convince George to give this to me." Ballantine handed Aaron the envelope. Inside was a leather-bound book, surprisingly slender, filled with careful penmanship. Aaron skimmed it to confirm that it was what they had asked for, not focusing on anything in particular; there would be time enough for that once the man was gone. Nothing jumped out at him, but he hadn't expected it would.

"If word gets out that George shared this, monsters will be the least of any of our worries," Ballantine said. "But that's not—" He paused whatever he had been about to say, looking at them more closely. "You both look terrible. What happened?"

"Hunts are messy things," Aaron said.

"Did you kill it?" Wild hope lit the man's face, and for a moment Aaron thought he was going to grab one of them, before Botheration shifted at Rosemary's feet, subtly putting his bulk between them.

"I'm afraid not," Rosemary said. "But it knows we're here now, which means it will be more cautious."

Or it would be driven to more direct violence, Aaron thought, but even he knew not to say that out loud.

Ballantine looked as though he were about to say something rude, only at the last minute remembering that there was a lady in the room.

Bother whined a little, sensing the tension, and Rosemary reached down to soothe him.

"My apologies. Mr. Ballantine, if you would excuse me. Our recent altercation with the uncanny has left him a bit agitated, and I feel the need to recompose myself as well, after our encounter. I leave you in Aaron's capable hands."

The day his sister needed to go to her room for a quiet lie-down after . . . anything, Aaron would expect to see pigs gliding overhead. But she was right; whatever Ballantine had to say, he would say it more freely if she was not in the room.

Aaron waited until the door had closed behind her before going to the sideboard where the hotel had graciously provided a decanter for those who were in need of something more supportive than tea.

"No thank you," Ballantine said when Aaron offered him a glass.

"If you change your mind," Aaron said, putting it down on the occasional table near where Ballantine was standing, then lifted his own glass in salute, taking a long sip. It wasn't particularly good bourbon, but it wasn't bad, either.

Ballantine shifted on his feet, rocking back and forth slightly. He was uncomfortable. Fair enough, so was Aaron. He could fake his way through a conversation well enough, but without a goal, a question to ask or detail to find, he tended to flounder.

"So what did you discover?"

Aaron had already sussed this man out, and Rosemary had agreed: he wanted straight talk and direct results. Unfortunately, they only had the first to offer him. "The uncanny is hunting your wife."

Ballantine did a faint double take, head tilting as though he wasn't quite sure he'd heard correctly. "Excuse me?"

"And her brother, but that attack was successful." He knew he was saying it wrong, and all Aaron could think was that Rosemary was going to murder him. But something about the look on the other man's face, as though he was offended the uncanny wasn't interested in him, amused Aaron enough that he was able to regroup and find a smoother way to explain it.

"We believe that your wife's family has drawn the ire of a particularly vindictive uncanny, possibly a succubus or something similar."

"A—a what?"

"A succubus." Aaron was about to explain to the man what a succubus was, when common sense caught up with his mouth, and he shut it with a hard click of his jaw. "It is not important the type." Particularly since they still weren't sure. "We know what it looks like, and how it attacks, so now we should be able to track it down. But if we knew how your wife's family encountered it, and what happened, that would speed things along significantly."

Aaron had absolutely no hopes that Ballantine would know; he suspected the only one who might know for certain was Franklin, and that man was not speaking—not even to a medium, according to Rosemary.

"It's not . . . it's not her. Or Franklin."

Aaron tried very hard not to let his exasperation show on his face, but honestly, why were people so insistent on denying what was obvious? "I understand that this is hard to hear, but—"

"It's not just them. That's why I'm here. We received a call this afternoon, not long after you left. There's been another attack." He swallowed and suddenly changed his mind, snatching the glass of bourbon and knocking it back in a single swift gulp. "Adam's dead."

Rosemary had just stepped out of her room, presumably to rejoin them, when Aaron came out of the elevator. She took one look at him and unlocked her door again, leaving it open for him to follow her in.

Bother was curled up on the bed, his nose resting on the pillow. His ear barely twitched at them, and he muttered deep in his chest as he chased uncanny in his sleep.

"You have a look," Rosemary said. "Like you're about to burst."

Aaron wished he'd taken the decanter with him. "Our

theory has a flaw. Another man was attacked and killed to-night. And a witness claims to have seen the same figure Mrs. Ballantine reported at the scene."

Ballantine had given him the terse details, then taken his leave, claiming a need to return home to be with his wife. Aaron, having gotten what he needed, had stopped listening at that point.

"Well." Rosemary sat on the bed across from Bother, one leg tucked underneath her, and rested her chin on the back of her fist. "That's an unfortunate twist. Still. The dead man was a friend of hers? Maybe there's a connection that way?"

He appreciated her attempt to maintain his theory, but it wouldn't float. "The connection's through Ballantine directly, said he'd known the man for years."

"Damn. And also, damn."

His sister rarely cursed, but he didn't have the energy to appreciate the moment. After going out into the hallway, he unlocked his own room and retrieved the *Compendium* from his bag, then locked up his room again and brought it back to hers, already flipping through the pages with the ease of someone terribly familiar with the contents.

The Blackburn Compendium was a history of the uncanny known to live along the northeastern borders, updated every seven years. Aaron had spent hours annotating the pages of this edition with his own notes, and the once-blank pages in back now contained details of the uncanny they'd encoun-tered who were not native to this region but had arrived at some point to make trouble.

"This would be easier if there were some way to cross-reference the types," he complained as he shut the door behind him. "Something that causes a sleeplike malaise, and looks human, and has that odd skin . . . That should be enough to identify it, but trying to find something that specific . . . Do you think the hotel would bring us up a pot of tea? It's going to be a very long night."

"Tell me about the new victim," Rosemary said, ignoring his grumbling with the ease of long practice. She had moved from the bed to the chair now, the datebook in her hands. "You said he was connected through Ballantine—another businessman? Maybe the shipping—"

"He was an academic of some sort. At Boston College."

"A teacher? Not the sort of man I'd expect Ballantine to be friends with." She reached for her pen and tapped it against the desk thoughtfully. "Oh. That's . . . wait. Boston College? That's a Jesuit school."

"Mmmm." Aaron marked the page he was looking at with his finger and frowned. He hadn't thought about that until she mentioned it.

Contrary to popular belief, most uncanny weren't bothered by religious symbolism, or so-called "holy ground." Faith was a particularly human construct. But the Jesuits were known to use more pragmatic weapons along with their symbolic ones, when dealing with uncanny threats, and in turn, most uncanny steered clear of them.

"Had Ballantine told him anything?"

"The man knew of Congdon's illness—Ballantine said he'd been to the house recently, but no, nothing else."

"You think he's lying."

"I think . . . there's something going on we're not being told." But he couldn't say why, or what. "Ballantine says that eyewitnesses said he seemed to simply keel over, but it was late; there were shadows; they couldn't be certain. And unlike Congdon, he died soon after."

"But you said someone saw—"

"Again according to Ballantine, one of the witnesses thought someone had come to help the man when he fell, but then they just . . . disappeared."

"That was when we were guarding the Ballantines' house. . . ."

"The uncanny saw us, and found different prey. Maybe. Yes." Or there was a pack, but that seemed unlikely. Smaller uncanny banded together, but in America, the larger ones tended to live and move alone. There were theories as to why, Aaron had entered into a correspondence with an academic who had written on the topic, but the practical reason was that most uncanny held their territory jealously and did not welcome competition from their own kind.

"It wasn't our fault, Rosie," Aaron said softly. Even if they'd known the uncanny would reach outside the family, they couldn't blanket the city, just the two them. Even with more Huntsmen to call, even if he'd asked Jonathan for help, they couldn't possibly have prevented this.

But that didn't make the weight of responsibility any less. A man was dead.

———————

They had been doing research, Aaron poring over the *Compendium*, writing down possibilities and then striking them off the list, and Rosemary looking through the datebook, when there was a knock on the door. Bother lifted his head, looking inquiringly at the door before checking with Rosemary for direction. But he seemed curious, not alarmed, and both Harkers relaxed slightly, hands moving away from their knives.

"Wait," she told the hound, while Aaron went to the door, opening it just enough to see who it was, but not so much that they would be able to see in. He exchanged low-voiced words with the person; then there was a faint clatter of china and metal, and the sound of the door closing.

The clatter came from the tray he was holding, the warm smells of bread and meat making both Rosemary and Bother take notice.

"I arranged for something to be sent up," Aaron said. And by "arranged" he meant he'd slipped the porter a considerable chunk of his remaining cash to ensure it, after Ballantine's visit. They'd eaten earlier, but hunts took energy, and he knew they'd likely be too busy to go out before the restaurants closed. "It's not fancy, but"—and he placed the tray on the desk, careful to move the *Compendium* out of the way, and removed the metal cover—"edible. And enough for Bother, too."

He took one of the plates and set it on the carpet. "Beef of . . . some sort, reasonably rare, rolls and butter, and what might have been runner beans, at some point in their lives." Rosemary wouldn't care, he knew; she considered food a necessary chore, occasionally enjoyable but more often an interruption in whatever she was doing. But he found himself oddly offended.

"Tea?"

"Thankfully, yes."

The food was warm but bland, and Aaron made quick

work of his, putting the plate aside for Botheration to finish. He watched his sister place food in her mouth almost methodically, her attention entirely focused on the book Ballantine had given them.

"Does it tell you anything?"

"That Mr. Congdon was a very junior member of the firm, which we already knew. And handled mostly new-money families."

Aaron frowned. "How do you know that?"

"The names," she said. "At a guess, and it's only a guess, they would all be considered parvenu. Immigrants made good, I'd suspect, Italians or Jews, or some other that would keep them from becoming clients of a more senior partner." She poked a finger at the list, almost accusingly. "I can't tell where some of these names come from. Zeelenska, Kowalski, Carvalho?" She stumbled over them slightly.

"Polskiy," Aaron said. "Or Ruskiy. Russian."

Rosemary tilted her head, thinking. "A junior lawyer, his sister the wife of a well-to-do businessman, and a Jesuit teacher. What do they all have in common?"

"Other than a murderous, unknown uncanny?"

"Other than that, yes. Wait." She pulled the datebook toward her, and Aaron hesitated, hand halfway over the teapot. "What?"

"Wait, wait . . . there. De Peña."

He stared at her, brow wrinkled as he tried to follow where her thinking had gone. "The name means something to you?"

"Vaz de Peña, that was the name of the girl who was there with Mrs. Ballantine, remember?"

He honestly didn't, until she jogged his memory.

"The maid said that her father was a friend of Congdon's. That the Ballantines treated the girl like family." Her brain was racing to connect the pieces, but it shuddered to a stop at the same time Aaron asked, "But where does the Jesuit fit in?"

Rosemary looked at her half-finished plate and pushed it away, a little regretfully. "I suppose we're going to find out."

He reached over and pushed the plate back toward her. "Not tonight, we're not. It's late. Eat."

The human place was large and uncomfortable. Too much stone, too much metal, too much noise. The uncanny dabbed at its wound and hissed, a watery sound of displeasure. It wanted to go home, wanted to be away from this place. But it couldn't go. Not yet.

There were lessons to be taught.

Fifteen

THE NEXT MORNING, Rosemary took Bother out for his walk, carefully skirting the parklet in favor of strolling along the storefront-studded street. The smells coming from a little bakery drew them in, and she walked out with a paper twist filled with small rolls the baker had called carcaça, split and stuffed with melted cheese. Bother had whined until she fed him one, nosing at her until she closed up the twist again. "No more until we're back in the hotel," she told him.

Once inside, Bother begged another roll, then settled on the floor to chew contentedly, while Rosemary got ready for the day.

Aaron knocked on her door a little while later. He finished the last of the rolls while she braided and coiled her hair and made sure her hat was securely pinned, then checked herself again in the mirror.

Aaron reached out and tapped her on the shoulder. "You look fine. What has you so twisted?"

"You're not?" She glared over her shoulder at him, then jabbed another pin into her hat. "Fine. Let's go."

Leaving Bother asleep in her room, they rode down to the lobby in the elevator, Rosemary only able to muster a tight-lipped smile in response to the operator's greeting.

She thought she was hiding her anxiety well, until they reached the lobby and her brother said, "We should take the trolley, rather than drive."

"Your driving is getting better," she said, trying to be encouraging, but knew he had seen the easing of her shoulders at the idea of not having to get back into the automotive just yet.

The trolley driver, a strapping young man with a drawl straight out of a more southern state, said that the college stop had just been added, reducing their walk from considerable to negligible. He let them off at the edge of the campus, a sprawling piece of land that still looked like the farm it had been until recently, flat fields and narrow creeks that could turn an ankle or break a leg if you weren't careful. But a wide expanse had been flattened and filled, a graveled path leading to newly erected buildings strutting their importance like royalty, edifices of carved stone set in a stately pattern around each other. Signs at the trolley stop pointed in a number of directions, the one labeled ADMINISTRATION directing them toward a building slightly less grand than its companions.

That was the logical place to begin.

Rosemary watched a handful of students, every single one of them male, all dressed in somber blacks and browns and carrying books either under their arms or in bags slung over their shoulders, and tried to imagine Aaron there. It was a horrifying thought.

"I would have chewed my arm off to escape," he said as

though reading her mind. "Assuming they didn't cast me from the nearest window—or into the nearest pyre, first."

"Don't even joke about that."

It hadn't only been Aaron's driving that had put her on edge. The moment they'd heard the dead man had worked for the Jesuits, they'd both been uneasy. Huntsmen's blood was tainted, according to Church doctrine. While it was unlikely that anyone here would ever have read that doctrine, much less thought it still relevant, nearly eight hundred years later, Huntsmen gave Rome and its outposts a wide berth, whenever possible. They certainly didn't hunt on Church-owned land.

"Standing here isn't accomplishing anything," Aaron pointed out, pragmatic as ever.

Rosemary nodded, not moving. "You go first."

With a dramatic sigh, Aaron took her hand in his and dragged her a few steps down the path, until she pulled free and followed at her own pace.

Following the sign's direction, they came to the administration building. Unlike the massive steeple-crowned building in the center, where most of the students were heading, this had a vaguely unfinished feel to it.

The doors were solid oak, half again as tall as Aaron, and wide enough to trot a pair of horses though without brushing the sides, if both were to open. They were closed, a weight of silence surrounding them, as though daring anyone to disturb their rest.

Rosemary might have been imagining that last. But Aaron lifted his hand to grasp the handle, then paused and let his hand drop again, so if she was imagining it, she wasn't alone.

"It's not going to bite you."

"Are you sure?"

No. She wasn't.

Annoyed with herself, Rosemary pushed past her brother to grasp the handle of the door. And if she had a half second of hesitation when her fingers curved around the metal, half anticipating a shock, she was not going to admit it. Ever.

The building was so new it practically squeaked, the stones still remembering the quarries they'd been hauled from, rather than the use of mere mortals. Inside, gray stone and Gothic arches made Rosemary wistful for the relatively simpler Victorian architecture of New Haven, with its bright colors and welcoming feel.

Or maybe it was the religious iconography everywhere she looked, from the carved stone to the tapestries to the crosses everywhere she turned, in stone, wood, and glass, making her feel like they would be better served by leaving.

"May I help you?"

They both startled, and the speaker took a step back, hands held up in apology. He wore a black robe, collared tight at his neck and belted at the waist, and his head was uncovered, thick hair slicked back against his scalp. Rosemary took all that in at a glance, then returned her attention to his face. He was waiting patiently, and when he saw he had their attention, offered a gentle smile.

"Let us try that again, shall we? I am Father Brian. May I help you?"

"Ah. Yes." Rosemary cast a quick glance at her brother, who looked as though he was about to bolt back out the doors, too. She tilted her head sharply, lifting her chin toward the priest, but when Aaron's eyes only widened, she sighed and turned back to the priest.

"I'm sorry, we're here to speak to someone about Adam Perris?"

"Oh. Yes." Father Brian looked stricken, and Rosemary was reminded that he had likely known the victim personally. "I'm not sure what I can tell you, ah . . . ?"

"My name is Rosemary Harker, and this is my brother Aaron."

"Miss Harker, Mr. Harker. May I ask why your interest in Father Adam?"

Father Adam? Ballantine hadn't said the dead man was a priest. Rosemary felt the urge to grab Aaron's hand and flee. But they had never run from a hunt before, and she'd be literally damned before a priest scared her off.

But words stuck in her throat. While they'd had a story prepared, they had expected an administrator, some sort of secretary or clerk. Not to be brought face-to-face with the living embodiment of a Huntsmen child's boogeyman.

"We're here at the request of Walter Ballantine. They were friends." Aaron stepped forward, literally moving Rosemary aside an inch to take the man's attention off her. She would have cried in relief, if she hadn't been so angry at herself. "He was hoping to learn more about the cause of death . . . ?"

The priest narrowed his eyes as Aaron spoke, and Rosemary's urge to bolt out the door increased to the point where she had to force her legs to stay still. Never mind that the man had only been polite, so far. It hadn't been that long since Huntsmen were among those "questioned" by the Church, their possessions and often their lives forfeited.

These might be more enlightened times, but they were still Huntsmen, and this man was Church.

"Please," Father Brian said as Aaron's line of patter trailed off. "Come with me."

Unhappy, but seeing no other option, Rosemary followed, Aaron close by her side. The priest led them farther into the building, one large room opening to the next. It was, she admitted, an impressive space, high-ceilinged, with delicate stained glass windows alternating with ordinary clear ones. The longer she looked, however, she noticed smudges shoulder-high on the walls and scuff marks on the wooden floors. It looked like a church, but it felt like a school, and somehow that calmed her.

He was just a man, despite his clothing. She had been charming information out of men since she was a child. They would be polite, they would get the information they needed, and then they would be gone.

A smaller but still ornate wooden door opened onto a long hallway, and he walked them past a row of offices, most of them open-doored and empty. "We are still in the process of moving from the old campus," the priest said, noticing where her attention had gone. "Which is why you are dealing with me, rather than any of our lay staff." He smiled at their surprise. "Yes, your dismay was that obvious. I was not offended. Now"—and he ushered them into an office that was clearly occupied, from the piles of papers on the desk—"what brings a pair of Huntsmen to investigate the death of a Jesuit?"

Rosemary bolted out of the chair she'd just lowered herself into, Aaron instinctively taking his usual position on her left, ready to fight their way out if needed.

The priest didn't move. Not frozen in fear, just . . . very still, very calm. "Please. Assuming you mean me no harm, I mean you no harm."

Aaron's left hand was curled at his thigh, elbow lifted, and Rosemary knew that he could have his pistol in hand and firing in the time it took the priest to say another word. And if her brother missed, which he wouldn't, not at this range, her knives would be out a bare second later.

But she held off, they both held off, as Aaron said in a voice dry as dust, "You'll excuse us if we don't take your word for that."

"Of course. The door remains open, you may leave at any time. But you have questions."

Rosemary let her own hand relax, but only a little. "And you'll answer them?"

"Assuming you answer mine, a simple one. Why are Huntsmen looking into Father Adam's death?"

She gave him credit, there was no nonsense of responding to Aaron rather than having to speak to a woman, as she'd more than half expected. She looked at her brother, a lifted eyebrow and tilted head asking and answering. The priest waited while they both, slowly, sat down again.

Aaron, at Rosemary's tiny nod, said, "We think it may be related to our hunt."

Father Brian steepled his fingers as though at prayer but otherwise made no reaction and did not ask for clarification. That was good: Rosemary wasn't sure she'd have let her brother give any more detail than that, even if he'd been willing to.

"I'm not sure how much more I can tell you, that your friend likely does not already know."

Aaron pulled the leather-bound notebook from the inside pocket of his coat and licked his thumb before using that digit to find an empty page. He looked at the stub of a pencil at the end of the ribbon and, without asking permission, reached forward and took one of the pencils waiting in a cup on the desk. "How did he die?"

"You know this already, else you would not be here."

The Harkers waited, and he sighed. "There was no indication of violence. He simply collapsed in the street. It was, by God's mercy, swift. One moment he was speaking with a colleague, the next he was . . . Witnesses said he did not suffer."

"But he had been in good health prior?"

"He had appeared to be, yes. But sometimes the Lord—"

Aaron shook his head. "We don't think God had anything to do with this."

"One of your . . . uncanny creatures?" He did not cross himself, but Rosemary suspected he wanted to. "But why?"

There was a mix of sorrow and curiosity in his voice that made the knot in Rosemary's throat loosen slightly. *Just a man*, she reminded herself. A man who was grieving. "Do you happen to know if Father Adam had any contact with a family named de Peña?"

He glanced at the ceiling, frowning in thought. "The name does not ring a bell, but I would need to check the school records. Father Adam worked with our younger students. He taught logic to our third and fourth years."

"Daniella said she had a brother," Rosemary said. "He might be a student here." Had he been older or younger? It hadn't seemed important to note at the time. It hadn't *been* important to note at the time.

Father Brian leaned back in his chair, the wood creaking slightly. "This would be easier if you could tell me what, or who, you're looking for."

Rosemary looked at him from under her lashes, trying to gauge his sincerity.

"I realize you have no cause to trust me. And I regret that. But I think that there was a reason you encountered me this day, rather than another of my brothers."

Aaron crossed his arms over his chest. "And that reason might be?"

"I am a historian. I know of your people, what you do. What you are."

Rosemary tensed. Here it was.

"And I do not believe that what you are is evil."

It should not have been such a relief to hear those words. Rosemary was immediately, irrationally annoyed at the emotion she felt, as though this man's belief made any difference whatsoever.

Aaron seemed unimpressed. "It is still the opinion of the Church that we are the spawn of devils."

"The Church is slow to change. But, inch by inch, theologian by theologian, we do. But I do not expect you to believe that, or to simply trust my word. Let us say then, instead, that we have a truce, for this moment. For the memory of Father Adam."

The Harkers exchanged another glance, and Rosemary nodded, ever so slightly.

"Let me—" Father Brian shifted to rise, and the Harkers tensed again. He paused, halfway out of his chair, and waited until they settled themselves again.

"Let me check with the clerk, have him check the relevant files."

He left, leaving the door ajar, as though to reassure the Harkers that they were still free to leave—or to keep an eye on them. Rosemary wasn't sure which, if either, it was, and the uncertainty made the tension worse.

"Do you believe him?" She kept her voice low, even though they'd seen and heard no sign of anyone else around.

Her brother gave a one-shouldered shrug, his body tense again. "Do I think he's all 'let's embrace the filthy demon-spawn as brothers and roast the fatted calf'? No. Do I think we can trust him to get the information we need? Maybe. We'll see. If he comes back and says he can't find anything, maybe he can't, maybe he can, but they decided not to share it with us."

"I don't think he knows anything more about the death than what he told us." She wasn't certain she trusted the priest, but she did believe he mourned the dead man and would rather know what had killed him than continue believing a lie.

"Maybe. I wish we could have gone with him, looked at his files ourselves."

That almost made her laugh. "I don't think he wants us strolling around their precious campus. And I'm all right with that."

He made a tsking noise. "We faced down a lunatic witch throwing storms at us, and a few buildings have you unnerved?"

She refused to rise to the bait. "Yes."

After a few minutes, Aaron got up out of his chair, pacing to the wall, then around the chairs behind Rosemary, then in front of her back to the wall, then repeated the cycle. He kept his hands in his coat pockets, the wool swinging around his knees with the motion. Rosemary ignored him; movement gave his nerves somewhere to go. Instead, she studied the desk in front of her, as though it might tell her something about the man they were waiting on. A few Latin texts she didn't bother trying to translate, a notebook filled with what looked like pencil sketches of leaves, and a stack of financial-looking papers she recognized from her own efforts at house-hold budgeting.

She was just about to give in to temptation and see what a priest spent money on, when she heard footsteps in the hall-way, and settled back in her seat.

Father Brian came back in, someone trailing just behind him. The newcomer was wearing ordinary trousers and a knitted sweater in mildly alarming shades of orange. He was bald-headed and round-bellied, and slightly out of breath, as though he had run to keep up with the taller Father Brian.

If the priest was surprised to see Aaron out of his chair, he didn't show it, instead gesturing to his companion as he reclaimed the chair behind the desk. "This is Jean-Michel. He keeps the attendance rolls."

"Yes. I am, yes." Jean-Michel pulled out a kerchief and mopped his face, then his scalp, before putting the kerchief back in his pocket. Not all that sweat could have been from trotting through the hallways; Rosemary wondered if Father Brian had told him what they were, or if Jean-Michel simply did not enjoy speaking with strangers. "You were looking for a boy, surname de Peña?"

He did not look at either of them as he spoke, but he did

not look at the priest, either, so Rosemary decided he must be one of those who preferred the company of books and ledgers to people.

"Vaz de Peña," Aaron said. "The father might have been a military man, rank of captain."

"Yes. Well." The clerk put down the book he had been carrying and riffled through the pages before finding the one he wanted, running his thumb down the list of names. "No, not there, either. There is no de Peña or Vaz de Peña listed. But." He closed the ledger and tucked it back under his arm, still not looking at either Harker. "But the name sounded familiar, and I was trying to remember why, as we walked here. And I think the boy may be one of Father Adam's charity cases."

"We do not call them that, Jean-Michel." Clerk chastened, Father Brian turned back to the Harkers. "Father Adam had a skill with children; it was part of what made him such an excellent teacher. At any given time, he had a handful of youngsters who were not attending our school, but he felt had particular promise or need that called for nurturing."

"The boy mentored by the priest, the girl by Mrs. Ballantine. That's the connection." Aaron frowned. "But where does Congdon fit? The maid said—"

"I think we need to talk with the family," Rosemary said, interrupting his thought. Her gaze flicked to Father Brian, who, unlike his clerk, looked back at her seemingly unruffled, but with a hint of concern in his eyes.

"Surely you do not think these children had anything to do with Father Adam's death."

"Directly? No." She hoped not. The girl was human; surely

her brother was as well. But the Harkers had learned too well that humans were not incapable of monstrous things.

"But it is possible they may shed light on it. Speaking with them, or their parents, could tell us more. I don't suppose you would know how to get in touch with them? An address or"—taking a guess at the family's economic status, if they hobnobbed with the Ballantines—"a telephone line?"

Not wanting to fluster the clerk beyond any ability to communicate, she directed her question to the air somewhere between him and the door.

"I am afraid not." He didn't sound particularly sorry, and when Father Brian nodded to release him, he scurried off into the hallway, ledger under his arm, the relief practically visible in his wake.

Father Brian looked after him a moment, then, shaking his head, turned back to the Harkers. "I'm sorry we were not able to help more."

She hoped the priest wasn't going to ask them to keep him informed; once gone from this place, she did not want to return. Instead, he simply escorted them back through the hallway, through still-empty rooms, and deposited them at the exit.

"Go with God," he said with no apparent sense of irony. Rosemary managed a polite smile before grabbing her brother's hand and towing him out into the fresh air.

There were more people around now, students and older men she assumed were teachers—and possibly more priests. Rosemary barely waited for Aaron to put his hat on before starting back down the path that would get them out of here.

"This is going to be fun," Aaron said as they walked.

"What?"

"Asking Mrs. Ballantine for an introduction to the family of the girl she treats as a daughter, because we suspect the girl of being involved in a murder, and her brother's illness." He paused, looking up at the cloudless sky. "You do it."

Sixteen

THEY HAD BARELY exited the building when Aaron felt it again, that sensation of being watched by something not human. Instinctively, he looked down and to his left, but they had not brought Bother with them. He had only his own instincts to judge by. The Sense, the ability to pinpoint exactly where an uncanny lurked, was a trait Huntsmen valued, so of course he had little of it.

But every human alive, Huntsmen or not, knew when a predator was nearby.

He took a slow breath in and tried to shake the feeling without being too obvious about it. Rosemary, walking alongside him, didn't seem to notice anything amiss. Then again, she was already upset by being here, by being in close proximity to a priest, however reasonable he had seemed; it was possible any further disquiet she felt she had chalked up to that.

It was also possible that there was nothing there, that he was creating phantoms. He had never been prone to such a thing before, but Aaron supposed it was possible, the pressure of the hunt and having encountered something unknown in the park combining to create paranoia.

Another few steps, and Aaron was certain that it wasn't his imagination. It was not only watching; it was *following*.

And it wasn't the thing that had attacked Rosemary in her guise of Mrs. Ballantine. It felt . . . different.

Although it was unusual for Huntsmen to encounter uncanny they were not actively hunting, it would not be unusual for there to be more than one in town. While they tended to carve out their own territories, there were a number of uncanny who gravitated to human habitations, either for access to victims or because it made their life easier.

Or, in very few cases, because they genuinely enjoyed being around humans, whether that was good for the humans around them or not. If such an uncanny were to notice that Huntsmen were in town, Aaron would not be surprised if they were to lurk, if only to assure themselves that the Huntsmen were not there for them.

There were two lines of thought on that, among Huntsmen. Most felt that any uncanny who took an interest in them, rather than hiding, was a potential threat. Others held a different view, that uncanny should be considered not-threats until they did something actively threatening.

Their parents had been in the latter category.

Of course, their father was currently living under a false name in a very carefully warded asylum, while the rest of the Huntsmen believed he'd died in the same hunt that killed their mother. So his might not be the best advice to follow.

Still. It had offered them no challenge, done no harm that they knew of. And they had an uncanny they needed to be worrying about already.

"You're thinking very hard. I can practically smell the coal burning."

He almost lied. Almost.

"We're being followed. An uncanny." He paused, taking her gloved hand in his own. "Since we left the building."

Without being too obvious, Rosemary slowed her pace, Aaron following suit, as they left the main walkway for a detour past a cluster of rosebushes, their thorny branches only beginning to show buds.

"I can't sense it." Rosemary was frowning, but she didn't challenge his claim. "Is it—"

"I think it's the same one Bother and I felt watching us, near the hotel." That was better than the other options, that the uncanny they were hunting was hunting them, or, possibly even worse, that they'd somehow attracted the attention of a third uncanny in as many days.

But it was also much worse, if his gut suspicion about the uncanny in the park was right.

Dear God, he wanted to be wrong.

"We're nowhere near that park."

"I know." That meant it was almost certainly following them, which meant nothing good. "Feel like a longer walk?" He squeezed her hand twice, and she returned it. A question: Did she want to try to draw it out? And her answer: yes.

Rather than turning left for the trolley station, they turned right, away from the main cluster of buildings, toward the yet unimproved grounds. Uncanny were not actually deterred by sanctified grounds, despite what the stories claimed, but there would be fewer people there, away from buildings, and therefore less likelihood of bystanders getting hurt.

"Oh. There it is," Rosemary said quietly, her nostrils flaring as though she could actually smell it. "I really dislike being stalked. It irritates me."

Despite himself, he grinned at her. "Let's let it know that, then, shall we?"

There were a dozen or more tricks of hunting, most of them designed to bring an uncanny out into the open. Choosing one was largely dependent on the type of uncanny—unknown, here—and the terrain.

The cobblestone road they were on ended a bit ahead, turning into a narrower dirt road, a patch of dry winter grass edged by shrubbery that looked long abandoned by human hand. Rosemary squeezed his hand again, letting him know she would be taking lead, then let go, striding forward as though to look at something. Two steps, then a third, and she let out a surprised cry, dropping to her knees.

"Rosemary?" He strode forward, bending as he did so as though to lift her up. It was a perfect ambush moment, both of them distracted, one possibly hurt. And it gave them cover to arm themselves, knives slipping from sheaths into hands with the dexterity of long practice.

But when he lifted her back to a standing position, knives hidden by the folds of her skirt and their coats . . . nothing happened.

They waited, keeping their breathing slow, alert to the faintest crackle or snap from the underbrush. Aaron could feel sweat dripping under his collar and down his back, and only training kept him from shuddering like a horse afflicted by flies.

"It's gone."

"What?" Rosemary wasn't doubting him; she was exasperated. "It follows us all the way out here, and then just . . . gives up?"

"Maybe it's just curious."

That wasn't as reassuring as he'd meant it to be, from the look she gave him.

"Are you sure it's not the same one that attacked me?" She shook her head, negating the question even as she asked it. "No, I'd have known. Wonderful."

Aaron knew better than to be hurt by the assumption that she would have known when he would not, but he shoved it down with the ease of long practice and put his blade away.

Rosemary likewise sheathed one knife but kept the other in hand, ready to throw the moment anything came at them.

"It's odd, though, that you knew it was there before me." She didn't sound accusing, merely curious, but he felt a spasm of guilt nonetheless.

"I think . . ." This was why he'd almost lied, because the moment he started talking about it truthfully, the whole truth would come out. He'd never been able to hide things from Rosemary, not for long. He'd never wanted to.

"You think it's an Elder One." Polite phrasing: Huntsmen weren't superstitious, but there was no need to call things to you if you didn't wish to see them. "That's why you were so cagey, before. You thought it then, too."

Hearing her say it was worse than his thinking it. Once

she said it, it was more real. "I had been very carefully not thinking about thinking about that."

The fey hadn't poked their noses into human business— at least not that the Huntsmen had heard, and they would have heard—in centuries. They had, according to all stories, signed the treaty, returned most of their captives, and disappeared to whatever realm they'd come from.

Uncanny were bad enough. The fey—powerful, mercurial, dangerous even by Huntsmen standards—were another thing entirely. Aaron did not want them to be the ones who had gotten the fey's attention again. For many reasons.

Rosemary tilted her head up, as though studying the clouds, the brim of her hat casting her face into shadow. "Do you think it's related to . . . that?"

"That" being the witch of Brunson, who had found a way to access the magics forbidden by the treaty and hidden by Huntsmen. She was dead now, but fear of the fey discovering that a human had broken a basic tenet of the treaty had forced the Harkers into silence about what had actually happened.

If it had all been for nothing, if the fey already knew, Aaron thought, Rosemary was never going to let him live it down.

"Let's hope not," he said finally. "Hunt now, worry about . . . that later."

Rosemary nodded and sheathed her knife, but her expression suggested that she was going to continue to worry about it now, thank you very much.

Fair enough: he was worrying, too.

Seventeen

*I*T HADN'T MEANT *to be there, passing from one place to another, but when it had smelled them, it had been unable to resist. The crackle and stink of magic drew it, magic and violence and the delicious delicate taste of fear.*

Small-cousins were fierce and sharp, fun to play with, but the hunters were clever. Clever was good. Clever was better. The figure pulled shadows out of the sunlight and wrapped them around itself, becoming leaf and trunk and bush, the better to follow, the better to listen. The hunters were clever, but it was clever, too, and old, so old. Old enough that something new, something interesting, was better than meat.

Siblings, pulsing bright the way all their kind did, not as bright as they had been, once, but brighter than the dull sparks around them. It hadn't meant to notice them at all, hadn't meant to be noticed, that first night. But the hunt-dog had sniffed them, the hunter had known them, and that was new; that was interesting.

It was old, so old, and little surprised it anymore.

But the hunter had stunk of magic, old magic but also new

magic. Human magic. Lightly then, deeper here. The hunter knew things he should not, had done things he should not.

This was something new, and maybe dangerous. Possibly entertaining.

It would keep an eye on them.

Eighteen

BY THE TIME they made it back to the Ballantines' home, Aaron was deeply regretting not having taken the automotive, but he knew better than to mention that to his sister. Unlike him, the longer they sat on the rattling trolley car, surrounded by strangers, including a child with very sticky hands, the calmer she became.

By the time they reached the house, he would never have known that she'd ever had a disquieting thought in her life, much less been edging on terrified just an hour or so before. And when the housekeeper took their hats and coats, and directed them not to the library but to a side parlor, Rosemary strode forward as though she herself owned the house. Despite himself, despite knowing better, Aaron couldn't help but believe that everything would go smoothly now.

The side parlor was clearly less used, the furnishings quality, but slightly out of date. Mrs. Ballantine had been working on needlepoint when they entered, but she put it aside and, taking one look at their faces, sent the housekeeper off for tea and told them to sit down.

Rosemary started to tell her what they had learned. She sat, stone-faced but for a faint twitch in her left eye, until his sister had finished, then asked, "Are the children in any danger?"

Aaron hadn't even thought of that.

"At this point, all we know is that the family, or some connection to the family, is what the victims all share. It's the first real lead we've gotten, and so we need to investigate. There is no reason to think that the children themselves are at direct risk." Only after he said that did Aaron think that maybe he should have let her think they were, that it would get them what they needed faster.

"You don't have children, Mr. Harker. I don't expect you to understand."

"The sooner we speak with them, the sooner we will be able to put this all to rest," Rosemary said. "Please. Give us their address."

"I don't know what you think those children could have to do with any of this, but they're not going to let you in, much less badger their children, simply because you claim I sent you. And no, I will not tell them this over the telephone—don't even think of suggesting it." Her disdain was clear, although it was difficult to tell if it was for the idea or the machinery itself.

Rosemary's face showed nothing but sympathetic understanding, but he could see from the way her hands rested in her lap that she was frustrated. His sister could be charming; he would lay money on her being able to reconnect. But it wasn't going to happen just then.

Aaron himself, used to dealing with strong-willed women,

had already bowed to the inevitability, because the only way they were going to find the children was if Mrs. Ballantine came with them.

Sure enough, a few minutes later, Mrs. Ballantine rang a bell and, when Macy appeared, told her to fetch her coat and hat and tell young Billy to bring their automotive around, while she placed a call.

Billy at least seemed pleased to see them, helping Rosemary into the covered portion of the automotive after Mrs. Ballantine and indicating that Aaron should ride up front with him.

"You must understand: they come from a very different sort of life," Mrs. Ballantine told them, as the automotive rolled through the streets, having to lift her voice over the sound of the engine, and Aaron wondered what sort of life she thought *they* came from. "Duarte de Peña was the captain of a fishing boat. Several fishing boats, I suppose. He and his brother, they did very well for themselves. Then his brother died, some sort of accident, and he sold his interests in the boats, and moved his family here. He wanted them to live a better life, not one dependent on how the sea felt that day." She lifted a hand in greeting to someone they passed on the street. "Those were his exact words, 'how the sea felt that day.' I believe he misses that life, but of course we do what we must for our children."

"Indeed," Rosemary murmured.

"The name . . . they are Spanish?" Aaron mentally prepared himself to switch languages, if it were useful.

"No . . . I don't think so? It's not something you ask a person."

Aaron had no idea why you wouldn't ask, but he thought that was probably not something he should ask, either.

The automotive turned a corner and slowed, the engine rattling and thumping as though in objection.

"We're here, ma'ams, sir," Billy announced needlessly, jumping out and turning to offer his employer a hand as she descended from the seat, Rosemary and Aaron following.

The de Peñas lived on a street of brick town houses. The houses were each lovely, with deep bow windows and wrought-iron gates that in the summer no doubt bloomed with roses, but the fortunes of those who lived here, while well above that of the Harkers, were obviously not quite that of the Ballantines.

Mrs. Ballantine sailed up the steps, the very picture of a well-to-do lady going a-visiting, from the beribboned hat to the polish of her boots, and Aaron shifted uncomfortably, suddenly aware that even their best clothing had suffered from being packed into cases and hung in hotel closets, even before they'd put them on. Rosemary had fared even worse, the fall she had faked leaving a faint grass stain on the cream fabric of her skirt. He wasn't sure if she'd noticed it yet or not, but his gaze kept returning to the irregularly shaped mark, as though it were trying to tell him something.

An elbow in his ribs made him look up in time to see the curtains twitch in the house next door. Someone was clearly curious as to who had pulled up, but Aaron only caught a glimpse of a pale face before the curtain was yanked back into place, curiosity no doubt receiving a scolding from propriety.

When he looked back at the source of the elbow, his sister's face was a portrait of composed respectability, and he took the hint, rearranging his own facade to match hers.

Once they'd gathered themselves behind her, Mrs. Ballantine gave the door a solid rap. The door opened almost immediately, someone clearly having been waiting for the summons.

The woman who greeted them was no housekeeper or maid. Tall, young, and elegant even in a simple shirtwaist and skirt, on seeing them, her face lit with a quiet pleasure. "Dorothy."

"Benedita." Mrs. Ballantine took the woman's offered hands, giving her a warm smile in return. "I'm sorry I was so mysterious over the telephone. May we come in?"

"Of course, of course, please." And the woman—Benedita—stepped back to allow them to enter. A young maid was standing just behind her, ready to take their coats and hats, and there was a brief moment of confusion while they were all sorted out.

"Benedita, may I present Aaron and Rosemary Harker? And this is Benedita Ruiz Vaz."

Rosemary cocked her head. "Ruiz Vaz? But I thought . . ."

Mrs. Ruiz Vaz had a laugh that matched her face, full of humor that made Aaron feel as though they were in on the joke, rather than the cause of it. "With marriage I am de Peña, yes, but . . ." She shrugged. "Our tradition honors both mother and father. Our children bear both Vaz and de Peña."

She had a slight accent, nothing particularly noticeable, but the words ran together differently than in English. It was almost familiar to Aaron, but not quite.

"You aren't American?" Rosemary asked, likely remembering, as Aaron was, the maid's scornful comment about the family. Mrs. Ruiz Vaz's skin was the same shade as her daughter's, certainly darker than the Harkers' but not so much that Aaron thought it would be remarkable, and if it were not for the accent, he would have been hard-pressed to notice anything exceptional about her.

"I was born in Portugal," she said, leading them through open pocket doors to a parlor, a bright, open space with cream-painted walls and a scattering of high-backed club chairs upholstered in a deep blue set around a low table where, Aaron noted, tea was already set for four. "Meu marido— my husband—and my children, they were born here."

Aaron had never thought to learn Portuguese. He wondered if it would be difficult. "Mrs. Ballantine says that he was a maritime man?"

"The de Peñas have long been fishermen. Duarte captained a fishing fleet, he and Rafael, his brother. But when Rafael, Deus rest his soul, died, my Duarte decided he did not want his son to risk his life on the sea. And so he sold the ships, and we came here. Please, be seated."

The chairs were solid and comfortable, the sort of chairs meant to be lounged in, not perched on. Even though the furnishings were nothing like theirs back in New Haven, Aaron could imagine himself reading a novel here, his feet up, Bother sprawled on the rug.

Rosemary settled herself in a chair and accepted a cup of tea with a brief smile of thanks. "You have a son and a daughter?"

Rosemary knew there were two children; she had something in mind, leading with that. Aaron dragged himself out of his pleasure in the fit of the chair, accepted his own cup of tea, and paid attention.

"Yes. Daniella and Joao. Please, what is all this about?" She addressed the question to Mrs. Ballantine, who in turn looked to Rosemary. But before Rosemary could say anything, the door banged open, making them all startle.

"My pardon." The man who'd entered looked as startled as they. "I did not know you had company, Nita."

Benedita reached out a hand to him. "My husband, Duarte, who occasionally forgets he is no longer on a ship filled with men with no manners."

"They had excellent manners, Nita, just not polite manners." It was clearly a good-natured exchange, if one worn thin over time. "Dorothy, as always, you are a welcome guest. And who might your companions be?"

Duarte de Peña filled every expectation of a sea captain: he was broad-shouldered and weather-browned, hair and mustache just turning to salt, with the carriage of a man accustomed to giving orders and having them obeyed without question.

"Aaron Harker"—Mrs. Ballantine did the introductions—"and his sister Rosemary Harker."

Aaron stood to shake the other man's hand, while Rosemary offered her hand from her seat, only to have the former captain bow low over it. "Friends of the Ballantines are welcome in our home."

"I'm afraid that this is not entirely a social call," Rosemary said, her hands folded back in her lap. "Captain de Peña, would you join us, please?"

"Duarte, please," he said, pulling a smaller occasional chair from by a side table and sitting down on it. "That title is gone, along with my ships." He held up a hand, stopping his wife from pouring him a cup of tea as well, and nodded to show that he was ready to listen.

Rosemary glanced at Aaron, but he simply raised his eyebrows in return. The captain, Duarte, seemed perfectly willing to listen to women; Rosemary might as well continue.

"My brother and I are here at the request of the Ballantines, to discover the cause of her brother's illness."

De Peña looked at Aaron. "You are a doctor?" He looked singularly unimpressed.

"God forbid," Aaron said with feeling, which made the other man's face crack with a hint of a smile. "No. But we do not believe that Mr. Congdon's illness is of natural causes."

A lie, if a small one; the uncanny were as natural as man or beast. But the general populace equated them all with devils and demons, and it was simply too much work to explain otherwise, the few times they'd had to explain at all.

"Not natural? But the—"

"He was poisoned?" his wife gasped, a hand going to her breast.

"Nita," the captain said, reaching over to pat her free hand. "Why must you think of such things?"

"Poison of a sort," Rosemary said. "But not the sort we tend to think of. Something has sent him into this deep sleep, and we need to discover who, so we can learn how to counter it."

"A devil has him?" Duarte's gaze sharpened, even as his wife and Mrs. Ballantine made protesting noises, although it was unclear if they were aimed at the idea of a devil, or her husband's mention of them.

"A medium came to see him," Mrs. Ballantine said, attempting to reassure the other woman. "She saw no shadows around him, only that he was not able to speak with us."

Aaron ignored the women's soft conversation, watching de Peña carefully. Devils and demons were nonsense, but at least the man had not refused to believe it could be anything other than purely medical causes. The modern age was fine, Aaron would not choose to go back to less technological times, but science also had much to answer for, in his opinion.

"Not a devil, no," Rosemary said, speaking to the ladies as well as Duarte. "But we believe it may be something that feeds on men much the same way."

De Peña narrowed his eyes and pursed his mouth, looking not like a man about to object, but one thinking very hard. "His illness is indeed a tragedy, no matter the cause. But why have you come to us?"

"Because there has been another victim." Rosemary said it gently, but her gaze was sharp on him. "One outside the family. And the common element between them is your children."

The Harkers had been fortunate, this far in their lives; their hunts had intersected only with adults, and never once in all those hunts had they been required to bring someone's children into it. But that streak of luck had ended.

Rosemary had no idea what to expect.

Even under the best of circumstances, telling someone about the existence of the uncanny usually included outbursts of denial, accusations of dupery, and outright hostility, often leading the Harkers to be shown the door, occasionally with force. She had hoped that Mrs. Ballantine's accompaniment would avoid that particular result, but what she was not expecting, at all, was for the captain and his wife to simply . . . deflate.

"You . . . aren't shocked by any of this?" Mrs. Ballantine sounded shocked, herself, by that.

Ruiz Vaz looked unhappy, but it was her husband who responded.

"By the idea that our children could be involved? Of course. I do not see how that could be possible. They are good children; they know better than to dip in such things. But that such things exist?" He touched his mustache with a forefinger, then lifted his shoulders in a faint shrug. "I am not saying that I believe the fairy tales," he said, watching his wife far more cautiously than he had the Harkers, "but—"

"It's nonsense," his wife said, her hand still tucked into his, but now clenching it tight enough for her fingers to leave marks behind. "Tales told by village avós, to keep children from wandering too far or speaking to peddlers and other strangers."

"Nita." His voice wasn't scolding, or particularly commanding, but she clamped her lips shut and looked down at her lap.

"It is not only the grannies who whisper such things. A sailor's life is filled with legends and stories, and my men were often superstitious beyond appeal. And I have seen too much to discount a kernel of truth in it, no matter how improbable the Good Friends may feel, surrounded by modern civilization."

His cautious, casual use of the indirect caught Rosemary's attention and convinced her, more than anything else, that he not only believed but knew more than he was telling. Folk who did not have firsthand experience were less careful about using an indirect address, if they even knew it at all.

"But even if such things were true, why would you think the children are involved?" their mother asked, vaguely frantic. "They're good children, well-behaved. They say their prayers every night."

And no doubt had crosses hanging on the wall over their beds, holy wafers on their tongue, and blessed water and ash dabbed on their foreheads, Rosemary thought. None of which had ever stopped an uncanny.

"It may be that we are wrong." Her voice was as reassuring as she could manage, showing none of the frustration she felt. "For their sake, I hope we are. But speaking with them, with your permission, may help us determine if there is indeed a connection, and if so, how to put an end to it. And in doing so, learn how to cure the illness Franklin Congdon lingers under."

Hopefully. They were working with the assumption that the death of the uncanny would release its victims. If the man did not recover, or worse yet, died? Not every hunt ended with perfect success; Huntsmen learned to take what victories they could. But she did not think the Ballantines would be so pragmatic, and the Circle would not be happy if the Ballantines were not happy.

"Of course," the captain said. His wife looked visibly upset but did not object. "They are upstairs. Nita, if you could fetch them?"

He watched her leave the room, fondness and worry clear on his face, but the moment the door closed behind her, he turned back to the Harkers, all softness gone.

"You think something has targeted my children?" His

voice demanded an answer, as though they were sailors under his command.

"It may simply be coincidence," Rosemary said, but unlike his wife, he did not want to be soothed.

"You would not be here, Dorothy would not have brought you here, if you truly thought that." He got up, pacing across the room, and Rosemary had to fight the urge to pace with him, keeping her legs still under her demurely draped skirt. She noticed a faint grass stain at knee level and rubbed at it absently.

"Nita scoffs now at the stories; she wishes to have left them behind when she came to America. But a sailor has no such excuse, not if he wishes to keep his crew. And I—I said my crew was superstitious; in truth, every sailor, even a captain, abides by certain rules as a matter of practice, or they do not prosper. In the cities, people may ignore the things at the corner of the eye, in the shadows of the moon. But that does not mean they are not there. My ships made offerings every time we left and each time we came back to port. The Good Friends have no cause to be upset with me or mine."

"It's unwise to think we ever understand what drives an uncanny," Aaron said quietly, but before the man could respond, the door opened, and his wife ushered her children in.

Rosemary's gaze flicked over the girl and landed on the boy just behind her. He was taller than his sister, if not by much, with the same strong-shouldered build as their father, but where she was dark-haired and dusky-skinned, his hair glinted wheat gold as the sunlight through the windows touched it. Despite clearly approaching manhood, his face was smooth and sweetly innocent.

If this wasn't the boy the clerk had seen with Congdon just before his attack, Rosemary would eat her best hat, feathers and all.

From the calculating expression on Aaron's face, he was thinking the same thing, possibly down to the hat.

"Mrs. Ballantine!" The girl, Daniella, was clearly delighted to see her, coming forward to drop a polite kiss on an offered check, then turning to the Harkers with wide, curious eyes. "You were there, last time I visited," she said. "But I was sent out of the room because you didn't want to talk in front of me."

Her mother winced, clearly mortified at the girl's forwardness, but Aaron stepped forward, taking her hand and bowing over it as though she were a princess. "I admire a young lady who speaks her mind. And as I am Miss Rosemary's brother, this must be yours?"

Rosemary hid a smile behind her hand; whatever Aaron's awkwardness with adults, he was far better with children than she could ever hope to be.

"Joao Vaz de Peña. Call me Joe," the boy said, offering his hand to be shaken, then turning to Rosemary and, after a moment's hesitation, offering her his hand as well. She took it, gratified to feel a firm grip, the same as he had offered to Aaron. "Mama said you wish to speak with us?"

"We do," Aaron said. "If you'd be so kind as to help us."

The children seemed to respond well to that, settling themselves on the settee next to their mother, their hands in their laps and attentive expressions on their faces.

"You know what happened to Mr. Congdon?"

"He's sick," Joe said.

"Yes. He had a sort of . . . a fainting spell, in his office."

Joe frowned, his eyes suddenly worried. "Like the fever? Might we be sick, too?" he asked his father. His voice cracked on the last word, making his sister giggle, and he shot her an indignant glare, even as his mother murmured something reassuring, in what Rosemary assumed was Portuguese.

Aaron, meanwhile, looked up at the captain. "You'd seen Congdon recently?" De Peña's name had been in the datebook, but not for several months.

Duarte nodded. "The morning of the day he fell ill. We had no appointment, but I had some papers I wanted him to look over, and Joao came with me to drop them off."

"And he seemed healthy to you then?"

Boy and father both frowned, their expressions similar in a way that would have been amusing under other circumstances.

"Yes," Duarte said finally, and Joe nodded, then shook his head, making his father do a slight double take. "No?"

"When we were waiting for you. I told him a joke, and he laughed. And then he coughed, bent over like this"—and the boy mimicked someone bending at the waist to cough into his hand—"and he said it was nothing, but there was red on his hand."

"Blood?" Aaron looked at Rosemary, a question in his eyes. Nobody had said anything about blood.

"Franklin used to cough blood when he was a child." Mrs. Ballantine's voice surprised Rosemary—she had almost forgotten the woman was with them. "He was a sickly child. But he grew out of it."

"Something brought it back up," Aaron said quietly, and Rosemary did a quick inventory in her head of any uncanny who might be able to do that. The only one she could think of were anhaema, who shook blood from human bodies, but they wrapped themselves around a host for hours at a time, leaving a shell behind. Even if an anhaema had been interrupted, the victim would not look as healthy as Congdon did, nor would they still be in such a deep sleep, days after.

Had the uncanny attack begun earlier than they thought?

"Mr. de Peña." When Aaron had the man's attention again, he asked, "Did you see Mr. Congdon eat or drink anything while you were with him?"

"No. I did not have an appointment, I'd only meant to drop the papers off, but he said he had been about to take his morning walk, and invited us to join him. We strolled around the block, and then came inside. I excused myself to use the washroom, and then we left."

If something had happened during that walk, surely the captain would have noticed. Rosemary thought he was the sort of man who noticed things.

"It's because of the shadow, isn't it."

"What?"

Every adult turned to look at Daniella, who suddenly became incredibly interested in the cuff of her blouse.

"Dani." Joao's voice was accusatory

"Filho, hush." Their father's voice was stern, brooking no argument. "Daniella, what shadow?"

"The one that's been following us." She looked sorry she had spoken but unable to escape her father's attention, unable to take the words back.

Joao scowled at her. "You weren't supposed to say anything!"

"If it hurt Mr. Franklin, I don't like it anymore!"

"Daniella." Rosemary slipped out of her chair and knelt next to the girl. She put her hand out, waiting until smaller, cold fingers slipped against hers. This, Rosemary knew how to do, years of coaxing and consoling a younger brother coming to the fore. "Tell us about the shadow. Please."

With a desperate, defiant glance at her brother, she did.

"It's always been there. Not always always, but I remember it way back before. When we lived in Payomet. It would hum to me, when I was falling asleep."

Mrs. Ruiz Vaz and Mrs. Ballantine looked horrified, as though they were half a breath from snatching the children up and running from the house.

"There are some uncanny who attach themselves to a household," Rosemary said, hoping to reassure them. "They do small chores or mind babies in exchange for shelter and food." Honestly, Mrs. Ballantine had invited a medium into her house to converse with a spirit; she had no right to pull that expression now. "If it was one of those, they're"—not harmless, no uncanny was harmless, but—"relatively benign. If you had offended one, they simply would have left, possibly spoiling all the food in your larder first."

They certainly would not attack someone barely connected to the household, much less do damage to another household.

"No." Mrs. Ruiz Vaz shook her head, her face set. "No, none of this, not in this house."

"Benedita." Captain de Peña put his hand on Joao's shoulder. "You saw this shadow, too, filho?"

Joao nodded reluctantly. "Not for a long time now. When

I was little, when we were by the water, sometimes. Just . . . a flicker, in the water. But then not again until we came here." His jaw tightened. "I'd see it on the street, when I was coming home from school. It never did anything; it just stood there. Watching. But if you looked back at it, tried to see it straight, it was gone."

Rosemary caught her brother's eye, lifting one eyebrow. Lurk and disappear. That sounded suspiciously like the uncanny that had been following them earlier.

De Peña did an excellent "disappointed in you" expression. "And you did not think to tell us?"

"Tell you what? There was nothing there!" Joao's grown-up facade cracked, along with his voice. "People already stare at us, I would not give them any more reason."

"It was a Good Friend," Daniella said, but her voice was less certain than it had been.

Her brother turned on her. "That's stupid! I told you: Good Friends can't come on dry land!"

"Joao!" The captain's voice was like a whip, cutting through the room, and both children, hovering on the edge of an all-out squall, subsided immediately.

Rosemary let go of the girl's hand and stood up, looking at the captain. "I think we need to know more about these Good Friends."

———————————

Daniella clearly wanted to stay and take part in the conversation, and Joao was just stubborn enough to not want to leave if his sister was staying, but their mother put a quick end to that, taking each of them by the elbow and marching them toward the door, speaking to them in a low voice. Rosemary didn't need to know Portuguese to know that they were being scolded within an inch of their lives for keeping secrets.

Mrs. Ballantine, with a worried look over her shoulder, followed the three of them out of the room.

De Peña watched them go, then sank into a vacated seat with a deep groan. "Poor Benedita. She wanted so much to leave all this behind, to fit with her neighbors, be accepted, and now . . .

"This is madness, some terrible madness, and I will wake up and swear never to eat cozido again, for the indigestion dreams it brings."

The Harkers waited for him to finish, not without some sympathy. He might have accepted some superstitions, known that there was more to the world than what was seen, but the idea that your children might have been stalked by an uncanny, not just once but over many years, was horrifying to consider, even if it had seemingly done them no harm.

But the uncanny was still out there, had attacked and killed, and they still didn't know why.

"Tell us about your Good Friends," Rosemary said, soft-voiced. "Please."

"It's a myth, a story." He swallowed. "I thought. Even when we made the offerings, I never thought . . .

"They're seafolk, merfolk. If you appease them, they'll drive the fish to you, whistle up winds to take you safe home. If you don't . . ." He made a face, although Rosemary couldn't tell what it signified. "But that's all anyone has ever agreed on. The stories say they can shift their shape, looking human sometimes, others with the body of a seal, or the fin of a shark.

Some stories say they will marry a human but leave them after a while. Some stories say they eat sailors who fall overboard, others say they will aid sailors in distress. Legends have a way of shaping themselves to what people want, and people want many things."

"The legends are based in truth," Aaron said.

"Ai, yes, I know! But why would it be following my children? Why would it even be here, on land? And to hurt Franklin, who has never once gone to sea? No." He shook his head, a lock of hair falling forward into his eyes, only to be brusquely shoved away. "No. There must be some other explanation."

"A deep-sea uncanny," Rosemary said, ignoring his protestations. "The one that attacked me, it seemed to come from nowhere, but what if it came up from the drains by the side of the road?" She turned to her brother. "It could have reached the priest the same way."

"The creek behind the house . . . it could have used that to come up to the property . . ."

The Harkers spoke at once, voices overlapping each other.

"It attacked you? And a priest? But—this is madness." De Peña broke into their excitement, a hand coming up to cover his mouth, as though he were feeling ill. "This can have nothing to do with my children." He saw the looks on their faces and visibly checked himself. "You believe that it does." It was barely a whisper, fear and resignation tangled in a knot. "But we made all the proper offerings . . . and I've sold my share of the fleet. I'm not a sailor anymore. Why would it follow my children—and why would it try to kill anyone?"

Rosemary felt the surge of heartbeat that came when a hunt picked up speed, even sitting quietly in her chair. "That is what we are going to find out."

De Peña shook his head. "How?"

"I . . . have an idea," Aaron said.

Nineteen

I HAVE AN IDEA." Aaron was reasonably certain that it was a bad idea, or at least that Rosemary would tell him that it was a bad idea. But it could work.

He thought it would, anyway.

Rosemary pinched the bridge of her nose with two fingers. "I'm going to hate this, aren't I? All right, what?"

"We use the children—"

"What?"

"No!"

Aaron held up both hands as though to stop a physical assault rather than a verbal one. "Not like that!" Although, considering Corpus Christi, he supposed Rosemary had cause to assume. "The uncanny appears to be invested in the children. If we were to suggest to it that they were in some way in danger—"

"No." De Peña's voice allowed for no argument, and Aaron regretted saying anything in front of the man. Although he supposed they would have needed his permission anyway.

Next to him, Rosemary was giving him that look again, the one that was half exasperation and half pity.

He hated that look.

"The children are the only connection we have," he pointed out. "Unless you want to wait for another victim—oh wait, we had one already, and he's dead."

Rosemary bit her lower lip, clearly trying to find some response to that. But there was none; they both knew it.

"Can you create another illusion?" Rosemary clearly hated the idea, but less than using the children.

Aaron shook his head, not without regret. "Wouldn't work. Illusions are based on the uncanny expecting to see what they're shown. You only get one chance—after that, anything with even a bit of native intelligence will see through it."

And this uncanny was definitely showing intelligence.

"It has to be real. But I might be able to do it without their being present." His thoughts were racing almost too fast to keep up, pages of lore flipping through his memory, scanning for the right receipt. When Rosemary started to say something, he held up a finger, willing her to be quiet until he found what he was looking for.

"Uncanny are creatures of instinct. If the lure was powerful enough to override thought, touch on that instinct, it should work. But it requires physicality, if not physical presence. Skin, flesh." Bone would be ideal, but Aaron knew better than to suggest that. "Blood. Blood and flesh, even a little bit, could stand in for the actual body."

Duarte put himself in front of Aaron, his height and broader shoulders intending to intimidate. "Not them. Me."

Aaron hadn't been intimidated by a human since he was eleven. "What?"

"They are my flesh and blood. And if this is . . . if it is a Good Friend, then it followed me originally, not them. Use me as your lure."

"Would that work?" Rosemary asked.

Aaron considered it, pushing the new factor into his calculations. "It might." Not as well, but not having to argue with Rosemary would be preferred. "Better if we had something of theirs as well. Something well-loved, that's been with them a long time." Part of it was physical scent; part of it was emotional: the stronger the bonds of ownership, the more powerful the ingredient.

De Peña stroked his mustache, then nodded abruptly. "Wait here."

"As though we're going to go anywhere," Aaron muttered, but only after the door had closed behind the other man.

The moment they were alone, Rosemary was in his face, a forefinger poking into his chest, hard. "I don't like this, Aaron. You're taking too many risks."

"In for a penny . . . ," he said, but she didn't blink.

"Where does it stop? Where is the line, and what are we going to do when you suddenly realize you're on the other side of it? Even if the Circle never finds out, how is what you're doing any better than—"

"Don't." Even the thought that Rosemary was comparing him to that madwoman was too much. "I'm being careful."

"No you're not."

They stared at each other, her finger still pushed against his chest, until Aaron blinked.

"Truly, Rosie. What I'm doing, it's called sympathetic resonance. There's a scientific argument for it, as much as a magical one. And it's the only way we even have a chance to lure the uncanny out, without using the children. So we either do this, or we give up."

And they couldn't give up. Couldn't, wouldn't. No Huntsmen would, shy of death.

Before Rosemary could try another argument, de Peña returned, holding a floppy-limbed doll with a china head, and a small wooden boat, painted in intricate detail.

He gave the doll to Rosemary, then hesitated, turning the toy in his hands as gently as though it were made of glass rather than wood and canvas. "This was my boat. The *Silver Dove*," he said, holding it so they could see the name painted on the side. "I captained her for seven years before Joao was born, then three after. But then Daniella came along, and . . . Having children, it changes you."

Aaron would have to take his word for it.

"Thank you," he said. "The best way, I think, would be for you to smear a little of your blood on these. If we can keep it wet until we are ready to call it . . ."

"Why not wait until then?" He caught the glance Aaron gave Rosemary, and his chin lifted, stubborn determination radiating from him. "I'm coming with you."

"No you're not."

De Peña gave Rosemary's immediate response a grim smile. "This is my family. My friends. That makes it my problem." He lifted the edge of his jacket to show the butt of a pistol that definitely hadn't been there before. "If you need my blood for this, I'm willing to bleed, but I'm going with you to do it."

Aaron saw no reason to argue with the man; he hadn't blinked at the mention of the uncanny, and Aaron had no doubt that he'd be able to handle himself if it came down to blows—or bullets. Rosemary could disapprove of bringing outsiders in all she wanted; even he knew she wasn't going to convince a father to stay at home when his children were at risk.

Their own parents would have done exactly the same.

"He's coming, Rosemary." It was a warning: if they squabbled in front of the captain now, they would lose authority. Her gaze narrowed, but she nodded once.

"Fine. But you listen to us. No heroics."

"I am not a heroic man by nature," de Peña said calmly. "You lead, I follow."

Aaron wasn't sure he believed that, but it would have to do.

"But if you intend to set the lure here, I will want to send Benedita and the children elsewhere first."

"Not here." Aaron had been thinking about that. "The children said they only saw it occasionally, almost as though it was checking on them. We need to go where it's hunting."

"But we don't know who else it might target," Rosemary objected. "Unless the captain has a very limited social circle?" They both turned to look at him, only to have him shake his head.

"We have made an effort to socialize, since coming here. Nita especially has been making friends. I could name a dozen or more who have been in contact with the children, and who knows how many more through their schooling."

Aaron had been afraid of that. "I think we need to go back to the Ballantine house."

"You think it will make another attempt at Dorothy? Or Franklin?" De Peña didn't look alarmed, merely calculating.

"It's a trait of the uncanny to be compelled to finish things. Its first attempt on Mrs. Ballantine was stymied by her not being home; the second failed because it was actually Rosemary. So yes. I think it will try to attack Mrs. Ballantine again."

"But she's here—with the children!" De Peña looked ready to race upstairs, halting only when Rosemary lifted her hand, shaking it back and forth to say no. "None of the attacks have happened when the children were present. I don't think that will suddenly change. If it is watching, it will likely follow the car back to the house."

De Peña nodded. "So we will go with her."

"We need to make a stop at the hotel first," Rosemary said. "There's something we need to pick up."

The Ballantines' automotive was larger than the one Aaron had rented, but even so, it was crowded, with the addition of de Peña and Botheration. Despite having Botheration stretched out heavy across their feet in the back seat, de Peña didn't complain. Of course, that might have been sheer caution, particularly after Bother, driven by some sense of mischief, had yawned wide enough to show every one of his teeth as well as the full length of his tongue.

"Pull over up ahead," Aaron said as they turned onto the street before the Ballantines, then threw open the door, urging Bother out before following. "Take Mrs. Ballantine home," he directed Billy. "We'll follow on foot."

The boy touched his cap, then threw the car into motion again, lurching forward the moment de Peña closed the door behind him.

When they reached the house, Aaron paused to check the sigils. They were faded but still intact on the gate, and Aaron frowned at them before turning away. Rosemary knew that it bothered him to leave them that way, but improving the lines would be counterproductive if the uncanny had to come in that way.

They passed quietly along the path, not wanting to alert anyone that they were there. At their back, the Ballantines' house glimmered, lights already shining warmly from behind curtains. Inside, Rosemary could imagine Mrs. Ballantine unpinning her hat, changing out of her day-dress, dropping a kiss on her husband's forehead before accepting a cup of tea. Would she tell him what was happening outside? Or would she try to hide it from him, pretend it wasn't happening?

"This is a bad idea," Rosemary said, her voice low but not quite a whisper. Whispers carried.

"You've said that."

"I'm saying it again."

At her side, Bother grunted softly, but she couldn't tell if the hound was agreeing with her or her brother. She rested her right hand against her thigh, feeling the reassuring solidity of the silver dagger in her skirt pocket, then turned her hand just so, to make sure she could reach it without getting tangled in the cloth.

Following behind them, de Peña was a tangible presence, the sound of his boots on the path oddly echoing louder than

Aaron's and Rosemary's steps combined. Bother did not like him back there, occasionally turning to glance behind, rather than keeping his attention on the chore at hand.

"Focus, hound," she told him, and he twitched his upright ear at her as though to say, *I know my job, human.*

They had already proven that the uncanny could be lured into showing itself. But if this was a Good Friend, the captain's story suggested a level of intelligence that meant they couldn't take anything for granted. It might take the lure—or it might simply decide that they were a threat and attack. And they'd brought an unknown element, without any idea how he might actually react once faced with an uncanny.

She loved her brother, but there were times she wanted to throttle him. If he hadn't agreed with de Peña, they might have been able to leave the man out of it.

"Do you think it was following us, too?" Aaron asked suddenly. "Back at the college?"

"That would simplify things."

"That's not an answer."

"I don't know," she said, exasperated. "Maybe it was, maybe it wasn't. Does it matter right now? Focus, Aaron."

The grass was slippery underfoot as they made their way to the stone wall, and Rosemary paused to hitch her skirt up slightly, not caring that the captain would see her stockinged leg. She had the suspicion he'd seen far worse, and cared less.

Once they were out of direct line of sight of the house, Aaron reached into his pocket and pulled out a fairy light, resting it on his upturned palm.

Rosemary disliked fairy lights the way she disliked all fey

tools, but a tungsten flash would be visible, too clearly a sign of someone where they should not be. The fairy light cast a different glow, the sort that folk would see out of the corner of their eye and tell themselves to ignore, if they knew what was good for them. And an uncanny might not think it was a human, if they took note of it at all.

"Laft, pfiift, pheeen." The words sounded more foreign than any foreign language Rosemary knew, and she couldn't repress a shudder as her brother whispered them, the fairy light suddenly casting its off-white light into the night.

"Damnation," the captain whispered behind her, then: "It doesn't burn? I'd make another fortune, selling those to the navies."

"You'd have to learn the secret for making them, first," she said. Fairy lights were artifacts, not rare but not easily replaceable. The Harkers only had the one, and for all that she might occasionally wish it down a well, she took as much care with it as Aaron did.

Aaron reached into his other pocket, pulling out his penknife and flicking it open. The blade was small but sharp.

"Captain. If you would?"

De Peña didn't argue with the title this time, already rolling up his sleeve and offering his left arm, while Rosemary held the toys ready.

De Peña barely winced as Aaron nicked the soft part of his wrist. Under the fairy light, the blood dripping onto the toys was a deep purple, almost black, and Rosemary found herself fascinated by the way it glistened, splattering the doll's white pinafore and shiny-smooth face.

Sympathetic resonance, Aaron had said. Uncanny were

creatures of emotion, not logic. The resonance should cause them to believe that the children themselves were injured and bleeding.

Ideally, that would cause the uncanny to rush in to . . . what? Defend them? Attack?

It didn't matter. *Be ready*, she told herself. Whatever happened, be ready.

When doll and boat were both smeared with the blood, Rosemary handed them to Aaron, then took out the supplies she had grabbed when they picked up Bother and applied a pad of cotton to the wound, then wrapped gauze to hold it in place.

"I'm fine," the captain said, moving his arm away. "Taken worse peeling potatoes."

Rosemary doubted that but didn't insult him by saying so.

"Shh!" Aaron's hiss sounded irritated, and Bother growled deep in his chest, making them all come alert.

"Get back," she told de Peña, not bothering to keep her voice low anymore, twisting her arm so that one of her throwing knives slid from its sheath into her palm.

"But—"

"Now," she said, even as she was flipping the knife in her grip, from resting to ready pose. The uncanny had arrived too quickly. They had been right; it had been stalking the house itself.

De Peña stepped away, but she heard the familiar sound of a pistol being drawn. He'd had the wrong pistol to use any of their bullets; ordinary lead could wound most uncanny, even if it couldn't kill them, but she doubted he would be able to get a shot off, if the uncanny did attack.

Trying to kill something, even something not human, was harder than most people understood.

The sound of water splashing made her tense, turning toward the sound. Had it been across the creek? Or was it doubling back, moving away? They would be better off without the fairy light marking them, but extinguishing it now would leave them blinded by the dark, too many deadly seconds before they could adjust.

More splashing, then nothing. Rosemary could feel sweat rising and cooling on her skin, leaving behind the faint stink of fear. No matter how many times she had done this, no matter how much they trained, there was always the knowledge that most uncanny were faster, stronger, and by the time Huntsmen went after them, more comfortable with violence. The only thing Huntsmen had in their favor was logic.

Bother pushed his bulk against her leg, then moved forward, putting himself between his humans and where he sensed the uncanny. Rosemary oriented herself by that, trusting his instincts more than her own senses.

Silence. The fairy light's glow showed her the outline of her brother's shoulder and back, the toys still in his hands. She silently willed him to drop them, to draw his own weapon, but he stayed motionless.

"Captain." God, she hated this plan. It was a terrible plan. "This is your cue."

———————

Aaron turned just enough, the fairy light clinging to his wrist catching the angles of de Peña's face, casting the rest of his body back into shadows. He had to admit, it could not have been better staged if Reinhardt himself had directed it.

"My Friend. Why are you doing this?"

He'd coached de Peña on what to say, how to say it, although Aaron would not have blamed the man if he'd forgotten all of it in the chill of the moment. But de Peña was made of sterner stuff, facing into the darkness as though he'd done it a hundred times before. Aaron supposed in his own way he had, bringing his ship through storms time and again, over the years.

They'd told him only to ask, politely, what the uncanny was about. But the captain took a step forward, causing Bother to stir, unhappy, and went on. "I was never less than respectful to you and your sisters. My ships made their offerings; my men were careful with their nets. Why do you haunt me and mine?"

At Rosemary's knee, Bother pulled back his upper lip, teeth glinting in the fairy light, and Aaron knew without seeing that Rosemary's hand would have dropped to Bother's head, telling the hound to wait. He second-guessed their decision to bring him; the hound was well-trained, but his instinct on seeing an uncanny was to rend and tear, not wait.

But if things went badly, they would need him.

There was silence from the shadows, even the sound of running water seemingly halted. Aaron could hear his own heart thumping steadily in his chest, the sound of air rising and leaving from his nostrils.

The captain switched to Portuguese, and Aaron's Spanish barely let him follow along, guessing at words he didn't understand.

"Why are you so far from your home, Good Friend?"

From the darkness, a voice responded. "Why are you?"

The voice was soft, sweet as the scents of apple blossom and salted toffee, and Aaron felt himself move toward it, even not knowing what it had said. But the moment his foot slipped forward, Bother's attention turned to him, a growl rumbling deep in the beast's chest. Not a threat, but a warning: you're heading into danger.

Brought back to himself, Aaron made a sound of satisfaction. He had been right; the uncanny did have the capability of human speech. Now to see if it also shared with humans the need to justify itself.

"This is my home now. Go back to the sea, Good Friend. Leave my family alone."

Aaron *thought* that was what the captain had said, anyway. But from the response, it was the wrong approach. The shriek rising out of the darkness was everything ungodly, filled with rage, as a figure lunged from the shadows. The fairy light on Aaron's wrist caught its features briefly: it was the same one that had attacked Rosemary in her guise as Mrs. Ballantine, the same or one as alike as to be its twin. Too-long fingers stretched for the captain, trying to wrap themselves over his face. He stumbled back, tripping over something and landing flat on his back.

The singsong voice still had Aaron's head muffled-feeling, but years of working with Rosemary had him moving toward the uncanny, knowing that his sister would be taking a defensive post until the captain was able to get back to his feet. Bother would be—he felt a heavy weight brush against his leg and grinned tightly—taking low point, to give the uncanny something to worry about, too.

He just needed the uncanny to move or speak again, and Bother would pin it down. But it did not move. They were at a stalemate.

Aaron thought several potential curses, biting his lip hard enough to raise a blister, but took the opportunity to shift his knife to his right hand, taking up the pistol with his left. They'd been trained to shoot with either hand, but his knife work was still best with his dominant hand.

He thought about calling out to his sister, get her placement, but that would give it away to the uncanny as well. Assuming it wasn't one of those that could see perfectly well in the dark. If it was sea-based, he could only hope it wasn't accustomed to drier air. Anything to take away its advantage.

For all his readiness, the attack nearly caught him by surprise; he would have sworn the uncanny had been to his left, not his right. He pivoted and bent at the knees, knife slashing up and making contact with something that snagged, then gave way, a warm liquid running down the edge of the blade onto his hand. It felt thick and gross, thicker than blood and worse than entrails, for half a second, before whatever it was began to burn like he'd grabbed the wrong end of an oven-hot pan.

Training alone kept him from dropping the knife, but the pain drove him to his knees—which meant that the uncanny's next attack went just over the top of his head. Before he could react to that—before he could even work through the pain enough to react—Bother was in motion, his chunky body suddenly fluid, muscles bunching and stretching as he launched into the air and came down with one of the uncanny's arms in his mouth.

Another shriek, loud and pained enough Aaron was certain the entire neighborhood would be woken, and the uncanny twisted, a wet, slurpy sound followed by a hard crack, and was free of the hound's grip, then disappeared back into the shadows.

Or mostly disappeared. Bother, breathing hard, sat down, the torn limb still lodged between his teeth before he spat it out with a clear sound of disgust.

"Good boy, Bother," Rosemary said, not sounding as though she was sure it was good at all. The hound had dropped the arm at her feet, where it twitched once, making all three humans jump back a pace—the captain scooting on his backside—watching it nervously. But it did not move again, and Aaron became aware of noises in the not-far-enough-away distance. A quick glance up the hill confirmed that yes, the lights in the Ballantine house were all on, and figures were moving within.

Aaron dimmed the fairy light, then wiped his hands against the dry grass, not wanting to get any of the ichor on his clothing if he could avoid it. Bending over, though, he felt bile rise up in his throat, triggering another worry: the blood—and other less mentionable bodily fluids—of some uncanny were toxic to humans; he needed to wash his hands, and every other bit of exposed skin, quickly. "Chances of getting out of here without them seeing us?"

"Unless you're willing to go over the fence, over the creek, and the long way around, carrying that arm? With the uncanny still maybe out there and severely upset with us? Not great," his sister said dryly, helping the captain up from the ground.

"That was what I thought." There was no way in heaven or hell he was going anywhere near that creek just then. "Back the way we came, then." He slipped off his coat, using it to gingerly wrap the arm up, to keep it from making contact with unprotected skin. It was heavier than he'd expected, but the acidic ichor dripping from it seemed to have congealed already. He would be thankful for small mercies. "How's the captain?"

"I think I broke an arm," he said for himself, teeth gritted, but standing upright. "And possibly a rib. Nothing worse than I've taken in a fight before, but I'd forgotten how much it hurts."

"Whatever you said to it, it made it very angry. Don't antagonize the uncanny, Captain. That's our party trick."

"I told it to go back to the sea. To leave me and my family alone."

"And it didn't like that," Rosemary said. "Interesting."

"I think—" And Aaron's words were cut off by another burst of nausea and a helpless roil in his gut.

"Aaron, what?" he heard his sister exclaim, and then he could do nothing but crouch over and helplessly vomit onto the night-dark grass, the bundle of detached arm falling to the ground at his feet.

Rosemary barely remembered how they'd gotten Aaron up to the house; she had a vague memory of the captain slinging her brother over his shoulder, while she snatched up the limb and directed Botheration to stay by her side. It seemed to her as though one moment they had been facing down the uncanny, and the next they were back in the Ballantines' kitchen, electric lights showing the grayish pallor of her brother's face and the worried lines in de Peña's face as he directed the maid to brew water, while Rosemary quickly bound up his arm and ribs.

"I'm sorry, Captain de Peña, it's—"

"Had worse, girl. Had worse. And we're well past titles; I think we've earned the intimacy of given names, yes?"

"Just don't call her Rosie," Aaron said, his voice weak. "She hates that."

Aaron was lying on a padded bench, the wall behind him all that kept him upright, and Rosemary kept half her attention on him even as she finished her makeshift work with the splint and bandages.

Ballantine had allowed them in but grimly refused to send for a doctor. Rosemary understood his logic: there was no way to explain what had happened without it sounding, at best, dodgy, and "dodgy" was not a word the Ballantines wanted associated with their name.

But watching her brother gesture for the basin, then emptying his stomach again, only strands of bile coming up at this point, Rosemary discovered that she didn't give a damn about keeping things quiet.

Ballantine had shown them to the kitchen, then left them to it. Mrs. Ballantine and the housekeeper had declined to show themselves.

"Water's ready," Macy said. Her hair was down in a single plait, but her apron was as spotlessly starched as though she'd not been woken up well before dawn, and her expression, unlike Ballantine's, was sympathetic.

"Let the mint leaves soak, then add the lemon rind and a pinch of salt," the captain—Duarte—ordered. "Old sea remedy to purge the stomach gently," he said at Rosemary's inquiring look. "Fresh lemon would be better, but I wouldn't trust any this time of year, for squeezing."

When Macy finished the preparation, she brought it over, and he gestured to Aaron. "Drink," he said. "Rinse your mouth with the first sip, then swallow the rest, but slowly."

The maid had to hold the cup steady for him as Aaron took a sip, then spat it out into the basin and took another, which he did swallow, making a face at the taste.

For a few minutes, the only sounds in the kitchen were the sounds of Aaron drinking and the soft noises of the maid busying herself getting ready for her morning chores. Occasionally she would look over at them, as though dying to ask a question, but before she could work up the gumption to do so, Ballantine returned.

"I was told that you were among the best at what you do." Ballantine was now fully dressed, standing in the entrance to the kitchen, arms crossed over his chest and a scowl on his face. "How difficult could it be to kill the thing, and why did you need to endanger someone else to do it?"

"I invited myself along," Duarte said, but Ballantine's glare said he wasn't impressed by that.

"They should not have allowed it. It was reckless of you, and criminal of them. You have children, and a wife, man. A business to run!"

Huntsmen are disposable was not quite silent in his words.

Rosemary caught Duarte's attention and gave a tiny shake of her head. She appreciated the fact that he was willing to speak up, but it would not mend matters. His own eyes narrowed, the exhaustion clearly visible on his face in the electric lights of the kitchen, but went back to watching Aaron take another sip, reaching his unbroken arm forward, despite the binding on his ribs, to catch the cup before Aaron went into another bout of vomiting. He held the cup silently, waiting, while Rosemary ached with the need to go to her brother and comfort him.

But Aaron would not welcome comfort, right now.

So far, there seemed to be no other effects from the toxic ichor, but Rosemary wouldn't be complacent until Aaron's body stopped trying to turn itself inside out. And possibly not even then.

Wounds they could stitch up; broken bones they could bind up. Damage done to their insides was harder to fix, if it could be fixed at all.

She banished that thought. He would be fine.

When Aaron finished vomiting and took the cup from Duarte with a weary nod of thanks, Rosemary turned back to Ballantine.

"Killing it would not have told us why it was here, or why it was attacking your family," she said as mildly as she was capable of.

"I don't care why it was doing it—I want it stopped."

Having delivered his opinion, Ballantine stalked off down the hallway again, leaving the three of them alone.

"I care," Duarte said quietly. "We injured it, but it's still out there. If a Good Friend, if that . . . thing . . . was following my children, I want to know why. And why, if I offended it, was it attacking others, not me."

"It didn't seem angry at you, at first," Aaron said, setting aside the cup, now empty. The maid took it up, refilled it, and handed it back to him with a stern look that, in other circumstances, would have made Rosemary smile.

"Not until I told it to go away," Duarte agreed. "It was calm, almost . . . conversational until then." His body gave a gentle shudder, as though suddenly realizing that it was cold. Rosemary wondered if he might be going into shock, and if he would be offended if she told him to move closer to the fire. Catching the maid's eye, she made a gesture toward where she had previously pulled down the liquor for Mrs. Ballantine's "special tea" and indicated the captain with a tilt of her head. The girl, quick-witted, nodded, fetching a glass and the bottle, and pouring him a dash of the amber liquor.

"Don't I get any?" Aaron asked, and both Rosemary and Duarte said no in unison.

He sulked for a moment, then took another sip of his tea. "I take it that was not what you were expecting?"

Duarte started to shrug, wincing as he was reminded of the splint on his arm and the bandages around his torso. "Legend has them as . . . physically appealing."

"Legends usually do," Aaron agreed dryly, then spat once more into the basin before pushing it away and wiping his mouth with a kerchief. "It had a lovely voice, before it started screaming. Definitely related to a siren." It was beautiful to his eye, but he acknowledged that the teeth could be disturbing.

"I'm suddenly very glad I've promised Nita I'd not go to sea again." It might have been the electric lights hung on the walls, but Rosemary thought the captain's complexion under his mustache was paler than it had been even after they'd bound up his ribs.

"But . . ."

"But?" Rosemary asked, when Duarte hesitated.

"Each attack, from what you have told me, and what I have seen, is different. Are we certain . . ." He trailed off, clearly not wanting to say what was on his mind.

"That there's only one uncanny?" Rosemary finished for him. "It was the same one that went after me, in the guise of Mrs. Ballantine. And it reached for your face, the same way it did mine . . . and the same way Mrs. Ballantine described what she saw over her brother's body. I think . . . I think there is something in its touch that pulls life force from its victims."

"And your brother's illness?"

"The same thing that took Franklin down, only it didn't finish the job," Aaron said.

"But . . . you don't know how to reverse it. To wake Franklin up."

"Not yet. But we have something to work with now."

All three of them glanced at the coat-wrapped bundle that had been shoved under the table, Botheration in full guard mode over it.

"Manny?" Aaron said.

"Manny," Rosemary agreed.

"Manny?" Duarte echoed.

"Emanuel van Horn. Coroner for the state of Connecticut, and resident expert on uncanny forms." What he was was a vivisectionist, but Rosemary had found some people tended to become queasy at the word. "If he doesn't recognize the species, he will at least be able to tell us something about it."

"Dare I ask how you intend to get the limb to this individual without it, ah, making its presence known to everyone nearby?"

"No need for that," Rosemary said. "Tell Manny we have an unknown uncanny here, and he'll strap himself into the nearest automotive to lay hands on it." She frowned. "Although I suspect the Ballantines may not be feeling generous enough to let us use their telephone, and it's not a conversation I'd like to have in the hotel's lobby."

"We have a telephone," Duarte said, then looked down at his bloodied clothing and splinted arm. "But best you use it before Nita sees me . . ."

Twenty

WHEN DOROTHY HAD come home, she had gone directly to the room her brother lay in, pulling the chair close to the bed and taking his hand, fingers slack, in her own. Ballantine found her there, waiting in the doorway for her to acknowledge him, unsure, as he was unsure of very few things, what to say.

"He's never going to wake up, is he?"

"He doesn't know you're there. All you're doing is hurting yourself."

She didn't look back at him, and the acid that had been churning in his stomach since they first brought the boy home rose into his chest, making his breath taste like vinegar. "Dorothy. You can't change anything, sitting here."

He had indulged her, the first few days. Had listened to her pleas that when Franklin woke, he would need to see a familiar face, that he would be confused and frightened. As though he was still the gawky boy he'd been at their wedding, all elbows and ears, not a man grown. Walter had tried to be patient, had tried to be understanding. But eventually he'd put his foot down, hired a perfectly capable nurse to sit with him, made Dorothy return to her bed, resume her responsibilities. He'd told her that he would take care of it, had called in favors, reminded people of their obligations to him.

McIntyre had made no promises. Had been quite blunt about the fact that he could make no promises, that they would do their best, and send their best, but no hunt came with a guarantee, and that there was no certainty that Franklin would ever wake up again.

Walter had done his grieving then. Had mourned his brother-in-law, had paid the sums McIntyre asked, to ensure that the thing that had killed Franklin would be brought down and destroyed. And he'd tried to move on. Tried to convince Dorothy to move on.

Instead, Dorothy had brought in a spiritualist, full of claptrap and nonsense, yet another hand out for coin, filling his wife's head with nonsense about spirits and voices.

"Dorothy." His voice was too sharp, and he could see her shoulders stiffen. "Sweetheart. Please."

"You don't think he's going to wake up."

"I wish he would. I truly do. But no. I don't think he's going to wake up."

"You're wrong. Madame said he's trying to come back to us. Once they kill the thing that did this, he'll be free, and he'll come back."

He stared at the curve of her back, willing her to turn around, to see him standing there. But she merely reached forward to brush the hair from her brother's forehead, placing a soft kiss there.

"He'll wake up. He will."

He had already lost his brother-in-law. If the Huntsmen didn't do their damn job, he was afraid he would lose his wife as well. If not to violence, then grief.

After closing the door softly behind him, Ballantine went in search of the brandy, and the telephone.

Twenty-One

THE CALL TO van Horn went almost to the word how Rosemary had predicted, the man practically falling over himself to arrange his travel north. It was arranged that he would pick up the package from the Ballantines' home, where it had been stored, with Macy's slightly horrified assistance, in the root cellar.

With all that, it was well past midnight by the time the Harkers returned to their hotel. The clerk, an older gentleman, bald save for tufts of hair behind his ears and over his eyes, didn't give them a second glance when they stopped in for their keys, wishing them a bored good morning before going back to his newspaper.

Rosemary suddenly realized that she had no idea what was going on in the world outside of the hunt. The urge to grab the newspaper from the man, search for news of recent events in Mexico and Europe, made her fingers twitch.

"You think Ballantine is going to snitch on us?"

She turned to look at her brother, distracted, eyebrows raised. "And you say I use vulgar slang?"

"I learned from you. Answer me."

Rosemary had been trying very hard not to think about it. "I'd be surprised if he hasn't already. He doesn't seem the sort to worry about waking other people up, if he needs to say something to them."

"Wonderful."

"Put some sleep under your ear and it will all look better in the morning."

"That never worked when mother said it, either. And it is morning."

"Sleep, Aaron." She patted her leg, calling Bother to her, and went into her own room, closing the door behind her.

Shedding her clothing took more energy than she had, but sleeping in her clothing, grass-and-sweat stained, wasn't an option. If she was only going to have a few hours of sleep, she was going to be comfortable for it.

Hanging the skirt up, her attention was caught by the small box on the shelf, half-hidden by a hat. She placed a finger on the lid.

Three vials left. The temptation was there, the sweet promise of energy, the ability to think her way through any knot.

"Take your own advice," she told herself sternly, pushing the box back behind the plumed hat before closing the wardrobe's door. Sleep was what she needed, not Blast.

Bother had gone to the door to the hallway and sat down, staring first at it, then back over his shoulder at her, as though to ask why he was in one room, and the arm in another.

"Stop it," she told him. "If I let you keep it, you'd be guarding it all night, and you need sleep, too."

With a huff, he lay down but did not stop watching the door.

"Fine, be that way." Rosemary slipped into her pajamas and went to the tiny sink to wash up for bed, leaving the hound to his duty.

By the time she finished, drying her face on a too-coarse towel, he had inched forward enough that his nose was touching the door, but was snoring lightly.

"Good hound," she said, and crawled into bed with a deep, bone-weary sigh. "Good night."

―――――――――

Aaron woke with a start, one hand going to his throat, still half in a dream where he had been strangled. It took several breaths, unobstructed, before he remembered that the soreness came from the repeated vomiting he had done the night before. He lay in bed for a few seconds, letting his body wake up more slowly, checking to make sure that the nausea of the night before had gone. His hands ached, however, and when he fumbled the light on, he saw that the palms and fingers were still red-striped and puffy from where the ichor had touched them. He poked one stripe, cautiously, and hissed in pain. He considered getting up to ask Rosemary if she had any salve to put on them, and he considered staying in bed and trying to go back to sleep, when a knock on the door reminded him that something had woken him up.

He frowned up at the ceiling, the lamp casting harsh shadows across the surface. Rosemary would use a double tap or, more likely, she would simply pick the lock.

The knock came again, this time sounding as though the

knocker was annoyed. Aaron rolled over and looked at his watch where it rested on the bedside table, then shoved the covers aside and got out of bed. Padding to the door, he rubbed sleep from his eyes and snagged his pistol from the table where he'd left it the night before. Checking to make sure the safety was on—he didn't want to accidentally shoot a bellhop, no matter how early they were knocking—he unlocked and opened the door.

"You two really stepped in it this time."

Jonathan didn't wait for an invitation, shouldering the door open all the way and stepping inside the room. Aaron stared at him for a moment, then, realizing he was standing in an open doorway in his pajamas, holding a pistol, he shut the door and put the weapon back down. Not that he was averse to shooting Jonathan, on principle, but Rosemary would feel the need to scold him if he did.

"Don't look at me like that—I'm not happy about being awake, either. But first I got told to stick around rather than going home, and then I got rousted out of bed by a decrepit-looking clerk telling me I had a phone call from the old man himself, and I'm not going to suffer alone."

Aaron skipped over the first part—he'd *known* there was something sticky about Jonathan still being at the hotel!—and focused on the second. "Davistky called you."

"He did, and I would appreciate never having that happen again in my life." Jonathan leaned against the desk, looking about as happy as he sounded. "Now go wake your sister up."

"Why don't you?" Aaron asked, even as he was pulling on his pants.

"Because I don't want a knife in the eye."

He had, Aaron had to admit, a point.

———————

Rosemary had already been awake when Aaron knocked, Botheration having decided at some point to abandon his guard stance for the more comfortable bed, in the process stealing her pillow.

"Get dressed," Aaron said. "Quickly. We have a problem."

She slid her knife back into the space between mattress and frame and got out of bed. When he used that tone, she listened. "What's going on?"

"I'm going to let Jonathan explain it."

"Jonathan?"

"Come on. No, Bother, stay."

———————

It took a few minutes for Jonathan's news to sink in, which Rosemary blamed on the early hour. But when it did, she let a few particularly pungent curses escape.

"So the Circle no longer trusts us, is that it?" She would blame exhaustion, later, for her bluntness. "They leave us out in the cold for months, then give us an impossible task— find an uncanny but we can't tell you what it is and you can't actually ask any questions that might upset the victim—and then when we actually finally are getting somewhere, they send you to take over?"

Across the room, she could see her brother's expression, half shock and half admiration at her losing her temper, and it made her snap her mouth shut, teeth grinding against each other with the effort.

"All I know is that Ballantine isn't happy with the way things are going, and that got Davistky moving. The old man told me to get it done. Nothing like the fear of losing a quarterly check to motivate."

And there was Jonathan's redeeming feature: he had a streak of sarcasm a yard wide and miles long.

"Look." He lifted his hands in a gesture of appeasement. "I know this is . . . not ideal. But you're not being removed from the hunt; nobody even suggested anything like that. They just want a different hand on the reins. And I was here already, so." He shrugged, as though that absolved him of any responsibility. "And before you ask, no, I did not object or argue; I've no desire to be the next Armstrong!"

It had been decades, but stories of Mercedes Armstrong were told to every new Huntsmen as a warning of what would happen if you became too much of a thorn in the Circle's side. Rosemary wondered uneasily if, in years to come, they'd tell stories of the Harkers, in warnings never to omit details from your report, even if it was for a good reason.

Jonathan glanced at Aaron and sighed. "For heaven's sake, stop looking at me like that. I don't know what your problem with me is, Harker, but I'm not the enemy. I personally don't care how strange you are, or what the gossip was ten years ago, you're both solid Huntsmen, and that's what matters."

Rosemary saw the wince in her brother's eyes, even if Jonathan couldn't. They'd still been in their teens ten years ago, their parents on a hunt that ended with their mother dead and their father's mind broken in two. There were days it felt as though everything they'd done, everything they'd achieved since then, was a desperate attempt to erase that past.

They were better than solid Huntsmen. They were excellent, because they had to be.

But excellent Huntsmen didn't have someone else sent in to take over.

She stepped forward, pulling Jonathan's attention. "Fine." It wasn't fine; none of this was fine. But Aaron was injured; even if he was downplaying it, she could see the way he kept opening and closing his hand, as though trying to stretch it out. He claimed it didn't hurt, but they still weren't certain the ichor wouldn't have a lasting effect.

And after events last night, having someone else in the picture with Ballantine would likely be for the best. She was the politic one, and she'd almost snapped at the man the night before; Aaron tried his best, but if Ballantine said something hurtful to him, he would respond in kind and be apologetic later.

And later would be too late: Jonathan might not have been sent in to replace them, but it could still happen. And then they might take Bother.

"You're lead, we understand," she said now to Jonathan, holding eye contact to make sure that he heard what she was saying. "But you don't know anything about this hunt, and we do. So you'll listen to what we say." She wasn't asking a question, and Jonathan was intelligent enough to know that.

"I'll want to see your notes," he said, which wasn't what she had been saying. Before she could argue, he looked at the watch on his wrist. "There are still a few hours left of the night, and I for one intend to spend it in my bed. We will meet for breakfast at eight-thirty, and discuss our next moves. Agreed?"

"Agreed," Rosemary said, and then stared at her brother until, grudgingly, he nodded.

Satisfied, Jonathan made his exit. The moment the door closed, Rosemary held up a hand to forestall anything Aaron was about to say.

"We don't have a choice."

"I know." He sounded as sulky as he'd been as a child, when something didn't go his way, but the sigh was 100 percent grown-up. "I know." He sat down on the bed as though his legs wouldn't hold him up any longer, then flopped backward, his head hitting the pillow with an audible thump. "It was my fault. I've been distracted." He lifted his head from the pillow then, staring at her in alarm. "We can't tell him about the other uncanny."

"God. No." She hadn't even thought of that, which was proof that she was distracted as well. Whatever the other uncanny wanted, if it was following them—following Aaron— that was nothing Jonathan needed to know, because if he knew, the Circle would know.

And if the Circle knew that they suspected a fey was here, was sniffing around her brother, neither of them would ever see another hunt. At best, they would be turfed out; at worst, they would end up in a small room somewhere, names erased, locked away for their own safety—and that of the rest of the world.

There was no good reason for the fey to pay attention to you, only bad.

Twenty-Two

DESPITE WHAT JONATHAN had said, there had been no point in going back to bed, even if Rosemary had thought she could sleep after the news; dawn light was already beginning to creep down the street, the sky outside shading from black to murky gray. Rosemary returned to her own room, and only after a reasonable amount of time had passed, which she mostly spent writing irate letters she knew she would never send, did she dress for the day and—leaving Bother to guard the room—meet her brother in the lobby.

"I don't think we'll be able to come back to this hotel," he said, standing to greet her. "It seems the maids have been talking."

"Hardly the first place to be glad to see us leave," she said. "Let me leave a note for Jonathan. The café down the street?" At his nod, she went to the front desk, noting that the clerk was indeed eyeing them with cautious distaste, but he took her note and promised to give it to the gentleman in question.

The café was quiet, only an older man seated in the back,

a newspaper open across his table and an empty plate pushed off to the side. Occasionally he would scowl at something, before turning the page.

Aaron waited until they were seated, and she had coffee in her hand, before asking, "How many letters did you write to the Circle?"

The urge to make a terrible face at her brother the way she had when they were children was almost overwhelming, and Rosemary put it down to the lack of sleep. But she took a deep sip of the coffee, savoring the bitterness, before she admitted, "Five."

His burst of laughter was almost worth the admission.

"Are you all right?" She had seen the way he was walking, lacking his usual easy stride.

"Eh. I feel as though I've been kicked in the stomach by a particularly obstinate mule, and gargled with sharp-ended rocks, but I'll live." He waited until the waiter had come by to take their order before continuing. "And yes, I'm very aware that if we'd killed the uncanny last night, instead of trying to get answers, we'd be heroes right now."

"Except for Mr. Congdon, asleep for the rest of his life."

"Ballantine's already written him off," Aaron said. "You know he has."

Rosemary hadn't known that, not until Aaron said it. But looking back over the events of the evening before, she thought he was probably right. He would put up a good facade in front of his wife, but he wanted this sorted and done with, and no longer disrupting his life.

"I don't regret what we did," Aaron said suddenly. "With what we knew . . . we had to at least give it a chance."

Before Brunson, they'd both believed, as they'd been taught, what they'd told Duarte the night before, that the uncanny were creatures of instinct, not logic. That they reacted rather than thinking things through, that even the ones who could speak, and make some show of rational behavior, were barely more than beasts themselves.

Some uncanny were like that, certainly. Most, possibly. But having the uncanny in Brunson work with them to stop a mutual threat had driven doubt into the idea that uncanny could only be stopped, not reasoned with.

She had known, had *known* that that doubt would come back to bite them.

"I agreed to the plan," she said. "We needed information. And Duarte deserved to know why the uncanny was following his children." She'd been there to kill it. But she knew what had been in Aaron's mind, because she knew her brother: he'd hoped there would have been a way to talk the uncanny down, to convince it to go away without harming anyone else.

She could see his expression change, his features going stiff, and sighed inwardly, aware that he'd somehow managed to read her thoughts on her face, again. "It's not sympathy for them," he said. "It's not—"

"I know." Her exasperation melted. She could yell at him, and he would feel bad for it, but it would change nothing. He was who he was. "Just . . ."

"Just stay out of the way and let you and Golden Jonathan clean everything up. I know." He looked decidedly unhappy at being left behind, and she couldn't blame him.

"We would still be chasing our own tail, without you," she

said, and meant it. Getting the children to talk, thinking of the trap, all of it, had his hand on it.

"I can be both hero and villain in this piece," he said, but that stiffness softened, just a little. "I am all right with taking the blame for this, Rosie. Let my reputation be useful for once."

"I'm not going to let you take the blame—"

"You're not letting me do anything. I was the one who came up with the plan; I was the one who was so curious I let an outsider get hurt, and the uncanny escape. Your only sin was listening to me, and they'll forgive you that."

She did not like the way his words sounded. "If you think for one second that I'm going to let you take the fall for this with the Circle, you're even more a fool than you sound."

His quick, bright grin caught her off-guard. "There's my spitfire Rosemary. And no fear, I've no intention of sacrificing myself, just letting the gossips focus on me for a bit, while the two of you finish things up."

"Three of us, you mean." The man in question had joined them at their table in time to hear the last bit of Aaron's comment. "I've always been curious to see a hound in action."

"I don't doubt that," Aaron muttered under his breath, wincing when Rosemary kicked him under the table.

"Of course," she said to Jonathan, mirroring his politely professional expression back at him. "Now"—and he signaled to a waiter to bring him a menu—"we need to make a plan."

Three hours later, Rosemary hated the plan.

No, she thought, watching Jonathan standing in the

morning sunlight, his jacket perfectly tailored, his hair perfectly coifed, his hands perfectly manicured, as though he'd never dug up a grave or tackled an uncanny, the plan was a good one. She didn't even hate Jonathan. She simply disliked him intensely just then.

They were standing on the lawn a few feet before it sloped down to the stone wall, Ballantine and Jonathan standing next to each other, Rosemary was a few steps away, with Bother between them. It was almost the same as they'd stand, her and Aaron, except Jonathan laid on the charm like her brother could never do.

"Molosser hounds were bred for the single purpose of eradicating the uncanny," he was explaining to Ballantine. "They're intelligent, but fierce, and once they have the scent, they never let it go."

Rosemary ground her teeth in impatience. She had wanted to start immediately; Jonathan had insisted that they report to Ballantine first. "We have to make nice," he'd said, and so that's what they were doing.

Certainly, Mr. Ballantine was eating it up with a spoon, and Rosemary supposed she should be watching more carefully, taking notes on how to properly handle a benefactor. But she was too annoyed with the way Jonathan was pretending to be the one handling Botheration.

She hoped that he didn't try to take actual physical control as well. That would not go over well, with her or Bother, and she wasn't sure how the Circle would manage the inevitable results.

On the other hand it might be worth it, just to see what his face would look like with his wrist caught between Bother's powerful jaws, being gently—or not so gently—shaken back and forth.

"It's certainly a rugged-looking beast," Mr. Ballantine was saying, eyeing Bother the way someone might a side of beef when planning a dinner party. "I don't suppose you'd be open to breeding him with a local bitch?"

"Molosser bloodlines are closely kept," Rosemary said before Jonathan could promise something he had no authority to give. "The breeders are all in Germany, and there is not enough money in the world to risk my upsetting them."

The Circle could not take Bother away, probably. But the breeders absolutely could. They bestowed hound pups, and they could remove them just as easily.

Jonathan gave her a sideways look, but she had said nothing untrue, nor had she been impolite about it.

Ballantine, stymied, switched direction. "And you say that it will be able to hunt down this thing? Even though it escaped you once before?" There was a definite sneer implied in that, and Rosemary bristled.

"I have seen Bother track an uncanny through wind, snow, and rain," she said. "But he is also deeply loyal and protective, and Aaron and Captain de Peña had both been injured. Protecting them became his priority."

If she had told him to, if she had given the order, Bother would have continued the hunt. But she had chosen not to. That had been their second mistake, and the one Rosemary, not Aaron, had to own.

"But we have an advantage we did not have before, thanks to that attempt," Jonathan said smoothly. "The hound was able to injure the uncanny." Jonathan withdrew a small, kerchief-wrapped chunk from a leather case and peeled back the edges of the kerchief, showing it to Ballantine, who leaned in, then pulled back with a look of disgust on his face.

Rosemary couldn't blame him. The chunk of skin they had cut from the arm before rewrapping it for Manny was becoming particularly pungent, and not even Jonathan's keeper-box could prevent the stench from rising, once opened.

Jonathan turned with the piece in his hand, obviously planning to offer it to Bother. Rosemary flirted with the idea of letting him go ahead, making a fool of himself in front of Ballantine when Bother refused his command, but that would do no one any good, least of all the Harkers.

They needed Jonathan, right now. Which was a lowering thought, but no less true for it.

"Allow me," she said, placing her hand over his, covering the cloth and chunk without flinching. She met his gaze, willing him to accept her intrusion.

Thankfully, understanding flickered in his eyes, and he relinquished the chunk of flesh without complaint.

"All right, Bother," she said, stepping forward away from the two men. "Come." When the beast padded over to her, she bent carefully, aware that she was being observed, and offered the kerchief and its contents at nose level. "Bother. Suchen. Suchen."

Bother had learned his commands in both English and German; Rosemary was simply being petty about it.

The hound lowered his head, nostrils flaring. He had likely been able to scent it even in the keeper-box, but he also knew where it had come from and that there was no threat from a patch of skin and flesh, unconnected to a larger body.

"Yes, you took a chunk off it, but it's still out there," she told him quietly. "The thing that hurt Aaron." She had no idea how much of what she said the hound actually understood. It didn't matter; he would do what she asked him to do, because that was what he had been trained to do.

She waited, hand outstretched, until Bother's large, blunt head pulled away from the offering and looked south across the creek, then back up at the house, and then back toward the creek again.

His head tilted, his upright ear flopping over briefly before he blinked, a slow movement, and looked back at Rosemary again.

He was waiting for his orders.

Her heart started to race. "Botheration. Hunt."

The hound set off, quickly enough that neither Huntsmen had a chance to say farewell to Ballantine. When she looked over her shoulder, he was standing there, watching them go.

"I am sorry about all this," Jonathan said, striding beside her.

"I know." Rosemary didn't mean to be brusque. She suspected he was sincere in his apology, but she wasn't certain what he was apologizing for—the takeover of their hunt? The way Ballantine had ignored her once Jonathan appeared, speaking only to him? The way he'd tried to play the part of Botheration's handler, despite having no idea how to command the hound? All of the above, or none of it?

Another time, she would care. Right now, her entire focus was on Botheration, forging ahead of them at a steady pace. Her knives were a comforting presence against her skin, the swing of her coat weighted by the pistol secreted there.

The grass looked bare, the trees innocent of menace,

but she knew, even before Botheration paused, that this was where they'd encountered the uncanny last night.

"There should be more blood here," Jonathan said, dropping to one knee to poke at the grass. "You don't cut off an arm and not lose a great deal of blood."

"Ichor," she corrected him. "It burned Aaron's hand, made him ill." His not remembering that made her angry; they'd told him all this over breakfast, her brother reluctantly showing the still-blistered skin on his right hand.

"And the civilian, did he bleed?"

"No. A broken arm, cracked ribs. Nothing broke skin."

"So any trace we find will belong to the uncanny."

"My hat is green, I'm not," she said with some asperity, pleased when the tips of his ears flushed red.

"I'm accustomed to speaking my thoughts out loud, and unaccustomed to having a partner. You will have to forgive me."

He was owed an apology as well, for her snappishness, but Rosemary couldn't find it in her to care.

She moved past him, catching the hound's attention with an uplifted hand. "Bother. Move on. Hunt."

With one last sniff of the ground, the hound lifted his head and took in a deep breath, practically gulping the air. Then, with a rough shake of his body, he took off at a fast clip toward the creek, the two Huntsmen having to run to keep up.

The moment Rosemary and Jonathan left the table, Aaron regretted agreeing to stay behind. It wasn't that he didn't think they were perfectly capable: he knew they were. It just felt wrong, her going off on a hunt without him.

Their waiter, his hands balancing the dirty crockery, lifted his chin toward where Rosemary and Jonathan were leaving together. "That your sister's fella?"

"Dear God, no." Aaron admitted his reaction might have been slightly overdramatic, but the thought of Rosemary going sweet on Scheinberg was vaguely horrifying. Thankfully, he was reasonably certain she had more sense and better taste than that. "No, we work together."

The man gave a conspiratorial smile. "Wouldn't be the first time a man's brought a coworker home and he ended up a part of the family."

Aaron frowned, both at the thought and at the way the waiter had suddenly become overfamiliar. Thankfully, his mood communicated itself, and the man scurried away, one hand placed protectively over the stack of dishes.

Left alone, Aaron poured himself another cup of tea, his frown deepening when he realized that was the last of the water in the pot. Since freshening the pot would require him calling the waiter back over, Aaron resigned himself to this being his last cup.

Rosemary wasn't sweet on Jonathan, was she? He hadn't thought she was interested in men at all, like that, but the idea, once in his head, wormed into his thoughts and wouldn't let go. They'd grown up around the Circle; she knew any number of eligible young men among the Huntsmen. But too many had gone off, either assigned other territories or, more recently, loaned out to European Circles to supplement the Huntsmen there. Nobody knew when they'd be coming home—or if.

"But Golden Jonathan, Rosie?" he said to himself, folding his napkin and placing it on the table before pushing his chair back to leave. "You could do so much better."

On returning to his room, he had thought to finish his novel while waiting for Manny to get back to them with the results of his exam. But the silence of his room quickly became too much to bear, the novel taunting him with characters who took action, while he sat in a chair and did nothing.

Tossing the book aside, he paced the room, the carpet underneath his feet muffling the noise of his steps, the artificial warmth of the air pressing against him, until he felt as though his skin might crack open and his insides flow out.

He was thinking too much, Rosemary would say. Chewing the meat too hard, his father had called it, when he was younger and working himself into a headache. His father had understood him. At the time, it had been a comfort. Now it was another weight.

His father was the reason nobody trusted them. Andrew Harker, who had killed his own wife.

Nobody said that. Not out loud. Officially, their mother had died on a hunt. Officially, their father had died from injuries sustained during that same hunt, the implication that he had gained those injuries trying to protect her. A tragedy, those poor children, left all alone. Poor Rosemary, left to be guardian to her little brother, the one everyone suspected (knew) was a throwback. Useful certainly, but still, keep an eye on him.

They would never have questioned Rosemary's report on Brunson, if it weren't for him. How many other reports had they scrutinized, looking for something held back, something omitted?

Had their parents felt the same scrutiny? All because of him?

"Enough." His pacing took him to the case that held their hunting tools, set at the foot of his bed, and he stared at it a long moment, not really thinking anything in particular, a vague white space filling his brain.

He lifted the lid, even though he knew the inventory by heart. Rosemary's bow was in there, unstrung and inert, arrows bundled by its side, a pot of resin for the string. There were more bullets in there, of various makes, and a cloth roll of throwing knives, as well as a longer knife, long enough to almost be called a sword.

He thought about taking it out, making sure the edge was still sharp, but he'd done that already, before they left home.

There was nothing to do. No one to speak with. Nowhere to go.

Aaron did not know what to do with his body.

If he stayed here, trapped within the room's walls, he thought he might go mad.

He grabbed his coat and hat, left the room, dropped his key off with the old man behind the desk, and headed outdoors.

It was warmer than it had been on previous days, although the threat of a late cold snap would linger for a few more weeks. He left his coat open, muffler hanging around his collar, and turned his face up to the sun, spring-weak but welcome.

The parklet across the street drew his attention again, and he hesitated before resolutely turning and walking in the opposite direction. He was supposed to be staying out of trouble, not looking for it.

Aaron had noted the hodgepodge of stores when they had first come to town, but they'd had no chance to explore. They never did, too occupied with the hunt and then rarely feeling the urge to linger once it was done. Now he drifted toward the town center, drawn by the bustle. Remembering the encounter with the pickpocket, he stayed alert to anyone who came too close or seemed to have ill intent. But people were content to ignore him, focused on their own business, and after a few minutes, he eased up. Women strolled, arm in arm, obviously enjoying the morning sunlight. A gaggle of boys who likely should have been in school knocked past him, one of them calling out a hasty "Sorry, mister!" as they disappeared into the Woolworth's.

It had been a while since he'd simply wandered, with no plan behind it. He strolled the aisles of the Woolworth's, then browsed through a bookstore and had his shoes shined until there was no speck of dirt or dust remaining, tipping the boot-shine boy generously enough the man doffed his hat in thanks. He had thought that being out and about would settle his soul, but something restless and ugly was still stirring sluggishly in his breast.

His sister was on a hunt. Without him.

Never mind that he knew why he was not there, that he had been the one to recuse himself. If he had insisted on accompanying them, Rosemary would have supported him. The uncanny had already proven itself dangerous, even wounded; three Huntsmen would be better than two.

He opened and closed his hand again, feeling the lingering

effects in the way his muscles did not quite want to respond. No, better he stay off this hunt, at least for now.

The restless and ugly feeling, having no care for logic, remained.

He needed to do something. Anything.

Without consciously deciding, he found himself walking back toward the hotel, then crossing the street and entering the little park. It hadn't rained, the grass should not have been any greener, and yet it was. He paced slowly along the path, pausing to inspect several of the bushes and trees.

They, too, were greener, tiny buds of leaves only just beginning to unfurl.

It might simply be the warmth of the day, of a few days further into spring. Nothing unusual, nothing uncanny.

Or.

Aaron reached a finger to one of the buds, watching as the slender twig trembled in response to the touch.

Or the sudden burst of growth might be due to uncanny influence.

One of the signs of the fey was out-of-season greening. That was what the books said. There had been no verified sightings in decades, at least on American soil. Europe, with its quillwork of borders and boundaries, would be easier for the fey to slip in and out of. But even there, if they were there, they stayed silent, out of the way.

The quiet in the aftermath of Brunson abided. They abided by the treaty. They did not interfere in human affairs. They did not stalk Huntsmen.

They could not know that he had been using magics.

Aaron was almost able to make himself believe that. Almost.

––––––––––

"Mr. Harker." Benedita Ruiz Vaz was not pleased to see him on their doorstep. She eyed him the way one might a dog you were not certain of, and she did not open the door all the way, nor did she invite him in.

"I'm terribly sorry for arriving like this." He wasn't sorry, but Rosemary said some lies were better than the truth, and he thought this might be one of those. "I was hoping to speak with the captain."

The woman studied him, her dark eyes shaded and suspicious. Aaron met her gaze, blinking slightly to keep it from becoming a contest. He supposed he should say something else, coax his way in, but instead he waited, watching.

Finally, she came to a decision, stepping back and opening the door all the way.

"You are not to upset him."

"I understand." The man had taken a hard knock; she was being protective. He understood that. "But it's terribly important . . ." He hoped she wouldn't ask him what he needed to speak with her husband about, because then he'd tell her, and she'd boot him out the door. But she simply sighed and turned away, walking down the hall in the assumption that he would follow without question.

So he did.

The captain was sitting in a leather club chair that looked woefully out of place in the sunroom, with its white-painted furniture and delicate cushions, as though an elephant had wandered into the garden. His arm had been rebound into a more professional-looking sling, and the way he was sitting told Aaron that his ribs were still giving him pain, but his expression was more welcoming than his wife's.

"Aaron. You came alone?"

"We are not always joined at the hip," he retorted. "She is following up another lead. But I hoped to speak with you"—he glanced back at de Peña's wife—"and your children?"

The captain's mouth tightened slightly at that, but he nodded. "'Nita, could you fetch them, please?"

Aaron waited until he sensed that she had left, then said, "She doesn't like me much."

"She's mostly upset with me. But she doesn't like expressing it. What is it you want to ask my children?"

He wasn't quite sure. Asking to speak with them had been a move of impulse, not planning. "I think we were wrong. About what the uncanny wanted, why it was here."

"You think—what?"

"I think we went down the wrong path." Saying the words made him feel more confident that he was right, the restless movement inside him stilling, like Bother scenting the air. "But I need to talk with them."

"Miss Daniella. Master Joe." He greeted them solemnly, remembering to use the name the boy preferred. They nodded back, after a glance at their mother as though to make sure it was acceptable. She still looked unhappy but made no complaint. "If it's all right with you, I'd like to ask you a few more questions about the Good Friend."

"Don't call it that." The girl, her lower lip stuck out slightly, sounded angry. "It's not good. It hurt Papa."

"Sweetheart. It's all right."

"No." And she burst out with something in what Aaron assumed was Portuguese, although he couldn't understand any of it.

"Daniella Maria!" The outburst was enough to make the girl hang her head, but Aaron suspected the rebuke would not last long, nor change whatever she was feeling.

"You understand why we say things like that, don't you, Miss Daniella?" he asked her "Because we know that they have power, power we don't, and so we speak of them politely, and to not draw their attention. It doesn't mean we actually think they are good."

He had both children's attention now.

"We call creatures like that the uncanny. Some of them are—" He couldn't in honesty say good. "Some of them are not bad. Some of them are. But mostly they muddle along, alongside us. Doing the best they can."

His teachers would be horror-struck at his words. He wasn't even sure Rosemary would approve, for all that she preferred to leave things like brownies and dryads alone until they caused actual trouble.

"But it hurt Papa."

"Yes. It did. And I'm trying to find out why. But to do that, I need to know why it's here. Your papa said that it usually lives in the ocean."

"On the coast," Joao said. "They live in the deep waters, but sometimes swim with ships and keep them safe. And you have to be careful not to catch them in your nets, because then they get mad. Did . . . Papa, did you catch one in your nets?"

"Your papa has not been near a net in a very long time," the captain said, his voice soft.

"We haven't been near the sea in a very long time," Daniella said, and for a moment Aaron thought that she was agreeing with her father; then the wording she had used caught up with his thoughts. Not "you haven't been," but "we."

Was she referring to her family having moved away from the seaport? Or—

"Do you like the sea?"

The girl shrugged, looking down at the carpet again, as though it was far more fascinating than any conversation they might have.

"Joe. Daniella. Do you miss it?"

"I did, at first," Joao admitted. "The smell, and the sound of the birds overhead. Papa took me on a voyage once. I got to help with the offering when we left the dock." He sounded like it had been one of the highlights of his young life.

"I miss my friends," Daniella said, and her brother nodded agreement.

"You haven't made new friends here?"

There was a pause, neither child looking up.

"Not at first," Joao admitted. "The others . . ." He shrugged, not quite managing the nonchalance he was aiming for.

Aaron lifted his gaze, catching the captain's eye. The other man frowned, then seemed to realize what Aaron was asking for and nodded once. Quietly, he took his wife's elbow, indicating that they should leave the room. She made a sound of protest, and the children swung around to look up in alarm.

"Your mother and I need to have a conversation. It's all right, filhos. You answer Mr. Harker's questions."

Two pairs of young eyes watched as their parents left the room, the door closing softly behind them.

"Your parents love you very much."

"Yes," Joao said, as though that should be obvious. "Don't yours?"

"My mother died when I was just a little older than you. My papa died soon after." When was a lie not a lie? Their father was effectively dead to the world, and certainly dead to his children. The one and only time they had tried to see him, it had taken three orderlies to calm him down afterward.

They had never gone back.

"You had trouble making friends at first, you said?"

"They made fun of us," Daniella said. "Because Papa was a fisherman."

"Because we're Portuguese," Joao said. "Where we lived before, so was everyone else. But here, we don't look like them. We don't know the same things they do."

Something in Aaron's gut squeezed in unwilling recognition. Different reasons, different causes, but oh, he remembered.

"But we're learning," Joao said, almost defiantly, as though expecting Aaron to argue with him. "Mr. Franklin is teaching us. And Father Adam."

"And Mrs. Ballantine," Daniella added. "She taught Mama and me both. And it became so much easier then."

Aaron sat back in his chair, missing pieces slotting into place, previously tangled thoughts suddenly snapping into clarity. The children weren't just the connecting point; the uncanny was going after people who *befriended* the children. But why?

And, more urgently, who else?

Twenty-Three

ARON RETURNED TO the hotel to discover that while Rosemary and Jonathan had not returned, there was a message for them from van Horn, the coroner.

"He was most urgent you get it right away. Made me repeat the message twice, to make sure I had it right." The clerk sounded put out, his competence having been challenged, but Aaron was in no mood to sooth his ruffled feathers.

He refolded the paper, his gaze resting on the simple clock ticking away time across the lobby. The message had been simple enough: van Horn had finished his exam, but he did not say what the results were.

The man did love to make a presentation.

Aaron should wait. Huntsmen worked alone, or with a chosen partner. But there was a structure and order to be followed, a chain of command as real as any the military might impose. And Jonathan had made it quite clear that the Harkers were not to make any decisions on their own anymore, that he was leading this hunt.

Jonathan and Rosemary weren't back yet.

"But they don't know what I know," he said quietly, arguing with a voice that sounded a great deal like Rosemary's. And he had no way to reach them, to tell them to hurry, or ask Jonathan's permission to go ahead.

Aaron made a face, the taste of that sour in his mouth.

He crammed the note into his pocket and passed the man behind the desk a coin of appreciation before turning on his heel and heading back out.

The address in the message was the next town over, but Rosemary and Jonathan had taken the automotive. He could go and come back with the results—but not if he waited for the trolley. He scraped through the remaining cash in his wallet, then walked to the hiring stand and acquired a driver to take him to his destination.

"Not many folk wanting to go to the morgue."

"No, I suppose not." Aaron looked out the window, hoping the driver would take the hint and stop talking. Thankfully, after a few more nonsensical comments and Aaron's terse responses, the driver subsided into silence for the remainder of the trip.

Exiting the cab, Aaron looked up at the building in front of him. Like so many buildings in town, it was built of a weathered red brick, looking rather as though it had been there for a hundred years and planned on attaining at least a hundred more.

There was a small metal plaque by the door that announced that this was the location of Middlesex (West) Morgue, and to ring the bell for entrance.

Aaron did so and then waited. And waited.

Finally, the door opened, and a man stuck his head out, a scowl on his face. His hair was stone white, his skin coal black, and his body was wrapped in a leather apron that had definitely seen better days.

"Yes?"

"Here to see Emmanuel van Horn."

"Oh. Right." The man stared at him a moment longer.

Aaron swallowed a sigh. "May I come in?"

"Oh. Right." The man backed up, holding the door open for Aaron to enter.

The man, who never introduced himself, gestured for Aaron to follow him down a Spartan, if clean, hallway. Overhead electric lamps flickered faintly, casting more shadows than they provided light, and the flooring under their feet echoed the tap tap tap of their shoes against off-white painted walls.

Van Horn had set up shop in a windowless, featureless room, looking up from his work when Aaron came in.

"Ah, young Harker."

Van Horn hadn't changed at all since Aaron had seen him last: a tall, rounded man, whose shaggy hair constantly fell over his wire-rimmed spectacles, and no amount of pomade ever seemed to help.

"Your sister not with you?"

"She's busy."

"Hmph."

"She will be sorry to miss your presentation." That was a lie; Rosemary was a champ at digging up bodies, and never flinched at a corpse, but there was something about the thought of them being cut up that made her turn pale. She would have come, she wouldn't have allowed herself to make excuses, but she would not have enjoyed it.

"Yes, well. As well she should. But this was a fascinating piece you gave me. I don't suppose we've access to the rest?"

"Not yet."

"Pity, a pity."

"Your findings?"

"Yes, yes, come over here, let me show you."

Aaron had no such hesitations about seeing bits cut open, so long as he was not required to touch it. His hands clasped firmly behind his back, he leaned over the table to see what van Horn was so excited about.

"Fascinating bit, aquatics. We know so little. But yes, aquatic, probably deep sea. You said the family it attached itself to was Portuguese?"

"Yes."

"Hmm, so yes, lamiak, almost certainly, although it's impossible to be certain of the exact species, even with the country of origin. Too many of 'em showing up, crammed into the bulkheads and holds of cargo ships like rats jumping continents. As though we didn't have enough of our own to worry about." He barked a laugh, then dragged a cloth across his mouth before discarding it in a half-filled bin beneath the table. "Sirens, sailors call 'em, all the way back to the ancients. Mermaids, if you want the fanciful term. Though there are all sorts, most of 'em we haven't categorized yet. See the coloration?" And he poked at the skin with a slender metal tool, lifting it so skin caught the overhead light, reflecting pale blues and greens. "I'd wager in the water, it turns one way or another, you won't be able to see it." Aaron blinked, but before he could parse that, the examiner went on. "Not scaled, definitely mammalian, but the skin's elastic, a layer of fat underneath, like a seal. Definitely deep sea, not our usual thing. Surprised it lasted as long as it did on land. Can't imagine what drove it here."

Aaron thought he could.

"Weren't sirens supposed to be beautiful women?" The face still haunted him, but the arm, cut open and dissected, made his injured hand itch.

"Hm, yes. Doubtful it could actually change species, we've yet to encounter anything that could do that, but you said the song made you cotton-headed?"

Aaron nodded.

"So hypnosis, make men think it was a beautiful maiden, men retell that as a song that makes them lose their minds because who wants to admit you went mad for a monster. The stories all come from somewhere, young Harker, you know that."

As scolds went, it was mild, and Aaron ignored it.

"So now you've an uncanny running about—or swimming about—with only one arm. You've gone and made it angry, young man."

"It was already angry," Aaron retorted. "It's killed one man, and sickened another into a coma."

"Hmm. Venom? That's fascinating. The claws did not seem designed to deliver it, did you happen to see its teeth?"

"Its blood burns."

"What? Oh, fascinating. Did you see it happen?"

In answer, Aaron unfolded his fingers from his palm and extended his hand to be seen.

"Oh. Oh dear." Van Horn tsked. "Young Harker. Idiot boy. Come here and let me deal with that."

"It's fine."

"Are you a medical doctor? You are not. Sit."

Aaron, grumbling, sat on the indicated metal stool and waited while the older man gathered a bottle of a clear liquid and a long cotton swab. "Be thankful it hit your hand and not your face. You're going to have some scarring."

Aaron shrugged, then cursed as the wetted swab hit his skin.

"Calm down, keep your hand steady," van Horn ordered. "Tell me how your sister is doing. Has she cast off her senses and run to join Miss Paul and her militant maidens yet?"

That made Aaron laugh even as the swab swept across his skin a second time.

Rosemary was not enjoying the expression on Jonathan's face as they came out the other side of the second, deeper creek, and she certainly wasn't laughing at it. That would have been crass and cruel. But she might have felt a little warm amusement, hidden as she bent to unlace her boots and slip off her sodden stockings, replacing them with dry ones drawn from the pocket of her coat.

Bother, briskly shaking out his own soaked fur, moved up the bank, waiting for them to be ready to move again.

"You didn't think to warn me?" Jonathan asked, looking down at his water-soaked boots.

"You didn't think that hunting a water-based uncanny might lead to wet feet?"

He looked up at the trees lining the hill above them, lacking a response to that. At least he'd had the sense to wear sturdy walking shoes, even if they were too short to keep the water out. Rosemary finished relacing her boots, shook her skirt back down over her ankles, and stood up. "All right, Bother. Go."

Released, the hound started forward again, not with an energetic leap, but a steady, almost deliberate pace, ignoring the squirrels who yelled at them from high-up branches. His nose dipped to the ground every now and again, but more often he sniffed at the air and scanned his surroundings, ears alert. A hound didn't rely on a single sense, but rather all of them working in concert. And, Rosemary had always suspected, something more. Like Huntsmen, hounds were not only what they seemed.

"I'm surprised they didn't send you overseas," Rosemary said, continuing the conversation they'd been having as they made their way up the opposite bank. A number of younger men had gone, the unrest in Europe creating opportunities for uncanny incursions the local Huntsmen were too stretched-thin to handle.

"I was asked. I said no."

"Really?"

"That surprises you?"

"A little." A great deal, actually. She would have thought he would leap at the opportunity to go. "No interest in hunting the old country uncanny?"

"No interest in the old country at all." She must have

looked surprised, because he shrugged and went on. "Europe will continue to squabble endlessly; it's their history and their nature. But that doesn't mean we should spend our lives worrying about it. And we certainly shouldn't spend our lives on it."

Rosemary frowned. "You endorse President Wilson's nonintervention policy, then."

His quick glance of surprise did not go unnoticed, but she kept her peace, waiting to see what he would say.

"I do."

He didn't ask what her opinion was, and she didn't expect him to. Even fellow Huntsmen who otherwise accepted her competence often failed to consider that she might know as much—or more—on a topic and have opinions. But it was good to at least be able to talk with someone on these topics. Aaron would rather disappear into a novel than read the news, much less discuss it. And the ladies groups back home in New Haven were more focused on local politics, and the question of the Vote, than what was happening thousands of miles away.

Rosemary had learned to form her own opinions and keep them to herself.

Squinting into the distance, she could make out the shadows of farmland, the fields still barren from the winter. She had no idea what they might grow here, or when planting might begin.

The hound sniffed the air once, then led them at an angle across the meadow, cold sunlight dappling the dirt and making Rosemary wish she'd brought a hat, no matter how much of a nuisance it would have become.

"The Circle thinks it will be war," Jonathan said suddenly.

"And how is it that you know what the Circle thinks?"

"You know how."

She did. He was being groomed for greater things, aspirations to a position in Boston or Ohio or farther west. Someday, possibly, if he lived that long, a seat in the Circle itself.

He looked at her, then looked out across the meadow, as though his life depended on studying the horizon. "You could be, too," he said.

A rude noise escaped her, in surprise. "A woman?"

"It's a modern world. Why not?"

It was an amusing thought, and Rosemary allowed herself to entertain it for a moment. But they both knew that Aaron would never be accepted into a position of leadership, even if Rosemary were to scrape her way in. And she wouldn't leave him.

"I'd thought a hound hunt would be different," Jonathan said, mercifully changing the subject. "More . . ."

"More action, more snarling and biting and victorious howling?"

He laughed, pausing to shake his foot as though to dislodge a pebble. "I suppose so, yes."

"There's some of that, eventually. Especially the howling. But hounds are trackers more than fighters."

"But they do fight. I mean, I've heard stories. . . ."

"From Huntsmen who worked with hounds? Or those who saw them in action once, or heard stories of seeing them take down an uncanny with one snap of their jaws?" She could hear the tone in her voice and attempted to soften it. "Hounds aren't weapons, Jonathan. Bother is our partner. You don't send your partner into a fight if you can avoid it."

She could see that he didn't understand. Even knowing better, he looked at Bother and merely saw a large dog. One with skills and training that complemented his own, that allowed him to do his job better, yes, but that was all he saw.

And that, she suspected, was why the breeders would never grant him a hound of his own.

Maybe this hunt would teach him to see otherwise.

And more likely not, she heard her brother's voice say with a sniff.

To each their own. Jonathan was welcome to his office ambitions. She would stay in the field, with Aaron and Bother. Doing what they did best.

Ahead of them, Bother had paused at a ditch, nosing carefully at the dried grasses around it. His square head turned, looking back at her without turning his entire body, and she saw the glint of something red deep in his eyes.

"He's got something."

"How can you tell?" she heard Jonathan ask even as she pulled the knife from her left arm sheath and moved forward cautiously. The ground had gone from dry meadow to a softer, wetter feel, and she placed her boots carefully.

Bother waited patiently until she'd reached him, then nosed again at the ground and stepped aside to let her see what he'd found. It was a puddle of something, not quite a liquid, not quite a solid. Remembering how the ichor had burned Aaron, she approached it cautiously.

"Don't touch it!" Jonathan said, and she paused a second to send a prayer up for patience.

"My apologies," he said when he'd caught up with her. "That was unnecessary."

"It was."

He'd found a stick, an inch thick and the length of his arm, that he used to poke at the puddle. The not-quite-liquid clung to the wood but did not sizzle or burn.

"Is it blood?" she asked. "Or some other bodily fluid?"

"It's too thick to be blood. But there's too much of it to be spit, unless it has larger reservoirs. Did you notice large cheek pouches?"

"We were a little busy at the time," Rosemary said acerbically, but she was trying to remember. "The face was . . . attractive." She felt somewhat embarrassed that that had been her first thought. "Scaled, or skin textured so it looked like scales, but the face itself was rounded. So perhaps, yes. I wonder—"

A low rumble interrupted their discussion, and they both stilled. Bother had shifted forward, all four legs braced under him and his head up, his erect ear on a swivel.

"It's near," Rosemary said, keeping her voice just above a whisper, to keep it from traveling. She felt rather than saw Jonathan draw a pistol, then the faint sound of a safety switch being flicked off.

"We kill it," he said, and Rosemary nodded her understanding. It hadn't been a question.

Twenty-Four

*I*T WAS WELL past lunchtime, and Rosemary and Bother—and Jonathan—still had not returned. Aaron sat in a club chair in the lobby, a newspaper open on his knee and a glass of tea on a small table by his elbow, but he hadn't read a word of the print, nor taken more than a sip of his drink.

He was not worried. He wasn't. Worry would suggest that he thought Rosemary and Bother couldn't take care of themselves, and he knew they could.

He even knew that Jonathan could take care of himself, and that the three of them together were a match for nearly anything they might come across.

But he, Aaron, wasn't there. And he should have been. For years, it had been first Rosemary and Aaron, and then Rosemary, Aaron, and Bother.

It was his fault he wasn't there. If something happened to them, that would be his fault, too.

And there was nothing he could do except wait to hear back.

Unless he decided not to wait.

"Bad idea, Harker. Bad idea." He picked up the newspaper again, intending to immerse himself in the news of the week, but the print blurred and ran in front of his eyes, leaving him with a faint headache. He hated newspapers, with their irregular columns of ink and annoyingly large headlines. A novel didn't shout at you; it let you proceed at your own pace.

His pace was not to sit and wait.

Van Horn had confirmed not only that it was an oceanic uncanny, but that it was not one of the local uncanny, nor one that had been reported in the region before.

So it was possible—highly probable—that it had followed de Peña's people here.

That was not an uncommon thing. Van Horn had said it himself; people came and brought bits of their homes with them: their belongings, their stories, their superstitions . . . and the things that fed those superstitions.

Aaron folded the paper in two and let it rest in his lap, staring out across the lobby without actually seeing any of it.

Uncanny followed, and sometimes they changed when they came to the new world. Imps had been dangerous once; in America they had devolved into nuisances, backyard scavengers. Yellow dragons had taken to city life, curling themselves around chimney tops, causing massive fires when disturbed. Brownies had picked up new trades, the better to hide themselves among human habitations. An uncanny accustomed to tribute in exchange for protection . . . how would it react when that tribute ended?

Aaron shook his head, irritated at himself. The uncanny was not attacking de Peña, nor those dear to de Peña, and it had every opportunity, if the children were to be believed—

and Aaron did believe them. It was attacking those at a remove . . . .

His fingers drummed along the pad of newspaper on his lap, lower lip caught between his teeth and his eyes gazing at something far past the wall in front of him. Puzzle pieces, scattered across the table of his mind, slotted together, one after another.

The uncanny was attacking those who were helping the Vaz de Peñas fit into their new world.

His breath caught at the idea.

It was ridiculous, contrary to everything Aaron had ever been taught. Uncanny might use humans as protection, as food, as stolen labor. But they did not *care*. They did not form bonds with those humans.

But if they did . . .

It was a revolutionary thought. And like all revolutions, Aaron knew, it was dangerous. They'd omitted details from their last report because the Circle did not want to know, could not know anything that upset the status quo. The idea that uncanny could care? That they might feel *possessive* over some humans?

Aaron had no regrets for the uncanny he had killed over the years. They had been dangers to the humans around them, and Huntsmen existed to protect humanity. But what if there was a way to prevent that danger? If an understanding could be come to some way to head off violence before it erupted?

Admittedly, his first try here had not gone well. But the uncanny in Brunson had understood that they had a common enemy, proving hundreds of years of Huntsmen lore was wrong.

The treaty had once seemed impossible, after all.

Aaron stood, abandoning the newspaper on the chair. He could prove it, once and for all. He just needed to reach the uncanny before Rosemary and Bother did.

When Aaron was very young, he had asked a question that had seemed terribly obvious to him: Why did they hunt, when it would be easier to lay a trap?

The answer he had been given, that a hunt could target a specific uncanny, while a trap might catch anything, had never satisfied him, particularly once he learned of sigils and how they could be used, even knowing all the reasons why they should not be used.

"They're just tools," he said out loud, looking down at the markings he had drawn in the dirt before bending down to correct one line and extend another. He had learned the basics at his mother's knee, the sigils to dissuade someone from looking at a thing, to keep them away from danger, or let him know if someone had poked into his belongings. And if these were more complicated than those, major sigils to minor, the base was the same.

Rosemary would kill him. Slowly, with her bluntest knife.

But that didn't mean it was a bad idea.

And he knew the uncanny they were hunting, now, so he wasn't flailing about blindly, the way— He cut that thought off, focusing everything on the lines chalked into the damp brown dirt. Satisfied now that he had them correct, he put the stick of calcite into his pocket and withdrew the tiny scrap of flesh he had saved before giving the larger chunk to Rosemary. It was tiny, barely the size of his smallest fingernail, and carefully scraped of any of the goo that had burned him the first time, but that scrap was all that he'd need.

The sigil for calling, the sigil for holding, and something to bind a specific entity to the actions. It was simple, really. Simple and precise. No risk of catching the wrong uncanny, and it would not harm the one he sought, only bring and bind it, so they could talk, without it lashing out again.

And this time, he had found a place away from town, surrounded by nothing but fallow fields. Not even a farmer would come here, midafternoon on a cold spring day.

"Not every uncanny is a mindless beast; we know that now." He spoke out loud, as though Rosemary was there to be his sounding board. "And this one is showing logic in who it attacks, and how it attacks. And it didn't really try to hurt us; it ran away the first time, and again when it could have killed de Peña."

He ran a hand across his mouth, aware that his hand was cold and damp with sweat. Aaron knew he thought differently from most people, but that didn't mean he didn't think at all. Whatever he might believe about sigil use, what he was doing was dangerous, and doing it alone was the height of folly. He should erase the sigils, go back to the hotel, wait for Rosemary to come back. And then, if she agreed—he could convince her to agree—they could come do this together. With Bother.

Except Jonathan would never allow it, and Rosemary would not . . . Would Rosemary choose the Circle over her brother? Aaron didn't think so, he couldn't let himself believe so . . . but he also couldn't take that chance.

Before he would second- or third-guess himself, he dropped the piece of skin in the space between the two sigils, and—

He paused, feeling the skin of his arms and neck prickle, as though someone had run an invisible feather along them, and his bowels tightened, a sure sign that his body wanted him to run.

Instead, he stayed very still, breathing through his nose until the urge to flee subsided.

Something was watching him.

No, not something. Someone.

"Go away," he whispered at it. "I'm not bothering you— don't bother me."

His gaze fell to the sigils again. Sigils weren't magic. Not the kind that was forbidden. Not like what they'd seen in Brunson, where a human had unleashed old magics, the kind that were definitely forbidden by treaty. There was no reason why the fey should be paying attention to him.

Throwback, a child's voice taunted.

Throat dry, Aaron breathed through the memory, replacing it with memories of his parents, bright and laughing as they retold stories of hunts past. Of Rosemary, her eyes half-closed as she concentrated with her bow. Of Jacob, teaching them how to track.

Huntsmen carried fey blood within them. But fey blood did not make them fey, did not define them. Not even him.

The presence didn't disappear this time, but it didn't seem to be coming closer, either. Aaron waited, forcing his breathing to calm, his heart to stop thumping quite so loudly.

"We kept quiet for your own good, too," he told the watcher. "If the Circle thought the treaty had been broken, they wouldn't be bound by it, either. Do you really want Huntsmen coming after you again?"

The last time was before Aaron's great-grandfather had been born, but the names of the dead were etched into stone, Huntsmen brought to see the giant slab at least once during their training. No one knew, or could say, how many of the fey had been destroyed, but estimates at the time said it was three for every two Huntsmen dead.

"Nobody won that war; nobody ever wins that war. That's why the truce happened. Don't do anything to break it."

Aaron wasn't sure if he was talking to the presence behind him, or himself, or the universe in general, but the feeling of something watching him eased slightly, and for only the second time in his adult life, he breathed a prayer of thanks.

He reached into his pocket again and pulled out a roll of matches, tearing one off and touching it to the striker until a tiny flame erupted, stinking of sulfur and ash. Before the breeze could kill it, Aaron shielded it with the cup of his free hand and knelt, lowering the flame to the piece of skin. He didn't need it to burn, just a little bit, enough for the sigils to use.

When the skin instead burst into flames, a cloud of putrid, greenish-gray smoke billowing into Aaron's face, he fell back on his heels, coughing, his eyes streaming with tears.

"Ugh. Ack." He turned his head to the side and spat, then worked more saliva into his mouth and spat again. It took him a moment to erase the taste out of his mouth, some faint bit of it still lingering on his tongue. When he returned his attention to the sigils, worried that the flame-burst would have ruined them, he was relieved to see that they remained intact, the smoke a thick cloud slightly larger than a billiard ball, swirling restlessly between them, the occasional tendril licking out, then being absorbed into the ball again.

He frowned. It shouldn't be doing that.

"Go," he told it. "Bring and bind."

As though they had been waiting for a command, several tendrils reached out again, narrowing and elongating until they snapped free of the ball and disappeared in ever-uncurling spirals.

An uncomfortable feeling stitched itself into his limbs. Sigils shouldn't require commands. Once drawn and given a focus, they had power. None of his reading had indicated major sigils worked differently.

Then again, he had never tried to use two in tandem before, either. That was likely it.

At least he was alone; if it went badly, it was only on him. And Rosemary would resurrect him just to kill him again.

Settling on the ground, he adjusted his coat so it protected his backside from the cold earth, then pulled out a knife and laid it down within easy reach before retrieving his pistol, making sure it was loaded and ready and placing it next to the knife.

Then he waited.

Rosemary was getting very tired of this uncanny and also had the vague suspicion that it was mocking them, as they followed it down into a thicket and then back out again.

Or rather, Jonathan and Bother followed it.

"Someone forgot to tell this uncanny it belongs to the deep sea," Rosemary said through gritted teeth as she yanked her skirt out of the clutches of yet another bramble. Paces ahead of her, Jonathan gave no sign of hearing, or slowing down, Botheration a few paces ahead of him and hot on the trail. A final tug, and she heard fabric tearing but couldn't worry about how ragged she would look at the end of all this. "Pants, Harker," she snarled at herself as she took off after them. "It's 1914. Next time care less about drawing attention, and wear pants."

They had been following the uncanny's trail through meadow and farm for over an hour now, if she judged the sun's position correctly, most often at a steady jog, dropping down to a walk when Bother had to pick up the scent again. Every inch of Rosemary's body ached, but she was only vaguely aware of it, the nervous tremor of the hunt overwhelming all else. And if it felt odd and uncomfortable to be hunting without Aaron, Jonathan's taller, more angular shape almost filled the hole.

Almost.

"I think it's in human form," Jonathan said when she caught up with him, Botheration in a wide-legged stance, body square and blunt muzzle lifted into the wind. "That's why the hound keeps losing the scent."

Rosemary wanted to snap a defense, but it was not a bad theory. Actual shape-shifters were rare, thank God, but if this uncanny shared ancestry with selkies or ushtey—or a nhang, God forbid—it was possible. She wondered what van Horn had made of the body part and if he'd been able to identify it.

She spared a moment to worry about what Aaron was doing, knowing full well that even if he'd had good intentions, there was no way he'd stayed in the hotel. Most likely, he had gone to pester van Horn. The old man was accustomed to him; Aaron would be fine.

"If it can shift, and it heads into town, we'll lose it. It must know that—why is it staying out here?" She heard the frustration in her voice, and from the way Bother's ear flicked backward, he could, too. Hunts were too often like this, rushing in without enough information, racing against the risk of more deaths. She hated it.

"You think it knows we're following?" Jonathan sounded surprised by the idea, and she wanted to hit him.

"Don't underestimate any uncanny," she said, watching Bother's head as it tilted, following something in the air. "They may not think the way we do, but they do think." A lecture, nearly word for word from their uncle, given when she was early twelve, her first knife heavy in her hands.

"They're not intelligent," he said. Then: "He's got something"—even as Bother's head went back, his jaw dropped open, and a deep, challenging howl rose from his throat.

"Holy mother of Jesus!" And she would have laughed at the way Jonathan nearly shot himself as he tried to cross himself with the hand holding his pistol, but Bother was moving again, and she was hard on his tail, skirts hiked nearly to her knee to keep from tripping.

"What the hell was that?" he shouted from behind her.

And she did grin then, a hard, fierce grin that she knew matched the one stretching Botheration's muzzle. "Exactly!"

The cry of a hellhound, telling its prey to beware.

Twenty-Five

WHEN HIS TIMEPIECE ticked over to the quarter hour, Aaron rose from the tree stump he had been using as a bench, letting his limbs unbend slowly, bringing feeling back into his extremities. Sitting had likely been a bad idea, but standing had become boring, and moving around too much was a worse idea; too much movement could spook the uncanny, and while the sigils might bring and bind it, he would not put the same faith in sigils he would in rope or ties.

But sitting risked being unable to move when the uncanny showed.

On the plus side, his unseen watcher had left, either because it had decided Aaron was no longer of interest, or it had been bored watching Aaron simply sit there.

If he was lucky, the watcher had been here on an unrelated matter and would have no further interest in Aaron or Rosemary. If so, Aaron would return the favor. Silence was in both their best interests: keeping themselves out of official notices, and the treaty intact.

The treaty had no name, it was simply The Treaty. Somewhere deep in the archives of the Circle there was a copy of it, allegedly written on unicorn hide. The terms had been simple: the fey would vacate human lands, and humans would refrain from the use of proper magics. Huntsmen had been given the responsibility of enforcing the terms on the human side. And they had, by means gentle and less so, until no sensible soul even considered magic possible.

And when an irrational soul ventured into areas they should not . . . that was the Huntsmen's responsibility as well. So it had been from the beginning; so it was now.

Aaron did not know who had been tasked with enforcing the terms from the fey side. He could only hope they would retrieve their wayward child soon, before anyone else noticed.

Someone like Jonathan, for example. Rosemary might argue that he wasn't a bad sort, but they'd known each other since they were teens, and Jonathan was a company man from the bones out. He'd told Rosemary months ago: they couldn't afford anyone in the Circle even thinking that the treaty had been broken from their side, much less the idea that the fey might. . . .

Even now, his brain stopped shy of thinking it directly, as though that would make it true.

"It would be foolish to think they've never had anyone poke their nose over," he told himself, arching his back until he heard something crack and pop. "So long as they don't have cause to think we've broken the treaty, and no one in the Circle has cause to think they've broken the treaty, everything will be fine."

He'd been telling himself that for months.

Aaron had just begun a series of shallow knee bends when

he heard it, a dry, coughing noise. Then another, definitely closer. Definitely not human. It could have been a mountain cat, or possibly a bear, but every instinct told him it wasn't.

Aaron glanced to where his knife and pistol lay on the ground a few feet away, trying to determine if he could reach them in time, and if he should even try.

Rosemary would definitely be using her bluntest knife, if she learned he'd done this again. But it had worked the last time . . . .

"I'm here to talk, not fight," he said, raising his voice to carry into the underbrush. He had to believe that the uncanny would understand him, that there was more driving it than animalistic rage. Experience told him it was possible. But his training was screaming at him to pick up a weapon, to be ready to kill, the moment an opportunity showed itself.

"We got off on a bad foot"—*arm*, his brain unhelpfully corrected—"but I just want to talk," he said again. He lifted his hands to show that he was unarmed, turning slowly in a circle, trying to determine where the sound had come from. "No games, none of your magic. If you kill me, Rosemary won't rest until she's taken your skin and re-covered a sofa with it. My big sister is fierce, and she holds a grudge. So why don't you just come out and talk to me? See if we can't settle this like civilized creatures?"

A rustle of leaves and the sound of something scraping across bark was the only response.

"Trying to scare me?" He didn't have to force a laugh. "Huntsmen don't scare that easy. We know you're dangerous. But so are we. And you have to know by now that we're not going to just go away."

The longer he talked without a response, the more he began to doubt. Had the uncanny in Brunson been an aberration, a sport, in its ability to use logic, to think beyond base impulses and needs? Had he been entirely wrong about what drove this uncanny?

There was silence, then another dry cough, this time coming from behind him. The uncanny had been circling. Looking for a point of attack? He should have left a note, so Rosemary would know where to come looking for his body if he didn't make it home.

"I'm sorry about, you know, the arm. That wasn't intended. Well, I didn't intend it, anyway. Bother takes protecting us seriously. But he's not here."

That . . . might not have been his wisest comment ever. Aaron was beginning to get irritated, the cold making his joints ache and the absence of Rosemary and Bother beside him leaving him feeling horribly exposed. He turned slowly, keeping his hands away from his body and lifting his chin so his voice would carry. "Answer me, damn you!"

A noise filled the air as though in response, but although the sound raised the hair on Aaron's arms, every mortal instinct warning him to run and hide, his rational mind recognized it.

He had just managed a heartfelt "Damn it, Rosemary!" when there was a fleshy thud, and a body crashed into the clearing, scrambling to its feet just as a hundred and ten pounds of red-eyed hellhound followed after it.

Cursing in three languages, Aaron dropped into a crouch and lunged for the weapons on the ground. His hand closed around the hilt of the knife just as the uncanny, curling in a move that human bodies could not mimic, swung its remaining arm at him, fingers scraping air inches from his face. He ducked again, rolling away from the uncanny, but it followed, that dry cough close enough to smell sweet-rot and brine coming from its breath.

Too long from the water, part of his brain observed, as the uncanny came for him again.

"Aaron!" Rosemary's cry was part fear, part surprise, and a sizable dash of irritation infused into his name.

"Less yelling, more helping," he managed to get out, slashing up with the blade in a desperate attempt to get the uncanny off him. It turned, and the shape shimmered, as though trying to disappear. *An illusion,* he thought, remembering what van Horn had said. Tricking the eye. He stabbed again, wildly, and felt the blade strike home, and suddenly the uncanny was inches from his face. Up close, the face was vaguely human in shape, but the eyes were thick black pools, without lash or brow, the nose more of a subtle snout over that wide, red-lipped mouth. Whatever song it had used to enchant him earlier either did not work twice, or it wasn't bothering.

"Get away," he heard Jonathan yell. "I don't have a clear shot!"

Then Bother was there again, massive jaws closing on the uncanny's intact shoulder, trying to tear it away from Aaron. The uncanny made that curving move again, sliding away from both of them. Aaron used the distraction to get a better grip on the knife, flipping it in his hand and stabbing up into the uncanny's abdomen, hoping to get lucky and hit something vital.

The uncanny let out a sound that hurt to hear, and Aaron

jerked away as liquid oozed from the wound, remembering all too vividly what had happened last time he came into contact with its bodily fluids.

"Damn," he swore, as the ichor coated his knife, sliding down the blade to the handle, and he debated the risk of holding on to it versus what it would do to his skin once it dripped off.

"Don't you dare shoot," Rosemary yelled, and Aaron looked up to see Jonathan across the clearing, arm outstretched, the pistol in his hand aimed directly at the uncanny—and Bother, teeth still dug in deep.

"Bother, leave it," Aaron said, wincing when his voice cracked like an eleven-year-old boy's. "Bother, leave it!"

Snarling, eyes lit like the fires of hell, Bother released his jaw hold and backed away, stiff-legged, hackles raised from neck to midway down his back. The uncanny, bleeding from the abdomen and already lacking one arm, looked for all the world like a sacrificial victim before the axe fell.

Given a clear shot, Jonathan couldn't miss.

But the sound of the pistol firing was matched by the uncanny pushing up and away from the ground with unnatural flexibility, a cannon-shot leap not away from the bullet, but *toward* it.

The uncanny went down, but so did Jonathan, pistol dropped to the ground, knees hitting first, then toppling forward, face down in the dirt.

And while the uncanny squirmed onto its side, scrabbling with one arm to get to its feet, Jonathan did not move.

"Hold still!" Rosemary's voice rang out, commanding enough that even knowing she didn't mean him, Aaron paused mid-action, then recovered himself with a quick head shake, grabbing his own pistol from the ground and training it on the uncanny.

"Rosie?"

"I'm fine." Her voice was firm, and you would have to know her well to hear the exhaustion underneath. "Check Jonathan!"

Aaron cast another glance at the uncanny, who had fallen back to its knees, upper body swaying. Bother was a menacing presence just behind it, lips pulled back from gums in a truly terrifying snarl. Deciding the dying uncanny was no longer a threat, he holstered his pistol and hurried to where the other man lay.

A quick hand to the base of Jonathan's throat, and another touch just below his nostrils, and Aaron frowned, then moved his hand down to rest over the man's heart, pressing down to feel the rise and fall of his chest through the layers of clothing.

"Aaron?"

"What did you do to him?" Aaron didn't bother looking at the uncanny, focused on getting the man's body situated, placing Jonathan's arms over his head and thumping his chest repeatedly, hoping to get his breathing started again.

"Come on, damn you, come on. Breathe!"

The sound of low, uncanny laughter reached his ears, something whispered in that horrible, beautiful voice, then the single retort of a familiar pistol. Rosemary, putting a final bullet in the uncanny's body.

"Aaron?" Rosemary's voice, tight and worried.

"Just . . . wait," he said, his words catching the rhythm of his hands, press and release, press and release, his arms and shoulders aching, counting under his breath and praying he wasn't doing it wrong, until there was a faint rattle in Jonathan's throat. When Aaron placed his hand under his nose again, there was the barest whisper of air being exhaled.

"He's alive," he said, sagging back on his heels in relief, then looked over his shoulder, noting the crumpled form on the ground behind his sister. "And you claimed the kill after all."

"Joint effort," she said shortly. "Don't think I'm not furious with you, whatever you were doing out here. Why isn't he waking up? Isn't death supposed to cure them?"

"Looks like we were wrong." He didn't mean it as flippant as it came out.

"We need to get him to a doctor."

Aaron looked back at the motionless man on the ground, calculating his weight, and groaned. "I don't suppose there's a handy wheelbarrow just lying around anywhere?"

"No such luck." But the grim lines on her face eased a little, and she whacked him on the shoulder as she came up next to him, checking for herself that Jonathan was still breathing. "You're going to have to carry him."

"Me? Why me?"

"Because you didn't just chase across half the county to get here, that's why."

As logic went, he couldn't argue with it. Getting to his feet, he whistled for Bother, who had been standing guard over the uncanny's corpse. "If we can build a travois, Bother can help me drag him back. We'll need a few branches green enough to bend, not break." The hound came to his side, nosing gently at Jonathan's still body as though to ask why the human wasn't moving.

"That's rude, Bother," Rosemary said. "What about the uncanny?"

"There's no way we can haul them both back. Cover it, and we can come back for it in the morning."

Nodding, Rosemary turned to go look for branches when she let loose with a string of curses that made Aaron blanch, even as both he and Bother sprang into defensive positions, half expecting another attack. But the clearing was empty.

Wait. Aaron blinked, as though that would change the scene in front of him, but the clearing remained empty, save for his kit, sitting by the stump.

The uncanny—the *dead* uncanny—was gone.

As unnerving as the disappearance was, Jonathan had to be their first priority. Aaron used his chalks to mark a few trees, so they would be able to come back in the morning and look, then loaded Jonathan's inert body onto the hastily built travois.

That lasted about halfway back to town; then Aaron did end up carrying Jonathan, half slung over his shoulder like a very long sack of wheat. They'd received more than a few odd looks as they came into the hotel, a hastily murmured lie about an old friend who had tried to drink his troubles away only appeasing a few of them.

Botheration's steely stare likely helped keep the others at bay. The last hint of red had thankfully faded from his eyes, but he was still a massively imposing beast when he chose to be.

Rosemary left them long enough to bustle up to the desk, tapping the bell for attention with enough arrogance only a fool would question her hastily rebraided hair or torn, muddied skirts.

"I need a message sent to Dr. Emmanuel van Horn." She took the pad of paper from the clerk's hand and wrote a quick note, then folded it into the offered envelope and passed it back, a bill tucked underneath. "Quickly," she said, and waited until the clerk nodded before turning back to the rest of her party.

"He's not getting any lighter," Aaron said under his breath as she joined them. "I say we take the elevator."

Rosemary glared at him, but since the alternative was hauling an injured man up several flights of stairs, she agreed.

They brought Jonathan to Aaron's room, Rosemary holding open the door and Botheration bringing up the rear. The hound's hackles had been raised since the uncanny's body disappeared, and once inside, he took up guard at the door, as though daring anything to come in after them.

Aaron laid Jonathan down on the bed, fussing briefly with arranging his arms and legs comfortably, then turned to Rosemary, his mouth open as though to launch into the apology she had refused to hear the entire journey back to town.

Rosemary still wasn't ready to hear it. Not yet. She went into the washroom and wetted a hand towel, then came back and laid it on Jonathan's forehead. His skin felt warm, as though he were running a slight fever. Remembering the cool, clammy look of Congdon's skin, she wondered if that was a good sign, or not. Every Sleeping Beauty legend said they were cool to the touch, as though in death, not warm or sweaty. But they hadn't been able to examine the victim immediately after contact, before.

Aaron was packing, muttering to himself. "How does it do it? It didn't bleed on him, or spit, or anything like that. How did it do it? What did we miss?"

Rosemary shook her head. She didn't know, and she didn't know that it mattered anymore. The thing was dead; Jonathan wasn't. He just needed to wake up.

She was not going to tell the Circle that they'd lost one of their shining stars to the Harkers' failure.

A knock on the door startled her, the dryness of the hand towel telling her she'd gotten lost in her thoughts for longer than she realized. She didn't look around, trusting Aaron to determine who was at the door and deal with it.

She pulled the coverlet up over Jonathan's still form, touching the back of her hand to his lips for a second, just long enough to determine that there was the faintest puff of breath there. Faint and faltering.

"Who's the patient, and are they alive or dead?"

"Alive, but not in any position to argue about your bedside manner," her brother said, ushering van Horn into the room.

The man must have lit things on fire to arrive as quickly as he did, although he looked cool and calm, as though he'd just strolled out of his own living room.

Rosemary gave up her spot to him, stepping back a few paces to watch as he set his black bag on the side of the bed and lifted the now dried towel off Jonathan's forehead, tut-tutting under his breath. "What happened?"

"The uncanny." She didn't want to say any more, and

thankfully he just nodded and didn't push. Instead, he opened his bag and rummaged through it, pulling out a series of tiny vials, stoppered with brown cork, and a handful of gleaming metal instruments she couldn't recognize and didn't want to know about.

"I just wanted to talk, damn it," Aaron said.

Rosemary didn't have the strength for this. Not now.

"Rosie?"

She hated that tone in Aaron's voice, the faint, wavering uncertainty that made him sound like the too-young boy he'd been, watching their mother be put into the ground. But she was also still furious with him—not for what he'd tried to do, that was pure Aaron and you might as well be angry with a flower for blooming—but for doing it without telling her, without backup, and without any apparent thought for how it would look to the Circle.

"Not now," she said, but reached out and took his hand in her own, squeezing once to let him know she wasn't mad at him, not forever. There was a hesitation; then he squeezed back: message received.

At least the uncanny was dead. She had put a bullet through its chest.

"Do you think there was another one," she asked, barely a whisper. "That it took the body?"

"Or maybe it disappeared once dead, like a jellyfish melting on the sand," he whispered back. "Don't borrow trouble when we still have a sackful."

They stood there, hand in hand, waiting, while van Horn finished his examination.

Finally, he put his tools away and closed the little black

bag, the metal latch making a tiny snicking sound. He shook his head, not looking up at anyone else in the room. "It's definitely a venom of some sort, possibly catalyzed by exposure to air. You say it was used as a defensive weapon?"

Van Horn looked at Aaron, who shrugged. "Don't ask me—I am apparently a seventh-level idiot without the sense God gave a carp."

Rosemary had called him that, and more, as they'd carried Jonathan's body back into town. She'd apologize. Eventually.

"Let me rephrase that," the older man said with the air of someone who'd seen everything, twice, and was no longer impressed. "Did it spit it at you before you made contact, or after?"

"It didn't spit. It oozed." The coroner's glare made him add, "After I cut it."

"Fascinating. Not a weapon at all, then, but a defensive mechanism. Possibly not even under the uncanny's conscious control."

"Except the first victim didn't attack it, didn't even have a chance to defend himself, from what the eyewitness said." Rosemary could not believe that all of this had been an accident.

"If I had the rest of the body to examine, I would be able to tell you more."

The Harkers glanced at each other, and Aaron actually shuffled his feet, like a guilty schoolboy.

"You do have the body, don't you?" Van Horn sounded terribly disappointed in them.

"I shot it point-blank, direct to the chest," Rosemary said. "It went down; it wasn't moving. We had Jonathan to worry about. And then it was . . . gone."

Van Horn shook his head, turning back to his patient. "So it's missing an arm, oozing poisonous sludge, is incredibly hard to kill, and knows what you two look like. I'm sure that's not going to be a problem at all."

Twenty-Six

THEY LEFT JONATHAN in van Horn's care and went down to the front desk to use the telephone there. The clerk on duty, clearly having heard stories, had stared at them, only granting them access once Aaron had peeled a bill from his wallet and placed it on the counter.

The operator connected them, and Rosemary looked up at the ceiling, as though to ask for strength, or patience, before identifying herself.

"Yes. It's done." From the terseness in her voice, Aaron assumed it was Ballantine, rather than his wife, on the other end of the line. He was saying something, Rosemary's hold on the telephone receiver getting tighter as she listened.

"We don't know." She glanced upward again. "No. I'm sorry. Yes, I quite understand."

She placed the receiver down in the cradle and looked back at her brother, both of them aware that the clerk was eavesdropping shamelessly. "There was no change at their end."

Franklin Congdon, like Jonathan, had not woken up.

"Let me guess: he doesn't think we did a good enough

job because we didn't work miracles?" He didn't wait for her to confirm. "I don't like wealthy people. Can we never be them?"

"I don't think that's going to be a problem," she said dryly. "Come on."

Daniella opened the door of the town house, her look of caution turning to worry. "Miss Harker?" Her gaze went to Aaron standing behind her, then back to Rosemary. "Mama! Papa!"

There was a flurry of activity, and the Harkers were swept into a side parlor, where the family had been gathering for tea. The captain stood to greet them, gesturing for them to join them, even as his son pulled additional chairs from the side of the room for them to sit.

"What news?" Benedita asked, half-hopeful.

"We trapped the uncanny, out in the woods." Rosemary stopped, looking down at her hands. "Aaron tried to reason with it, to convince it to stop, but . . . it was very angry."

"And it's still out there?" Benedita pulled her daughter closer to her, as though to protect her by proximity.

"It's dead." The words brought silence to the room; then Daniella let out a sob, muffled by her mother's breast.

"But . . . you will need to be careful." Rosemary looked at Duarte, willing him to understand what she was saying, needing to impart the seriousness of the situation but not wanting to frighten the children. "We killed it, but when we took our eyes off the body, it disappeared."

He heard what she hadn't wanted to say. "You think there is another one out there."

"It's possible. Unlikely—being out of salt water this long was harming it. I can't imagine any others would be faring better. But there is still a risk, not to you, but to those around you. If we are right"—and she was almost certain they were—"the uncanny thought it was protecting the children."

"Protecting?" Benedita's voice sharpened, and she paused, visibly collecting herself. "By attacking their father?"

"Nita. I was hunting it at the time. You do not blame the shark for biting the fisherman."

"No, I blame the fisherman for dangling his feet in front of the shark."

Aaron looked down at his own feet, biting the inside of his cheek. It wasn't funny, but at the same time, it was.

"Please." His sister's voice was calm but stern. "This is important. The uncanny was going after everyone helping you adjust to your new life here. You need to be careful."

"Everyone?" Daniella's voice trembled. "Our teachers? Our friends? But why? Why would a Good Friend do that?"

"Because I broke my vows," Duarte said. "Because I left the sea, took us away, took you and your brother away. Four generations served the sea, but I took you away."

"You can't blame yourself," Rosemary said. "Trying to understand why an uncanny does anything is . . ."

She had been about to say *useless*, Aaron knew. *Pointless*. Instead, she reached out to the girl, touching the top of her hand, making her turn to look at her. "It wasn't your papa's fault, and it wasn't your fault, nor your brother's. You couldn't explain that you were happy here; it wouldn't have understood."

"You don't know that. You hurt it." Her lower lip trembled, but no tears fell.

"If you had never made tribute, never participated in that foolish superstition, this would not be happening." Mrs. Ruiz Vaz did not let go of her daughter, but her body shifted toward her husband, addressing her words to him. "If you hadn't tangled us in this—"

"If I hadn't given tribute, we would never have done so well to be here," he said, matching sharpness for sharpness. "We would still be living in a cottage that stank of fish, your hands sore from sewing nets. Is that what you wanted? Is that what you wanted for Joao and Daniella?"

"Joe."

"What?"

Joao's face was set in mulish lines, but there was a suspiciously watery redness to his eyes. "I want to be called Joe. I've told you that."

Both parents turned to their son, his mother's mouth pulled into a tight line. "Now is not the time, Joao."

Aaron lifted an elbow, pushing it into Rosemary's side. "And that says it's time for us to go."

"Yes." Duarte placed a hand on his wife's arm, squeezing it before rising again. "I will see you out."

The door closed on mother and son arguing, and Duarte sighed. "We wanted for them to fit in, to be part of this world, not their old one. But even so, it is hard, to let them go."

They paused in the entrance hall, and Duarte offered his left hand first to Aaron, then to Rosemary. "It has been an honor to sail with you."

"And with you, Captain," Rosemary said, her cheeks tinged pink with a faint blush as he released her hand. Aaron would have to remember to tease her about that later. For now, he opened the door for her, turning to say one last fare-well to Duarte, when Rosemary's eyes went wide in shock. She dropped to one knee, her throwing knives slipping into her hands even as the uncanny pushed through the door in a blur of greens and blues, slammed into Duarte, and knocked him to the floor.

Rosemary's first knife landed in the uncanny's back even as Aaron was lifting his pistol, trying desperately to remember what bullets were loaded in the chamber. He gave it up to God and sighted, but the uncanny's body was already twitching in clear death throes.

Aaron, unwilling to fire the pistol indoors if he could avoid it, slipped the safety back on and shoved the pistol back into his pocket.

Stepping carefully, he grabbed the uncanny's feet—shoeless and webbed, he noted almost in passing—and dragged it off Duarte, who, with his arm in a sling, had been faring poorly in their struggle.

"Did any of the ichor get on you?" he asked, bending down. "Did you breathe any of it in?"

"No, no I don't— Get back," Duarte yelled as doors opened down the hallway, the household's attention drawn by the commotion. "Nita, keep the children there, I'm fine." He tried to sit up and groaned, falling back with a heavy thump. "Ai Deus, everything hurts again."

"Be glad you're alive to hurt," Aaron advised, his hand itching under the ichor scars. He used his other hand to help Duarte up, both of them careful to avoid the puddle of ichor staining the floor.

"Aaron." Both men turned their heads at Rosemary's

voice, strained and . . . Aaron refused to identify that note in her voice as "scared." She was looking at the uncanny Aaron had just dropped, and Aaron turned to follow her gaze. It was dead; he didn't see what she was— He stopped mid-thought.

"It has both arms," he said. "Rosie, it has both arms."

Using a gloved hand, she pulled her knife from the body and wiped it against the side of her skirt, then moved to the doorway, her movements slow and cautious as she looked outside, then stepped down to the street.

"Another? So there was more than one?"

"Apparently so." Aaron wanted to be outside with his sister, but someone needed to guard the doorway, in case anything got past her. She would be fine, he told himself. She would be fine. But it was still the longest forever he could remember, until she stepped back inside and closed the door.

He caught her gaze, and she shook her head once, even as she made the knife disappear back up her sleeve. "Nothing out there."

Duarte was muttering something under his breath; Aaron wasn't certain, but he thought it was the rosary.

"That isn't going to help," he said.

"Then what is? There may be more of—" And Duarte cast a look at the body, which, unlike its kin, had not disappeared. "Dear God, we need to get it out of here."

He had a point. "Do you have a garden where we can stash it?" Just until van Horn could come by to pick it up, which he would no doubt do the moment they alerted him, delighted to have a specimen after all.

"I . . . there is a root cellar."

"That will do." With a sad thought for his gloves, which

were new, he pulled them on and went to hoist the body, careful not to let any of the drying ichor touch exposed skin this time.

"If nothing else," he said to Rosemary, "this will give Manny a better chance to find a cure for the ichor sleep."

"Silver linings," she agreed, her gaze focused on Duarte, who had started praying again.

"All I wanted," he said finally. "All I wanted was to give my children a better life, a chance to become important citizens, with opportunities. For Daniella never to have to mend nets, or Joao to never have to risk his life in a storm, just to keep food on the table. I vowed this, every time we left the harbor. But those . . . those things, they're what made it possible? And now they've come to demand repayment, by refusing to allow my children that future?" He let out a bitter laugh. "Can you never escape your past?"

"Uncanny are not the devil," she said calmly, resisting the urge to shake him. That wouldn't help, and the man was already injured. "They're just . . . creatures. With rules and expectations that don't always fit in our world. All they knew was that you had left them."

"And killing those helping us, to make me come back?"

"Trying to understand their thinking . . . take my advice and don't," Rosemary said. "But . . . be careful," she warned him. "And if you can"—and she cast a look down the hallway, thinking of his wife's reaction—"you might want to consider making those offerings again. Eventually, hopefully, your Good Friends will understand that Joe will not become a fisherman. Or maybe he will grow up and decide that is exactly what he wants to be. Buy them time to consider their options."

The uncanny, wrapped in a tarp, had been rolled into the root cellar, and Duarte had promised to guard it until van Horn could come by with a truck. Rosemary stood, without judgment, and watched while Aaron chalked protective sigils on the front stoop of the town house.

"It won't stop them," he said. "I'd need to do something stronger to stop them. But it might make them reconsider stopping by."

He put away his chalks and held the gate for Rosemary, then closed it behind them. "Two uncanny, maybe more. A school? Or would they be a pod?"

His fascination with the minutiae of lore usually amused Rosemary. Less so this time. "I wonder if there were other victims we never heard about. Or if they went after other sailors who left the seas."

"It will all go in the report, and the Circle can handle it from there," Aaron said. "We did our job. This hunt is over. Managed discreetly."

"Without escalating things," Rosemary agreed, slipping her arm through his and leaning against his shoulder. "Diplomatically. Mother would be so proud."

And if their laughter was a tinge hysterical, neither of them were going to mention it.

On their way out of town, they made a detour, pulling in alongside a small, single-story house set back from the side of the road. There was a small sign, ISAAC REEVER, BOOK-

SELLER, and a graveled path that wound from street to door, passing under bare-branched sugar maples.

Rosemary twisted in her seat to study the building. "It doesn't look open."

"Good. No customers means he'll be more amenable to making a deal." The Circle would happily reimburse them for any purchases they made, as well as removing the volumes from the Ballantine home, if the books were deemed too dangerous to be loose in the world. Anything here they did not deem as such, Aaron would happily add to his own collection.

They got out, Rosemary giving Botheration the command to stay. This might take a while, and though Aaron didn't think anyone would take off with their belongings, she was right: there was no reason to be careless with them, even if Bother could be a useful tool in negotiation—of intimidation, if it came to that.

But as they came closer to the building, Rosemary frowned. "Didn't Mrs. Ballantine say this man had sold books to her parents?"

Aaron had to think; a lot had occurred since that conversation. "I think so, yes."

"Not the kind of man to close up shop overnight, then."

Or a man at all.

With his longer legs, Aaron reached the door first and pushed at the metal handle. It opened easily at his touch. There was no tinkling bell overhead, no sound of greeting, or, conversely, no voice telling them to go away, that he wasn't open yet.

There was nothing. The space inside was empty. Not only of books, but everything: books, furniture, people.

Aaron took a step back, almost bumping into his sister, who put a reassuring hand against his back.

"They said he was odd."

"And old."

They both backed out of the house then, hands instinctively touching weapons for reassurance, although neither actually pulled a knife or pistol. Once clear of the threshold, Rosemary turned around, while Aaron kept facing the house, a low whistle alerting Botheration, waiting in the automotive, to be on alert.

It was entirely possible that the man had died, or moved, and the Ballantines, in their own personal chaos, had not heard. It was possible that the gossip had not reached Ballantines' staff, likewise. Possible, but not probable, not if he was that much of a character, that much of a long-time fixture. Adding to that the fact that he had been in possession of, and selling, books that he should not have had, for generations . . .

Some towns never saw an uncanny. And some towns seemed to collect them.

"Bother would have told us if he was still around," Aaron said in not quite a whisper, meant only to carry the distance to his sister's ears. She nodded, but neither of them relaxed until they reached the automotive, Botheration standing in the back seat next to their luggage, his eyes alert but body soft.

"Get in," Aaron told her, and went to crank the engine.

Not every uncanny needed to be hunted. Some just needed to be left alone.

———

As the metal monstrosity rattled down the road, taking the hunters with them, a shadow watched them go.

The small-cousins were dead. It could have warned them; hunters kill small-cousins, that was what they did. They would kill it, too, if they could.

It knew better than to linger long enough to be found. It was old and cunning. But it was also curious. They smelled like old days, better days. When it hadn't needed to hide, when small-cousins and humans were more fun.

It would keep an eye on them. They were interesting.

Acknowledgments

SEVERAL PEOPLE IN particular made it possible for this book to reach readers' hands, and I would be remiss in not singing their praises directly.

In no particular order:

Jess Parnell, for helping turn my Max into a good canine citizen.

Janna Silverstein and Amanda Cherry, for convincing me to be social even when people-ing seemed too exhausting to even consider.

Katherine Cordick, for the daily commiserations.

Jéla Lewter, for staying on top of things.

Thank you all.